The Night Always Comes

Another Story from the Adventures of Harry and Paul

Paul John Hausleben

Cover design and cover concept by Paul John Hausleben
Photographs of the author by Paul John Hausleben

ISBN: 978-0-9886336-1-2

DEDICATION

To number twenty-seven, wherever he is now

CONTENTS

In Memorial of Mrs. Marianne Rogers

"People never really go away forever. Even when they die, they return to us, somehow. We remain together forever with the people that we love."

Paul John Hausleben, December 2012

ACKNOWLEDGMENTS

I would like to thank my family and friends who all supported my efforts in writing this story. I really cannot be thankful enough to all of you for your support and feedback. I would also like to thank all those fellow hockey players whom I chewed the same ice with many years ago. I do not believe that I could write this novel if not for those players trying to tear my head off or making their best attempts to send me from my net-minding spot to the emergency ward. In a very strange sort of way, thank you to all of you!

The Night Always Comes

Preface

This novel carries the subtitle of *Another Story from the Adventures of Harry and Paul,* because I feel as if the word, "adventures" captures the essence of the stories. I can even make the case that you can look at each chapter as an individual adventure. I rather enjoy using that word within the subtitle, as opposed to other words or descriptions. Indeed, in my opinion, they are adventures and I am a "storyteller" of them. Collectively, the books tell of the adventures and the lives of two lifelong friends who have a special bond.

One is a bombastic, overwhelming, lovable person, who along with his fun-loving family attacks life every day, and his best friend, is smart, steady, reliable, and athletic, who also is very calm, intelligent, religious, (but not outwardly so) and conservative. The stories tell of their adventures together as well as their families, friends, the women who they grow to love, their emotions, and of the people who were part of their lives.

Most of all, they tell of them growing up during the wonderful time of the late 1970s and beyond, in the unique and strange place known as northern New Jersey.

While they are all fiction, with strange names to places, sports teams, cars, products, music, and other spoofs, I must confess that at times, the characters, situations, and events have some amount of truth to them. I would say that they are fiction with a little nonfiction interjected here and there.

I would be remiss not to confess that there was, and in fact, still is a Harry M. Redmond Junior. There is also a Paul, as I am living proof of that!

We are still friends to this very day.

The character of Harry in the stories is a mirror image of my real-life friend, whose name is actually Harry M. Rogers Junior. I confess to embellishing Harry a little here and there, and (please forgive me Harry) I changed his last name, but a large part of his character is quite accurate. The character of Paul John Henson, however, is mostly fictional, except for the hockey goaltender angle, long hair and beard, his love of music, and a few other nuances that are indeed factual.

In a reflection on the actual episodes that inspired most of the story lines of this book, it is sometimes hard for me to believe that some of this could have happened to two young men growing up on the outskirts of the City of Paterson in northern New Jersey.

However, I bet many people could say that about their own situations and lives.

Everyone has a story to tell, it is a shame that nowadays, we choose not to share stories as we did years ago. Life was sure a lot simpler back then.

These stories contain a great amount of humor, but they have at times, some hidden meanings, as well as some introspective thoughts at how ordinary people interact, support and love one another, achieve greatness, share kindness, or are just plain wonderful persons. In some cases, the chapters depict heart-warming times, as well as situations of great sadness.

I think that is how life really is, or at least it should be. Humor should be a large part of our lives and we should mix life with some serious times, and of course, there are inevitable times, when life becomes quite sad. We always take ourselves too seriously these days. That is what I tried to depict through these stories, there is nothing here that is very complex. The stories are tales of very simple events but contain unique characters that all blend and interact with one another in a special way. I have written about strictly the human element of life in a very simple time.

I decided to keep the theme of *The Time Bomb in The Cupboard,* and I wrote *The Night Always Comes* in the same type of narrative format, from the character of Paul John Henson's own stream of memories and consciousness. His narrative contains authentic northern "New Jersey speak" with subtle bad grammar, twisted words and phrasing, and the common northern New Jersey slang emitting from within his own mind. I wanted it, to a certain extent, to seem as if Paul John Henson is speaking directly to the reader with his own northern New Jersey language and accent. Paul maintains his steady, calm composure throughout the stories, despite the fact that his best buddy Harry as well as Harry's family, his own family, his eccentric relatives, their mutual friends, all turns his life constantly upside down. Outside influences always place him in outlandishly strange situations that are always just out of his control. It is great fun to ride along with Paul as he makes his way through all of it.

I hope you enjoy this book and the various adventures of Harry and Paul. If you were lucky enough to have grown up or lived during this time, or even luckier to be from northern New Jersey, then I hope these stories transport you back to that magical time, and you can relive your own stories and memories. If you were not from that time or from that place, then as Harry would say, "It is one adventure after another, so come along for the ride and see where it all takes us."

I hope you enjoy this book as much as I have enjoyed putting these adventures together.

Thank you for reading them.

Paul John Hausleben

December 2012,

Prologue

In life, sometimes, by chance, perfect mixtures of people meet and unite for no apparent reason. Perhaps it is just fate, luck, or chance that may have influenced the situation, and contributed in joining them together. It could be the hand of God, or whatever higher power you choose to believe in that guides these types of things. In sports, the team that finally has that perfect mixture of players wins championship after championship, but once one or two of the key team players leave and move on, the team is never the same. In the business world, a business could be not quite clicking, and new people are hired, and they all just jell like never before. The new ideas they come with, the passion they have for the work, all blend just right. It is perfect, and success becomes a by-product. Once some employees responsible for the success move on, then the business flounders, and the success the once business enjoyed, fades away, and becomes difficult to maintain. It happens quite often in the world of music when successful musical groups begin from random meetings of people. Is it pure chance or random luck when a few musicians join because of indiscriminate or arbitrary meetings to make wonderful sounds together?

On the other hand, is it something else that steers and guides us all?

Perhaps it is sometimes pure chance, but it is indeed a strange and fascinating aspect of life. The right people, the right personalities, the right time, the right place, and when it all comes together, it is fabulous.

When it falls apart, it is heartbreaking.

The late 1970s were a magical time. The Vietnam War had finally ended and America tried to heal. The economy was difficult and money was tight, but people were special. They worked hard, were respectful to one another, wrote letters to each other, they sat and talked around kitchen tables and on front stoops and on porches; they partied hard and had fun; they spoke openly of God and religion, and they shared stories and interacted with each other, rather than type texts or send emails. The music was so special too; it invoked spirit and the simple, plain messages of love, peace, kindness, and of simply having a good time and enjoying life.

It is on the backbone of some of these things that lives were built, hearts were crushed, music was played, dances were danced, but through it all, there was a bond, a bond so strong for some people that it endures forever.

The Night Always Comes

1

1979 Trans Whizzer

I still remember all of these events as if they happened just yesterday or even maybe an hour or two ago. I have etched it all into my mind forever. I can never, ever, shake them from my mind, no matter how hard I try. And what began it all was a car. Not any old ordinary car, but a once in a lifetime, magical car.

There it was in front of 20 John Street in Paterson, New Jersey, sitting there like a shining billboard of muscle car glory. It was a metallic brown color with golden trim, removable T-top roof, and golden honeycomb pattern wheels. Four speeds on the floor, with the Trans Whizzer high output, supercharged, 475 cubic inch Dragon engine, and all the other options that the manufacturer had offered. It had a premium sound system, cruise control, air conditioning, the car included every single accessory or power option available with not a single option omitted or overlooked. The golden Dragon logo sat on the hood along with all the other decals spread out over the car, just sitting there oozing with sheer horsepower. There it sat, a beacon of testosterone for a single nineteen-year-old male. It felt as if an invitation for a speeding ticket should come with the car ahead of time so that you could just get it out of the way right away. That way, you will not feel quite as bad when the inevitable does happen, and the police officer peels off the ticket, and hands it to you with a smile. It would have lessened the impact considerably.

A brand new, fantastic, and surreal, 1979 Trans Whizzer,

and it just so happened to be that it was Harry M. Redmond Junior's brand-new car.

Growing up, Harry M. Redmond Jr. was my best buddy, in fact, he still is my best buddy, even to this day. We were like brothers and very seldom apart. He was big, tall, and strong, with a beer barrel chest, longish blonde hair, a little thin, blonde mustache, and a devious, but joyful smile. He was a wonderful guy. Harry was a very good-looking guy; tall, stocky, and rugged with a powerful build. Harry had a good job, with which he earned a lot more money than the rest of us could even imagine at this point in our lives. He had many girlfriends, and the world was truly his oyster. Harry and I played ice hockey together for years and his reputation for being a rough and tumble guy both on and off the ice, certainly was a reputation he earned and deserved. In reality, he was a joyful, playful, and carefree guy, who as the rest of the Redmond family did, he lived to play and laugh at the world as life went by.

Harry had suffered a devastating injury in an ice hockey game in the early winter of 1978, which was a year or so before he bought his new car. A deflected hockey puck hit him dead on and hard in his mouth, and the injury he suffered turned out to be devastating. He lost all of his front teeth, broke his jaw in five places, broke his nose, and suffered some cheekbone damage. He was in the hospital for about a week and the recovery period after that was a long and painful time. Harry quit playing serious hockey after that, although he still played in casual leagues here and there to stay sharp and in shape. Harry was a tough cookie, and it took a lot to keep him down. I continued in my hockey career, and actually was lucky enough to have signed an agreement in 1978 for a semi-pro team out on Long Island, New York, and I was making a few dollars here and there. This was summer and the off-season for me, so I had plenty of free time after my full-time job.

Harry was a unique guy, and cars were an important

part of his life, in fact, they were a major piece of his ego puzzle. Now, he had a fantastic Sonicmobile that he had for a few years, and I thought that car was really the ultimate car in which Harry could never surpass, but Harry was the kind of guy who always needed a new stimulus. He grew bored with things very quickly. One day in June 1979, the Sonicmobile was gone, no warning, no one last cruise in it for old time's sake, just gone on a sudden Harry whim.

Harry often acted on a hair trigger, which was part of his magic.

"Come on over," Harry said to me on the phone, "I have something new to show you!"

"Click," the phone went dead.

My old man looked up at me from behind his newspaper, "That was a short conversation!"

"Yeah, well, it was Harry, and he said he has something new to show me."

The old man pulled his paper back up over his eyes. "Oh no, not again, I hope it is not another pet ferret, or that he has taken up skydiving or skeet shooting again. Those were real disasters."

"I will see you later," I said, and out the door, I went. My old man was used to Harry and all of his, as we liked to call them, "phases." After all, we had been best buddies for ten years or so and my parents knew all of his family. The Redmonds were legendary in our neighborhood for their backyard parties, holiday gatherings, and overall fun and friendliness. "Something to show you" was, of course, this fantastic piece of automotive prowess. I did not know what to say as I stood there staring at it in front of Harry's house. The entire neighborhood was out in the street admiring it and taking pictures of the car as it sat there gleaming. Harry had just purchased it for cash that afternoon from a Dragon dealership out on Route 17 in Paramus, New Jersey, and he had driven it straight home. I walked over and read the sticker in the window, and my jaw dropped in awe and shock as the price of ten thousand, eight hundred dollars soundly jumped off the paper and knocked me over. While the rest of us labored away earning meager wages, Harry actually earned a very good wage, and he made a lot of money. What a great feeling to be this young, no responsibilities, no debts, and you had the entire world as your canvas to paint upon in any way that you may have wished.

Harry was like a game show host, beaming from ear-to-ear, walking around, and showing everyone his latest, and perhaps greatest triumph. This, of course, was the era of the 1970s and the famous movie, Dragon Road Race starring Barry McGirk, had made the Trans Whizzer the car to have, while he tore up the movie screen with the beautiful Harriet Dudley at his side. Now Harry was just like Barry, well sort of, just like Barry, as he did not exactly have Harriet Dudley, but in his mind, Harry thought that he and Barry were just about on the same level.

We were both nineteen-years-old now, and Harry had just finished a long term, off and on relationship, with a gal named Joyce. He was a free man, with lots of extra time and cash, and that alone may have been enough to call out the New Jersey National Guard to protect single females under the age of thirty in the entire state. I knew this car was the major piece of his rebound plan to bounce back from the pain of his recently ended relationship. You see, with Harry it was all about an image and this new extraordinary set of wheels would fit the bill just perfectly.

Harry came over and put his arm around me. We both stood there admiring the Trans Whizzer, and Harry smiled.

"She sure is a gorgeous vehicle, isn't it, Paul?"

I nodded my head in agreement while still finding it difficult to come up with adequate words to describe the car.

"Can you imagine the fun, chicks we will meet, and the adventures we are going to have in this baby?" Harry said as he rubbed his hands over the rear spoiler. "These summer nights will be all ours, we will be kings of the road. We work hard during the day to buy these cool things, but my friend, the night always comes and we will be there together forever." Harry gave me a big bear hug, and I knew that this was going to be the start of a lot of excitement.

Little did I really know where it would lead us.

Therefore, it began; the wonderful Trans Whizzer phase of Harry Redmond's life. The Redmonds were famous for going through various phases, which dominated their lives with some special interest or, in many cases, an actual different lifestyle. It was, in many ways, part of the appeal of them as a family as well as quite comical. Harry lived with his dad and since his mother had passed away; his oldest sister and her family lived with them too. It was one big, huge, large house of fun. A house full of large, happy, fun-loving people, tons of mayhem, along with parties and endless action, all crammed into a small, old, Cape Cod house set in the middle of urban America. The Redmond family worked hard, and they played even harder. They were the most eclectic, lovable, and wonderful people I have ever known.

The Redmonds were all large, gregarious persons, in both size and personality. To say that the Redmonds enjoyed life would be a gross understatement. Part of the mystique would be whenever the Redmond clan was riding the wave of another phase. The first intense phase I remember was the "baseball phase" when Harry was about fifteen years old. There were many mini-phases along the way when we were younger, but none of them stuck in my mind, or I did not notice them until the "baseball phase" came along. Even though Harry played hockey, he loved baseball, and the fact of the matter was he was just not that good a baseball player. He was, however, a great hockey player, but his love of baseball remained long after he conceded that he really was a poor baseball player. The entire Redmond family for this one summer became embroiled in the New York Bugs baseball team. The Redmonds could not just get into something; they fell hook, line, and sinker and float while it enveloped their lives.

If you really wanted to understand the magnitude of a particular Redmond phase, such as the baseball phase was, then you needed to realize that the phase would reshape and totally transform their entire lives. They would cease all other activity except for work and eating in order to focus only on the new interest.

Mr. Redmond did not just go out and buy a New York Bugs baseball cap; he bought an entire uniform! Soon after, the rest of the Redmond clan which included Harry, his sisters, Linda and Patty, his brother in laws, Ronnie, (otherwise known as Ronzo) and George, (also known as the Big Spike), nieces, nephews, and even the family pets, would be wearing Bugs uniforms. On days after work and on weekends, the entire gang would walk around wearing their full New York Bug uniforms; they even would go shopping in them. The Redmond house would be transformed into a replica of Bugs Stadium, with banners, the Bugs logos, Bugs bats, baseballs, coffee mugs, Bug lights strung with multiple, little, Mr. Bug lights (the team mascot) glowing back at you in the night, beer mugs, soda cups, napkins, paper plates, and just about every form of New York Bug memorabilia that you could find. They even painted the living room blue and orange like the Bug team colors! Mr. Redmond and Harry went half each to purchase a six-feet-by-six-foot framed, autographed, color picture of the great Bugs pitcher, Jim Beaver, that they hung on the living room wall right next to the television. The record player would be playing the Bugs theme song, "Buzz with the Bugs" constantly.

It was amazing!

They did not really seem to care whether the Bugs won or lost the games. I never really noticed that anyone was even aware of where the Bugs were in the pennant race. The love of the New York Bugs and baseball overall triggered this phase. It had no real rhyme or reason. The entire family crowded around the television and watched every televised baseball game on the tube. I could always tell when the game was on, because if the weather were good, then the crown jewel of the Redmond's New York Bugs memorabilia collection would be out on the front porch. Harry had found, via a mail order company, and then purchased, a seven-foot high life-size, blow up balloon of Mr. Bug, who was the team mascot of the Bugs. He would tie the balloon up on the front porch with a rope so that it waved in the breeze but would not blow away. Mr. Bug was really a large baseball head on a man's regular body, and he had this dopey look on his face, with this scary, giant, baseball head with a Bugs cap on top of it. As far as team mascots go, I found him slightly disturbing and a little creepy.

There he was on game days tied to the Redmond's porch waving in the wind to the entire neighborhood. I never dared to tell any of the Redmonds that most of the people living in our neighborhood were not very fond of poor Mr. Bug! The house was filled with the voices from every television and radio of Blabber Viscardi, Johnny Mclaughy, Ralph "the Rocket" Lenard and Bob McGee as the play-by-play announcers for the Bugs. The announcers became as if they were old neighborhood friends. The "baseball phase" lasted all the way into the next spring, when the Redmonds capped the phase off with a huge family trip. The entire crew of Mr. Redmond, Harry, Linda, Patty, Ronzo, George, and all the children, all went down to the New York Bugs training camp in Bloody Hot City, Florida to participate in the New York Bugs dream camp. Harry actually signed up as a participant in the camp. In exchange for an exorbitant amount of money, he received an actual Bugs uniform, and the team allowed him to play on the field as a "make believe" actual New York Bug. The Redmonds loved it all! They took a million pictures of Harry playing third base for the fraudulent Bugs team and spent a fortune. It was a legendary time in the Redmond family legacy.

Then, as suddenly as it began, it ended.

For no apparent reason, other than boredom, the "baseball phase" was over. One day, shortly after they all had returned from Florida, I visited Harry's house, and the picture of Jim Beaver was gone from the wall. Harry and Mr. Redmond were finishing painting the living room walls and the ceiling an off-white color, and they had thankfully removed Mr. Bug from the front porch and stored him in the basement.

"Aren't you guys into the Bugs anymore?" I asked Harry.

"Oh yeah, we are, just not as much as we used to be," Harry answered. That was a little vague, as I never really had run into anyone who had been quite into something as much as the Redmonds, but I shrugged my shoulders and chalked it up as having passed. It was just another wonderful, fascinating, and quirky aspect of the Redmond family, and their whirlwind approach to life.

Following close on the heels of the wild period of baseball madness was the bizarre and wild, "photography phase." Unlike the baseball phase, this phase had a clear-cut trigger, which caused the entire family to become wildly obsessed shutterbugs. This phase was triggered by Harry's dad, who purchased a top-of-the-line Substantial Industries, super deluxe, auto focus, X2-1-9 camera with all kinds of attachments. All of Harry's family worked very hard and while they were not wealthy, they did all earn a good income, especially when compared to the rest of our neighborhood. As a result, they did have a lot of extra money to spend on various toys to support them through their numerous phases and interests. Mr. Redmond was still a widower, and he liked to travel with a number of different lady friends that he knew through his church. Off he went to Hawaii one summer, with one of his ladies and his trusty camera, with one hundred lenses, cases, shade filters, and all the bells and whistles.

When he returned, he wore nothing but Hawaiian print shirts for months on end and he showed the family all kinds of fantastic photos that he had taken while on the islands.

That was all it took.

Soon Harry, then Ronzo, then George, all ran out to the stores, and purchased loudly printed Hawaiian shirts and big straw hats. Then, they all dashed off to the camera store to buy the same Substantial Industries X2-1-9 top of the line cameras.

Soon, they were all wearing the same kinds of shirts and they were all snapping merrily away. Then the ladies followed, and before long, the entire clan wore loud, Hawaiian print shirts and had the big, fancy cameras hanging around their necks twenty-four hours a day. They transformed the house into a maze of cameras, lenses, film canisters, photography magazines, and tripods. You could not go anywhere near any of the Redmonds without having your picture taken. The walls of the house had nearly every square inch covered by framed photos that every member of the family had taken.

I made the big mistake of giving Harry and his family extra tickets to an ice hockey playoff game for a team that I was playing goal for at the time. The entire entourage showed up with cameras in hand. The area in the stands where they were all sitting was alive with constant non-stop flashing as they snapped picture after picture. It looked like the surface of the sun, and I had to be careful not to look up at them, when they waved at me to turn around so they could take another photo, because of the fear of being blinded by the camera flashes, and not being able to see the puck and play goalie that night.

To this day, I still have about four or five thousand pictures, which the Redmonds had given to me of that game with me in the net playing ice hockey.

I learned one unique and frankly scary aspect of the photography phase when we had a tropical storm sweep through northern New Jersey at the end of the summer. A seventeen-year-old, brave, and fearless, Harry, along with Ronzo and Mr. Redmond, set about into the flooded and windswept streets of Paterson, Haledon, and nearby cities and towns, to take as they called them, "disaster pictures."

The three of them went out during the height of the storm, and the team would send Harry on numerous precarious missions, such as crawling or climbing out on some downed tree limb in the middle of the Passaic River, to take a photo of some poor soul's house floating away due to the high waters. The three of them would row boats out into flooded streams and risk life and limb, all in the name of snapping a disaster picture. They would proudly display the developed photos inside of what they called, "disaster books" that would be labeled with the name of the event on the cover. They would keep the collection of albums on the living room coffee table and an unsuspecting visitor would arrive, and the Redmonds would proudly show off the book contents for hours upon hours. You could open it up to see thousands of photos of flooded houses and roads, collapsed bridges, as well as Harry, hanging as if he was a circus acrobat from some tree limb with his camera in hand, inches above death from some turbulent river rapid. After the big storm passed, the Redmonds would revert to common ordinary pictures, such as empty beer cans and the family dog, but let a snowstorm, ice storm, a blizzard or a thunderstorm roll through, and they would all dash with cameras into the field in a mad quest for more disaster pictures.

The walls of the entire house soon became littered and filled floors to ceilings, with books and shelves to hold all the photo albums as the sheer volumes of pictures overwhelmed the Redmond's household.

Then, almost as soon as it had begun, the era of "photography phase" went the way of Jim Beaver and the Bugs. The cameras went away, as did the tripods, the lenses, the film, and all the other goodies they accumulated during this phase. Ronzo and Harry took down all the bookshelves and boxed up the photo albums, and all of it was stored down in Harry's basement, which over the years began to overflow with the remnants and leftovers of the many phases that had come and gone.

A trip down into the basement of the Redmond's family home at 20 John Street was like a walk back into time, as you waded through artifacts of leftovers from the various phases. An added dilemma for a trip down into the basement storage area was that you always had to be careful of not putting an accidental hole in Mr. Bug, while he stood partly deflated at the base of the stairs. From his secluded storage spot of exile, he was there . . . still smiling at you with his dopey face and creepy eyes.

There were many other phases that came and went, some of them were major, some of them were minor, like "fishing phase" when the house was filled with all kinds of rods, reels, hooks, lines, sinkers, stuffed trout, catfish, and bass. The Redmonds were always at the doctor's office receiving tetanus shots after digging misplaced fish hooks out of their bodies.

The house looked like the inside of a fishing tackle store.

There was a "billiard phase," when the Redmonds actually moved their dining room table out into the garage and set up a pool table in its place. They then proceeded to turn the dining room into a dimly lit pool hall, and all of them took turns hustling each other, hustling me, and then all the neighbors.

Along came, "bowling phase" when Harry and the rest of the family joined teams in nearby bowling leagues and the house was filled with various bowling balls, the television was always turned to pro bowlers competing in tournaments and the famous, Bowling for Money television show on channel sixty UHF out of New York City. There were bowling bags all over, as well as smelly, old bowling shoes scattered here and there. Trust me; those leagues were never the same once the Redmonds descended upon them.

On and on it went, with, "archery phase," "hunting phase," "chess and checkers phase," "golf phase," "watercolor painting phase" and one of my particular favorites; "opera phase." That was when the house filled with loud, blaring opera music while all the Redmonds leaned into the record player and tried hard to understand what on earth the singers were really saying, and the story was all about.

The clutter and leftovers from the various phases had filled the entire basement by the time Harry and I had reached eighteen years of age or so. Now, it was spilling out onto both sides of the front porch. The Redmonds always kept the middle lane from the outside exterior door to the interior door free of clutter, but as you passed through, you could see the piles of items sticking out, as reminders from the various eras of the different interests. You could spot a bowling ball, an old New York Bug beer mug, a fishing pole, a film container, a bow, or an arrow sticking out here and there; it was a virtual cornucopia of some obscure testimony to the different eras of the Redmond's lives. Just when it seemed like the foundation of the Redmond family home would crack from the weight of disposed of clutter from the previous phases, along came the pinnacle of phases.

In many ways, it was the final and preeminent phase, a grand finale over the previous lost phases! This one rose above all others, to become a way of life for Harry and the Redmond family for a long, long, time.

This phase came along and started innocently enough. It was the result of being a carryover of one of the famous Redmond's theme related Labor Day backyard picnics and barbeques. No one in the world threw a backyard party as the Redmonds did. It was filled with food, music, endless beer, and soda kegs, laughter, horseshoes, a big backyard swimming pool, and it went on and on for days. The family would never allow a holiday to be just a one-day event or some type of quick celebration. A holiday on the Redmond's calendar went on and on for days! Every Labor Day, Linda and her sister Patty would create a new theme for the party, and invitations went out encouraging attendees to dress and act in a lock step with the party theme. One year it was a Hawaiian Lau, the next year it was patriotic, the next it was a Caribbean party on the islands, and on it went from year to year. Then in 1978, it was country and western and that was the fateful trigger!

The late 1970s brought citizen band radio, country music mixed with rock-and-roll, and movies that depicted and glorified the cowboy and western lifestyle.

For the Redmonds, this became a serious matter. They loved it!

Harry and his entire family went all out for this party, and this particular theme arrived. It became so wildly popular that it stayed. The party ended, but the way of life remained. It was one of the greatest of all the Labor Day bashes. There is nothing like a bunch of folks from northern New Jersey trying to speak and act like western cowpokes to be the epitome of weirdness. The music, the food, straw hats, big belts and western belt buckles, leather cowboy boots, vest and western shirts. It all went on and on, with every piece of western garb they could put on their bodies. Ronzo even tried a set of spurs on his boots until he realized the huge scratches, they were putting on the floors of his house!

I will reluctantly admit that I wore the cowboy hat that I bought for the party quite often while riding in my old MJ-17 Jeep with the ragtop down and latched. The Redmonds had pulled me into this phase because it was hip at the time and I had to admit for a time—it really was a lot of fun.

So, there you had it.

A full-blown, outright, country and western phase began right before all of our eyes for Harry and all the Redmonds. All of their attire changed. All they wore from this point forward were boots, ten-gallon hats, wide belt buckles, jeans, and western shirts with bolo ties for the men. Country music played twenty-four hours a day . . . it was never any other kind of music that you heard blasting away in the Redmond's house. If by some slim chance or twist of fate, the country music records ran out, then they tuned their old table radio into W.N.H. 1000 on the A.M. dial from New York City. That was about the only country station in the area broadcasting serious country music. It was comical, while you listened to all of these hard-core deep northern New Jersey accents as they tried hard to say, "fixin," and "I reckon" as they walked around in ten-gallon hats with pointy cowboy boots on.

Then the fun part began, when the entire family took up playing country music live. Harry learned to play the banjo, Linda sang, Patty and the Big Spike played washboards and jugs, Ronzo played the fiddle, and Mr. Redmond strummed the guitar and blew into a harmonica.

They were simply amazing and never, ever, did anything halfway, and that was part of the joy of being with them. You just could not help but love them all.

2

The Adventures Begin

The latest phase had been in place for almost one year, and it showed no real signs of fading from the Redmond horizon, unlike all the previous imposters beforehand. In all honesty, this phase fit perfectly with Harry and his new car. Like his hero in the Dragon Road Race movie, Harry wore a cowboy hat as Barry McGirk did in the movie, and he in fact, looked very good in his hat. Harry would throw his banjo in the trunk, he would take out the T-top for the Trans Whizzer, throw on a pair of black studded cowboy boots polished up like a mirror, and with his hat on his head. Harry looked quite the part. It was now July in 1979, and Harry had stopped at a local establishment and had the Trans Whizzer washed, polished and ready to roll. Saturday was our big cruising and party night. Harry and I both had to work on Saturdays so that made Friday nights just a regular work night for us. Harry was going to pick me up at my house on a Saturday night in early July. It was just a few days after the big Fourth of July celebration over at the Redmond's house, and we planned tonight to be one of our first big cruise nights in the new car. It usually took folks a week or two to come around after that party, so things were low key around the Redmond's household during the recovery period anyway, so it was a perfect night to hit the road.

A loud knock occurred at the back door; my mother glanced from the kitchen table, and saw that it was, Harry.

"Oh hello, Harry, come on in," my mother said. "I am

having some tea, would you like some tea, Harry?" The door opened and in walked Harry, his boots clicking on the floor, a big, wide, western belt buckle gleaming around his waist and he was wearing his big, black, ten-gallon hat. Harry was looking good as he was sporting a fresh haircut, and he was wearing black dungaree pants, a white, pressed, western shirt with silver studs along the shoulders and a black leather vest. My old man was sitting at the table reading his newspaper and drinking a Big Boulder beer.

Now my mother is of English descent and my dad well, he is from lack of a better description; he is of Paterson, New Jersey heritage. You could never have picked a stranger couple to get together than these two. A street-smart New Jersey tough guy who fell in love with a sweet, proper English gal, quite an interesting pair!

"How y'all doing tonight?" Harry bellowed as he strode into the kitchen, took off his hat, and bent over to give my mother a kiss on the cheek. "No thanks on the tea ma'am."

"Oh Harry, you are quite the character, now, aren't you?" My mother laughed as she always got such a kick out of Harry and his antics.

The old man put down his newspaper, stared at Harry, and shook his head.

"How y'all doing?" The old man asked, mocking Harry and his newfound phony accent. "What's with the cowboy riding the range act, Harry?" The old man continued to confront Harry on his new way of life. "As far as I know Paterson is a long way from Texas, unless I really failed my geography," he said as my old man picked up his newspaper once more and continued to read it.

"Oh, leave him be," my mother came to Harry's defense.

Harry just laughed and said, "Well, I reckon you can guess why there, Mr. Henson. You have to do what you have to do to get chicks. You do remember those days now?" The old man never even looked back up from his paper and beer mug. My mother got up from the table and moved towards the storage pantry in our kitchen.

While she opened the door, she explained, "Harry, I bought a box of dog treats last week for our dog Skippy, but for some reason he does not like them." My mother handed Harry a box of dog treats that she had taken out of the pantry and continued, "Maybe Cocoa would like to try them, I hate for them to go to waste."

Now, Harry had the world's smartest dog whose name was Cocoa. He not only was the world's smartest dog, but he also ate almost anything. A few years back, when we were working on the Sonicmobile, Cocoa came along and ate a tube of grease and we had to take him to the vet to get his stomach pumped.

Harry took the box and studied it.

"Why thank ya Mum, I reckon, Cocoa will love them. He eats almost anything. Hmm . . . I wonder why old Skippy would not eat 'em?"

Upon hearing his name, our family dog Skippy, came in the kitchen, sat down, and looked at Harry holding the box of treats. Harry opened the box, stuck his nose in it, and sniffed deeply. Then, to everyone's horror, he grabbed a dog treat and popped it in his mouth. We all stood there and watched as Harry crunched and crunched the treats and seemed to be studying the flavor in his mouth.

It sounded as if he was eating a bag of rocks.

Harry swallowed and answered, "Yup, Cocoa will like them, they are good, a little on the beefier side of the flavor spectrum, but I reckon he will enjoy 'em. Thanks!"

My old man just shook his head, Skippy turned and left the room, and even my mother did not know what to say. Sometimes, words cannot describe a situation, certain things become etched in your mind forever, and it is best not to say a word. I grabbed Harry by the arm and led him towards the back door.

"Y'all have a good night now!" Harry bellowed out as

we barged out the door and down the back steps.

"Be careful, boys," I heard my mom call out as we walked towards the Trans Whizzer and we both climbed in.

Music was an essential part of our lives at this point, and setting the proper mood was a prerequisite for a successful summer evening while cruising for chicks. Harry played country music quite often, but unlike the rest of the Redmonds at this moment, he would also listen to other types of music. A lot depended upon his mood, but if he wanted to cruise, then he would rock out. It was simply rock-and-roll all the way.

However, Harry had a weak spot, and I knew it. Despite his tough and rumble exterior, deep down, he actually was very emotional. When he was mellow, or in stress, or sad over the latest breakup of a relationship, then his weakness came to the surface.

About a year earlier, a famous movie had hit the big screen, and it was very popular. In fact, it was the most popular movie to come along in a very long time. It was a musical called Cruising starring the gorgeous and talented Crystal Zirconium. The flick was about a group of teenagers in the 1950s that cruised around in hot rod cars and got in ordinary trouble with love and life. It was a typical love triangle movie involving teenage angst. The star of the movie was Crystal Zirconium, who was also a very popular singer at the time, whom Harry just adored. There was a famous scene in the movie where Crystal's character goes through a makeover from a humdrum ordinary gal into a raving sex machine. She appears on a staircase in her new, black leather, skintight outfit and sets the world on fire!

When Harry and I went to see the movie with two young ladies on a double date, Harry nearly exploded and blasted off into outer space without a rocket ship at the scene where Crystal makes her famous appearance.

Harry's atrocious behavior embarrassed the two young ladies so horribly that they walked out of the movie house. We never saw or heard from them again, and it took me the better part of an hour to get Harry to come out from under his seat after he fainted at the sight of Crystal.

Harry, like many young males of our age, never fully recovered from the sight of Crystal Zirconium. In fact, generations of men remember how they felt after seeing Crystal at that stunning moment on the big screen, even to this very day! Harry as a continual reminder of her, always kept a number of Crystal cassette tapes handy that he would pull out every once in a while, just to, shall, we say, stir up some of his competitive juices or pick him up if he was in a sad, mellow, or a melancholy mood.

As I sat in the passenger seat, I watched as Harry was thumbing through all his tapes in his boxes and I wondered where he would land, and what the goal would be for tonight. Hmm, Crystal, pure hard rock, progressive rock, folk music, country. Where would he end up? I thought this was going to be a semi-mellow night, so I was leaning towards Harry picking some folk music. Just when you thought you could predict Harry's mood, he turned the tables over on me, and pulled out the Greatest Hits by the Electronic Transistor Orchestra!

Now this band received a lot of criticism from music critics, but no one wrote more catchy hooks, melodies, and better music that was perfect for cruising summer nights in the 1970s than did the Electronic Transistor Orchestra. The tape deck in the Trans Whizzer exploded as the opening bars of, "Sad, Sad, Woman" resonated from the speakers.

This was going to be a spectacular summer evening!

"What is the plan?" I asked Harry between songs.

"We are heading to Lord Crudley's Bar," Harry answered as he was going through gears in the Trans Whizzer and merging out onto a main road. Now, there was a slim window in the laws back then in New Jersey when the legal age for drinking alcohol was nineteen. It lasted just long enough for us to reach the age of twenty-one when the laws changed to the higher age.

Therefore, we were off to a watering hole about two towns over called Lord Crudley's Bar. It was an old shack tucked away on a hillside just off a main road. It was nothing special; a gin joint that had a cover band, a small dance floor, and that was about it. We did not go there very often, so I naturally was assuming that Harry had something planned. Harry's plans usually included something to do with young ladies, but he generally gave me some warning when that was the case.

After all, this same guy once pulled off a day where he dated seven different women in one day! That is a whole other story, better left for another time and place.

Tonight, he had not mentioned a word, so I had thought we were going to cruise and then hit the gin joint. I really did not expect us to meet any gals at Lord Crudley's bar.

"I have a gal I would like you to meet," Harry explained, between beating on his steering wheel to the tunes of ETO. Harry was a very exuberant listener to music, and he had this nervous habit of drumming the palms of his hand on the steering wheel to the percussion beats of the music.

"Oh, who is this?" I asked, while slightly surprised at the turn of events. I should have known better than to attempt a "Harry prediction."

"Well, I reckon she already has sort of kinda' met you already. After one of your games, she saw you leaving the ice and was interested in meeting you. You were awesome that night in the goal. I think that was the greatest game that I ever saw you play. In fact, it was the playoffs! You shut out the Colonials and that evil, loudmouth jerk, O'Malley. She was interested in you at first sight, man."

Harry was always continually exaggerating the truth, working deals and angles behind my back, and never really letting me know what the entire plan was. After all these years, I was on to him and I was very good at putting the pieces of the puzzle together on my own.

"So, let me guess, you were there with her best friend and this gal just happened to notice me without any assistance at all from you?"

"Well, sort of. Y'all are right that I am dating her best friend. In fact, I am dating her, and one or two others that I have my eye on at the moment!"

I shook my head because Harry would never change. He was with his steady gal Joyce for many years until they grew apart, he now was on a typical rebound full of young man angst, and this Trans Whizzer phase was allowing him to sow his wild oats and forget Joyce.

Harry spun the sports car into the parking lot at Lord Crudley's and gunned the big engine up a little hill in the entrance, as a bunch of people turned around to look and admire the car as he swung it into a parking spot. Harry jumped out, grabbed his big hat from the front seat, and closed the driver's door. I climbed out of the passenger seat and we joined up to walk to the front door.

"Fantastic car!" A young lady gasped at Harry as she stood there gawking at the Trans Whizzer.

"Why thank ya little lady," Harry drawled in his worst New Jersey phony western accent. The young gal looked at Harry a little funny as her eyes went up and down him, while she was gazing, first at his fancy boots, and then she gazed all the way to his big ten-gallon hat, but she did not say anymore. We all continued towards the dimly lit gin joint.

"It sure would be nice, Harry, if you had told me about this blind date. I really would have dressed a little nicer. Come to think of it, I really do not like blind dates."

I was complaining to Harry the entire way as we walked towards the front door of Lord Crudley's. My complaints were falling upon deaf ears. I was wearing my favorite tee shirt purchased from my recent attendance at a concert of my favorite progressive rock group, which was the musical group, "No Way." The shirt had the group's famous space age logo on the front. I was wearing a pair of faded black dungarees and I had on my old and trusty black canvas, high-top sneakers with holes in them on my feet. In addition, I had not trimmed my beard, hair, and mustache very nicely at all; in fact, it had been a few weeks since I had groomed. I looked like a hippie bum! I wore my hair long at the time, after all, this was the 1970s. I had my hair all tied back in a little tail behind my head. I looked like a typical 1970s hippie guy, and to be honest, I did not look too swift to be trying to impress some young lady.

"This is not a blind date," Harry answered, as we got in line at the front door for an ID check and pay for the cover charges. "She has already seen you and knows you."

I went to open my mouth in protest at the logic when the bouncer at the front door looked at Harry and said, "Hey there Texas, that will be three bucks." Harry slapped him on the back, whipped out six dollars, and said, "Howdy partner, this here dough covers my buddy here in the No Way tee shirt too." The bouncer had almost fallen forward when Harry slapped him since Harry was a big strong guy. The bouncer frowned when he looked at me.

"Let me see your identification there, No Way man." I showed him my credentials, and the bouncer waved me in.

"Geez Harry, you almost knocked him on his backside you slapped him so hard."

I spotted a proud, sly smile on Harry and he retorted, "Yeah, well, he looks like a wimp, anyway." Harry strode confidently across the bar room floor for his grand entrance into the joint. I followed him as he picked a table in the corner next to the stage. He clicked his boots on the wooden floor, adjusted his big hat, and imagined that every young lady in the entire bar was checking him out. We both sat down, and shortly afterwards, a young man came by and we ordered some drinks. I would nurse a Big

Boulder beer for a few hours and Harry always ordered Wall Crawlers. The Wall Crawler was a very popular mixed drink at the time, but I could not really ever tell what was in it to achieve the horrible bright red color that appeared in the glass. I was afraid to find out, but Harry seemed to enjoy them. The waiter delivered our drinks promptly, and he placed them in front of us as we scanned the inside of the bar for any action or familiar faces.

"Do you mind telling me this gal's name that I will be meeting?" I had finally decided to get up the courage, meet my fate, and ask.

"Sure, Binky is her name, Binky Hobnobber."

I almost spit my Big Boulder beer out over the table.

"Binky Hobnobber? Come on Harry, you have to be kidding me? It sounds like what I called my little teddy bear or my baby blanket when I was a little kid. Seriously, Harry, her name is Binky?"

"What?" Harry looked at me, feigning that he was puzzled. "She is a great gal, totally gorgeous, and has a great figure too. Knockout chick. Please be cool man, I am seeing her best friend Rose, and I do not want to mess this up. I have not been able to get Rose to come out without Binky, so I told her we could do this double date thing with you. Besides, Binky is just a nickname. I think her real name is Sarah, or something like that. You will love her. Besides, it is easy to remember the two names. Just think, well, Stinky and Toes."

Harry was working hard to make a joke and put me at ease, but I was getting a really bad feeling about this one, like it was a huge setup, and I was the scapegoat in another devious master plan of his.

"What is Rose's last name?"

"Rose," Harry said without even a second delay.

"So, we have Binky Hobnobber and Rose Rose?"

Harry sipped his drink, lifted his eyes a little over the glass and gave me a one thumb up signal while saying, "I reckon you got it now ole buddy." He elbowed me in the side and pointed. "Relax, here they come. Binky is the tall one on the left with the blonde hair, and Rose is the shorter gal with the black hair. I told you Binky is a knockout. Her old man is some big shot politician out in Bergen County . . . they have loads of dough. She drives this big, brand-new Galaxy 2000. I am telling you for a poor boy from Paterson, she is a good catch for you." I stared out into the dimly lit bar and vaguely caught the glimpse of two young ladies making their way through the crowd to our table while Harry stood up and waved his big hat so they could see him.

"Over here, Rose darlin'!" Harry shot up from the table, removed his ten-gallon hat, went over to meet them and grabbed Rose by the waist, and spun her around like a top. Harry then tilted her over and gave her a long kiss on the lips right in front of everyone. 'Harry is always the showman,' I thought, as I stood quietly next to the table like an awkward fish out of water.

The three of them approached the table and Harry bellowed out, "Binky and Rose, I want you to meet my best buddy in the entire world, the famous number twenty-seven, Paul John Henson! He is also the greatest ice hockey goaltender in the entire world!"

I still felt like a meager, worthless dope as I reached out my hand over the table, shook Binky's hand, and softly said, "It is very nice to meet you." Binky smiled and shook my hand, and she then started to sit down.

"This is of course Rose, but I guess you have figured that out already by the way I greeted her!"

I smiled at Rose and said, "I did make that assumption, based upon the greeting that Harry gave you. It is nice to meet you too." I reached out and shook her hand and she smiled back at me, slightly embarrassed at the grandstanding kiss from Harry.

Now, it was not nearly as bad as I had imagined. Binky

was very pretty, tall, slender, with shoulder length, perfectly groomed, blonde hair. She had stunning, clear, blue eyes and a nice, shy smile. While Harry tended to exaggerate quite a bit, in this case his description of Binky being a knockout, was much less of an extension of the truth than he was usually prone to. She was actually close to being even more than a knockout; she was more in the range of a Hollywood movie star! Harry was also correct, as she had a perfect hourglass type female figure. She also seemed well mannered and very shy.

I had immediately spotted the proverbial fly in the ointment for me. To my horror, she was dressed very nicely, especially in comparison to my hippie outfit. She was wearing a fancy, frilly, white blouse with a black shawl type sweater over her shoulders, and a nice black skirt, which was long and tumbled down below her knees. Rose was dressed, a little more casual, but still very nicely with a printed blouse and a nice pair of dungarees.

I was the only bum in the bunch!

I was very tall, about five inches or so over six feet, and Harry was also tall as he was right around six feet. I knew right away that Rose was a little self-conscious because she was very short. It was very strange, but I had become very used to following people's eyes. As a hockey goalie, I was always keenly aware of watching a shooter's eyes for a clue as to where they may shoot the puck. I saw Rose's eyes dart up and down nervously as she looked at Harry and me.

As we stood around the table, Rose said, "My goodness, you both are so big, I had no idea how tall you were, Paul, until now. You looked so different in all that equipment, when we saw you on the ice in that hockey game." Rose sat down quickly in her chair, smoothed her hair out, and chuckled. She had short, jet-black hair, cut in the short, wavy style that was so popular in the 1970s. She wore large hoop earrings and had a very nice, wide smile. Rose was very pretty, with dark brown, almost black eyes set deeply in her head.

She had distinct features of some Italian heritage, and as Harry would have said to classify her, "She is one of them, there Hollywood type chicks." It was true. Rose was very attractive. She laughed easily, and she seemed to be a fun-loving person who might, just might, be able to stand up to the whirlwind life of Harry. Maybe. . ..

Some background music was playing. The house band was not coming on until much later.

"I reckon y'all must be thirsty! What would you little ladies like to drink?" Harry asked.

Rose answered first, "A Purple Pirate beer please."

Binky smiled and said, "A Martini. Shaken not stirred please." Hmm, just like the famous fictional English secret agent, Ian Leadfoot drinks. Very interesting, I thought. Harry ordered the drinks for the ladies and they arrived quickly.

After some small talk, Harry suddenly jumped from his seat upon hearing the opening bars of, "I Heard It in My Cowboy Hat" by the Riding the Range Boys Band.

"Come on little lady, this is one to cut the rug to!" Harry put on his big hat, picked Rose up out of her chair, and rushed her out onto the dance floor for a dance. Harry was out there on the floor putting on a show and whipping poor little Rose around like a rag doll.

The moment of truth arrived, as I found myself alone at the table with Binky, and I have to say, my comfort level was not very high. Now, I had been dating here and there, but between hockey and my job, I never really had time to have a serious, steady relationship.

I was generally comfortable around women, but this was different. This was a blind date, I was unprepared, not dressed nicely, and I was feeling duped by Harry, and his ploy to gain more time with Rose. After what seemed like more than just a few minutes, I finally spoke up. After all, Binky must have felt awkward too. She did seem quiet, shy, reserved, and frankly, like she was very nice. I searched my mind for an appropriate opening line or two. I felt that a compliment would be a fair way to start, and Binky was dressed so nicely, I thought it would be a good way to break the ice.

"You sure do look nice. That is a very nice outfit that you are wearing."

Binky turned, looked at me, and answered, "Well, thank you. I sure am dressed a lot better than you are, wearing that dumb No Way tee shirt and you are all untrimmed, with some dirty old sneakers on. Why, I had no idea that you were a hippie, when I saw you on the ice in that game. I really cannot stand the band No Way anyway, all those weird lyrics and loud horrible keyboards. What on earth is, 'Close to the Crevice' all about, anyway? It seems like a bunch of spaced out, psychedelic nonsense to me."

Oh boy, I sunk down in my chair, as that went over like a lead balloon. The SSN Binky just torpedoed and sunk the USS Henson, and it was not pretty.

"Well, I would have dressed nicer, and I do apologize, but Harry really did not tell me that we were going out to meet you and Rose tonight." I stammered in a vain and hopeless defense. The one thing I was most self-conscious about and Binky nailed me on it right off the bat! Binky just sat there staring at me with wide eyes and a defiant look on her face. She was so incredibly gorgeous, but now she seemed to have a bit of a wild side to her. So much for my incorrect initial assessment that she was shy and reserved, it seemed like she had no trouble at all in speaking her mind.

"I am sorry." I started to speak, but Binky cut me off.

"I did check into hockey after that game I attended, and I did extensive research on the sport. In my opinion, it is a brutal game, and not a game that a refined gentleman would play, but the goaltender position that you play is quite unique. All my research informed me that the goaltender is courageous, fearless, and athletic, but the persons who play the position, tend to be strange, eccentric, and outright weird in their personality. After all, who, in their right mind, would want to stand in front of one hundred mile per hour projectiles being hurled at them?"

I sat there like a dope as I was being berated and pummeled by this young lady, who had some obvious dark sides to her personality, as well as some serious, pent up anger issues.

Out of the corner of my eye, I watched Harry whirling and twirling Rose around the dance floor, laughing, and having the time of his life, while I sat here tortured by this psychotic whacko. To my horror, Binky took a sip of her drink, swallowed, and then continued with her diatribe.

"The fact that you are a hippie type person, who is into the rock group No Way, fits with the description that most goaltenders are usually eccentric persons."

I almost was hoping that she was drunk, but since she was not slurring her words, and only had taken one or two sips of her drink. I could not chalk her behavior up to that fact.

"Even though you are not dressed appropriately for an evening out with a young lady, and your hair, beard, and general grooming is atrocious, I have to admit that you are a very attractive man. I am surprised at how stunningly handsome you are close up, as my research told me that most goaltenders generally suffer from cuts quite often, and have large scars from injuries suffered, while playing that brutish position. But you seem to have escaped that fact, except for the faint scar above your right eye, which is obviously a previously stitched up injury of a fairly recent nature."

My goodness! This chick analyzed things like an amateur detective. However, she was indeed correct, because I had suffered a deep cut above that eye from a slap shot on my mask during the last game of the past season. It was a bad scene on a hard shot that I could not flag down or track through a screen in front of my net. It came through some legs and skates, hit me dead on in the mask, and cut me fairly deeply. I was proud of the fact that I kept my wits after the impact and held the puck for a faceoff before I skated off to have the doctor stitch me up! It had taken about ten stitches to close it up. It was obvious to me that Binky was pretty sharp, and that she did not miss a trick.

Binky then finally stopped speaking; she took a long breath and just stared at me as if she was awaiting my reply. Now, I still only had ever spoken those two sentences, which started this whole long disaster. I was indeed a bit shell shocked as I wondered what on earth, I could say that would not invoke another session of verbal assault? I think somewhere in all of her speech was a backhanded compliment as to my appearance, but I was not going to risk pursuing that.

Harry had done it to me again, and this time he had paired me up with some wild-eyed, anger filled, weirdo, chick. I reached down, took a sip of my Big Boulder beer while Binky still stared at me with piercing, deep-set eyes, as if she was waiting to pounce on my next thought or word.

This was indeed the longest four minutes of my entire life. Suddenly, I thought of what Harry had told me about her name and thought that this would be a safe escape route. Go for it, Paul, just ignore the criticisms and go for some safe, funny, reserved, small talk.

Good safe strategy!

"So, how did you get the nickname of, Binky?" I smiled at her and looked straight into those amazing blue eyes. My smile faded in horror as her eyes widened, and her face turned into a display of immediate and powerful anger.

Oh, oh, a bad strategy!

"Nickname! WHAT NICKNAME? MY REAL NAME IS, BINKY. IT IS NOT A NICKNAME!" Binky was now standing up, leaning over the table and shouting at me at the top of her lungs. The entire gin joint was staring at us! Oh boy, this was getting worse by the second, and I prayed for the end of the song, for Harry and Rose to rescue me.

My goaltender training took over, and I finally decided to defend my net and fight back a little bit.

"Wow, I am sorry, take it easy, Binky. Harry told me Binky was a nickname and that your real name was Sarah. I meant no harm, it was just a misunderstanding, please, sit down."

I put my hand gently on her arm. She seemed to relax, and she slowly sat back in her chair. At least I knew the root of her anger issues; it was that her actual name was Binky, and now everyone inside of Lord Crudley's knew that her real name was Binky too. Binky seemed to recover a bit as she sat straight up, smoothed out her long hair while she continued to stare at me.

She half-smiled a bit, and spoke up softly this time, almost in a low whisper, "If you continue to drink beer, please do not think that I will kiss you at the end of the night, because I hate the smell of stale beer on a person's breath."

Binky had annihilated and destroyed my self-confidence. Within a short four-minute time frame, I learned that I have stale beer breath, I am a weird, sadistic person who gets joy at being tortured by hockey pucks, I am eccentric, poorly groomed, a hippie flake, I play a brutal sport, I listen to unusual music that makes no sense, and I insult people by not knowing their correct names.

Other than that, I had a lot going for me.

Maybe I should give up now and shave my head, find an order of monks to join up with, and spend the rest of my life copying manuscripts.

The world's longest song finally ended, and Harry and

Rose came back to the table, arm-in-arm with big, huge smiles on their faces.

"So, I reckon that your real name is Binky?" Harry asked as he came to the side of the table. Harry grabbed his drink and took a long sip of it and looked at Binky and then at me. No one answered him, so he simply said, "What?"

I shifted uneasily in my seat and picked up my beer to add more intense volume to my staleness.

"So, you guys are getting along great! This is a fantastic night, let's get some more drinks, and all dance a little. Binky, you know, Paul is a fantastic dancer. He is so flexible from all that goalie stuff. You cannot believe how good a dancer he is! Yep, ole twenty-seven, as everyone calls him by his hockey jersey number, is just about the greatest natural athlete, y'all will ever see!" Harry was working hard to diffuse the tension and he really was the ultimate optimist.

I was thinking that I would rather dance with Jack the Ripper, when I watched a young lady wander over to our table, smile, take a piece of paper, and slip it in the top pocket of Harry's shirt. I recognized her as the gal who had admired Harry's car when we pulled into the parking lot. Rose glared at the woman as she sauntered away. The woman was working hard at wiggling all of her assets, and she looked back coyly over her shoulder to make sure Harry was watching.

As Harry stared her down, he let out a loud bellow, "Well, howdy there, ma'am!"

Rose was not very happy, and she glared at Harry.

"A friend of yours?"

Harry laughed, sat down at the table, laughed again, and pulled out the paper. He showed all of us that it had the young lady's telephone number on it, and he crumbled it up and tossed it on the floor.

"Hey, what can I say, I am a celebrity you know!"

All of a sudden, within a few seconds of the young

lady's exit, a huge, burly, young man with slicked back, black hair, numerous gold chains hanging around his neck along with a large, golden crucifix and a short-sleeved black shirt that exposed bulging muscles and multiple tattoos on his arms, appeared at our table. Mr. Burly ominously stood next to Harry. He had tight black pants on that looked as if he had painted them onto his body. He wore pointy, black polished shoes and a large, golden belt buckle around his waist. The features and attire were a dead giveaway that he was of Italian descent. There were many Italian-Americans in this part of New Jersey.

Sure enough, he started to speak with the typical, thick New Jersey Italian accent. "So, Wyatt Earp, jsuta whoa ya think ya flirting witha, she isa my girla."

Tonight, was slowly turning into a disaster of legendary status. The big man poked Harry with his finger at the very top of his shoulder. Harry stared down at the big guy's finger as it landed on his body. Oh no, I knew Harry all too well. The big guy just made a major error in calculation.

Harry looked up at the large Italian guy, smiled, took a sip of his drink, and answered, "Hold on there, spaghetti, I reckon that your gal came over to me. I am here with my best buddy and these ladies and not bothering anyone. It is not my fault that she prefers a cowboy over your garlic-filled lifestyle."

Harry was a tough guy, as I had mentioned, he played hockey for years and had suffered many injuries, as well as working his way through many fights both on and off the ice. He and I had fought our way out of many a tough jam here and there, and while we may have suffered a few scrapes here and there, we did not lose too many rounds. Those stories and adventures are definitely better left for relating in other tales down the road. This particular encounter looked like it was going to be anything but ordinary.

The big guy had just woken up the sleeping cowboy and

it could turn really bad very quickly. Harry cracked his knuckles; I dug my sneakers in under the table and looked around to see if he had any buddies moving in for a potential ambush. Binky and Rose simply sat there with horrified looks on their faces.

Now that horrible hockey injury that Harry suffered always came back to haunt us once in a while, and tonight was one of those times. I cannot emphasize enough how horrific an injury it had been. The force of the hockey puck striking Harry in his face and mouth knocked him unconscious, knocked out most of his teeth, broke his jaw in four locations, broke his nose, blackened his eyes, and the doctors had to stitch him with about one hundred stitches in his face and mouth. He was in the hospital sipping gelatin and soup for two weeks, and the surgeons ended up reconstructing his right cheekbone with plastic surgery. I remember visiting him in the hospital and the best way I could describe his appearance was that he looked like a Halloween monster. It was the worst hockey injury that I had ever seen. He was fine now, but he had a false teeth plate in the front of his mouth and if you looked hard at his face, you could see some scars here and there. All in all, the doctors had done a remarkably good job of putting him all back together.

It was quite obvious that Harry's comments had enraged the big guy, and he picked up his fist and shoved it in Harry's face.

"I thinka I willa knocka your teetha out, cowboy!"

Harry quickly stood up, and now the entire bar focused on the situation while the bouncers rushed over to the table. The big guy stepped back just a little because he was surprised at the actual size of Harry once he had stood up. Harry held his hand up to indicate that the bouncers should stop.

He adjusted his big ten-gallon hat, looked over at me, and said, "Twenty-seven, please, slide your beer over here."

Puzzled, I slid my beer mug across the table and Harry took it. He sucked deep in his mouth, opened up his mouth, removed his entire front plate of false teeth, and dropped them in my beer!

He then turned and smiled a wide, toothless grin at the Italian guy and proudly proclaimed, "I reckon it looks like you are a little too late there, spaghetti, a hockey puck beat you to it. Now, just in case, you think that you will break my nose, then here, let me show you this too."

Harry never was very politically correct, and while he was usually a happy-go-lucky, jovial guy, you did not want to get on his wrong side. When he was riled up, he actually could be very insulting and brutal. Since Harry had pulverized his nose in the hockey accident, his nose for lack of a better description was, well, very flexible. He could move it back and forth very easily on his face.

Still standing up next to the dazed Italian man, Harry grabbed his nose with both of his hands, wiggled it, and with a loud, horrible crack, he popped his nose down so it was lying on the side of his face. He then turned and smiled at the horrified Italian guy with his bent nose and toothless grin.

"So, now, what do y'all want to do to me there, garlic breath?"

The big man's jaw dropped down on the floor and he took a few more steps back in horror at the sight of Harry and his hockey badges of courage. The suddenly, fear-filled man, waved his arms quickly across his body, almost as if he was indicating to Harry to stop. I think he was afraid that more parts and pieces of Harry would start dismantling before his eyes.

"Youa crazy!" The big guy walked away talking to himself, waving his hands in the air and shaking his head.

"I thought so," was all Harry said as he popped his nose back into place with a loud sickening crack, while shaking his head to make sure all the parts were still there. He then took his teeth back out of my beer, put them back into his mouth, and sat back down. Harry slid the beer mug back over to me, smiled, and said, "Thanks, Paulie."

I sat there staring down at my beer that no longer had any real appeal to me. The bouncers walked away and Harry clapped his hands together and asked, "What do you say we blow this joint and take a ride in the Trans Whizzer?"

Binky was sitting there just staring, and she finally managed to say, "That was the most disgusting thing that I have ever seen in my life."

Rose was equally stunned, and Harry smiled and said, "Yeah well it sure took the wind out of old garlic puss's sails now didn't it! I reckon that we ought to blow this joint!"

He pulled out a pile of dollar bills, threw them on the table, motioned to me to put my wallet away, and stood up. I was more than ready to leave, so I stood up, as did Rose and Binky, and we all started to walk out. I noticed out of the corner of my eye as the girls walked ahead that Harry bent down and picked up the crumbled paper that had the gal's telephone number on it off the floor. He then put it in his vest pocket. He looked up at me, winked, and put his fingers to his lips to signal me to keep my mouth shut. Harry was truly amazing. Sometimes, he even amazed me at how he worked the angles!

3

Ewing Ave and Other Oddities

Harry walked confidently by the bouncer at the front door and dropped a twenty-dollar bill in his front pocket.

"Here you go there, pal. You are on my payroll now, partner."

"Hey, thanks, Big Tex!" The bouncer tapped his top pocket and smiled. "Are you looking for a job? We sure could use a tough guy like you around here."

"Sorry, partner. I have other fish to fry, but y'all have a good night now," Harry answered him. "Hey, keep an eye on that new Galaxy 2000 in the corner there, will you partner? We will be back."

The bouncer nodded to Harry and gave him a little flip of his hand to indicate that he was cool.

The bouncer then turned around to Binky, Rose, and me and said, "Goodnight, guys. Goodnight, Binky," Obviously, the bouncer had been paying attention tonight. Since Harry gave him a nice tip, he was good to go, and on our side now, after all, twenty bucks in 1979 was not a bad little chunk of change for a tip.

"Rose darlin,' I will bring you and Binky back for the car, but right for now let's jump in the Trans Whizzer, I want to show y'all something."

As bizarre as the now famous teeth and nose incident was, I was almost thankful for the interlude, as it broke up the tirade that Binky had been laying upon me, and for that I was truly relieved. I was surprised that Rose and Binky agreed to continue to hang out with us, as I thought for sure, based upon her very clear expression of her feelings towards me, that Binky would have pulled Rose aside and asked her to call it an early night. Harry and Rose got in the front seat and Binky and I climbed in the back.

The heat of the day had passed, and it was a wonderful, clear, starlit, July evening with no humidity at all; it was fantastic.

It was a perfect summer night.

Harry took out the glass from the T-top of the roof of the car and stowed the glass in the carriers in the trunk. As soon as we climbed in the car, sat down, and Harry brought the big engine to life, Binky piped up.

"I have to say, Harry, while that gentleman of Italian heritage was clearly wrong in approaching and confronting you, and inciting the provocation, I found your aggressive handling of that situation horrifying, appalling, and almost Neanderthal in your behavior."

Harry slipped the Electronic Transistor Orchestra tape back in the deck and turned around to face us. "Oh yeah well, thank you, Binky, I reckon I did a pretty good job at diffusing the situation myself." He then laughed and turned back to face the front of the car. "I reckon he is actually mighty lucky that he made the right decision! I hate cleaning up piles of spaghetti all over my floors too!" Rose elbowed Harry in the side as he put the Trans Whizzer in gear, backed up out of the spot, and peeled rubber out of Lord Crudley's parking lot.

Binky folded her arms across her body in anger because she was miffed at Harry's smug response. She then leaned over to me and whispered, "You do not have all those false teeth or one of those trick noses from playing that horrid sport, now do you?" I shook my head back and forth adamantly, to indicate that was not the case, and Binky seemed convinced and satisfied. I wiggled over as close to the window as I could in hope that Binky would feel I was out of comfortable shouting range.

Harry put his arm around Rose in the front seat and they were laughing and singing together to the song, "Telegraph Signals" blaring out of the tape deck.

"Where are we heading to, Harry?" I asked.

"Paul, I am going to show you one of the strangest things you have ever seen, you are going to love this. It is a little weird and it may freak you out, but man it is cool." Harry was winding the Trans Whizzer up now and he pulled it onto Route 208, which was a highway that rolled from Passaic County all the way to the outer reaches of Bergen County in northern New Jersey.

It was awesome rolling up the highway through the night, in this extraordinary vehicle. The big engine was moving us effortlessly along, while the music was blaring out, and the wind was blowing through the open roof. Binky seemed to be calmer now, and she was enjoying the ride, as she stared silently out the window with the wind blowing her long blonde hair. I stole a stare or two at her out of the corner of my eye and saw that from the side, she had a great profile. I was careful not to allow her to catch me stealing a glimpse or two of her. I could not help but notice how when she did not have a sneer on her face, she actually was stunningly beautiful.

"So, Binky, what kind of music do you listen to?" Harry asked as he glanced back at us in the rear-view mirror. "Man alive, can you guys get farther apart back there or what? Do you want me to tie one of you on the lid of the trunk?" Harry was needling us and laughing as he spotted our seating arrangements in the mirror from the front seat.

To my surprise and absolute astonishment, Binky laughed and answered, "Oh, I like a lot of music, and right now, I have decided to get into the band No Way and the album, 'Close to the Crevice.'" My head spun around and I must have let my jaw drop to the floor of the car. Binky turned to me, then winked and smiled.

She really had caught me off guard!

"No kidding! Well, you two were made for each other, as Paul is one of the biggest No Way heads that I know of. He knows every song, lyric, hook, and detail about them."

This was certainly one of the strangest nights I have ever experienced. Either this young lady was a schizophrenic, or the bartender spiked my beer with a hallucinogen.

"Here we are! The Ewing Ave exit in Shadow Lakes," Harry proclaimed as he took the exit and geared down the car on a long turn. Harry guided the Trans Whizzer slowly down the long slope of the exit ramp of the highway and slowed the car to a final stop at the stop sign for Ewing Ave and the exit ramp. The exit ramp was actually a long downward hill of a road, and gradually the car leveled out at the stop sign. I had no idea what on earth he was doing, and this seemed like another wild Harry adventure of some sorts. Rose turned to Harry and asked the question that was on the rest of our minds.

"What are you doing? Why are we stopping here on this exit ramp?"

Harry smiled one of his famous devious smiles. "Watch, but I need to make sure no other car is in back of me." Harry checked his rearview mirror, then pushed the clutch in, put the car into neutral, and took his foot off the brake. "Now, watch!" he shouted. The Trans Whizzer was in neutral, and slowly, the car rolled backwards and to our amazement, the car continued to roll backwards and slowly went up the slope of the exit ramp!

Harry pounded on the steering wheel and yelled out, "Is this awesome or what? We are going up a hill backwards! It is totally freaking me out!"

Rose gave a little scream and Binky shifted into her detective-like observation mode as she studied the situation while looking out the window.

Binky then said, "It is an optical illusion. This is not actually a hill."

I looked out the window and even though the car was

barely moving, it sure looked like we were going backwards up a hill to me.

I ventured out into dangerous waters, as I had to disagree with Binky's observation, but I had to call it as it was, at least to my eyes.

"I don't know, Binky. It sure looks like a hill to me," I managed to say.

Harry spotted a car coming down the ramp behind us, so he put the car into gear and pulled the car back up to the stop sign. He then made a left-hand turn out onto Ewing Ave.

"I will go around and down the highway and we can try it again. Weird, huh?"

Harry was in fine form tonight, he had a plan, and he was working it to perfection.

"The story is that a girl was walking, and she was struck by a hit-and-run driver and killed here years ago, on that road, before they built the highway and the exit ramp was there." Harry continued, "I reckon she died right where the stop sign is at the end of the ramp, and when a car stops and stays there for a while, she doesn't like it. She then pushes the car up the ramp and away from where she died. Some people have even seen her ghost there at night. Last year, I came up here myself and tried this when it was around Halloween. It was a frosty, cold night, with a lot of moisture, and after the car rolled up the hill, I got out and checked the front hood of the car with a flashlight, and I noticed that there were handprints on it in the frost."

Harry finished his explanation, smiled a little grin, and I saw his eyes lick back and forth in his head as he caught a stare at Rose to gauge her reaction to his ghost story.

That was it!

Rose jumped, screamed, and grabbed Harry around his neck. Binky then unlatched her seat belt, slid across the seat, plowed tightly into me, smiled, and put her arm through mine. She then picked up the middle seat belt, pulled it over her, and buckled it. Binky reached behind my head and pulled the little tie I had on the back of my hair and yanked it out and placed it in her purse.

"You have nice, long, hair. You should not tie it all back like that. Unless, of course, you were playing in the net in a hockey game. For optimum safety, you would not want all that hair blocking your vision."

Harry looked in the mirror and saw that we were now sitting right next to each other. He chuckled and shifted the big car back out onto the highway. Down and around, we went, and right back to the Ewing Ave exit ramp. Once more, we duplicated the same scenario, and the car rolled up the hill, while Harry and I laughed, and the two girls shrieked in horror. Binky was holding my arm so tight that she was cutting off the circulation in my arm, and Rose had a death grip around Harry's neck.

"Oh no," Harry said as he looked in the rearview mirror and we all turned and saw the red lights of a police patrol car flashing and coming up behind us. Harry grabbed his ten-gallon hat, put it on his head, and pulled the Trans Whizzer over to the side, shut the engine off, and put it in gear so it would no longer move.

"Stay cool guys, I reckon that I have this all under control," the forever-confident Harry proclaimed. Neither the girls nor I said a word as the policeman strode out of his car and walked slowly up to the side of the Trans Whizzer. "Howdy Officer!" Harry shouted at the patrolman.

The officer was surprised at the sight of Harry and his big, black, ten-gallon hat. You could tell he was not prepared to run into a make believe, New Jersey cowboy on an exit ramp in affluent Shadow Lakes, New Jersey. He was a large, tall policeman with a drill instructor type hat on his head and a big, beer belly that hung over his gun belt.

"License, registration and insurance card there, cowboy

man," the officer said as Harry handed him the documents. The officer looked them over, and then took his flashlight, looked at all of us, and looked around the interior of the car.

"This looks like a brand-new car. Are you broken down here? Why are you hanging out on the exit ramp?" The officer asked.

"She sure is a beautiful car, isn't she, officer?" Harry answered, but the officer just folded his arms, stared back at Harry, and then handed him back his paperwork.

"Up here from Paterson, eh? Now, what business might you Paterson boys have all the way up here in the suburbs? Some type of no-good business I imagine?" The officer looked at Harry and once more, he folded his arms across his chest.

"Well, I will be honest, officer. I was just showing my buddy and the girls the ghost ramp."

"The ghost ramp, I see . . . the ghost ramp. By the way, what is with the big hat and cowboy act? Have you been drinking, son? Please step out of the car." It appeared that the officer was not buying what Harry had decided to sell.

Harry opened the door, and the officer looked him up and down. "No sir, I had one Wall Crawler hours and hours ago, at Lord Crudley's. I am as sober as a preacher would be. I will take any test you can muster up and then some."

Binky leaned over and whispered in my ear, "Should you do something Paul, is this going to be an adverse situation for Harry? My research last week told me that this town has a higher-than-normal rate of arrests than the neighboring towns."

I tapped her arm and said, "Relax, Harry can sell ice to an Eskimo. Let's wait and see how it all shakes out."

I thought to myself how this gal spends an awful lot of time researching every aspect of life; she is a walking statistic book. Harry went on then to explain the story about the ramp, the ghost, the entire tale. On and on he went, turning on the best charm he could ever turn on. Harry was amazing; he could work a crowd or an individual like the best politician. There was just something about him that made people follow and believe him.

It was very hard to explain.

The officer listened intently to the story, pulled his hat back on his head, and looked at Harry. He suddenly seemed to be engrossed in the facts that Harry had just presented and was ignoring the fact that Harry had just confessed to going the wrong way on a one-way street.

"No kidding. You mean to tell me, son, that this big, heavy sports car will go up this ramp? All my years here on patrol, I never heard this story. I have to say I never heard of cars that go uphill."

Harry moved quickly and offered to back up his testimony with a demonstration.

"Yup! Here let me move the Trans Whizzer and y'all climb in your car and try it."

Harry climbed back in the Trans Whizzer, winked at all of us, and moved the car over so the policeman could pull his car up to the stop sign. This was really getting good. Only Harry could convince a policeman to violate the rules and laws of the road.

We all got out of the car and watched as the policeman pulled his car up to the sign and tried it. Sure enough, the car rolled up the hill, until the policeman could take no more. You could see him shaking his head in the front seat in amazement. He put the car into the parking gear and jumped out of the police cruiser. Binky and Rose were both hanging on my arms, shaking, as the summer air had turned colder, and the atmosphere had become spooky. Harry met the policeman next to his car.

The officer was clearly nervous as Harry laughed and slapped him on the back.

"I reckon it sure is strange ain't it!"

The officer shook his head and said, "I cannot explain it, but it really is kind of scary."

Harry reached in the Trans Whizzer and grabbed the box of dog treats that my mother had given him.

"I sure have rustled up a mighty hunger. Are you hungry? Have you eaten yet?"

"No, as a matter of fact, I am a little hungry," the policeman said as Harry handed him a treat. The two of them sat there on the side of the exit ramp like the best of friends, crunching dog treats together, talking about the ramp, the strange story, the Trans Whizzer, being a policeman, and any other subject you could ever think of.

"These are good, what are they?" The officer asked between bites.

"Oh, just some snacks my buddy's mom gave me," Harry answered vaguely. Harry was one of a kind, and the three of us walked back to the car and got inside. Harry exchanged some more small talk, the two of them shook hands, and Harry got back in the car and started it up.

"This place gives me the creeps! Let's go, Harry," Rose said.

"He sure was a nice guy. What a great guy," Harry was very excited. Binky reached up in the front seat, grabbed the box of dog treats, and looked at the label. She shook her head and placed them back where they had been. Once more, words really could not capture all the nuances of the strange behavior of the world-famous Harry M. Redmond Jr. and his unique approach to life.

We rode back down Route 208 and rolled through the night. It was late now, and this crazy adventure and evening had finally waned. Binky seemed very tired. She rested her head on my shoulder, and did not say anything all the way back down the highway. We pulled into Lord Crudley's parking lot and Harry waved to the bouncer, who nodded back. He then pointed to Binky's car as if to say he had it all covered. We all got out of the car and walked over to the Galaxy 2000. Harry pulled Rose off to the side and he was talking to her softly, when the two of them suddenly disappeared around the corner of the car, out of our sight.

I very awkwardly reached out to shake Binky's hand. "Well, it was quite a night. I am sure none of us will forget it anytime soon."

Binky ignored my hand, while she looked around nervously, smiled weakly, and laughed a soft, almost inaudible laugh. She then looked down at the ground and kicked mindlessly at some stones on the surface of the parking lot. Binky seemed now to be shy and searching for some words to say. She then took a small piece of paper out of her purse and placed it in my hand.

"Please call me, I really would like to see you again," and with that she looked up and suddenly gave me a quick kiss.

Binky caught me totally off guard by her reaction.

"I guess I don't smell like old beer after all," I said with a smile. I heard her mumbling some words very softly and low, but not quite low enough that I could not hear them. I listened carefully and then I caught her clearly saying, "We all get up, we then we all get around."

I then recognized that she had been reciting verbatim, the closing lyrics to the song, "Close to the Crevice." I then realized that Binky had duped me.

"Hey, you really do know the music of No Way, don't you?"

She did not answer, but she smiled at me, then went straight to her car and got in. I closed the door for her and Harry escorted Rose into the passenger side and closed the door. We waved as the big Galaxy started up, the headlights came on, and Binky pulled out of the lot and drove up the road. Harry came over and put his big arm around my shoulders. The two of us stood there for quite a while, watching while the taillights of the big car disappeared into the night. It was obvious that Binky had warmed up to me as the evening went on, and I to her, but as I stood there recalling this very strange evening and all that had transpired, I still could not help but wonder why on earth her parents had named her Binky.

"What a night, eh buddy, ole boy? I reckon twenty-seven, that those are two of the prettiest gals in all of New Jersey." Harry walked with me back to the Trans Whizzer. Neither of us had to say a word as I reached down into the tape collection, fished around in the box, pulled the Electronic Transistor Orchestra tape out of the deck, and slid in a Crystal Zirconium tape.

Off we rode into the night, back to good old Paterson, with Crystal's soft voice serenading us.

"Please, hear me, my love, please," Crystal, pleaded from the tape deck as she melted our hearts.

It provided us with the perfect closing to another perfect Harry and Paul day.

4

Harry's Theory

It was a week or so after the famous nose and teeth night, and Harry and I had both been busy with work. Even though I had the best intentions of calling Binky, I had blown it and had not gotten around to doing so. Harry and I had no real plans, but since we had both been busy with work and some overtime projects, we really had not met up in a few days. After all, this was 1979, and the economy was brutal. During these days, you took every chance you could at working a little extra and making a few dollars here and there.

I left work at a normal time on a Thursday and decided to stop by the Redmond's house and see what was going on. I drove an old MJ-17 body jeep at the time with a soft ragtop.

It was not fancy, but she rolled.

I parked the jeep in front of 20 John Street and Ronzo, who was hanging out in front of the house weeding a fence line, immediately greeted me. He was wearing his big straw cowboy hat, big boots, and dungarees with his wide belt buckle.

"Howdy Paul, where have you been hiding these days? I have not seen you since the big Fourth of July picnic . . . well, what I remember of it, that is."

"Hey Ronzo, yeah, I have been busy, working you know. I see Harry is home. Maybe we will have a few days to ourselves this weekend."

Ronzo tossed a few weeds in a bag at his feet, stood up

and took a long sip of Dingleberry beer from a can he had on the front steps. He leaned back on the front railing of the porch and seemed to be thinking.

Perhaps Ronzo was pondering his lost youth.

"Hey, enjoy it while you can, I remember those days, you are only young once, and with that car of Harrys, I reckon the world is your oyster."

I patted Ronzo on the back and smiled. He went back to his weeding, and I went up the front steps, in the front door and walked into the living room. There was a country and western record blaring away on the record player. There was not a soul around except for the Redmond's dog Cocoa who greeted me with his favorite toy, the famous rubber Piggy. I knelt down and petted him. He dropped Piggy on the ground and licked my face. He was really like a second dog to me next to my own dog, Skippy. I loved Cocoa, and I was sure that the feeling was mutual.

"Hey where is everyone, Cocoa?"

Cocoa, who really was, smarter than most people were, barked at me, wagged his tail, and then picked Piggy back up. Cocoa then led me out the back door, and out on the patio where I found Harry and his sister Linda sitting around the picnic bench.

Harry was playing his banjo and Linda was singing.

"Hey buddy, we were just working on our song here, the one about all of my favorite old cars. It is really coming along. I think it is a potential super hit."

Linda stood up from the table, smiled at me and said, "Hello, Paul. Harry, let's quit for now. I have to get supper going, anyway. I think we need to rework the second verse, but we can work on it later."

"Hey, Linny," I said as I waved to her and sat down.

"See you later, Paul," Linda said as she went through the back door of the house.

"So, this is a really big deal, this song you two are working on?"

Harry ignored me as he put his banjo in the case, closed it, and never answered the question. Harry took off his ten-gallon hat and set it on the table.

"You know that Binky is devastated that you have not called her. What is with you? I introduce you to each other, and she dives head over teakettle for you. Nice move twenty-seven, to get this great and downright gorgeous chick interested, and then disappear and never call her?"

Harry was pacing a little back and forth now, and I could tell he was still going to let me have it.

"Did you not see the stars she had in her eyes for you that night? Tell me, Paul—that even though you are under the influence of the Old Lady Syndrome that you did not check out her fantastic figure? I swear, I think you are blind sometimes to all of this! I know that I surely did, and a lot of other guys in that joint would have lined up to trade places with you!" Harry seemed to be more than a little upset with me, so I tried to muster a little defense.

I felt bad because that was not my intention.

"I didn't mean to not call her. We just have been busy since we went out to Lord Crudley's Bar. After all, you and I both have been working a lot of overtime."

Harry sat down on the edge of the picnic table, sighed, and looked at me.

"Yeah, we have, but I bailed you out as usual, because Rose told me the girls wanted to know if we would take them to the shore on Saturday. I told them they were in luck since we both had a Saturday off for a change. You need to call Binky tonight, though. She needs to hear from you. The poor gal is a mess thinking that you do not like her and are not interested. You know . . . it is time that you and I had an open discussion, buddy."

Harry grew serious, and he pushed his big hat away, sat on the edge of the picnic table, and faced me.

"I need to teach you about Harry's Theory, you, of all people, need to pay attention and learn from this."

For the first time in a long, long, time, I noticed that during this entire conversation, Harry was speaking regular, "New Jersey" to me. Phony, western drawl, twang words had miraculously left his language for the moment.

"Oh boy, is this one an official type Harry Theory of yours or just hypothetical?" I joked.

"This is serious. What I am going to say may be a little rough, but I am saying it because I care. I hate to tell you this because we are like brothers, you and I have been through an awful lot together since we were little kids, but I have to teach you this."

I leaned in a little because I was very intrigued. It was not often that Harry actually showed a serious side or offered advice of any sort to me; it was usually always the other way around.

"You are the smartest, nicest, most caring guy I know. You have a decent job, you are a great athlete, you are a good-looking guy, have a great personality, you speak well, you can talk about any subject on Earth from history to music with intelligence, you have a ton of things going for you. But the trouble is that you are too nice of a guy. I think it was that baseball manager who said nice guys finish last, and it is true. You, my good brother, are a doormat. You are a loser with the chicks because you are too nice a guy. You are too reliable, too honest, as well as caring, and trustworthy. Chicks can count on you to come through all the time. There is no mystery to Paul John Henson."

Harry slid off the edge of the picnic table and leaned on the side of the table. He looked down, and then back at me, to make sure I was paying attention to him.

"You are the kind of guy that women want to marry and stay with forever, but you are not the kind of guy they want to date!"

I was a little uneasy. Harry's logic seemed to make sense in an odd sort of way.

"Well, isn't it good to be all those things?"

"See you do not get it, because you are a nice guy!" Harry stood up straight now and was excited as he preached, "If you would just open your eyes and see that the chicks all study you and check you out, you may be able to understand how to use what you have that God handed to you, Paul. I watch, I see, and you are oblivious, because nice guys like you are too kind and reserved and do not flaunt themselves in front of women. You should see the gals check out your backside and whisper about your hair and athletic body. You just walk by like a little reliable, kind, nice, dodo bird, as it is not the right thing to do to allow yourself to be an object of female desires."

Oh boy, Harry was letting me have it with a painful analysis. "Women our age, hell, all women of any age, they like the dangerous guy, the guy with the tattoos, the mysterious guy, the bad guy who shaves his head, and was in prison, the guy who has a hard edge, women eat that stuff up. The boring, reliable guy, he can be found mowing lawns on Saturday mornings all across America, cleaning his gutters, taking the kids to school in his family sedan, helping his wife carry the groceries in from the car, and running errands for her. All the while, his wife couldn't care less, as she has her eye on the make believe bad-ass, mean guy next door, who just got out of prison, has no job, still lives in his parent's house, has tattoos all over his body, has a motorcycle, kicks his family dog, and has an alcohol and drug problem."

I was really having a hard time with Harry's Theory now and cleared my throat to speak, but Harry held up his hand to indicate that he was not done.

"That is why I get all the gals and you get shut out, because I keep them guessing. Half the time they do not know if I am from Texas or New Jersey, I wear my hockey scars like a badge of courage, I drive fast cars, I keep them always thinking about who I am, how tough I am, and they never really can get close enough to me to figure me out. These women, they love it, and that is why I have them lined up for miles, and you can only get a date or two here and there."

Harry was now shaking his head back and forth and he sighed a little.

"Here is what will happen, since I can predict the actions and moves of my best buddy, Paul John Henson, to the letter. I know what you will do. You will call Binky, apologize, and tell her how you have been working extra hours to save up extra money. Binky will think how wonderful you are. A reliable guy who works hard, earns money, and brings home the paycheck like a good, little, reliable robot. In her mind, she will say, wow, this is the kind of man that I would like to marry someday . . . but not right now. He is handsome, steady, reliable, and honest. I would love to marry him, but I sure would like to sow some wild oats first."

Harry was now waving his arms in the air and pacing back and forth while he preached his sermon on his theory.

"She will hang up the phone and then dream about the shaved down, tatted up, drugged out, dangerous, guy around the corner and how she could get a date with him rather than be bored to tears with the reliable and predictable, hippie goalie guy."

I felt uneasy now. I could not help but to think there might be some actual truth to Harry and his wild theory.

I asked, "What should I say to Binky? I mean, instead of the truth?"

Harry sat back on the edge of the table and continued, "Tell her you were busy all week shopping for a new motorcycle for you two to ride on, and she could rip her top off, and go topless on the back of your new bike if you decide to buy it! Or tell her that you went down to the tattoo parlor for them to ink you up, but you could not decide if you should get the skull and crossbones or the naked lady. Better yet, tell her that you rode in your jeep to Seashore Heights with the rag top down and got caught in a thunderstorm all the way home on the Garden State Parkway. For the love of Pete, tell her anything, but do not tell her how you were working to earn extra money like a good little boy, and you were so busy and tired that you could not call her!"

I sat down on the picnic table now as Harry had hit a nerve for me. He did peg me as a steady, predictable, reliable guy, and while I did have a few dates here and there, I certainly did not have them lined up as he did.

"Look, Paul, believe me, someday you will find a great gal who wants exactly what you offer and I hope that you two lovers stay together forever, and that she never grows bored with a nice, reliable, steady type guy. I have to tell you that some of the greatest lessons that life has taught me until now, came out of the worst times that I have lived through. I learned from certain situations like when my mother died, when my relationship with Joyce finally ended, and when I was hit with that hockey puck and landed in that hospital bed, sucking gelatin out of a straw for a week that I was not going to stay down for long. I vowed to take something away from those tough times, and I think I did. I know that I am going to live this life as hard and as fast as I can, and it is going to be one adventure after another. I will not waste one minute of it!"

I thought as I listened that he was doing a pretty good job of living up to that vow—that was for sure!

"I am only teaching you for now, so that you can get over this stigma of always being the steady, calm, reliable, boring, buddy of crazy, wild Harry."

I stood up now and said, "I appreciate the advice and you sharing, Harry's Theory, and I guess there is some truth to it, but I am not buying it all. I think that a nice gal like Binky is, well, she would look at a man for what he is now. I do not think she is looking that far down the road."

Harry was shaking his head in disagreement. I decided to turn the table on his way of life and theory.

"What will you ever do, if you find a gal who you would like to settle down with, and those hard and fast times are interrupted by a young lady who steals your heart?"

Harry chuckled, grabbed his big hat, and reverted to his country and western alter ego, "I reckon that will be a cold day in Hades! That girl would really need to be special and different to catch old Harry."

"Or she would need to be Crystal Zirconium," I came back, catching him a bit off guard.

"Oh yeah!" Harry yelled out, "Then, Hades would be frozen over!"

We made plans to meet early on Saturday and to pick up the girls. I jumped back in my jeep and headed for home. On the ride home, I was running Harry's Theory repeatedly in my mind. It just seemed so upside down, so contrary to what I was as a person; it was really hard for me to believe. I came home, ate some dinner, and fished around in my desk drawer for Binky's phone number.

It was hard to have any kind of private conversation in our house, because we only had one phone and it was right out in the middle of the dining room, where everyone in the house would pass by and hear every word. I ran a number of wild scenarios in my head of what I would tell her, just in case Harry and his crazy theory proved to be correct. The tattoo idea was too wild. I did not have enough dough to buy a six-pack of Big Boulder beer, let alone a motorcycle, and I never take the top down on my jeep. It could get wet if a sudden storm came along.

Harry was right. I was a loser!

I was nervous as a cat as I dialed her number and tried hard to think of what to say. Just as I was about to dial the last number, my old man came in and stopped in front of me.

"Are you going to be long? I have a problem with a

machine at the shop and I need to call in."

"No, just a few minutes, I will be off in a minute."

The old man nodded and went back to the New York Bugs game on the television. I dialed the number again, and a man answered on the second ring. The voice was deep and to be honest, he sounded like a gangster type guy.

"Hello . . . may I please speak with, Binky?"

"Yeah, who is this?" The man asked gruffly.

"Paul, this is Paul John Henson calling."

The gangster voice never said another word or returned, but I heard the phone receiver fall down as if the gangster-voiced guy placed it on a table or something. I could stand in front of one hundred miles per hour hockey pucks without even an ounce of fear, and now I am calling this chick and my knees are knocking together.

Thanks Harry, old buddy, old pal.

I remembered Harry telling me that Binky came from a wealthy and important family. They were involved in politics. I thought to myself—that explains the gangster voice on the phone, after all this is New Jersey.

I heard the receiver pick up, and I heard Binky's voice say, "Hello, Paul."

"Hey, Binky. How are you? I am sorry, I have not called, but I have been busy all week." I hesitated for just a moment, "At work, we had some mandatory overtime."

I folded like a cheap tourist camera.

Harry was right.

I had scripted the conversation to perfection, exactly as he had predicted I would.

"Oh, that is fine, I understand. Work is very important. But I hear that we are all set for the weekend to go to the shore. It will be nice to see you."

"Yeah, yeah, yeah, we are all set, it will be great."

Just then, the old man appeared from the other room and stood right over me with his arms folded, as it was apparent that I had used up my meager five seconds of allowed phone time. I explained to Binky that I only had a minute to speak because my father had to use the phone for a work emergency. We confirmed the time and place we would pick them up on Saturday and it was over. Binky told me that she understood about the short phone call, it was so nice to hear from me and once more, she emphasized that work was very important and we hung up.

"Geez Dad, I was only on the phone for a few minutes." I complained as we switched places.

The old man had a puzzled look on his face.

"Binky? Are you for real? The girl's name is Binky?"

The old man, of course, had been eavesdropping.

"Is that a nickname?"

I walked away shaking my head and saying, "Take my advice, if you ever get to meet her, don't ask."

Saturday arrived, and weather-wise, it was a great day. It was clear, warm, but not too hot. I made a point of dressing better, with a nice pair of black dungaree jeans, casual but clean moccasin type shoes, and a nice casual, clean, button down, summer type shirt. I combed my hair, trimmed up my beard and hair, and put on a nice pair of sunglasses. I did not tie up my long hair as I remembered Binky's suggestion. I thought that I looked vastly improved over my last disastrous appearance. I was not about to be burned twice. Harry and I packed some bathing suits, extra clothes, socks, sandals, and some towels in a hockey equipment bag of mine. We wanted to be prepared, just in case we were going to hit the water and sand, but Harry was not sure exactly what the plan was.

Now, there were many choices for beaches to enjoy along the New Jersey shoreline. Some were famous for certain things, like the music scene along the northern shore points, or some pristine, shallow water beaches way down near Delaware, or others were a mixture with a music and bar scene, boardwalks, amusement rides, and nightlife along with pure, clean beaches. For the ultimate mixture for folks our age, in the 1970s, the clear choice was to go to Seashore Heights. It had it all, including a huge boardwalk with rides, amusements, as well as bars, and a music and dance scene.

Seashore Heights was today's destination.

We rolled out in the Trans Whizzer, picked up Rose first, and then went over to Binky's house, which was in a well-to-do town about twenty miles north of where Harry and I lived. The Hobnobber estate included a huge mansion, set on a hill, with a long driveway leading up to a large four-car garage. The house looked like it had a hundred rooms. You could see a large, in-ground swimming pool, tennis courts, and a smaller house set out on the property nearby the courts and pool. It looked like something we had seen on television that a movie star would have lived in.

"Holy smokes, what a joint this is! I reckon ole Binky and her clan, sure has a lot of jingles stashed away somewhere!" Harry was amazed at the size of her house. He pulled his hat off and scratched his head as he admired the property.

"Now Harry, please do not dwell on it, you know how self-conscious and defensive Binky can be," Rose warned.

I leaned in from the back seat and added my opinion, which was primarily in the interest of self-defense and preservation.

"Oh boy, please do not rile her up Harry, it could make for a long day for me, buddy."

Harry and Rose both nodded in agreement. Harry pulled into the long driveway, just as we saw Binky walk out the front door and head for the car. I went to get out of the car to let her in, but she already slipped in the back door of the car and sat down before I could even get out of my door.

"Howdy there Bink-a-roo-ski, how y'all doing?" Harry

bellowed as Binky got in the car.

She smiled and said, "Hello."

Binky then turned to me, slid over across the back seat to be closer to me, and asked, "How are you?"

I nodded, smiled, and said that I was fine. Binky nodded, and all seemed well. Harry was already down the driveway, out on the main road, and flying off before we even had a chance to settle in the backseat.

"It is going to be a great day, youse guys, we have a little longer ride here to make it to Seashore Heights, but it is worth it. I have all kinds of music, just say what you want to hear. We can have a blast on the ride down the road. If y'all become a little hungry, then we have some snacks and we have a cooler with sodas in the trunk. We are rolling!" Harry was very excited to begin our adventure.

Binky was dressed very nicely in dungarees and a summer type blouse. I had noticed that she had not carried a bag of any sort, only her purse. Before I could even ask if we were going to go in the water or on the sand, Binky started to speak.

"Now, I want to be clear on this as we are going to the seashore and beach," she said, as Harry turned the music down to hear her. "Rose and I had a long discussion before we planned this trip, and we both decided that we will not go in the water. I do prefer not swimming in the dirty ocean because it ruins my hair and nails, but even going on the beach will be out of the question for today."

I sat back as I had been down this road before and I knew this would be some type of detective agency, evaluation of the situation by Binky, based upon her latest research.

Binky continued with her instructions for the day, "Rose agreed that being on the beach with Harry would be uncomfortable. We are certain that he would be observing all the young women in their swimsuit attire, ogling over them, making loud and lewd comments to them, and being generally offensive. I did not want to have Paul and his athletic physique and stunning appearance out on the beach being observed by competitive young women, who would be watching him and making me uncomfortable so early in our relationship, so we both have decided that a sand and water visit is out of the question."

I did not say a word. I knew better and noticed that Rose was nodding her head in agreement. In fact, Rose had started to nod her head at the point when Binky said that Harry was going to be, "Generally offensive." I held my breath waiting for Harry's reaction, started to pray softly to myself, as Binky leaned in, and stared at Harry with one of her wide-eyed stares waiting for his response.

After what seemed like forever, Harry laughed and yelled out, "I reckon I am guilty as charged! I think that was a fairly accurate prediction of what would have happened. In fact, you may have underestimated it a little bit darlin,' as I planned on being really, really, offensive."

Rose smacked Harry in the arm, and I breathed a sigh of relief as Binky leaned back into the seat. She grabbed my hand, smiled, and she seemed satisfied that Harry had agreed with her and even embellished it a bit more. I just sat there, smiled, and did not say a word. We had safely dodged one potential bullet, so I was hoping for a perfect day.

The Trans Whizzer rolled onto the highway, but we first had to find our way through the streets of the city of Paterson, and then eventually to the Garden State Parkway. Harry and Rose were chatting in the front seat, and Binky and I were involved in our own conversation in the rear. We talked about my work, my family, and general things until I finally got around to asking her where she worked. She told me that she worked for her father in his business office as his assistant. She also told me that her father was an attorney who had become involved in politics, about ten or so years ago.

It was a pleasant conversation with no repeat of the previous episode of her berating me. I thought it was going so well that it was worth the risk, so I ventured out on a dangerous and previously visited limb.

"You sure, do look nice today, you are dressed so nicely," I said and sat back waiting for my fate.

Binky turned and said, "Thank you, you also look extremely appealing and very handsome. I really like your shoes and your beard looks so trim and neat. I must say that you clean up even better than I could have ever imagined."

It was obvious that I would need to measure success with Binky in very little steps.

Harry was flying down a two-lane road right outside the outskirts of the city, weaving in and out of traffic, speeding just a little and showing off even more. Suddenly, he had to slow down and hit the brakes.

"Idiot!" Harry screamed and pounded the steering wheel as he down-shifted and gunned the Trans Whizzer to go around a small car, which had slowed in front of him. The traffic congestion had built considerably, and it forced Harry to slow down and stay in the lane behind the slower car.

"Take it easy, Harry, it is just a little traffic," Rose said as she rubbed his arm and shoulder.

"Yes, Harry, slow down there. It is cool, it is not even eight in the morning. We have all day to get to the shore. There is no real rush." I jumped in to settle the big guy down.

"I cannot stand when people drive like this and clog up the road like a bunch of slow pokes." Harry then came down with both hands on his horn, pushing the horn button for a long, long, time.

He was being a little obnoxious.

The car in front of him ignored him and it did not speed up at all, but just kept poking along. The slow speed of the car in front of Harry successfully enraged him even more. Harry finally spotted a break in the traffic next to him, gunned the big engine, and roared out into the next lane and around the slowpoke car, while we all held on for dear life.

When Harry got alongside the car, he pushed the button for the passengers' window to go down. He turned and yelled out the window, "Hey, you, big dope, where did y'all get your driver's license? At a supermarket? What are you, some kind of slow, stupid, jackass?" Harry then let a string of obscenities fly out the window as he sped by the car. He seemed to be relieved and impressed by himself, now that he had blown off a little steam from his Harry relief valve.

The flow of the traffic being what it is in congested New Jersey and luck being the way it is, resulted in Harry only going a few feet until a traffic light turned red, and he had to grind to a halt. Of course, the way luck is, but who pulls up right next to him on the passenger side . . . but the slowpoke car. Harry pushed the button for the passenger's window to go down for round two. As the window went down, and he turned to let the driver have it, we all noticed at the same time that the driver of the slowpoke car was staring straight at us with his window also open.

The other thing that was painfully obvious was that the driver of the slowpoke car was a priest in full clerical garb.

"Harry, he is a priest!" Rose said as Binky and I gasped in horror.

The priest was looking straight at Harry when he yelled out the window, "Harry M. Redmond Jr.? Is that you, Harry?"

Harry's eyeballs almost popped out of his head, and his ten-gallon hat almost blew off from the steam that released from the top of his head.

"Father Mark! I am so sorry, Father Mark. I am so sorry! I did not know!"

I leaned over and whispered to Binky that this was not just any ordinary priest, but he happened to be the head priest at Saint Peter's Catholic Church that the Redmond family attended. The Redmond family and Father Mark were very close; he even visited many of the famous Redmond family gatherings. In fact, he and Harry's father were very close friends. Binky squeezed my hand and shook her head. Rose sat stunned in the front seat. I learned very quickly that she also was Catholic as she started to cross herself repeatedly and started to recite The Lord's Prayer aloud.

Father Mark shook his head and wagged his finger to Harry at his displeasure at his behavior. As the light turned green, the priest made the sign of the cross out the window to Harry, yelled to Harry, to say ten Hail Mary and say The Lord's Prayer and that he would see him at confession this week. All kinds of cars were now honking their horns at both Father Mark and Harry. Harry almost lost it again for a second, and started to yell back, but he caught himself when he saw that Father Mark was still watching him, and he was still shaking his finger back and forth in a warning motion.

Binky leaned in and said in my ear very softly, "Methodist, I am a United Methodist."

"Lutheran," I answered, and she sat back and nodded her head.

Rose let Harry have it with both barrels of her Rose verbal shotgun. She was red-faced and angry with the big New Jersey cowboy.

"Now, I too, have to go to confession this week, because you have to be as Binky says, a friggin' Neanderthal! I cannot believe that you swore like that at a priest." Rose folded her arms across her chest in anger.

Harry was a little stunned, but I knew he would recover. "Well little lady, I reckon he is more than just a priest. He baptized me, gave me first communion, buried my mother, taught me in school, and has been our family priest since I was a little guy. He is also one of my father's best friends. So, for me it is a little bit of a worse situation that I am in with the big man upstairs."

Then good old Harry, who is always the first person to try to wiggle out of tight or adverse situations, put a little escape twist on the situation. He smiled and turned to Rose and asked, "But I reckon isn't that what confession is for?" Since Binky and I were not Catholic, we both were working as hard as we could not to laugh at the situation.

The luck and irony of the person being a priest was strange enough, but the fact that he was from the Redmond's home parish and a family friend was too much to take. Rose buried her head in her hands, Harry now fully recovered, chuckled, down-shifted, and we headed for the highway. Some things never changed for Harry and me. This was going to be just another normally wild day!

Rose overcame the impact of the incident with Father Mark quickly, and soon, they both were laughing in the front seat and things seemed normal in relative terms once more. Harry was such a jovial and adventurous soul that it really was hard to stay mad at him for very long. It sure seemed that Rose had an easygoing way of going along with his outlandish behavior and not dwelling on it for very long. By now, many of Harry's previous young lady companions would be fleeing in terror and running for cover. Rose just laughed and smiled. Could it be that she was just a little more than just enjoying his company on a casual basis? She seemed like she was falling for the big guy. I made a mental note to pay more attention to her body language and interaction with Harry.

This could become very interesting indeed.

We were now driving down the Garden State Parkway in the Trans Whizzer and it was a pleasant and relaxing ride, as Harry had selected some jingly, jangly type rock-and-roll from a band named, The Blue Whales and their famous, “Rocking Dreams” recording as a musical backdrop for this part of the ride. Binky and I settled in for the long ride, and we engaged in some very interesting conversation that included a variety of topics. In fact, we seemed to be covering every topic under the sun and then a little bit more. Binky actually went on and on, explaining some of her projects, interests, and her latest research of music by No Way, as well as the sport of hockey. She seemed to be working hard to understand what I enjoyed, and what made me tick, while I enjoyed learning more about her and what her interests were. Despite her unusual and quirky personality, she was great fun, very intelligent, and once she was relaxed, she had quite an engaging personality.

I mostly listened, which I was very good at doing. I said very little, but I found myself really enjoying her companionship as well as her extraordinary beauty. I interjected some of my dry humor occasionally in some very careful and strategic intervals as I tested the waters very carefully. I was not looking forward to a repeat of some of our initial conversations. I was surprised indeed, when I was able to make her laugh, much more than I thought I would be able to. She put me on the spot, occasionally asking me questions about specific hockey rules and then some difficult questions about the meaning of some very obscure lyrics in some songs by No Way, but her intensity was much different from our first meeting.

Every once in a while, she would lean in and check Harry’s speedometer, and then warn Harry of the latest statistics according to her research for New Jersey state troopers and the issuing of speeding tickets, but for the most part she was calm and relaxed.

At times, the four of us would engage in some group conversation, and there was no doubt that a special chemistry existed and was growing among all of us. As each mile rolled by, the four of us grew closer; there was some type of perfect interaction between us. I know I felt it right away, and I had a feeling that it was very special. Even though we had only been together as a group for a short amount of time, I felt that it was almost as if some kind of destiny had brought us together, to be with each other at this time, place, and moment. Perhaps it was a by-product of the intense friendship between Harry and me, or it could be that Binky and Rose were also very close, so that it all just intertwined.

I could not really say exactly what it was, just that it existed.

As time went on, and I studied the relationship between Rose and Harry even more, I could not help but think that Rose was perfect for Harry. She laughed at all of his jokes and actions, she managed his ego, and she was easygoing, pretty, and very smart. Rose was also just a lot of fun. I felt they were really a great match. The only question that remained, was whether Rose could really keep up with his never-ending, topsy-turvy lifestyle and hectic pace.

It could be exhausting.

We had driven past most of the northern New Jersey cities alongside the Garden State Parkway and had now ridden far enough south that the roadway had changed into gentle rolling landscapes, and we enjoyed the more scenic areas of central New Jersey. We stopped for gas and a rest stop, but then quickly resumed our trip. Soon, the Garden State Parkway had narrowed down to a two-lane, scenic highway as we rode parallel along the ocean line. We grew closer to the Seashore Heights exit, and Harry started to pick up the pace in the Trans Whizzer. He had been cruising fairly steadily, but now he got on the car a little more and started to weave in and out of the traffic and pick up some speed. We did receive many horns beeping at us and thumbs up from admirers of the Trans Whizzer as we rolled along. The car attracted a lot of attention and Harry ate it all up. As Harry moved from the hammer lane to the slower lane, he hit a stretch of open road, with no other cars in sight for miles.

All of a sudden, in the hammer lane appearing like magic alongside us was an immaculate, black sports coupe with the windows rolled down.

The driver was a middle-aged, very distinguished looking gentleman, wearing mirrored sunglasses, a perfectly groomed fresh haircut, and a dark mustache and beard. Alongside of him, in the front seat, was a woman who might have been slightly younger than the driver might be. She had long blonde hair blowing in the wind, dark sunglasses on, and you could tell she was dressed to the hilt. She was drop-dead, knock down gorgeous, like a movie star sitting in the passenger seat.

The car had New York license plates and a highly polished finish that we could see the reflection of the Trans Whizzer in as the two cars rolled side-by-side.

It was a gorgeous car!

Harry looked over as the two cars were almost exactly even with each other, and his eye caught the woman sitting in the front seat. He tipped his big ten-gallon hat, pushed the button for his window to go down, and let out with a loud, "Hoowee, howdy there, little lady!"

Rose immediately hit Harry in the arm and yelled, "Stop it, Harry!"

Harry was beside himself, and as predicted earlier by Binky in her speech, he was quickly moving into his offensive mode. "Wow, you are gorgeous!" Harry yelled to the woman as Rose continued to try her best to control him.

I was a bit of a car aficionado; I looked at the car, studied it, then said, "Do you guys realize that is a 1977 Volcano Advantage? You know the car that the secret agent Ian Leadfoot drives in the movies and his books!"

Binky looked at me, and then at the car, and she said, "It is fantastic. What is with the driver and that woman? They look as if they might be famous movie stars or celebrities."

"Maybe they are. That car is worth a pretty good chunk of change," I added.

Harry was still eyeing the woman, and she smiled back at Harry and winked. Harry let out another cowboy type yodel; he then down-shifted the Trans Whizzer, toyed with the gas pedal to make the big engine roar, and then looked over to the driver of the Volcano to see if he was up for the challenge. I sensed this was going to be something that Binky would object to, and I prepared myself to hear a laundry list of data and information about racing and its adverse impacts, provided by Binky's latest research.

I could not have been more incorrect.

To my utter shock and surprise, Binky unlatched her seat belt, leaned up and over the front console right by the stick shift and yelled, "Go get him Harry, see what he can do!" She was leaning into the driver's compartment, she was very excited, and then she sat back, buckled her seat belt, grabbed me by the face with both of her hands, gave me a big kiss, and hugged me around the neck.

Binky whispered to me in my ear, "I love racing and speed!" I was outwardly shocked at the Jekyll and Hyde transformation of Binky, as I think Rose and Harry both were too, at the conversion of the normally, prim and proper, Binky, into a speed and racing freak!

As we recovered from the shocking outburst of Binky, the driver nodded back to Harry to indicate that he was in. When the driver of the Volcano shifted and hit the accelerator, it caught Harry off guard. The Volcano let out a puff of smoke and took off while the big engine of the Trans Whizzer slowly roared to life. I watched as the tachometer almost redlined and Harry shifted.

"Shift it, Harry, shift!" I yelled. The Volcano had exploded; it had taken off like a rocket ship. That was no real surprise; after all, it was one of the world's most elite foreign sports cars. The Trans Whizzer generated such horsepower that the force pinned all of us into our seats.

The force and power of the Trans Whizzer were frightening to all of us . . . except for Binky. The Volcano was starting to move away when the Trans Whizzer gained tremendous speed. It was now right alongside of the Volcano and moving ahead a little, as the big 475 cubic inch engine was now wide open.

One thing about Harry was that he could really drive. He was an expert and could handle a big, powerful car as well as anyone could. The Trans Whizzer was pulling away now, and the big engine was roaring and still gaining speed.

Binky was beside herself, screaming and cheering Harry on!

I watched as the driver of the Volcano, in desperation to catch up, decided to shift and try an overdrive gear. A big, choking puff of smoke came out of the back of the Volcano and it sputtered and then stalled. Remarkably, it looked like the engine on the Volcano Advantage had failed! Harry slowed and allowed the Volcano to glide over in front of him, and cruise to the breakdown lane. The Volcano limped to the side of the roadway and slowly came to a stop in the breakdown lane.

Harry maneuvered the Trans Whizzer close by them and cruised by slowly within earshot of the broken-down vehicle. He then rolled by with the windows open and yelled out, "Hey, bad luck there, old boy, but you were losing anyway! You should have saved a whole load of dough there, secret agent guy, and bought a Trans Whizzer!"

The driver of the Volcano shook his fist at us, and he yelled back, "Get lost, cowboy!"

Harry let out another holler, shifted, and left the Volcano Advantage and the two movie stars on the sideline. Harry was living his Dragon Road Rage dream; all that was missing was Harriet Dudley and Barry McGirk.

There was a lot of laughing and celebrating inside the

Trans Whizzer and Binky returned to her normal, "refined" state and sat calmly next to me. She slipped her hand inside of mine as it rested on my lap, fluffed her hair, straightened her blouse, and she peacefully sighed as if nothing had ever happened.

Binky then confessed.

"Everyone, I do apologize if I became overly excited during the racing challenge, but I am quite fond of the excitement that racing offers," Binky said as she looked at me and smiled. I just sat there and tried hard to hide my shock at this hidden element of her personality. I thought to myself that they label us goaltenders for being eccentric and strange. Binky was certainly a very intriguing and different woman!

Rose was still recovering from the incident, and Harry just went on and on about how his beloved car had taken out, "That, there fancy, overpriced, car driven by them, there, movie stars."

Harry popped out the music tape, grabbed the "Tell me all about Dreams" cassette tape by The Soda and Beer Caps Band, and slipped it in the tape deck. No more mellow times, the rest of the ride to Seashore Heights was going to be a full-blown rock out. I knew we all were going to have to hold on tightly.

When Harry was on the loose, then nothing was safe and Seashore Heights was in his periscope sights!

5

Harry Conquers the Hammer

We arrived at Seashore Heights without any further racing challenges from elite English automobiles driven by movie stars, irate verbal barrages hurled toward poor, defenseless, clergymen, or disclosures of our hidden elements of our inner personalities.

It always amazed me at how many strange and unusual events that Harry and I could pack into a mere three-hour period.

We found an all-day parking lot close to the boardwalk, and we worked a deal with the lot attendant. We paid him for the day and some nights at a slightly reduced rate. I paid for the parking. I was carrying a little more cash than I usually did because of my working extra hours as the stereotypical reliable, steady, boring guy straight out of Harry's Theory.

The four of us strode towards the boardwalk, with Harry in the lead with Rose, his head on a swivel rotating almost 360 degrees around, as he was looking at all the young ladies walking around in swimsuits, making lewd comments, tipping his big hat to the ladies, and clicking his boots on the wooden decking. It was comical to watch as Rose elbowed him and turned his head back in a vain attempt to control his wandering eye. Before this day ended, Harry's lust circuit breakers may overload and blow.

I think our gals had forgotten that young ladies in swimsuits also walked the boardwalk.

Binky and I walked behind them, and she shook her head in disgust at Harry's behavior, while she commented, "Your friend can be so out of control sometimes, his respect for women and for Rose is abominable."

I nodded my head in agreement, feigned my best display of surprise at his behavior, and just played it cool.

I was now used to from years of experiences, of how words like offensive, atrocious, loud, rude, lewd, and disrespectful, were common descriptions used in describing my best buddy in the world. I took no real offense to it, as it now was commonplace to me and actually quite normal.

"I reckon I could go for one of them, there, Big Bob's orange frozen custard treats, how about y'all?" The big guy was now hungry . . . after all, racing, verbal tirades, and ogling women was hard work, and "Rustles up a mighty hunger!"

The four of us picked up the frozen custards and sat on some benches facing the ocean, enjoying the food and the view. It was a magical scene, the weather was gorgeous, and the sky was a clear, deep, blue color. There was just the faintest little; white, puffy clouds dotting the blue sky here and there. We had picked a winner of a day to make this trip! The ocean was calm, and the waves were gently rolling and tumbling to the shoreline. The beach crowd was just starting to grow in size, but it was still early in the day. It was going to be a great day.

Harry put his arm around Rose and I did the same with Binky. The four of us sat there on the bench for quite a while, enjoying our snacks and not really saying too much. We were all soaking up the sunshine and at the same time, a cool gentle ocean breeze, waved over us, teasing us with a taste of seashore magic.

For two poor street schleps, well to be honest, one poor schlep, and one with a lot more dough from Paterson, New Jersey, we were not doing too badly, not bad at all as a matter of fact.

Harry M. Redmond Jr. was one of the world's most famous boardwalk game players. He loved it, and the sight of the games and thrill of the pursuit of some inferior quality, giant teddy bear prize, made in Sri Lanka with a poorly sewn mouth, and weird eyeballs, was too much for him to handle. He drooled all over himself at the very sight of a game of chance. Harry had a collection of prizes such as, green, orange, and red colored ten-foot-long felt stuffed snakes, whirlybirds, pinwheels, lions, tigers, those cheap plastic imitation beer mugs, that always leak and say, "New Jersey Shore" on them, as well as hundreds of other prizes that he had won over the years.

He stashed away all of his prizes in his basement alongside the other memorabilia from the Redmond's various phases.

Boredom crept into the world of Harry within about five minutes. The only actual time he was not pursuing some type of adventure, excitement, or entertainment was when he was asleep or perhaps in the restroom.

Harry had enough of this peaceful, serene scene, and his eyes wandered over to the game area on the boardwalk. I saw the eye of the tiger appear in his eyes. He removed his hat, wiped his mouth, and his eyes darted back and forth in his head like little windshield wipers. He cracked his knuckles, (not his nose thankfully, but his knuckles) stood up, and I knew he was ready for battle with spinning wheels of fortune, undersized basketball hoops, rigged and fraudulent pitching and rifle targets, floating plastic frogs on lily pads, and other assorted games of chance.

Harry stood up, "Let's go, youse guys! I want to check out the games over here!"

Ah yes, the prediction was correct! Let the games begin!

Now, I knew the story well, but of course, the girls did not. The reason he loved the games so much was because he usually won. The reason that he won most of the time was that he had the famous Redmond family, "inside scoop," on how the games were rigged. All the Redmonds were famous for dropping the names of famous folks, they knew, met, or rubbed elbows with, to obtain the coveted "inside scoop." They were also always obtaining and seeking secret information, working angles, and always pursuing, as they called it, "the inside scoop."

As we walked, I leaned over and whispered to Binky, "Any minute now, Harry is going to tell a story about his brother-in-law Ronnie, and how he worked these games as a hawker, before he went over to Vietnam."

Binky looked at me, a little puzzled, but she saw me nod my head, and then she smiled. She appreciated the warning and seemed to get a kick out of how well I knew my best buddy.

Harry was walking briskly now towards the games as his eagerness was starting to overtake him.

"Now y'all watch me play these games, especially you little ladies. Paul knows these tricks too, from hanging around Ronzo and me."

Harry began to tell his story and reveal the covert secret information.

"You see, I have the inside scoop on how these games are rigged in favor of the operators. They let folks win, just enough to keep dopey people and random suckers interested, but I learned all the tricks from Ronzo, err, I mean Ronnie. He is my brother-in-law."

When Harry said, "Ronzo," Binky squeezed my hand tightly, and she laughed softly.

Rose was intently watching him. Her smile was broad, and her eyes were twinkling. She was falling completely for Harry's magic.

"Yeah, Ronzo lived, and he worked on the New Jersey shore as a game hawker and barker for a summer or two, just before he was drafted and sent over to Vietnam. He learned all the tricks of how it is all rigged and then taught me how it works. We come down here and clean up, before the operators get wise to us, and ban us from playing any more games. Here, let me show you."

Harry headed straight for his number one target, the game where you take the giant, heavy, wooden hammer, aim, swing, hit the lever, and the little hockey puck slides up and down the track in an attempt to ring a bell mounted on the very top of the track, which results in winning a prize. Alongside the track, from the bottom to the top, are printed various words, descriptions, insults, and praise that match with the level of which you made the hockey puck travel. The bottom has words and phrases such as, "wimp," "weakling," "are you kidding?" Then as you progress higher and higher, it is printed with, "not bad," "strongman," and "don't mess with you!" On the very top of the track right next to the bell, the track had printed big block letters, "SUPERHERO!"

When we got close to the hammer game, Harry motioned for us all to huddle up together. We all gathered in a circle. Harry looked around and started to speak very softly, so that just in case the secret agent, movie star guy, had his Volcano Advantage repaired and was tailing us, he would not steal the secrets of winning boardwalk games.

Harry could work a crowd like a fine violin.

"Watch as all these, here, big, muscle bound, dopes, swing the hammer up over their heads, and try with all their might, to bash the little lever. I reckon they will wear themselves out trying to impress their girlfriends and the spectators. The inside scoop is how the mechanism of the lever works, it is betting on you hitting it hard and not fully even on the face of the lever."

Harry made a little motion with his hands and arms to demonstrate a hammer swing and continued with his revealing of the secret inside scoop.

"The trick is to just drop the big hammer perfectly flat and even and full on the lever with a little, tiny, swing, and the weight of the hammer and the flat, even, blow sends the little hockey puck up like a rocket ship and rings the bell. They want all these jerks to swing hard and uneven so that the mechanism does its thing and holds back the travel. Handfuls of idiots get lucky once in a while and hit it flush. I reckon just enough of these, here jerks, nails it to keep people interested enough to keep them all spending their dough. Once in a while, you see some little dopey kid, or Grandma Moses who, can hardly even pick up the hammer, hit it correctly and win. The game barker hustles them out so that no one figures it out and chalks it up as a fluke to the crowd."

Harry stood away from our huddle, he looked around once more just to make sure no one was listening or eavesdropping on us. He then finished his lesson.

"It is a money-making rip-off racket! It has nothing to do with strength."

I almost expected all of us to have to cut our fingers and make a secrecy pact in blood together not to reveal the inside scoop, but we broke the huddle at Harry's motion and he led us to the side of the game and said confidently, "Watch and learn."

We stood on the sideline watching the hammer game, and the game operator who was a little, tiny, young guy with a very heavy, New Jersey accent, and who had a nervous habit of pacing while he yelled at the crowd.

The game hawker shouted and encouraged big, strong guys as they walked by, "Give it a trwwy! You look like a big strong bruwwte, come on, win your gurl a prize."

He hawked at little skinny guys, "What are youse guys afraid of? Or are youse guys too cheap to try? Or too weak to even tink 'bout it?"

On and on, the little guy worked the crowd, throwing a mixture of encouragement, then sporadic insults or taunts to try to entice someone to plunk down a quarter and grab the hammer. The young man was surrounded by a collection of various stuffed animals, figures, sports team's pennants, and other assorted cheap looking, junky prizes. Sure enough, a giant, hulking, brute type of guy came by, paid the charge, and picked up the hammer. He worked his grip on the handle of the hammer like a professional baseball batter. He then pulled the hammer high over his head and bashed it down with a loud, "thunk!"

"Woooooooo."

The little puck went up a few feet to the "wimp" range and then slid down.

"Oh . . . too bad, there muscle man, not as trong as youse look," the little insulting guy yelled out. "C'mon, yoo need practice, give it another trwwy!"

The big hulk plunked down another coin and gave it another whack. Up, up, up, then oops, it lost momentum and down it went. This time, it reached the "winkie-dinkie" level. Embarrassed, the hulk left to try to salvage his pride on some other less demanding game elsewhere.

On and on it went, for about fifteen minutes, with a variety of different sizes and shapes of men, a few gals, and a father of two little kids with his wife, all giving it a bash or two and failing miserably. Due to the influence of Harry and his theory, I imagined that the young father was really working to regain his youth and prevent his wife from staring at the bad guy who lived next door to them at home.

One by one, starry-eyed contestants gave the game a try and all of them failed terribly, and for their efforts, they received a trickle of some encouragement, followed by some New Jersey accent-laden insults from the little guy here and there. The game, for the most part, was cleaning up. One guy did reach the "not too bad" level, but he only gave it one try, and then he bailed.

It was the moment of truth as Harry turned to us and said, "It is time, gang. I am on." Harry waited until quite a crowd had gathered in front of the game, so he could work it for maximum impact and hero status for himself. He moved in for the kill with his coin at hand. I had seen this act many times before. I knew that Harry wanted as many folks around as possible, so that the game barker would put his foot in his mouth, and Harry could lure him into the trap of having his secret revealed to the entire world.

Up to the game, the ever-confident Harry strode, as the three of us moved in closer to watch the show. He puffed out his big chest; his big hat was on his head, perched at just the right angle, for maximum dramatic effect. He was clicking his boots upon the wooden boardwalk and making his grand entrance like the sheriff riding into town with his white hat on his head, while riding the proverbial white horse to save the day.

"Howdy there, Shorty!" Harry bellowed out. "You sure have a lot to say there for a little feller, I reckon you never stop flapping your jaws! I left my microscope at home, so I reckon it is a little tough to find ya there, Shorty!"

The little guy sneered a little at Harry, then checked him out, identified him as a born sucker, and swooped in for the kill shot.

"Well . . . hi dare big, giant, goofy, cowboy guy! You look big and trong, but I doubt you can do this. That big hat looks like it gets in your eyes. Where did you tie up yawwr horwwse?" The crowd erupted into laughter as it looked like the little guy was going to make fun of Harry and beat him like a drum.

Harry laughed, took off his hat, and put it on a post in front of the game machine.

"I will tell you what, Shorty, here is a quarter, but I want to know what I will win, if I ring that bell."

The little guy picked up a medium size teddy bear at random and proudly proclaimed, "Dis!"

"What do I win if I do it two times in a row?"

The little guy stared at Harry, then walked over and picked up a larger sized, phony looking; stuffed bunny that only vaguely looked like a bunny and said, "Dis! I doubt yoo could even pick up the hammer, though."

The crowd was now moving in closer, and the laughter at Harry's expense was loud.

"Come on around folks, the giant, goofball, cowboy tinks he can hit the bell twice in a row. When he fails, then someone else can come on and youse guys can show him how it is done!"

Harry interrupted the little guy, "What if I do it three times?" Harry was now leaning in closer to the little guy without a smile and a deeper and more serious tone in his voice.

The crowd went silent, and a couple of voices wandered in and amongst the crowd asking, "Who is this guy? Can he really do it?"

Binky and Rose looked at me, but I was just standing there stoically with my sunglasses on. I held Binky's hand with one hand and Rose's hand with the other. The little guy was a little nervous now, you could see he was no longer as confident, and he was not quite sure of whom on earth this phony cowboy was, who was calling in his cards. He was in a pickle because he still wanted to work the huge crowd that had gathered. He went back to the prize boards and picked up this enormous, stuffed, Dinky the Orange Teddy Bear character from that stupid cartoon series of the same name, and he held it up. It was ugly, it hardly resembled Dinky at all, but it was the largest prize he had.

"You win, dis cowboy!"

"Deal!" Harry yelled out, clapped his hands together, and he grabbed the big hammer. Now, there was a huge crowd around, and everyone, including the three of us, moved in close around the fence surrounding the game as Harry grabbed the hammer, and walked over to the front of the machine by the target lever.

Being the master showman that he was, Harry propped

the hammer up between his legs, spit on his hands, rubbed them together, and then placed his hands carefully on the handle of the hammer.

The little guy erupted into a tirade of insults directed at Harry, "Look at this act, youse guys! He is stawwlling; he cannot even lift up the hammer after all that big tawwk!" On and on he went, while Harry took a deep breath and stared up at the bell.

Rose leaned in and asked me, "He can do this, can't he, twenty-seven?" All of a sudden, she had lost confidence and became a doubter in her hero's abilities.

Playfully, I contributed to the tension and simply answered with, "Just watch."

The crowd gasped as Harry lifted the hammer, took another deep breath, and violently swung it high and hard up over his head. Harry let out with a loud blood-curdling yell at the top of his lungs, and just when it looked like he was going to bring the hammer down with a crushing blow, he used the big, powerful, chest muscles of his, to stop in mid-swing! He then gently lowered the hammer directly over the lever from about a foot above it, eyed it carefully, lined it up, and simply dropped it right on top of the target.

The hammer landed squarely on the lever and, "WHOOOSSHHH!" The little hockey puck went up the track like a rocket ship and the bell gave off a loud, "ding!"

There was a quiet hush of stunned silence over all the spectators, but Rose let out a loud cry of, "Yeah, Harry!"

The three of us began jumping up and down and cheering. The crowd followed our lead and erupted into cheers and applause. The little loudmouthed guy stood there stunned, his eyes were bugging out of his head, and his mouth was hanging wide open as he shut up in mid-insult.

Harry stood there smiling and fist pumping in the air to us. He bent over and bowed to the crowd in three directions, and then grabbed the hammer and counted out a loud, "One!"

"No! No! No! Here, here, here!" The little guy ran over to the massive Dinky stuffed prize, grabbed it, ran over to Harry, pushed it in his arms, and confiscated the hammer.

"What?" Harry made believe that he was surprised. "I reckon that I still have two more tries there, Shorty. Your big mouth said that I could not even pick up the hammer!"

The little guy glared back at Harry and said in typical New Jersey fashion, "Get lawwst will yoo?"

Harry laughed, waved his hand, picked his hat off the post, and glared back at the little guy. The crowd of spectators now charged towards the little guy as folks were waving quarters at him to try it.

The little hawker was now overwhelmed, and he put a sign out on the fence that read, "OUT TO LUNCH."

"Sorry folks, break time! Sorry, come back layder. I have to have lunch and a cup of cawwfeee." He then ran off behind the game machine and disappeared behind the wall.

Harry walked over to us carrying the enormous imitation Dinky stuffed animal. It was at least seven feet high and three feet wide. I could not help but think that it was even creepier than the inflatable Mr. Bug that was on the Redmond porch during the baseball phase. He placed it on the boardwalk as Rose came over and gave him a hug and a kiss.

"That was awesome, Harry! The way you put it to that rip-off artist was fantastic."

Binky and I came over and congratulated him, and Harry was beaming ear-to-ear, "It was just as I told you, nothing to it!" Harry loved nothing better than being the star of the show.

Leave it to me to spoil the moment and enter some reality into our lives. After all, someone had to have the job and do it when you were dealing with Harry.

"One question, gang. What on earth do we do with that huge, creepy Dinky thing?" I asked.

Binky piped right in, "Please keep it away from me, Paul! I did some research and checked into those cheap prizes, and they all come from strange oversea countries. I read just last week that the USDA found dangerous chemicals in the dyes, bacteria infestations upon them, and one shipment, even had banned insects from some foreign country living inside of them. They are disgusting!"

Binky stepped away from the giant Dinky and she forcibly pulled me by the arm to stay away from it as well. The four of us now stood there staring at this seven-foot high, potential disease, pest infested, stuffed monster, and we all took two steps back away from it.

Harry looked at the Dinky, and then over at Binky, as he asked her, "You really research stuffed toys and their origins?"

Binky nodded her head very rapidly up and down a number of times to indicate that was indeed the case, but she did not say anything else.

The imitation, enormous, Dinky the Orange Teddy Bear sat there looking back at us with a dim-witted, phony look on its face, and spinning eyeballs, while we steered clear of it as if it was a loaded hand grenade.

"Why not just ditch it in the trash Harry, you already have tons of this stuff at home from beating these games, hundreds of times," I suggested.

Harry stared at the Dinky for a while, tilted his hat back, and frowned, while saying, "I reckon that I could do that twenty-seven, but this prize is kind of special the way I went around it and beat the game. It now has memories attached to it."

"It may also have potential hazardous materials associated with it," Binky reminded us.

Harry as big and tough as he was . . . now had an undying affection to a stupid, stuffed, Dinky the teddy bear.

"I thought you hated that stupid cartoon? You used to moan and groan all the time when your sister Patty would make you decorate her Christmas tree with her special collection of Dinky Christmas lights."

"I reckon that is true there twenty-seven, but Dinky is not so bad. I never liked that, there talkin' fire hydrant guy. What was his name? Y'all know the character that the male dog used to pee on all the time."

Binky, of course, knew the answer, undoubtedly, due to her research efforts, and she offered the answer, "Plugger, his name is Plugger. The dog that used to very rudely urinate on him is named, Sniffy."

"Yeah, I reckon you're right there, Bink-a-roo-ski, it was Plugger, but I kinda like ole Dink-a-roo-ski youse guys."

Every once in a while, Harry would slip up on his phony western accent and an authentic New Jersey word or two would slip in there.

We had a profound conundrum facing us, as it looked like Harry was not willing to give up on his prize, but since Binky had planted the seeds of doubt in our heads; it seemed like it might not be worth the risk of keeping it, and all of us coming down with some unknown, foreign, stuffed Dinky disease.

"We cannot possibly transport it inside the Trans Whizzer due to the potential troubles that it may carry. Realistically, it is too large to fit with all of us inside the vehicle." Binky reasoned. "I would not even hold it to carry it as something could come off on your clothing and cause multiple troubles."

Harry started to brush off his shirt, and Rose came over to help him, as he realized that he had carried it from the game stand over to us.

I was a problem solver, that is what I did the best, and hanging around Harry, I always had many chances to prove it. I noticed out of the corner of my eye, a young man rolling a two-wheel hand truck, making a delivery of some supplies to one of the boardwalk concession stands. He had his truck loaded up with food boxes and some rope, which held the boxes on the hand truck. My old man was also the most famous of the many legendary dealmakers in our entire neighborhood, and he had taught me a trick or two throughout the years.

"Wait here you, guys. Hey, Harry, please throw me your car keys, take everyone over there to that stand, and buy everyone some pizza or something. I will be right back."

"Where are you going?" Harry asked as I caught the keys.

I did not answer him, but instead I ran over to the young man rolling the hand truck and said, "Hey pal, you have a minute? Do you want to make an extra ten bucks?"

"What?" The young man seemed puzzled, but the prospect of a little extra jingle had caught his attention. This was of course; New Jersey and street deals are a way of life.

"Yeah, here is ten bucks. I need some of that extra rope and your hand truck for ten minutes."

"Okay, but I really need it back very fast. I have a lot of work to do." The young man stood the hand truck up, took the boxes off it, and pulled at the rope. "Hey, how do I know you will not run off with it, steal it, and then I will get fired?"

"See that big guy over there wearing the big, cowboy hat with those two really pretty girls? If I do not come back in ten minutes, go over to him, and he will give you a hundred dollars."

The young man stared over at Harry and said, "That is the big guy who almost knocked the bell, right off the hammer tower! Yeah, man, here is the hand truck. I want to talk with him, anyway. He is awesome! Is he from Texas?"

"Go for it, guy," I said as he handed me the rope and the hand truck. I did not answer the question. After all, Harry was a true celebrity. He would work it out. I grabbed the hand truck and rope, strapped up the infected and creepy Dinky on the hand truck, and began running towards the parking lot where we parked the Trans Whizzer. I sure got many looks and laughs from onlookers, this long-haired, hippie guy sprinting along with a hand truck that had a giant Dinky strapped to it, but it was just another ordinary day for me in the adventures of Harry and Paul.

It was the off-season for me, but I was in good shape, and this run was nothing for me, I had been a sprinter in high school and had won my share of races. I had ten minutes to do this, but I hoped that Harry laid it on so thick; the young guy would forget the time, anyway.

I made it to the car in no time flat, carefully handled Dinky with the tips of my fingers (after all, Binky does do a lot of research), and chucked it on top of the Trans Whizzer. I then tied it down securely with the rope, grabbed my extra dress shirt from my bag as I knew I would be a little sweaty from this jaunt, and headed back to Harry and the women. I was running hard and fast. I had to bring the hand truck back to the young man in time, to save Harry from shelling out some major dough.

Many people, who may have never seen anyone run that fast, were cheering me on. People could see I was on a special mission and they cheered loudly while rooting me onward! I returned in no time flat and handed the hand truck back to the young guy. The little run and the exercise actually felt pretty good! Harry, Binky and Rose had seen me take off, I was now out of breath and a little sweaty, but I had solved the problem.

"Wow! Thanks! That was fast. Look, I got his autograph," the young guy told me as he proudly showed me a paper with "Big Tex" written on it.

"Nice, kid, thanks." I said as the young guy went away happy. "Big Tex?" I asked Harry. He shrugged his shoulders and continued to chomp down on the pizza slice.

"We got you one too." Harry pointed to a slice that Binky was holding for me. "Thanks for taking care of the Dinky for me, twenty-seven. I guess you tied it up on the car?"

"Yeah, I did. It is on top of the Trans Whizzer. Let me tell you, it looks pretty weird up there, but it is there. Let me change into this fresh shirt and wash up in the restroom. I will be right back." I returned from the restroom, Binky put my old shirt in her purse for me, and we sat and finished our lunch.

"I reckon you gals see why Paul was a championship sprinter in high school. You have never seen anyone run like he can run, that is for sure." Harry had a big ego, but on rare occasion, he did slap some praise on other people.

"I knew you were quite the goaltender, but my goodness, I have to agree with Harry, you are an amazing, all-around athlete, Paul," Binky smiled at me as she also paid me a compliment.

Wow! A nice comment from Binky. Things were going pretty good between us. We sure were a long way from that rocky start we had back at Lord Crudley's Bar. I thanked her and was hoping that she did not quote a few one-hundred-yard dash world record times or some type of other statistics.

She took a tissue out from her purse, and was wiping my forehead, and checking my face.

"You did wash your hands well after touching that horrid thing. I hope you did not handle it much."

I assured Binky that was the case, I would pass Dinky disease scrutiny, and she seemed satisfied after performing an inspection of me for any strange or foreign matter.

After eating, we moved onto other games. Harry showed us which buttons the game operators rigged to stop the wheels of fortunes, and which ones were just dummy buttons. He showed us how they fit the toy rifles with defective sights to make you miss the targets, and he showed us how to identify the prize frogs in the plastic lily pad pond to pick out the correct one to win a prize.

Binky had made it clear to me not to waste any money on winning her any prizes, even if I knew how to do it, as she wanted nothing to do with any of those, "Disease infested, foreign, imported products" that are given away.

Harry learned his lesson and did not select any other stuffed animals for prizes, but he stuck to safer prizes that were washable. Soon, all of us had our arms full of New York Bugs flags, New York Canaries pennants, soda and shot glasses that said, "Seashore Heights" on them, imprinted beer mugs, more pinwheels than we could hold, as well as other assorted junk, until the four of us could no longer carry any more items.

6

The Flipper Strikes Back!

Harry announced that he was finally finished with his game tour and we carried all of his junk back to the Trans Whizzer. We dumped all of it in the trunk. Stuffed Dinky proudly sat atop the Trans Whizzer in all of his obscure glory, tied with the ropes to the front and back bumpers. I think Binky was secretly hoping that someone would come along and steal it.

We all walked back to the boardwalk when Rose said, "Let's go on some rides!"

Binky nodded her head rapidly. I thought for a moment her head would fall off her shoulders from the ferocity of her violent head nod.

"I love the fastest ones!" Binky announced, while she got that same crazed look in her eye that she did when the race was on. Apparently, our two dates were enthusiastic amusement ride aficionados.

Off we were, making our way over to the ride pier and I have to admit it was with some trepidation that I agreed to head over there. Harry rolled his eyes at me since I knew the ride pier was not exactly Harry's favorite place to visit. I had a bad experience with sitting next to Harry on an amusement ride once, as his stomach does not fare so well whenever he spins, twirls, or flips around on these rides. He also has a tendency to lose his false teeth when he spins or when he flips upside down. A year or so ago, at a local carnival, in the late spring, it took us about three hours to find them after one ride on a large Ferris wheel. We had to have the operator shut the ride down while everyone helped us look around on the ground for his wayward choppers under the wheel. I did not want to give his secret away and let Rose know that her superhero indeed had a weak spot. By the same token, I was not looking forward to a repeat of those adventures.

Harry pulled me aside as the girls looked over a chart to decide which rides, they wanted to go on that would inflict the maximum level of torture on us that would be humanly possible.

Harry whispered to me, “Look, I will tell them I cannot go on the rides, but you will take them on anything they want. But you need to keep them busy and away from the water park for as long as you can.” Harry continued to watch the girls to make sure they did not come over by us.

“Why, are you going to the water park? Are you going on some rides there?” I asked. “You will need the stuff out of the equipment bag if you want to. . ..”

“No, no, no, there you go, not following or knowing anything because of your terrible affliction with the Old Lady Syndrome!” Harry angrily interrupted me. “I am going to hang around on a bench at the base of the big giant water slide, because that is where the force of the water knocks the swimsuits right off of the ladies as they come down the big water slide.”

Harry looked over my shoulder to check on the location of the ladies.

“It is a blast, and good for at least ten exposed breasts, backsides, and other parts per hour! It is fantastic! The force of the water sometimes knocks the bikini tops clear off them! It is worth the slight hit that I need to take on my image because of a winky dink tummy and the fake choppers!”

“Oh, I do not know about this Harry. Why do I have to be involved in your crazy schemes? Rose is such a nice gal, and besides, I get dizzy going on all of those stupid rides.”

"Oh, come on, buddy, do it for me. Just keep them busy for a while, that is all . . . it is no big deal."

I was not happy, but I finally agreed to his scheme, just as the girls settled on the roller coaster for the first go around.

Harry came over and put on his best effort at a fraudulent humble and timid act as he began his confession.

"I reckon that Paul will need to take you girls on these rides. I do not do so well on them. You see, it is a little embarrassing for me, but I reckon that I have a weak stomach for these kinds of things, and with my false choppers, they have a tendency to fall out, which can be a bad scene for me."

Rose immediately moved into a sympathetic mode of poor, poor, Harry. She touched his arm gently in sympathy at poor Harry's plight.

Rose had bought the sob story.

Even Binky bought it, as she had a sad look on her face at hearing of his ride induced ailments, and the loose, bothersome, and tricky chopper syndrome.

"Oh, we understand Harry, but we feel bad that you will have to stay on the ground here and be bored while we go off and have such fun," Rose sympathized. Harry whipped up some fake sadness, put his head down, kicked at some sand on the wooden boardwalk, and put his hands in his pockets.

This was some act even for Harry, and I had seen him pull off some winners.

"Oh . . . I will be all right. I will watch from here and wave at you guys. I will go get a soda or something."

Oh brother, I thought, the girls have such exhilaration about these stupid rides they have forgotten who they are dealing with here.

Harry had woven a silk cloth of flim-flam and the girls had bought it.

Now as far as my thoughts and feelings went, riding on amusement rides was just not my favorite thing. I was not afraid of them. I could go on the largest and most imposing of amusement rides without even flinching. They did not make my stomach sick, but some rides that spun around made me very dizzy. I was simply not a big fan of the rides—if I had my choice, I would pass on them. However, since it was for Harry and our women, I could give it a whirl and take one for the team.

Rose gave Harry a kiss and off we went in different directions. While Harry went off to watch embarrassed young ladies with accidently exposed bare body parts, my fate was to head off to various torture chambers under the disguise of amusement rides. Harry gave me a covert hand wave, a wink of the eye, and we headed off in different directions.

We waited on a twenty-seven-mile-long line for the roller coaster, which was a large, old, rickety, wooden thing with the happy and nostalgic name of, "The Seashore Cannonball." I had ridden this old, wooden mess many times before. Under the false pretense of fun, it gave you huge welts and cuts on your rib cage as it tossed you around like a rag doll in the car. The stitched padding on the inside of the car was like a tissue, it was so thin and feeble. Its only purpose was to give you a warm feeling that the operators of the ride actually cared about your safety and comfort, but one ride full of welts and bruises would change your mind.

After what seemed like hours, we finally approached the coaster. Since we had three of us in the car together, the tossing about inside the car should be minimal, or so I thought. We started to climb in the car and the ladies stopped to argue who should sit where. Binky wanted me in the middle and she wanted to sit on the end, but Rose was not happy about being on the end. The ride attendant became annoyed as the debate lingered.

He looked at me as the ladies debated and he commented, "They sure are pretty, but you have to listen to this all day? It is not worth it, pal."

I did not answer him. Finally, the gals settled the debate, and I landed in the middle with the girls on the ends.

Rose leaned over and told me. "I love rides, but I have to warn you that they terrify me and I may scream a little."

Binky laughed as she had already transformed into her alter ego, speed freak, personality. She simply said, "I love the entire experience. I looked it up the other day, and this coaster reaches speeds of over fifty-five miles per hour."

Joy, joy, joy, I thought, and off we went.

Clank, clank, clank, up the obligatory big hill, then down the other side we went, zipping along at zillions of miles per hour, with our hearts in our throats and welts on our rib cages. Binky was an "arm raiser" and "seat stander" coaster ride, and she was beside herself with the thrill of the ride. When she moved, she left a little void, which caused Rose and me to shift and bang around. I was not about to mention to Binky that she should remain seated, I just was not going there. Rose, on the other hand, had indeed provided an extremely accurate description and warning, when she said she would be terrified. As soon as the coaster started to move, she crossed herself multiple times, and then from the moment we took off, until the end of the ride, she clung to my neck and arms with a death grip and screamed a loud, high-pitched scream, directly in my ears.

Boy, this sure was fun, I thought.

The coaster stopped, and I tried hard to hear exactly what Binky was saying, but since I was nearly deaf now, it was a bit difficult. Binky climbed out of the car and then gave me a big hug. She thanked me and, of course, provided a summarized and detailed analysis of the entire coaster ride and experience.

"I know that riding these coasters is nothing compared

to being a fearless goaltender like you are, while you are standing in those nets. You did not even flinch or yell once, which is, of course, what I expected of you. Nevertheless, for Rose and me, it is scary. Scary or not, I just love the speed!"

"Oh yes, it is nothing," I spouted aimlessly.

Binky was a covert thrill seeking, speed freak, chick, hiding behind that prim and proper front. Rose apologized to me for the red marks on my neck and arms and for screaming a "little."

I just smiled and sensed a potential escape route out of continued amusement park ride madness, I said, "Well, if you are that scared, I understand . . . and we do not have to go on any more rides." It was worth it to me, to try the fake caring angle in an effort to get out of riding anymore.

"Oh no, I am terrified out of my wits, but I love it," Rose answered. Outstanding logic. However, who am I to judge? I am nothing but an eccentric, strange, and weird goaltender.

Off we went towards the next ride. Binky and Rose skipped merrily along, dragging me behind them with their hands latched onto mine as they pulled me along. The next ride they selected was some horrible, torturous ride created by some sadistic engineer, who received joy out of spinning his victims high in the air on a simulated black octopus' thingy. Same deal . . . Binky loving it and losing all of her refined personality, and Rose screaming bloody murder in my ears.

Then we were off to spinning teacups, which spun you around until it felt as if your head had unscrewed from your neck, then a mad dash off to the Wild Rat, as we zipped up and down and all around, in a little, reckless, car that looked like it would go off the track any second. Then we were all stuck on the inside of a wall, within a hollowed-out circle, and they put leather straps around us to hold us, and we spun around a million miles an hour, while the floor dropped out.

On and on it went, from one torture chamber to the next, each ride having a little different way of extracting louder and more consistent screams out of Rose, thrilling Binky a little more, inducing a bit more deafness to my hearing, and accumulating, ever more red marks on my rib cage and body.

I was having a wonderful time and found myself daydreaming of where I might be able to find an emergency room to check into for treatment. The moment of escape was near as the girls checked the ride map, and it looked like my ride experience was joyfully ending.

"Well, I guess it is time to go find Harry. All that is left are the kiddy rides," Binky moaned.

I whipped up the best, phony, sad tone I could muster up and said, "Oh, wow, what a shame, it was so much fun," I said as I touched the red welts on my neck. "Well, let's find the way out of here."

Just when it looked like we were reaching the end of the road, and we had finally ridden all the adult rides on the pier, Binky stopped as we were walking out and looked up at a ride.

"Oh Paul, you are the greatest! You found the Flipper! I love the Flipper!"

Rose and I stopped, because I was confused, since I was not aware that I found anything. I was just inching my way toward the exit and thinking about where I could buy some first aid ointment and a hearing aid.

Binky turned and jumped on me into my arms and almost knocked me over. So much for her refined and dignified personality.

"Let's go, let's go!"

Binky yelled out as she ran towards the ticket line. Rose and I stopped and looked at the ride that towered above us. This ride was the ultimate monster of ominous mayhem. A towering spindle of madness that loomed at least two hundred feet straight up into the air.

The very top of it was inside a cloud bank.

It had one immense metal tower anchored to the ground with a boom type of arm attached to the middle of the main tower. Cars covered in heavy steel cages lined up along a track mounted on the outside of the boom and the cars eerily sat there, as if they were miniature, spinning, vortexes of torment, mined from the pits of Hell. Not only did the boom rotate around and around, just to add some more fun and joy to your life, the cars also rode the little track on the outside of the boom and went around and around, while the entire thing spun.

"Oh Binky, I do not know, this looks very bad," Rose remained frozen in place and her feet would not move.

Binky stopped walking, turned around, and said, "Dear Rose, now come along, it is nothing. The Wild Rat was much worse in thrashing intensity and the potential for ribcage bruises, and you loved that. The Flipper is fun. Twenty-seven, help Rose along now."

Rose looked at me and she was as white as a ghost was. I decided to appeal to Binky on behalf of poor Rose and maybe, just maybe, we both would escape the wrath of the Flipper.

"Binky, I do not think that dear Rose is quite up for this, she is really scared."

Binky came back and grabbed Rose by the arm, "Nonsense, we came all this way to ride the rides. You will regret it if you miss the Flipper. I checked into the incident rates for accidents for all of these rides last week, when I researched the park and they are all very safe. The design engineers reworked the original design on the safety latches for the cages to prevent people from falling out and plummeting to their deaths. There is nothing to be afraid of, my dear Rose. Don't you agree with me, Paul?"

"Sure, Binky, your research made me feel more comfortable. This looks like a nice, safe, enjoyable, ride to me."

I felt bad about fudging that statement, and if I had been Catholic, I would be heading off for confession. In fact, I thought if I survive this experience, I just might go, anyway.

At the coaxing of her friend, Rose managed to say, "I gggguesss Binky." Off we went to certain deafness and potential annihilation.

Oh well, at least Harry was having the time of his life watching young ladies lose their swimsuits.

I walked up to the ticket booth and read the sign: "This ride takes 142 tickets each." Next to the ticket requirement on the sign, was a painted black skull and crossbones logo and underneath the logo, was a small coffin image.

'Oh boy, a big boy ride, and highway robbery,' I thought, while I dug down in my pockets for the last of my overtime. I bought our tickets, and the three of us started to climb the staircase to the center of the ride where you were loaded into the caged cars to fulfill your death wish.

As we climbed this fun amusement ride, there were various warning signs posted along the way.

"Do not ride this amusement device if you have a heart condition, are less than four feet tall, are afraid of heights, have high blood pressure, or are pregnant, ill, scared, nervous, smart, under the influence of alcohol or other mind-altering substances." The next sign read, "Be careful of your step, you are climbing two hundred feet in the air." Wow, even the staircase is dangerous. I halfway expected to find an undertaker stationed on the staircase with a tape measure to pre-check your dimensions for a coffin. We climbed a little higher and read another sign, "If you have reached this level, then you must be under the influence of alcohol or other mind-altering substances."

Rose was scared stiff, and I helped her along the way as we climbed higher and higher into the bowels of the Flipper. Binky skipped along at a merry pace, holding my hand, working hard to drag Rose and me faster. Rose and I would have preferred a slower pace, and a drum roll beat as if we were heading for the gallows.

We finally reached the top; the ride operator was sitting upon a little stool in front of about four million controls, levers, and flashing lights.

He greeted and smiled at the three of us and proudly announced, "Welcome to the Flipper!"

Well, at least he was a happy and carefree fellow.

After all, what a wonderful job . . . they pay you a wage to sit in the sun at the seashore, hundreds of feet in the air, while you send a long parade of victims off to sheer terror under the disguise of fun and amusement. The Grim Reaper and this guy should get along swimmingly.

The ride stopped and a little car swung in front of us. A young man with eighty-five tattoos on his arms and neck and who had no teeth was helping load victims in the cars. He unbolted about forty-seven safety bolts and locks. He then smiled a toothless grin, held the car from swinging, and signaled for us to enter the torture chamber.

The main operator leaned over and said to me out of an earshot of the women, "Lucky guy, riding with two pretty chicks like that."

"Yes, very lucky," I agreed with him.

"I will keep you on an extra-long time, buddy, so you can eh, grab a hold of some things," The Grim Reaper winked at me and smiled.

"Oh thanks, but you don't have to do that. . .." Before I could finish speaking, they shoved me into the caged car. I was between Binky and Rose, and we had about seventy-five straps and harnesses locked down over us to hold us in the seats. Then the cage slammed shut like a jail cell door, and the safety locks snapped back into place around us.

Rose was terrified, and she said, "I do not like how this looks guys."

Before we could say another word, the ride started and

off we spun into outer space. Right on time, Rose lost it at the top of her lungs and Binky yelled in joy. Binky held my neck on one side, as she whooped and hollered at meeting her now fulfilled speed and danger quota. Rose, on the other side, held my neck and arms in a death grip, while working hard to puncture my eardrums.

I felt like I was in a vise.

Higher and higher, we climbed. Looking down, the ocean and the people on the ground looked as if they might have been over in Europe somewhere. Up, up, up, we went, and then we flipped over and came back around the other side. Down, down, down, we went a million miles above the surface of the Earth at close to, if not, over the speed of sound. Around and around, we went, tumbling repeatedly, flipping back and forth, all in the name of fun and amusement.

While the big, main arm spun around like a high-speed mix master, the little caged cars that contained multiple horrified victims, flipped, spun, and turned around.

The wonderful and inspired double turning action, combined with the flipping and spinning of the caged cars, to turn your vital, internal human organs into mush. I felt a Big Bob's Griddle Frankfurter that I had eaten at a Labor Day picnic at the Redmonds about three years ago begin to stir from somewhere deep down inside of me. I slowly felt my eardrums melting and my head felt as if it was unscrewing from my neck. Just when it seemed like we were going to launch to the moon, the ride stopped with us on the underside of the main arm, and our caged car swung from the track parallel to the ground. We swung back and forth while hanging upside down. Rose was now screaming so loud that people two hundred feet down on the planet Earth could hear her, and they stopped to point up at us on the ride.

"Is this great or what?" Binky yelled.

I somehow managed under a great, intense, internal

pain to squeak out, "Great."

"Come on Paul, help me rock the car," Binky said, as she moved her body as best, she could under the harness. Binky wanted to get the car moving more while we faced straight down, looking at the earth.

"Nooooooooo!" Rose yelled.

"I think that may be a bad idea, Binky. Rose seems to be having a bit of a rough time with this."

I looked over at Binky, who was having the time of her life. I asked myself, is this really the same gal who was scared stiff by Ewing Ave and Harry's ghost story? Just then, the ride started moving again, and the anguish began all over, but this time for fun, variety, and pleasure, we were now going in the opposite direction!

Harry and his words, "It is no big deal," echoed inside my head.

The evil, vicious jerk running the ride was true to his word, as he left us on forever. His plan was to keep us on longer, based upon his assumption that I was a perverted dope. He really thought that I would subject myself to this ride for the chance of grabbing young, unsuspecting ladies in the wrong locations, while under the charade of having fun, in this out of control, chamber of horrors. The only body part that I wanted to grab was his neck.

I thought, if I somehow managed to get off this ride alive and intact, I would stomp the life out of him, and squeeze his neck, until his eyeballs popped out.

I was becoming so deaf and dizzy now that life was a blur, and just when I was preparing myself for death and meeting Jesus, the ride stopped. The car stopped swinging, and the operators climbed over us, undid the two million safety devices, and used the vise of life tool to extract us from the car.

Even Binky was suddenly quiet, as I am not sure that she actually realized the ride had stopped.

The Grim Reaper posing as the Flipper operator and his

toothless assistant pulled us out, and as I stood there spinning around, I looked at him and said, "You sir . . . are lucky that I am so dizzy, or I would choke you until your eyeballs popped out of your head!"

He laughed and led us to the staircase as he proudly proclaimed, "I get told that a hundred times a day!"

Off the three of us went, climbing down the stairs, not saying a word. We all were so dizzy and spinning, it was a miracle that we made it to the ground safely. I held both my arms out as the girls both held onto each of my hands as I worked hard to guide us all safely to the ground. I was faintly aware that we had climbed back down the two-hundred-foot staircase, but I was so dizzy, I was not really sure exactly where we were. We stumbled together to the ground level, found our way out of the fence for the exit, and made our way to the closest bench. The three of us collapsed onto each other and wrapped our arms around each other, in order to hold us upright.

The world was spinning a million miles per hour, and Rose, Binky, and I were stationary on this little, safe, happy, bench.

Yes, indeed! That is, it! I have it all figured out in my scrambled mind somewhere. We are now safe and back on planet Earth! Rose started to come around, as did Binky too, and they both clung to me and then kissed my opposite cheeks.

Rose was reciting, The Lord's Prayer aloud, and then she said, "Thank you, Paul, for saving me," repeatedly. I could not really understand what Binky was saying, but she collapsed and put her head in my lap.

After a few minutes, Rose asked me, "Where on earth is Harry?"

Harry, Harry, Harry . . . deep in the inner recess of my fuzzy mind, I recalled a guy named Harry. He acted like a cowboy, wore a big hat, and had a cool car.

Harry . . . Harry . . . Harry, who?

Due to my scrambled brain, and the fact that I could not focus correctly, I said, "If you cannot find him, then look in the water park at the base of the water slide."

At the mention of a water park and the slide, even the fuzzy minded Rose, could connect the dots in this game. Her eyes rolled in her head and she sighed loudly.

She got up slowly and said, "Wait here, I will find him and bring him back."

Binky and I sat holding on to one another on the bench as we slowly came around and crept back to a normal state. As my brain activity stabilized, and my mind slowly returned to normal, I became aware of the fact that I had not covered for Harry and sent Rose off seeking him. She was sure to find him at the base of the water slide and subject my best buddy to incomprehensible tortures.

I felt like a turncoat.

Oh well, I did my best. I was under extreme Flipper impairment, anyway.

Binky also recovered slowly, and she worked hard at bringing herself back to her usual normal state of prim and proper behavior. She sat up and returned to her normal Binky mode of operation.

Binky smoothed her clothes out, took a brush out of her purse, and brushed her hair.

"The Flipper sure was great, twenty-seven."

"Great," was all I could manage to say to Binky. I felt that the two of us had moved to the point in our relationship where I was comfortable sharing some more of the "inside scoop" with her. I told Binky where I thought Rose was going to find Harry and why he was there.

She shook her head and said, "Really Paul, really?"

I nodded my head, and she picked up my hand and squeezed it hard.

"You know Harry is quite the character, and I know you two are very close, but I sure am glad you are so much different from him."

She rested her head on my shoulder, and we just sat there listening to screams from the next round of sufferers high above the ground on the Flipper.

High up in the air, I am sure, The Grim Reaper and his toothless assistant were enjoying themselves.

Binky and I sat there watching the Flipper going around and spent victims stagger out of the exit, when all of a sudden, we saw Rose walking towards us with her arms folded across her chest. She looked pretty angry. I spotted Harry a few feet behind her and he was saying something, although we could not make it out.

"Oh boy, Binky," I said, as we both stood up from the bench.

"Hello, guys," Binky said, doing her best to break the ice. It was almost dark now, the lights of the pier and the boardwalk were flickering to life, and the nightlife was just beginning.

"Do you know where I found him?" Rose seemed to be slightly upset with the big guy. She waved for me to stay away, leaned in, and whispered in Binky's ear.

Binky did a great job at acting surprised and she reprimanded Harry, "No! Harry! How could you? That is disgusting and deplorable behavior!"

Harry just stood there looking at us and did not say a word. He walked over to me and whispered, "I thought you would keep them busy a little while longer, it was just getting really good."

I could not really fathom that Harry thought he could stay a little longer and get away with it. I looked at him and he must have sensed my anger because his eyes became really wide and large.

"Harry, any longer and I would have died! You have no idea what I did just so you could check out some gal's exposed breasts, backsides, and other body parts!"

Harry looked remorseful, and he said, "I am sorry, twenty-seven, thanks for how hard you tried, I just got a little extra caught up at the moment."

Rose, for a little gal, was quite the pepper pot when she was livid. She stomped over to Harry, got up in his face, and yelled at him.

"I should tie you and your stupid hat up on the outside of that ride over there and let you spin around for the whole night," Rose screamed as she pointed up to the Flipper.

Harry turned around and looked up at the Flipper. "Wow, only nutcases would go on that ride. I heard that four people were killed on that ride a few years back."

Upon hearing the death report, Binky opened her purse and pulled out some papers, which she began to study.

I heard her mumble, "Hmm . . . I thought it was only three deaths. I must have missed the fourth death while conducting my research on the rides."

"You better go to confession after this behavior! I am going to call Father Mark myself. To make matters worse, Harry was not alone! He was with a large group of young, married, fathers who were all doing the same thing as he was. Whooping and yelling at the tops of their lungs when some embarrassed woman's bikini top fell off, and her chest was exposed. All of their wives were there rounding them all up, and I found it disgustingly shameful."

Harry jumped in here, never missing a chance at a hapless defense of his actions, as well as, an effort to promote his world-famous theory, "That is because all of them, there, young fathers got wives checking out the backsides of all the bad guys who live in their neighborhoods."

We all just stared at him and no one answered as Harry shook his head up and down in support of his theory. I wondered where a little gal like Rose found the strength in her voice to be able to scream after the afternoon that we had been through today.

Harry reached out to Rose. "Aw, c'mon darlin' forgive

me, let's all go get something to eat, and have a great night before we have to roll home."

Rose resisted at first, but she slowly melted. We all had to admit that we were very hungry, so we headed for the boardwalk to find a place to eat.

The girls walked together ahead of us, and Harry and I lagged behind. Harry looked over at me and zoomed in close to check out my neck. He pulled my collar down on my shirt and he was examining my battle wounds obtained while covering for his escapades.

"Hey man, what happened to your neck, it is full of red marks?" He then leaned back, let go of my collar and smiled a broad devious Harry grin. "So, old number twenty-seven, I reckon you and Bink-a-roo-ski are really getting along now eh," he said as he put his arm around my shoulders.

I took his arm off my shoulders and said, "No, it is not what you think, or what you want it to be, in that devious mind of yours. Harry, someday, I will tell you the whole story, but right now I am hungry, and thirsty for an ice-cold beer, so back off." I seldom became angry with Harry, but when I did, he usually got the message.

There were two people on Earth that I knew Harry did not ever want to mess with, even as big and strong as he was. One was his sister Patty, (who I also would never want to tangle with) and the other one was yours truly! It took me a long time to become angry, but Harry had tested my dangerous waters today.

We picked a place with a bright neon sign that stated, "Surf Club" in yellow letters on a brightly painted blue banner area above the front door, and we entered. We had a quick identification check with an older gentleman at the door who stared at me for a second and then smiled at me as he waved us in. A young hostess then led us to a table, and we all sat down. It was nice to relax and be in the air conditioning. It had been a long, warm day. Since it was still early, the club did not have many people in it yet, and they had some soft music that was playing in the background. It was an attractive décor inside; there was some ocean and seashore related paintings on the wall, as well as some Seashore Heights and New Jersey memorabilia. I admired it all while we sat and we started some general table conversation. I shuddered a little when I spotted a full color oil painting of the Flipper ride, mounted in glory in a prominent location of honor near the bar. I wanted to go up and look close to see if the painter had captured little individual victims being tortured on the ride just for an element of realism. The club also had a long bar, a dance floor, and an open, raised stage for a band to play. It was a step up from a typical gin joint.

An attractive waitress walked over and she took our order. I saw her stare at my neck and then over to Binky, and she smiled and winked at me. I hoped that Binky had not spotted her reaction and thought about how these remnants of my ride experience were going to linger for a while.

Binky ordered a shaken not stirred Martini. I asked for a Big Boulder beer, Harry picked his usual Wall Crawler, and Rose ordered a Purple Pirate beer. When the drinks came, we all raised our glasses and made a toast to our day. Rose reached over and gave Harry a hug, and all was well in their world once more. I put my arm around Binky and pulled her closer to me. She seemed happy now that Rose and Harry had patched things up and we were all back to normal.

Once more, Rose had shown how I felt she was a good match for Harry. She was able to go along with his obnoxious and sometimes atrocious behavior and forgive him rather quickly. In fact, she now was even laughing at his behavior! She really was falling for the big guy, and Rose realized that he meant no real harm. Harry just could not help himself sometimes. I just wondered if it would finally wear her down or not, but time would tell.

We were all very hungry, so we ordered some burgers, more drinks, and other fare. Everyone started to relax now as the food arrived and the drinks floated around in us.

The conversation over the table recalled some many adventures of the day, as it was now a lot easier to laugh at certain things than it was before.

"Harry tells us that you are a fantastic dancer, Paul. Do you think we will ever have the chance to see you out there on the dance floor, or what?" Rose asked me.

"Oh no, I cannot really dance that well, you know Harry and his stories and all of his many exaggerations."

I was embarrassed and did not want to dance.

"I reckon he is being his usual, modest, and shy self, there, gals! Y'all don't believe him, he and his older sister won dance competitions together. I have seen them dance together and ole twenty-seven is the best dancer there is!"

Leave it to my best buddy in the world, to work me into a situation that, of course, I would rather not be in today. I just wanted to relax and enjoy a few beers here, and we all could unwind. Now, I could tell the pressure was on for me to demonstrate this supposed wonderful dancing ability.

I laughed it off in a weak defensive mode. "Oh no, I really cannot dance. I am a goaltender, not a dancer."

Binky stared at me, and her facial expression changed to a determined look. She suddenly had a deep allure to her face, and her body language changed to a posture of attraction. She fluffed out her long blonde hair and made it tumble over her front shoulders. I had never seen this before, and I must say she looked more than appealing! Honestly, parts of my body began to twitch.

Binky leaned over close to me, got up in my face, and asked, "Will you dance with me, twenty-seven?"

I think she was feeling the Martini drinks. Her invitation startled me and knew that it had more meaning than just sharing a simple dance. The Harry Theory swam around in my thick skull. I heard a little voice deep inside me, coaching me along. "Don't blow it, you dummy!"

I mustered up some inner strength.

"Well, I guess, but I am not that good really, besides I am a little sore from running the Dinky out to the car."

"You jerk," the little voice told me. "You are blowing it!"

I was making excuses and luckily for me, Binky was not buying it. She knew that I was an athlete and in tip-top shape. I was not sore, and Binky frowned a little at my hesitation and fake excuse. She leaned in even closer, and those clear, blue eyes opened even wider.

I started to come up with another excuse, "Well. . .."

"Fast or slow?"

She interrupted me and it was clear that she was not backing down. I looked at her and she had that same wild-eyed stare that she had when she wanted an answer to a question, so I knew she was serious.

"Either, but I will lead."

Binky leaned back satisfied, fluffed her hair, and she took a long sip of her drink.

"Done deal, Paul. Next song, no matter if you like the song or not, a deal is a deal, there will not be any backing out now."

I smiled at her and said, "Done deal."

Harry and Rose had been watching our exchange carefully, and they both smiled broadly. Harry became excited and loud. He clapped his hands and waved his big hat in the air over his head.

"Oh yeah, now you will see what old number twenty-seven can do!" He yelled and most of the club turned to look at us. "Turn that music up, let's dance!"

Rose, who knew a little something about Binky, turned to us all and revealed, "Binky is no dancing slouch either. She can really get out there and shake it all up too!" Rose had jumped in there to let us all know that this could be quite the scene.

I felt like I was in the net and getting ready to face off in a big game with the pressure on. I sat back, wondering what I had just agreed to. I am a progressive rocker and this was a disco club. I wondered what I had just roped myself into this time. I held my breath as the song that was playing ended, and I hoped and prayed that some gruesome disco song would not come on.

It was a pre-programmed tape, so it was really the luck of the draw as to what song was coming on next. The faint music tones started, and the manager of the club must have known that something was going on due to Harry's loud outburst, because he increased the volume on the sound system.

Harry's Theory had classified me as a loser and a doormat, but I was not going to blow this one or back down on a deal. This was my chance. Maybe my one and only chance with Binky, to shed that image of always being the reserved Mr. Nice Guy and a hapless victim of the Old Lady Syndrome.

As soon as I heard the opening bars of the song, I grabbed Binky's hand and led her out on the dance floor. I didn't even know what the song was yet, but I stared her down like a shooter closing in on my net. I was relieved as my musical encyclopedia of a mind, which had many songs in it, recognized the swooping violins, Spanish guitars, horns, and castanets to announce the arrival of one of my favorite songs, "Living Love" by the Electronic Transistor Orchestra.

Great song and very lucky on my part!

It was going to be a fast to medium speed dance, with some interesting tempo changes. I could handle this one and knew I could nail it. The question was, what type of dancing partner was Binky?

Despite my downplaying of my dancing abilities, Harry was correct when he said that I had won some dance competitions. I had taken many lessons, and my sister and

I had indeed danced for quite a while together since we were younger. My lead abilities would tell me rather quickly what kind of dancer Binky was.

It did not take very long for Binky to answer my questions!

The unique, Spanish influenced opening bars of the song began, and I smiled, as I realized by her initial moves that she could really bring it. She squared off to me, smiled, fluffed her hair, and cast a sex appeal felt all the way back up the Garden State Parkway in good old Paterson. In fact, a little earth tremor back home may have knocked over my mum's teacup. I was not going to blow this one and that little voice inside of my head went away satisfied.

I swept in and held her as the tempo of the song built up. I spun her at just the right moment, and we faced each other off at the end of a spin with almost perfect timing. Binky was an attractive young lady, and she had a fantastic female figure with gentle curves and glorious breasts. I suddenly realized that just like when she shed her prim and proper behavior for thrills and speed, she also could do the same on the dance floor. She knew how to move and shake her body as well as her individual parts in all the right ways out on the dance floor.

She really was downright gorgeous.

I am sure there were a number of young males in the club who were enjoying this scene! I could hear Harry yelling and carrying on from the table whenever Binky moved in an alluring manner.

For two people who never, ever danced with one another before, we made it happen. Whirling, twirling, and shaking, Binky followed my lead, as I was loose and feeling the flow. I was in the net making the saves and feeling the game. The old goaltender moves were serving me well! It was pure magic to a purely magical song. As the song came down to the final bars, I pulled Binky in close, held her, and then spun her for a final clasp and a dramatic, perfectly timed ending. It sure helped that I knew every beat of that song. Thank you to the composer of this song wherever you were, you sure wrote a good one!

What Binky and I did not realize was the size of the audience that we had attracted during our dance. When the song had ended, the limited number of diners in the club, waiters, and servers, Harry, Rose, management, and even the kitchen staff who had come out to see what was going on, all stood up and gave us a loud round of applause. It was something special, a chance meeting of the right song, the right setting, and the right people.

I was embarrassed at the end of the dance, and as we walked to our table, people came up to us and congratulated us. The server came over, placed another round of drinks on the table, and smiled.

"These are on the house from the manager. That was fantastic, youse guys! You must be professional dancers."

Harry was still standing, and he was beaming from ear-to-ear. He was whooping and hollering in typical, bombastic, Harry style as only he could do and get away with it, "Why thanks little lady, I told y'all, what a day this has been, yeeehaw!"

We all sat back down, and Binky looked at me and smiled. She took my hand very gently and looked straight into my eyes.

"Well now, that was not bad dancing for a long-haired, hippie hockey goaltender who does not know how to dress on a first date when he meets a young lady."

I laughed and smiled.

"Not bad dancing either, for a young lady who loves scary rides, high speed races, and thinks that all goaltenders are eccentric, weird, and obscure."

Binky leaned in close, kissed my cheek and whispered to me, "All of them, except this particular goalie."

We had a great time, we danced a little more, and Harry and Rose went out there on the dance floor to, as Harry would say, "Cut a little rug!"

The club suddenly became jammed packed with people and the dance floor was no longer wide open like it had been, and it became an effort to move around out there. Binky and I stayed at the table while Harry and Rose spent quite a bit of time out there on the dance floor. I spotted Harry during a dancing break, speaking with the manager of the club, chatting up a storm, pointing back to our table and laughing with him. He was always working the crowd and all the angles. Back he scurried with Rose for another dance out on the floor, and when that song ended, Harry and Rose came back to the table and sat down.

"I reckon it is time to hit the road gang. It is a long roll back, and it is getting late now."

Harry was correct. It was late, and it sure had been a grand day. We paid our tab and started to leave. As we made our way to the door, the older gentleman who was the manager came over to us.

He tapped me on the arm and extended his hand. "Thank you for coming. That was some dance with your young lady. It sure broke the ice tonight."

I smiled, said thank you, and started to move towards the door, but he held my arm, so I turned back to him a little puzzled.

"Excuse me, I may be wrong, but I only am here at the shore managing this place during the summer, I go back up north to near Paterson after Labor Day." All four of us were now listening to him as he continued, "I am a big hockey fan, I go to all the local games, and I think you are the young goaltender for the Long Island Roosters, aren't you?"

"Well, yes I am. How did you even recognize me?"

The older man smiled. "I thought it was you when you first came in, but I was not sure. When you were out on the dance floor, it came to me, the hair and beard . . . you know. You always tie all that hair up for games, but you let it down when you are not playing. I heard that your gal here likes it that way. The way you were moving out there, along with the hair made me put it together." He was a little guy, with thick, slicked back, black hair, and beady little eyes, but he had a happy and friendly manner to him.

The manager walked over to the edge of the bar and grabbed a paper and a pen that was there.

"Hey, do you mind signing this for me? That playoff game when you shut down that idiot O'Malley, and the Colonials was awesome, you were like a whirlwind that night."

The man handed me the paper and a pen, as he added, "Just in case you make it to the big time! I would have your autograph from when you first started out."

His request surprised me. These things happen to Harry, not to me. Not too many people ever had asked me for my autograph in public before this time. Previously, I only had a few fans ask me after a game at the rink. I took the paper, signed it, and put the number twenty-seven under my name.

"Could you please date it?" This old guy was a serious collector. I put the date on it and handed it back to him. He smiled at me and patted me on the back as I handed him the paper. "You sure, are a big guy! You look a lot bigger in person than you do in the net! Thanks, and youse guys have a great night."

We left and Rose was all over it. "That was incredible! You see, Harry. You are not the only celebrity around here!"

"I told y'all that Paul was the best. I hope you ladies know how lucky y'all are to be out with us! It is one adventure after another, so come along for the ride and see where it all takes us!"

Binky and I did not say a word as we turned up the boardwalk and headed for the parking lot. She only smiled at me, put her arm through mine, and pulled me close.

After all that had happened, there was not much to say. Her body language and facial expression told me all I needed to know about how she felt.

The night was clear and cool and although it was dark, you could hear the ocean waves crashing out along the beach. We walked and turned into the parking lot, which because it was now growing late, had a lot fewer cars parked in it now. The Trans Whizzer, parked in the corner of the lot, stood out from all the other cars.

"Oh no, my prize is gone!"

Harry let out a yell and ran to the car. Sure enough, the creepy Dinky was gone from the top of the car. The thieves, who had hoofed it, left only the ropes that I had used to tie it on the roof as a sad reminder to its once glorious presence. The lot attendants were all gone for the day, so there was no one to ask if they had seen the evil, shadowy figures who had stolen it. Rose, Binky, and I all faked our sadness to Harry for his loss and got into the car.

Binky whispered to Rose and me, "I hope the thieves realize the potential danger that they procured."

We both shook our heads in acknowledgement of the danger, and Binky was satisfied. Harry sat in the driver's seat and felt his pockets for the keys.

"I have them, Harry. I kept them from when I tied up Dinky."

I pulled out the keys and handed them to Harry.

He looked at me and said, "Hey, you know what, Paul? Keep them. Do you want to drive home? I am tired, and Rose and I can relax in the back and you can have a Trans Whizzer driving experience!"

This was fantastic! I had driven the Sonicmobile many times, but never, ever, had Harry offered before tonight to let me drive the Trans Whizzer.

"Sure!"

We all got out, reversed our seating, and I sat behind the wheel of this awesome machine. Binky climbed in next to me, and she clearly loved this. I started the big engine up, put it in gear, and we were off. I did not require any coaching, as I reached over to the tape box, pulled out the Crystal Zirconium tape, and popped it in. There was not much conversation now, as everyone was exhausted. I was feeling it though. I was in a flow, and it felt good.

It was not long before everyone was sound asleep in the car and I had the open road and the music to myself, with a backdrop of some soft snores and breathing. I punched the gas here and there and shifted the overdrive on the gears when I could. I changed lanes and gauged the flow of traffic as I hurtled north up the roadway through the clear, perfect summer night air. I was in charge of this glorious machine and I felt the power under my control.

I imagined myself on the speedways facing a hundred Volcano Advantages driven by wild-eyed, secret agents, as well as beating other sports cars driven by movie stars to the finish line. Car number twenty-seven, victorious again! I looked down at the custom shifter, the Dragon logo on the steering wheel, and felt that rush you receive when you are in charge.

I looked over at Binky sound asleep next to me and thought how gorgeous she looked, even in the dark, with her head resting on the seat. She was quite the gal, and she seemed interested in me. Let me see now; pretty gals, fast cars and road races, some cold beer, a captivating dance with a gorgeous woman, and a great day at the New Jersey shore. To cap it all off, I have a fantastic automobile under my control.

'Oh yeah, the end of another perfect Harry and Paul day,' I thought as I drove north up the road, and we disappeared into the night.

7

The Gold Key

Life had been going along well for us. The summer came and went, and we worked our way into the fall and the early winter of the year. Harry and I cruised many a night in the Trans Whizzer and we had many adventures and great times! I will leave the stories of those adventures for another time and place—they would fill multiple volumes of pages! Harry had many dates with many women, including the young lady who slipped her number in his pocket that night at Lord Crudley's Bar. While he ranted and raved about this girl and that girl in typical Harry fashion, he always seemed to go back to Rose. While they both would not admit that they did not want to date anyone else, I had a feeling that was really the actual truth.

Harry and the rest of the Redmonds were still embroiled in the country and western phase, and this time, it seemed like a phase that may never end. It had gone on so long now that it was as if it was finally a permanent way of life.

It may have been my imagination, but it sure seemed like they were actually losing their New Jersey accents and adopting authentic western drawls.

I was busy with work and the hockey season had resumed, so I did not have as much spare time as I did in the summer and the off-season.

I had warned Binky of how my schedule would change once the hockey season started, and that I would not have a lot of free time between my regular job, practices, and then actual games. She had only answered me when I told her those facts with a simple smile and a coy answer that I always remembered.

She looked at me and said, "That is fine, I can wait." I did not know exactly what that meant or how to take it. More importantly, for some reason, I chose not to ask her. Perhaps I did not want to face what the answer could potentially be.

I did stay in touch with Binky via the telephone in between my busy schedule. We went out together on dates when I had the time, and she attended all of my games, along with Rose and Harry. It was hard to tell if hockey was growing on her or not, but let me tell you that her research bug had made her an expert. She knew the rules of the game better than old twenty-seven did, and I lived and breathed the sport! Since I really did not date anyone else, I guess you could say she was my only gal, but I never really asked her if she ever went out with anyone else. For me, it just was not that serious a relationship. However, I always had a strange feeling that for Binky, it was very serious.

I was indeed afraid to ask, and I was very content to leave well enough alone. I enjoyed her company, and she was a great gal, but this was hockey season. I was playing well and beginning to develop into a solid goaltender.

The Long Island Roosters had promoted me to the starting goaltender position this year, after my success in the playoffs last year, and I was taking it very seriously. Playing the goaltender position at high levels of ice hockey competition required a commitment in training and concentration. If you did not prepare yourself mentally and physically, you could not only play poorly, but you could also get hurt badly.

I was packing my practice gear in my equipment bag on a Friday night when the phone rang. My mother answered it and since she was laughing very hard, I knew that it had to be Harry.

"Paulie, it is Harry, come get the phone," my mother yelled. "He is too much. He is still working on that song on his banjo dedicated to all his favorite old cars," my mother explained as she handed me the phone.

Sure enough, as I said, "Hello," I could hear Harry picking his banjo as Linda was singing in the background.

Harry stopped playing to speak to me. "Hey come on over. You do not have a practice or game this weekend, right?"

"No, I am off for this weekend. We played on Tuesday night, remember. You and the gals were at the game."

"Yeah, yeah, yeah, that's right, nice game there twenty-seven, y'all looking good this year. Hey, shave, groom that long hair of yours, look nice, pack some warm, outside clothes as well as a suit and tie, and some overnight stuff. Bring some extra jingle too. Wear casual, but nice clothes right now, please do not wear any No Way tee shirts or hockey jerseys. Come over quick, I have the ultimate cool for us this weekend."

"Click." The line went dead.

Typical Harry.

He provided little or no details, no supporting information, and just some vague, wild gibberish that undoubtedly will lead to some incredible adventure. Harry never spoke truer words than when he said, "It is one adventure after another, so come along for the ride and see where it all takes us."

I changed into some decent looking casual clothes. I packed one of my nicer equipment bags with the clothing and items that Harry had instructed me to. I did not own a suitcase, but I selected a bag that had my uniform number stamped on it, along with our team logo. I thought it was good looking and kind of unique. I took my only dress shirt, a nice tie, my suit pants, suit jacket and put them on a hanger and covered them with a plastic bag. My dress shoes, I tossed in the equipment bag.

I passed the old man in the hallway and told him, "Hey Dad, Harry and I and the girls, are going away for the weekend. I will see you late on Sunday night. Do you or Mum need anything before I book out?"

The old man stopped in his tracks, thought for a minute, and then said, "No, I am good. No hockey or work this weekend?"

"No, Dad, I played on Tuesday night this week, remember? I shut out the Rockets, you and the guys from the shop were at the game."

The old man seemed like he regained the memory of the game and he smiled. "Yeah, yeah, yeah, you looked sharp. Hey, when do you play the Colonials? Some guys from the shop want to go with me and taunt that loon, O'Leary."

"It is O'Malley, dad, the guy's name is O'Malley."

"Oh yeah, I meant O'Malley. When do you play them?"

"I don't know, Dad. In a couple of weeks, I guess, I will let you know. Hey, I will see you."

"Make sure you take that tie out of your hair. Bunky does not like that."

"Binky, Dad, her name is Binky."

I headed down the stairs as I heard him yell out, "You should get a haircut, it is a lot easier!"

For late November in New Jersey, it was unusually cold out. In fact, it was going to be way below freezing tonight. I very seldom wore a winter coat, but I did bring one along with my suit jacket just in case. I breathed deeply, looked up at the clear night sky, and thought about how much I loved the cold weather. I opened up my jeep, tossed the bag and my winter coat in the back, put the suit down carefully on the back seat, and headed out. I arrived over at 20 John Street and noticed that the driveway did not have many cars parked in it. I tapped on the front door.

"Come on in, twenty-seven!" I heard Harry yell from inside. I walked in and to my surprise; the house was quiet.

"Hey, Harry, so where is everyone?" Harry was busy

with his nose down in a suitcase, and he was working hard to try to zip it all up.

"Oh, they all went out, except Ronzo and Linda. They are upstairs watching television. My old man, the Big Spike, and Patty took the kids to a movie, and then they were all going over to Patty's house for the weekend. It is nice around here for a change. At least that stupid 'Dinky the Orange Teddy Bear' cartoon is not blasting away on the television." I had to admit it was one of the few times in about fifteen years, in which Harry's house was not utter noise and chaos. The change was eerily quiet. Even Cocoa was asleep on the floor in the living room, with his trusted Piggy tucked under his nose.

"I reckon this here stupid suitcase is defective!" Harry was frustrated, and he was struggling with zipping it all up. "Did y'all ever notice that I always get the defective zippers on stuff? I also always pick out a shopping cart in stores that have a bad wheel. I always git, the one cart in the entire dump that drags, wiggles, squeaks, or does not spin. I reckon I always git them!"

Harry looked at me for an answer but I did not know how to address his troubles. In fact, I didn't even know why this conversation had come up! This was starting out to be a very strange night.

I did however; have to admit that he was correct. He always did seem to pick out a shopping cart in the store with a bum wheel. It would scrape along the floor, wiggle, spin around like a top, not turn at all, or make some other wacky noise as we struggled up the aisles with it. Harry would usually become frustrated with it and ditch it in an aisle. He then would look around for a guy not paying any attention, take the poor soul's stuff out of the cart that he was using, and switch it with the one with the bum wheel. Harry then would roll away merrily and leave the other guy with the cart with the bum wheel. He also always did have zipper troubles, and I always had to remind him to check for "malfunctions" after he made a restroom visit. It was just another weird and wacky aspect of life with Harry!

I came over to assist him, and saw that the suitcase was fully packed and was overflowing. The two of us finally managed to get it all buttoned up, but it was not an easy task. I also saw that Harry had a suit under plastic, draped over a chair back in the dining room, with his banjo case sitting next to it on the floor. In addition, his super expensive, highly polished, black cowboy boots with the silver studs on the side sat on the floor next to the chair, while reflecting the dining room light above them in the boot tips.

"So where are we going that we have to bring all these fancy, dress clothes and suits?" Harry looked at me, did not answer the question, and smiled. Instead, he hammered me with a bunch of other questions.

"You did bring your suit, right?"

"Check."

"Nice shoes too?"

"Check, Mum."

"I reckon y'all better pull that tie thingy out of that hair of yours, Binky hates that thing. When y'all going to cut that mop of hair off, anyway?"

"Well, that confirms my suspicions and answers if I was going to see Binky this weekend, so one question has been answered. Do you care to reveal any more details, or do I still have to play twenty questions?"

Harry put his ten-gallon hat on the table and said, "Yup, we are going out with Stinky and Toes. It could be our biggest, most incredible adventure with them of all time!"

He was very excited, but Harry said this when we would go to the gas station, so I needed some more details before making any final judgment.

"So, the girls already know about this, and it is all planned. How come I am never in on any planning?"

Harry rolled his eyes at me, as if the answer to my question was so obvious.

"Because, you are too nice a guy and you would never think of these cool things and places that I come up with that is why. You would pick boring, nice, wholesome, family type places to go to for a weekend getaway. I cannot tell you where we are off to, you see I promised Ronzo, so let me see if he can come down now."

"Ronnie?" I was puzzled.

Harry stood at the base of the stairs and yelled up to the second floor, "Hey Ronzo, can you come on down now? Paul is here!"

A second or two later, I heard Ronnie yell back, "One minute!" Ronzo came down the stairs with a huge smile on his big, round, happy face. He was carrying a bag and a small black box in his hands.

"Howdy, Paul! How y'all doing? You had better take that tie thingy out of your hair. I hear Binky does not like it when you tie all your hair back like that."

I wondered exactly how many people in the world were aware of the fact that Binky did not like my hair tied back.

"Come on over here men, and I will give you the stuff y'all need for the weekend."

Ronzo led us to the dining room table. He placed the small box on the table, along with the bag. He opened the bag and handed Harry a bunch of papers, while he explained, "I left special and detailed instructions with the front desk, so remember, y'all Redmond and Boatmann. The both of you will have a special assistant assigned to you for the entire weekend. He will take care of your every need, plan events, and handle if there is any trouble, he will guide you along."

Ronzo shuffled some papers around that he had on the table. "His name is, let me see here." Ronzo was studying the papers. "His name is, Howard Pailet."

The big guy continued to go through the papers and

identify them to us. "This is for the ski resort, this is for the hotel, and here are the tickets for the grand ballroom. I reckon you need this here, blue-colored pass for the entrance to the cocktail lounges."

Ronzo looked down into the bag and pulled out a cardboard cutout of a key. "Oh yes, the parking pass, put this in the window of the Trans Whizzer."

The cardboard was about a foot long and six inches wide, shaped like a key, and it was printed gold. As Harry took it, I saw the distinct logo of the famous Black Bear Club on it, along with the words, "Black Bear Club Parking Pass. EXCLUSIVE GOLD KEY MEMBER."

"The Black Bear Club. We are going to the Black Bear Club?" When I asked, Ronzo turned and looked at me with a big, wide smile, but he did not answer. He then picked up the black box and opened it up. It was similar to a jewelry box, but a little larger, and looked as if it could hold a necklace.

"Finally, you will need this! Just hold it up wherever you go and you will have the world as your oyster!"

We peered down into the box and inside we saw a little golden key about six inches long. Molded on the end of the key was the shape of the famous Black Bear from the club logo. It was highly polished, bright, and I had to admit, very impressive! It could have been a piece of fine jewelry.

"You boys are not just taking your gals to the Black Bear Club, but you are taking them with a gold key. Now, this will cover the costs on everything for you and your gals, food, drinks, hotel rooms, shows, and even tips. Remember the gold key member does not tip! Be careful though, there are a few things that it will not cover, and this joint is expensive."

Now, even poor bums like us from the city of Paterson knew of the club. It was a legendary place in our neighborhood. We never dreamed of ever going to the Black Bear Club! The resort, country club, and hotel were located in the far northern tip of New Jersey, right next door to a ski area called Great Ravine. The club was about an hour and a half north of Paterson in Sussex County, New Jersey. We as young, testosterone prone men, mostly knew it for being famous for the very pretty, scantily clad, young ladies dubbed, "The Black Bear Ladies." They worked the floor as eye candy, wait staff, and other assorted positions. Young, as well as old men from everywhere, would dream of attending a function there, just to check out the famous ladies.

I wondered where Ronzo had managed to obtain an exclusive key and membership. The Black Bear Club was for super high rollers. It was out of our league that is for sure, but I had a feeling that possession of this gold key made us kings, or at least the equivalent thereof.

Ronnie worked as a maintenance electrician in a large department store in downtown Paterson. He made a good wage, but I did not think it would be anything near to what you would need to be a member of the Black Bear Club, nonetheless a gold key holder. I would think that the dues and fees alone would be all of Ronzo's entire annual salary.

"I reckon we have kept Paul in the dark long enough, Harry. Let me tell the story of what this is all about."

"Thanks Ronnie, I am not following this too much, other than we are going to the Black Bear Club."

Ronnie was beside himself with excitement. You could tell he wanted to clue me into the details of why he was in possession of the coveted gold key. I knew by his actions and expression that even for the Redmond family this was going to be an unusually strange and outlandish story. He pulled a chair out from the table and motioned for us all to do the same. The big guy settled down in the chair and he leaned in close to us with his hands on the table.

"A week or so ago, I was talking with one of the big shot owners of the store that I work for downtown, and he decided to tell me about this strange trouble out at his house with this electrical problem. He did not think it was a big deal and said that he just wanted to ask me about it, but he would figure it out on his own. I told him that I did not like the way that was a'soundin', so I better git on out and have a gander at it for him. He has this here, big, mansion out on the border of Shadow Lakes and Wayne; it has about twenty acres in the front yard alone."

Ronzo made a big square in the air as if to demonstrate how large the property was to Harry and me.

"I checked it out and after a little troubleshooting, I found half of his house is going dark and the power is going off. When I took the cover off one of the electrical services, I found half of it was burning up and smoking!"

Ronnie became very excited now, and he turned to me. "Paul, you being in the trade yourself . . . ya know how serious a situation this can be!"

I nodded my head as Ronnie was indeed correct. A smoking electrical panel could mean that a fire is right around the corner.

"I shut it all down, got a hold of him, and showed him. I showed him how it was only a matter of time. Dang man, it could have only been another few minutes, and it could have caught on fire and burned the whole mansion to the ground!" Harry, who already must have heard the story, could not contain his excitement even while hearing the story again it had him worked up.

Harry clapped his hands together, pushed back his hair from his forehead and piped in, "That is incredible, Ronzo, you saved the day for him!"

I had always heard that Ronnie was a top-notch electrician, and his keen sense of the original description had led him in the right direction. By all accounts, it seemed as if he had arrived just in time to intercept a potential tragedy.

"Anyway, I replaced the electrical service for him and had it all fixed in a few hours. I reckon, he was a lucky man to have run into me at the store and told me what was going on. The next day at the store, he comes up to me and hands me an envelope, with a check in it for two thousand dollars!" Ronzo looked like he was going to fall out of his chair, because he still was so excited about the situation. Harry was shaking his head back and forth. Clearly, the chain of events amazed Harry.

"I reckon I have never heard of such a thing. What a great guy, eh Paul?" Harry was in awe.

I was shaking my head in agreement and said, "It is unbelievable guys, it really is." I reached over and patted Ronzo on the shoulder.

"Get this, youse guys. The big chief then says to me, I have another envelope here for you. I know you and your family are big into entertainment and shows."

I had to laugh a little to myself as I wondered in a tongue-in-cheek manner how the chap determined that they were into shows and entertainment.

Ronzo continued with his story, "He tells me that he is a charter member, and one of the big shot directors at this club up in northern New Jersey, and they have a lot of country and western headliners all the time. He says, Ronnie, I signed you up with the maximum membership, a gold key membership for three years! At first, I did not want to take it. I told him the money was more than generous. He told me, nonsense, and that he could never repay me for what I had done for him. He shook my hand and thanked me again as he said that I not only saved his house, but I also might have saved some of his family's lives."

Ronzo finished his story, leaned back in his chair, and exhaled. He was clearly still amazed at his good fortune, as well as his ability to perhaps save not only the mansion, but the big boss was indeed correct; Ronzo could have also saved the lives of a lot of people.

It was an amazing story.

"You are a hero Ronzo, you should be very proud of yourself. I know that I am proud, just to know you!" I said as I stood up and gave him another pat on his shoulder. Ronzo also stood up now, reached out, and shook my hand. He was beaming a huge, wide smile.

"Why thank ya' there, Paulie, as an electrician yourself, y'all know that sometimes you just git a feeling when something is a goin' wrong! As a gold key member, I can designate my family members and friends to use my key and they obtain all the same rights and privileges that I have. Linda and I have plans for this weekend. When Harry told me that, for a change, you are off from work and hockey, I thought Harry and you could bring your dates and have a great time. I know y'all never, ever going to see a joint like this in all of your lives, guys. Linny and I have been going every chance we git, since we were signed up. This place will knock your socks off. Those gals of yours are gonna love it."

He sighed and looked at us. "This will be a weekend, y'all and your pretty little gals will never forget, I just know it will be."

Harry stood up from his chair and walked over to where we were both standing. I was grateful to Ronnie for the kind gesture and his generosity.

I told him, "Thank you, Ronzo. This is really nice of you. I do not know how to thank you enough."

Ronnie walked over to gather up all the papers and handed them to Harry. He then tugged at his pants and adjusted his big western belt buckle. "Ah, no need to thank me, boys. As I told you, a while ago, I was young once like you guys, but I grew up, way too quick over in Vietnam. The war stole my youth from me, so I want youse guys to experience some of what I missed."

Ronzo's facial expression suddenly changed from his previous wide smile to a little tinge of sadness. His mouth twitched a little, his hands were shaking, and he sighed, then he wiped his mouth. I noticed a little mist appear in his eyes. He was undoubtedly recalling some very tough times that Harry and I could only relate to, but we could never fully understand.

"You know, I was just about your age when I saw my best buddy, get shot and die in my arms. They shot him right through the chest, with a high caliber bullet . . . musta been from a sniper as we lay in some God forsaken, rice field, for who knows what reason. I crawled over to him and held him until he died there in my arms. Right there in my arms, and he was the same age as Harry and you are right now. God bless you, Jim McNeer, God bless you."

Ronzo stopped speaking. He then put his head down and he spoke softly, "I know what we missed, so if I can create a memory for you two guys, then by God, I am going to do it. Never waste a minute of it you two, please never waste a minute of it." He put his head back up and smiled at us both with a tear rolling down his cheek.

I was very proud to call Ronnie Boatmann my friend and to proclaim him a hero, because in my eyes he was both. That horrible war had stolen an awful lot away from way too many people.

Ronzo hid his eyes from Harry and me for a few seconds, then cleared his throat and continued, "I reckon that I can live some of what I missed through you two. Harry has shared some adventures with me and it sounds to me like you boys are doing pretty dang good at it."

The big man smiled once more.

"Besides, the kids and the old man are out for the weekend. If I get rid of ole ten-gallon here, I got Linny and the house to mahself. I am not that old! I may be big and slow—but I can still catch her!"

Ronzo was an awesome man.

We all laughed and gathered in so Harry and I could thank him again and shake his hand. It was very apparent that Ronzo appreciated our friendship and companionship as much as we did him.

A good part of my life as a youngster, my teenage years, and beyond, I spent around this man, and I will cherish those memories and the times we spent together forever. He was a special guy. The big man just stood there, beaming at us now.

"Now you boys go pick up, them, there, young ladies and have the time of your lives."

I nodded my head. "We will Ronzo, you take care, and just in case we forget to say it enough, thanks for what you did for all of us over there in Vietnam."

"I was no hero, Paul. I just did what I had to do!"

I thought to myself, yes you were. Thank God for you and all the others who answered the call.

Ronzo smiled and waved as we double-checked that we had all the papers and the gold key. I grabbed all of Harry's gear and out the door, we went.

As we were heading down the front steps, one of the second-floor windows opened up in Harry's house and Linda stuck her head out, "Hey Paulie, do not forget to pull that hair tie out, you know Binky hates that thing!"

I stopped and waved, grabbed the tie, pulled it out, and chucked it out in the road.

Linda waved back and yelled down, "Be safe out there, boys!"

We grabbed my gear from my jeep, and we were off in the Trans Whizzer. Harry was just about as fired up as I have ever seen him.

"Can you imagine this, Paul? We are going to be high rollers for the weekend! We are kings, and the girls will be queens."

I couldn't agree more. It sounded like a place that Harry and I could only have ever imagined, and now we were actually going to visit.

"I bet the girls are excited."

"Oh yeah, this is it for us. It may be the greatest

weekend ever, Paul."

I decided to put Harry and his famous theory and proclamation to a test. "I wonder why when you came upon this whole gold key weekend, that of all the chicks that you have at your fingertips, you always revert back to Rose. Now, before you try to use it as an excuse, you cannot tell me it is because of Binky and me. That is long over. Binky and I do our own thing when I can, so it is no longer that Binky and Rose have to go out together. Could it be that this gal has finally stolen your heart and you just will not admit it?"

It was a funny thing when Harry was serious, and when he wanted to talk one-on-one with me. He lost the western drawl and his alter ego, and reverted to being an ordinary New Jersey guy. He stared straight ahead and kept both hands on the steering wheel. He was thinking long and hard before answering my question.

I wondered if I had actually struck a nerve or not.

He finally answered me, "Paul, you know me better than anyone, and I have to admit that I do like Rose . . . she is the best. She is really pretty, no, I take that back, she is beautiful. She is fun, smart, and she puts up with my antics. I always go back to her, because she is the only girl since Joyce that just goes with it. She does not have big hang-ups or requirements."

Harry cleared his throat. I guess speaking in his native accent was a strain or he was just nervous.

"But as much as I like her and she likes me, I can honestly say that I do not feel it will be long term. I could be wrong and I do not know how to describe it, but I just have to find someone who . . . who, I do not know what to say to describe it, Paul."

I interrupted him and added, "She does not consume your soul yet, Harry. You need to find someone that you love unconditionally."

Harry stole a quick look at me and took his eyes off the

road for a second.

"I love that, Paul. You always know where to pull the right words from! You are right. Right now, Rose does not consume my entire soul. When I find the right woman, she will consume my entire soul, and I will not think about playing the right music, fancy sports cars, combing my hair the right way, acting like someone that I am really not, being the big shot, and all the other things I do. I will only think about her and she will think about only me. We will become as if we are like one person forever."

Harry never ceased to amaze me. People who did not know him as I did, would see a big and somewhat shallow, egotistical character, but nothing could be farther from the actual truth. He just put up these defense shields in front of him while he searched. He searched for the right woman, in the right situation, who when he found her, he would no longer have any shields up at all.

"Do you know, something, Harry? You just described true love."

"I did?"

"Sure, you did. Think about a mother and her baby. The baby consumes her entire soul. She loves the child like nothing else in her life, because to a mother, a baby comes from within her, and it is part of her body and soul. When you find the right woman, Harry, and you will my friend, despite what you say all the time, she will become a part of you, and you, a part of her, and she will consume your entire soul."

Harry whistled a soft whistle under his breath.

"Paul, you are the smartest person I have ever met, and if I do not say it enough, then let me say it. Thank you for being my best buddy all these years. No one has put up with more of my antics than you have. Wherever we end up, I know we'll be together forever. For Harry and Paul, the night always comes, and that is when we are out there, running around, doing the things that we always do, and taking on the world together. Let's go get, those girls and have the time of our lives!"

Harry put his big hat back on, returned to his alter ego, down-shifted, and off we were into the night and onto our next adventure.

It was a cold and clear, starry, late November evening. The cold air had only become a little more intense as the night went on. We stopped and picked up Rose first, Harry helped her load her luggage into the trunk, and off we went to pick up Binky. To say Rose was a little excited would be a very weak description. She was about as fired up as Harry was about the weekend we had planned.

I had never pulled into Binky's driveway, when she was not running out the front door to meet me. In fact, I had never gone into her house or even met any of her family.

This time was different, as she did not meet us or even open the door.

We waited in the car, and when we did not see her, I opened the car door and said, "Wait here you, guys. I will go see where she is."

I walked up the long walkway to her huge house, a soft glow of the house lights, and some walkway lights guided me along.

The front door was ornate and impressive, with brass hardware and a large door knocker that had "Hobnobber" stamped upon it. I did not see a doorbell, so I picked up the knocker and gave it three short taps. I wondered if that strange man with the gangster voice was around somewhere. I never did find out who he was, nor did I have the courage to ask Binky who he was.

The door opened right away, and a thin-faced, bald headed man opened the door so fast that I was a bit startled.

He bellowed out to me, "You must be, Paul! Well, come on in!"

The man swung the door wide open, and I stepped into

the foyer of a grand entrance to the home with a long, winding, center staircase in front of me.

The home was beautiful.

It was a mansion, inside and out.

"I am, Senator William T. Hobnobber. I am Binky's father."

Oh wow, I knew he was a big shot, but I did not know he was a senator!

He extended his hand out and I shook it.

"Nice to meet you, sir. I am Paul John Henson."

"Oh boy, strong handshake there, son! I can tell you are an athlete. Wow! I think you broke my hand!"

"I am very sorry, sir. I didn't mean it."

"Oh, no trouble. It will heal. Binky is upstairs. She is running a little late. Come on in and sit down. Binky has told me a great deal about you. Indeed, it seems as if you are the primary focus of her latest research efforts."

Mr. Hobnobber led me to a large living room with very expensive-looking paintings, furniture, and furnishings.

"Sit down, Paul," he said as we sat in two pleated black leather guest chairs close to the entrance doorway a few feet apart.

"She drives me bananas with all that information and research. Sometimes, I just want to stick a big sock in her mouth to shut her up! Does she drive you crazy also?"

"Well, sir . . . I do not know. It actually seems to be part of her charm."

Mr. Hobnobber looked at me and he said, "All those hockey pucks in the head must have scrambled your brains son, because she drives me crazy with all that information and data."

I did not know what to say, so I just sat there and took the insult like a man.

"Do you really know what the lyrics to that obscure, 'Close to the Crevice' record might be all about? Binky tells me you like that weird group, No Way and that you can tell her what it is all about."

"Well, sir, I have tried, but I am not really sure that I have it all correct. Binky never mentioned that you listen to the music of No Way."

"I try not to, because I cannot figure it out. But Binky told me all about you, and that you are quite the hockey goaltender, so I looked you up and did a little research on your sporting background."

Mr. Hobnobber seemed to be reciting all of this from a book, but apparently, it all was committed to his memory.

"You are six feet five inches, about one hundred eighty-five pounds, a championship sprinter in the one-hundred-yard dash and two twenty-yard run and set the records for pull-ups at Passaic County Vo-Tech with thirty-two. 1978 MVP of the Metropolitan Hockey League, Rookie of the Year, playoff MVP, a two point, one zero, goals against average, four shutouts, including one in the playoffs when you shut down that rat fink O'Malley. This is all quite impressive."

I now knew where Binky obtained the research bug.

"I played some hockey in my day also, and I always dreamed of taking a shot on a real goalie and scoring a goal, it is a long time wish of mine."

"Well, that is great sir, I am very happy to hear that you like hockey."

"Like it! I love it, son, and I want to shoot on a real goalie. Do you think you can let me shoot a puck on you, son?"

After he asked, he leaned in with that same wide-eyed stare that Binky performs when she wants an answer, but he was even more intense. He zoomed right in on my face.

It seemed to me that Mr. Hobnobber was a nutcase, so that explained why he was a successful politician.

"Sure, I guess you could take a shot or two on me. I could arrange for you to come down to a game."

Mr. Hobnobber stood straight up and quickly motioned

for me to get up from the chair.

"Actually, I have my sticks and a puck right out here on the back deck. We could shoot around right now."

"Now, now, Father. Paul has come to pick me up for a nice weekend retreat. He has not come here to shoot hockey pucks around with you."

I turned around, and it was Binky standing in the living room.

Binky had saved me!

"Hello Binky, you look great."

I really wanted to grab her in my arms, kiss her, and make a beeline for the front door to get away from her lunatic father. But for now, a simple greeting was all I could come up within my mind. So much for an in-depth conversation with her father to find out why they actually named their daughter Binky. But I think I now had some more clues. I started to hope and pray that her mother did not come in to meet me. For all that I knew, she may be wearing a full Long Island Roosters uniform somewhere in the house while practicing her slap shot.

Mr. Hobnobber frowned, and he looked disappointed, but he cheered up and said, "I understand, dear Binky. You two have plans, maybe some other time. I have to go and ice down my hand that Paul broke, anyway. So, have a great weekend and we will see you soon."

I reached out my hand to shake his, but he held his hand behind his back and laughed.

"Oh, I am very sorry, Mr. Hobnobber. It was very nice to meet and chat with you, sir. Thank you."

"It was my pleasure, Paul, and be sure you do not tie back your hair. Binky hates that hair tie thingy. Did you know that?"

"I do know that, sir. Quite a few folks have mentioned it to me recently."

Binky and I headed over to the door and she showed me her suitcase.

"Here is my luggage, Paul. Please, you need to bring it to the car. It is a little big."

I stared at an enormous black suitcase in front of me that looked like Binky was going away for at least seven years. I picked it up, and it took all my strength to muscle it out of the door and down the front walkway. As I struggled with the luggage, I heard Binky speaking with Mr. Hobnobber. She then kissed her father goodbye, and the door slammed behind us.

I finally made it to the car and Harry popped out when he saw me heaving the giant case down the walk. "What is that thing, a safe? What the heck took you so long? I reckon I was about to send in a rescue squad. Did you meet her folks?"

"Only her father, and don't ask. Give me a hand with this thing, will you? It weighs twenty tons."

I saw Harry look up over the suitcase to make sure Binky was still far away and not within earshot.

"I reckon her old man is a whacko, huh?"

I just nodded my head while working as hard as I could to drag the luggage closer to the trunk of the car. Harry unlocked the trunk, and it took both of us on each end of the luggage to get it in the car.

"My goodness, what on earth is in this thing . . . bricks?" The end of the Trans Whizzer sagged down about four inches when the luggage landed in the trunk.

Harry closed the trunk, and we met Binky while we were walking down the walkway.

"Did you get it in the trunk? It is a little heavy. I noticed that it was a little heavy when I carried it down from my bedroom."

Harry and I just looked at each other. I opened the door for Binky, and she floated into the back seat. Harry and I climbed in. He started the car, when we noticed the garage door go up on the Hobnobber's house, and a big Galaxy 3000 started to back out.

"Oh, that is just my father—he is going to the emergency room to have his hand x-rayed, because Paul broke it."

Rose turned around from the front seat in horror and asked, "You broke Binky's dad's hand?"

I shrugged my shoulders and did not answer her question. It was not worth going into. We had not even gone more than twenty miles from our house and this adventure had already exceeded the total strange, weird, and bizarre quota for all of our other adventures put together. The recovery time from the meeting with Mr. Hobnobber was going to be a little more than I initially thought, but I slowly became more involved in the conversation. The girls were certainly excited, and they were making all kinds of plans for shows, dancing, dinner, and activities.

Harry gave us all a synopsis of what the resort was like and he described some major points, and it sounded like something that we never dreamed of being able to visit in a million years. We rolled up Route 23 and headed north into Sussex County.

"Now remember, Ronnie has arranged for us to have a personal assistant to guide us and help us with all the events and details. It is part of being a gold key member. I am a'thinking his name is Harold or something like that."

I thought; what is going on here tonight? Did everyone take an amnesia pill?

"No, Harry, the guy's name is Howard, Howard Pailet," I said from the back seat.

"You know, I reckon you are right there, buddy, Ronzo did say Howard."

Binky was sitting right next to me holding my left hand, and I turned to her and whispered, "By the way, have you ever mentioned to many people that you do not like it when I tie my hair all back."

She looked at me a little strangely and said, "Why no, like whom?"

"Ronzo, my old man, Linda, and an awful lot of others." Binky was shaking her head back and forth to indicate no.

"I would not recommend speaking to others about such personal wishes within special relationships such as ours. My research last week, indicated to me that it could lead to hard feelings and some elements of discourse."

Of course, Binky had already researched the subject.

"I thought so, thanks."

I knew who the broadcaster was. Another strange, but true, mystery of life with Harry was that he knew and spoke with everyone and I do mean everyone! Harry spoke of any topic that he could come up with, as his mouth had no filter on it at all.

I swear I could go on a trip to Moscow and someone would come up to me and say, "I heard you are Harry's best buddy. How is Harry doing?"

Harry turned down the music, held his hand up, and called out, "Time out gang, I have an announcement to make! Rose, darlin,' this is mostly for you, but Binky will also be very proud of me. Paul is too nice a guy to say anything to me anyway, so he does not count."

Rose looked at Harry and asked, "Oh no! You really did not buy that horse you were looking at last week, did you?"

Harry shook his head. "No, no, come to think of it, this is more like an oath rather than an announcement. You gals do realize that here at the Black Bear Club, we will run into and encounter quite a large amount of very pretty gals dressed in very little clothing. I reckon they all work the tables and are part of the culture here. They are called the famous Black Bear Ladies."

Harry stole a glance at Rose to see if she had any initial reaction, but Rose was just staring at him very intently.

"Well, the last time we all went out and were in a similar environment with the opportunity to view scantily clad ladies like this, was at Seashore Heights. I did not behave so well on that day and I reckon I did get a little offensive. This time around, I make a pledge and promise to conduct myself like a gentleman, and be under control and be respectful, considerate, and polite to all the young ladies and to not gawk at or ogle them."

Rose had folded her arms across her chest when Harry had reached the part where he mentioned that, "He did not behave so well."

She shouted back adamantly, "I am not buying that for a second. I will believe it when I see it. You around those Black Bear Ladies!"

Binky leaned in and said, "I agree with Rose, of course."

"What! Don't I even get a chance at a fair shake? C'mon, Paul jump in here buddy and support me."

I started to say something, but both Binky and Rose yelled at the same exact time, "Paul is too nice a guy, he does not count!"

I was indeed doomed.

The stereotypical Nimrod trapped within the endless paradigm of Harry's Theory. Off we rode into the night, the big engine of the Trans Whizzer humming along and the four of us dreaming of the weekend.

The lights of the ski area grew closer on the horizon, twinkling at us through the tree lines in the clear night sky. We were right down the road now from the club and within a short amount of time; we would test Harry and his solemn oath.

8

Binky Defends Her Turf!

We pulled into the front of the club and followed the signs for the hotel check in. It was huge, fabulously decorated, and lit up like a beacon in the night, in the middle of nowhere, with the ski slopes as a backdrop. It was like something out of a picture postcard. I had never seen such a fantastic facility in all of my life.

Harry had taken the big cardboard key cutout-parking pass and placed it in the windshield of the Trans Whizzer. He pulled the car under an enormous, brightly lit canopy at the front of the hotel. The canopy had frames of gold, with fantastic, gold crystal light fixtures hanging on chains down from the roof of the canopy. In front of the canopy, facing the road, was a huge statute of the famous Black Bear that you see on their logo. It was about twenty-five feet tall and lit with a bright spot lamp. There were at least twenty men dressed in black suits outside, standing at attention.

Harry stopped in front of the hotel and shut off the engine. A tall man in a perfectly fitted black suit pointed at the key in the windshield and he yelled out, "Gold!"

About ten men ran up to the car and opened all the doors for us. Ten more men ran out the front of the hotel door and surrounded the car in a semicircle.

The tall man opened the driver's door and said, "Good evening sir, and welcome to the Black Bear Club." He then stood at attention next to the open door.

Harry grabbed his big hat, swung his legs out the

driver's door, stepped out, and stood up.

"Well, howdy there, my good man, Gastone. How y'all doing tonight? Y'all are on the ball and provide some good service, I see."

There were now two men cleaning the car, one on the front windshield, and the other on the rear glass. The club's workers seemed to descend upon us from every direction. A man ran up to Binky and me and stood right next to us, as well as one next to Rose. The man was dusting off my shirt with a little dust brush and checking my shoes.

Harry clearly loved the attention. "Come on over here, Rose. This here, is my little lady, and that, there, hairy guy is my best buddy and his gal. Y'all got to get the gear out of the trunk here, so let me unlock it for ya. You boys are going to need all of this, here manpower, to carry one of those pieces of luggage. I reckon it weighs about twenty-two tons. I had all I could do to make it up the highway and I have a 475-cubic inch Dragon engine in this puppy."

Harry slapped the tall man in the black suit on the back.

"Say, loosen up there, Gastone. Y'all seem a bit stuffy."

The tall man never acknowledged Harry's observation, but he remained stoic and stiff. He stood straight up after Harry's comment and spoke loudly, "We will park your fabulous automobile in our exclusive garage reserved for gold key members!"

Harry looked at him out of the corner of his eye while he was checking the front windshield on the Trans Whizzer. "Wow, y'all a loud one there. Did you swaller a microphone or something? Hey, look here, Gastone, one of your boys missed a spot here."

Harry was pointing to the glass and the tall man snapped his fingers for the glass cleaning crew to return. The glass cleaning crew dove back into the task while Harry nodded his head in approval. A man was following Harry and dusting off his shirt, vest, boots, and hat, while he opened the trunk. Teams of other men were now vacuuming out the car interior.

The Black Bear Club meets Harry M. Redmond Jr.

This is going to be good.

Binky was thrilled, "My, Paul! This is some place. I knew it was nice, but I had no idea, it was this nice!"

She put her arm through mine and hugged me close. Harry opened the trunk and a group of men began to take our luggage out as the four of us walked in the lobby of the hotel, followed by an entourage of escorts checking our every move. The inside lobby was unbelievable. It had a stone fireplace that went from the lobby floor all the way up through the hotel to the roof, with openings on each floor. Each level had a blazing fire inside of it on this cold night. It had cascading waterfalls, mirrors, plush pile carpets, illuminated fountains spewing up water, hanging chandeliers; black bear statues spitting water out of their mouths, ornate furnishings and furniture, on and on it went. Binky, Rose, Harry, and I just stood there admiring it in wonder. Even Binky, whose own house was no little shack in the woods, was in awe as she looked around and she squeezed my hand tightly.

I spotted a man with a bulky, two-wheel hand truck run out the front door and it looked as if he was heading to the Trans Whizzer, but he went behind the wall and I could not see him any longer.

We walked up to the front desk, where a staff of about fifteen men and ladies dressed in black service suits jumped to attention. The tall man in the black suit from the greeting crew had followed us to the desk. He leaned over the front counter to the staff and simply said, "Gold" to them. The entire front desk staff all sprang to attention and gathered around the front counter.

A middle-aged woman behind the front counter who was dressed perfectly and did not have even a single hair out of place smiled and said, "Welcome to you and your associates. Welcome to the Black Bear Club."

Harry strode up to the counter, like the sheriff riding into town on his big white horse. He clicked and clacked his expensive boots on the fine marble floors. The three of us followed and stood next to Harry at the counter.

"Howdy, ma'am . . . evening to you too. I think this is what y'all have been panting over us for and y'all need to see."

Harry took out the gold key and placed it on the front desk. Harry took out the papers that Ronzo had explained to Harry were for the hotel and handed them to her. The key had a number on it and the woman studied it, then she looked at a list.

"Oh yes, here it is. Once more, welcome, Mr. Yall Redmond Boatmann."

Rose said, "Who?"

"Yes, Yall Redmond Boatmann. Is that you sir, or perhaps, it, is you?"

She first looked at Harry and then at me.

"There must be some typographical error. The names are, Redmond and Boatmann," Rose said as the woman handed her the paper. It then hit me that Ronzo and his phony western drawl, with a New Jersey twist, must have said, "Y'all" before the names when he called it in. The poor person speaking with Ronnie then added a Y-a-l-l to the front of our names.

Once more, I solve problems, so I stepped in here, "No, please just take the Y-a-l-l out and it will be correct, this is Mr. Redmond here."

I pointed out Harry to the woman.

"Thank you, sir. He must be from Texas. Is he from Texas?"

"No, actually, the north side of Paterson."

She looked at me a little strangely, wrote something down on the papers, excused herself, then stepped away, and started to stamp the papers.

"Oh, twenty-seven, I love the way you step in and

handle problems when they come up, it is very efficient, Paul," Binky said, as I watched a team of about five men using the hand truck, struggling to wheel Binky's luggage over to us. Harry looked at me and pointed at them, as he was watching them as well.

The woman walked over to us and explained, "I see here that Mr. Howard Pailet has been assigned to the men for this visit. Mr. Pailet will be here within five minutes. We have just announced your arrival to him. The women, Ms. Hobnobber and Ms. Rose, are in room 505 and the two gentlemen, Yall Redmond Boatmann, will be in room 510. Here is your gold key back, a box of Black Bear cigars for the men, a box of our famous Black Bear chocolates for the ladies, your papers, and the room keys."

So much for solving problems, I thought.

"Mr. Pailet will provide for your every need and requirement during your stay, and he will explain your schedule and itinerary. Thank you so much for being an exclusive gold key member and visiting with us this weekend." The woman turned and pointed over the counter. "Yes, here is, Mr. Howard Pailet, arriving right now."

Binky leaned in and whispered to me, "Please note that kissing me is out of the question if you smoke one of those wretched smelling cigars."

I nodded my head up and down very quickly while Harry opened the box up, took a cigar out of the wrapper, and stuck it in his mouth.

"Good evening, ladies and gentlemen. Welcome to the exclusive, world famous, Black Bear Club and Resort. I am, Mr. Howard Pailet."

We turned around to see a shorter gentleman of about sixty years of age, standing up straight as an arrow. He, too, wore a black, perfectly fitted suit, with a white shirt and a black tie. He had thinning black hair with more than a touch of grey in it, thick, black-framed glasses, and a long, narrow, thin face. He had dark eyes that were almost black, and his face showed no emotion. Only a flat expression defined his face. After he spoke to us, he placed his arms and hands at his side and stood at attention like a soldier in formation.

Harry moved in close to Howard and nearly blew him over as he greeted him. "Howdy there, Howie! We are not your usual stuffy, pompous type guests, so I reckon I had better warn you of that ahead of time. From here on in, we will be using your first name only there, Howie."

Harry tapped Howard gently on the shoulder. "This is some nice dump that youse boys run around here. I am Harry M. Redmond Jr., here, live, and in the flesh. This, here, is my lovely, smart, and gorgeous gal, Rose. That, there, long-haired, tall guy is Paul John Henson, the best hockey goaltender in all the tristate area, and the gorgeous chick with the great figure, big chest, and long legs next to him is his gal, Binky."

Harry leaned in close to Howard and whispered, "Watch out for Binky, she will recite all the statistics for this joint from the year it was built, to y'alls total yearly revenue if ya let her."

Harry stood up and rolled the big cigar over and over in his mouth.

"Do y'all have a match there, Howie?"

Howard instantly produced a lighter and lit the cigar for Harry. Binky started to wave her hands in the air before Harry even took a drag.

Howard then repeated the introductions as he greeted each of us and shook our hands individually. "It is indeed my great pleasure to meet everyone. Hello, and good evening, Mr. Redmond Junior."

Howard studied Harry and asked, "Should I leave the junior off your name for the weekend?"

"Sure, Howie. Sounds good. It's like I am even a bigger deal than I already am."

"Thank you, sir. Consider it done except for formal introductions. Good evening, Mr. Henson, number twenty-seven, I do believe. I hate to digress here, but thank you for shutting out the Colonials in the playoffs last year and stopping that wretched human being, O'Malley. Ms. Rose. You look positively lovely this evening, and Ms. Hobnobber, you are stunning. You are indeed accurate, Ms. Hobnobber. The main resort facility was built in 1967, with the lobby renovation being two years ago, last fall, and therefore, your research is quite correct."

Binky fluffed her hair, smiled, and said, "Thank you, Howard, I was just about to ask that, but you have confirmed it for me ahead of time."

Howard glanced down at his paperwork and then back to us. "There was a typographical error on your paperwork, with an errant y-a-l-l added to your names, which I have removed after some confirmation research as to the origin of the mistake."

Wow, this guy knows everything and is Binky's research equal!

"I will be here at your beck and call to provide for your every need during your stay. I have your itinerary here, your favorite drinks, your favorite foods, and how they are to be prepared, as well as all the information about the four of you that I require for expertly performing my service duties. I am your total information and guiding resource for the weekend. I do need to measure the two gentlemen for their tuxedos for the grand ballroom dinner and dancing for tomorrow night, but we can do that right before dinner this evening, which is at eight o'clock sharp."

I was in awe of Howard and his incredible efficiency.

"I am sure you and your ladies would like to go up to your rooms, wash up, and prepare for dinner."

Howard turned and faced the ladies with his hands folded in front of his body. He showed almost no emotion or any slight element of disorganization, or the slightest misstep in his delivery.

He was spot on all the time!

"Ladies, in your room, you will find a fresh Martini, shaken not stirred, for Ms. Hobnobber, and for Ms. Rose, a chilled Purple Pirate beer, not too cold, it will be around forty-two degrees, as she enjoys it. There is also very fine, vintage champagne on ice."

Howard then turned towards Harry and me. "For the men, a Wall Crawler for Mr. Redmond, and a very cold Big Boulder beer for Mr. Henson, as well as some champagne. Please call me on extension twenty-seven for refills or anything else that you require. I strategically selected extension number twenty-seven, so that it matched Mr. Henson's uniform number, and would be easy to remember even under difficult situations, or if you were intoxicated."

Hmmm, it was nice to be famous for something even if it was in such a roundabout way. My uniform number would be a key, just in case we were bombed or in trouble.

Howard still was standing straight up and he continued with his immaculate delivery. "Please gentlemen, suits, jackets, and ties for dinner, and dresses for the ladies. I would like to please meet back here at seven, forty-five sharp. That will allow me some time to measure the men for the tuxedos. Please, let us set our watches together, as not to cause any delay or mismatch of time, which could interrupt this evening's dinner."

Howard glanced down at his watch and then looked at Harry and then directly at me. Harry did not wear a watch, so I made sure I was looking down at mine and I nodded my head and announced, "I have six twenty-five, Howard." He looked down at his watch and nodded in approval. Howard was like a finely tuned machine.

"We will bring your luggage up to your rooms immediately, however, I do apologize, as there will be a short, delay in the arrival of Ms. Hobnobber's luggage, as the wheeled device that we were using to transport it has broken and a larger replacement is on the way. As a reminder to Mr. Henson, please do not tie your hair up, as Ms. Hobnobber does prefer it to be long and loose."

And . . . I was just beginning to like this guy.

Harry took a long puff on the cigar and blew a bomb of smoke out that enveloped Mr. Pailet. He did not even blink or flinch.

"Sorry there, Howie," Harry said while he waved at the smoke floating all around Howard's head. "I reckon that you sure have things together there, Howie. Y'all should have used one of them, their Substantial Industries hand trucks. Those cheapo, Chungwoo brands ain't gonna cut the old mustard on Binky's luggage. You are on the stick-a-roo-ski, Howie! That, there, introduction was amazing. I think you covered everything except my shoe size!"

"That would be a size fourteen, men's extra wide, Mr. Redmond," Howard answered instantly.

Howard turned towards the lobby elevators and pointed.

"Please, this way to the elevators."

The four of us followed Howard, and the elevator operator guided the ladies' hands as they stepped into the car. No one had to say a word as Howard took us to the fifth floor and instructed us to turn left towards our rooms. Howard brought us directly to our doors and once more, reminded us to call him if we needed anything and that he would meet us in the lobby. Howard bowed slightly to us, and then smiled a stoic, almost rehearsed smile. We all thanked him. Off he went to the elevators, and he was gone.

Rose was very animated, and she broke into an excited speech. "This is an absolutely incredible place. Thank you so much for this weekend. It already has given me a lifetime of memories. It is fantastic!"

Rose was more excited than I had ever seen her as she

reached up and kissed Harry. Binky and I were standing in the hallway and both of us were nodding our heads in agreement.

I was still a little awe struck at the entire situation and turned to Harry and spoke, "Yes, thank you, Harry. Binky and I are also thrilled. I agree this is something else. It is like nothing I have ever seen."

Binky was still nodding her head in her typical rapid head nod, but she did manage to say, "Howard is simply amazing." She took my hand and you could see she was feeling the excitement building. "I feel like a queen," she proclaimed with a starry-eyed look in her eyes towards me.

Without even thinking, and giving it a second thought, I just turned, looked right at her, and said very adamantly, "You are a queen, Binky."

I then realized what I said, and I froze right there in place. What a nice guy, dumb thing to say! It was right in line with Harry's theory. I was very embarrassed. It just came out! I must have turned ten shades of red as Harry, Rose, and Binky looked at me. They all seemed shocked because it was so uncharacteristic of me to speak a comment of that nature aloud like that. Binky smiled widely. She pulled me close and hugged me.

Binky gave me a kiss on the cheek as she pulled me down to her level to reach my cheek. She loved this moment for sure.

"Oh, Paul. That may be the most romantic thing I think I have ever heard you say, thank you."

I did not know what to say, but Harry sensed I was in trouble and jumped in to save me. I felt embarrassed about my outburst and comment.

"Well, I reckon we need to hustle off to get ready and meet Howard in time. We will meet y'all out here at seven forty. See you!"

The ladies agreed, and they waved to us and headed for their room. Harry grabbed me. We headed off to our room and Binky and Rose went to theirs. I could hear Rose and Binky giggling at my dumb, nice guy comment. They knew that Harry had stepped in order to save me from my embarrassment.

Inside our room, it was the same fabulous decor as the rest of the club, with the best of furniture and furnishings. The room had two huge double beds that were fit for kings. The bathroom was practically gold-lined, with gold fixtures, faucets, and ornate furnishings. Just as Howard had promised, the drinks were there, as well as our luggage.

Harry finished his cigar and flopped down in a chair.

"What a dump, this place is awesome. Can you imagine what the dinner is going to be like there, twenty-seven? Not bad for a bunch of bums from Paterson." Harry took a long sip of his Wall Crawler and smiled. I was sipping the beer when Harry wandered over to me.

"You are falling for her, Paul. Y'all got more on your mind other than hockey pucks don't ya? That queen comment was the nice guy coming out again."

Harry was shaking his head almost in sympathy to my nice guy mistake.

"When will you ever learn that you've got to play it cool, be unreachable, be mysterious, and be in control? That compliment just gives you away as a loser my friend."

I nodded my head, as I knew I would hear it later from Harry, the moment that I had let it slip.

"It just came out, Harry. I do not know why—it just came out."

Harry looked at me over the top of his drink glass and pointed to me with his fingers as he took a long sip. "I will tell you why it came out. Because you are falling for her, and you are honest, nice, steady, and reliable. You see Paul, nice, romantic, comments like that are what nice guys always say. Bad guys make lewd, suggestive comments about their gal's body parts, and what we would like to do with them. Nice guys, like twenty-seven, give them titles of worship just like you did!"

Harry was shaking his head.

"Someday, you will thank me for my advice and see that I am right. But for now, we need to shake our doodles to make dinner on time. I reckon we better get washed up and be ready for the meal of a lifetime."

Harry held his glass up and we toasted to the night.

"I reckon the night always comes for us, Paul, and this one we will never forget. I will buzz ole Howie and get us some more drinks."

Just as Harry said that, there was a knock at the door.

I opened it up and there stood Howard, with another server carrying another round of drinks. He handed them to me and I said, "Thank you, Howard."

"Thank you, Mr. Henson. I know from my research that it takes about seven minutes for you both to finish one round of drinks and the ladies, about twelve minutes. I also calculated some time for a lecture on the Old Lady and Mr. Nice Guy Syndrome from Mr. Redmond, since I knew you would not be able to resist a romantic compliment towards the gorgeous and stunning Ms. Hobnobber. I will be delivering the ladies another round of drinks in just a few minutes or so. They are a bit behind their time, giggling at your romantic interlude."

It was nice to know that I was so predictable.

Harry and I took showers, and we both dressed to be ready for dinner in time. I did not own much in the way of a dress wardrobe, but I actually did have a very nice suit that I had sprung for last year when I won the MVP award and other awards from our hockey league. I attended the ceremonial dinner for the league to accept the awards, so I wanted to look decent for that big event. It was custom fitted by a tailor up the street from us in the old neighborhood. For my price range, it was indeed a very high-quality suit. It had cost me a few precious coins that I had saved up, which in my current pay grade had been a major investment and decision. The suit was a solid black, and I had selected a black tie along with a fitted white shirt. The tailor had been extra kind to me, and when I told him what the occasion was for purchasing the suit, he labeled my shirt cuffs with the number twenty-seven.

My parents had given me as a gift for winning the MVP award, a little gold tie tack molded in the number twenty-seven, which I now wore along with the suit. I wore a nice pair of black shoes, polished up like mirrors after a quick call to Howard for some "polishing" assistance. I did not dress up often, but when I did, I did my best not to look like a hippie hockey goaltender. I made sure I combed my hair, trimmed my beard, and my mustache, and, of course, no hair tie!

Harry dressed in his finest suit, which was a black, western-type jacket, cut long in the back, with his finest, studded western shirt, his fantastic black, silver-studded cowboy boots, a wide, gold belt buckle, big, ten-gallon black hat and a bolo tie. He looked beyond awesome. He made Barry McGirk look like a bum!

We polished up nicely for two poor kids from the streets of Paterson. We stepped out in the hall right at seven forty and made our way down to the ladies' hotel room. Harry was about to knock on the door when the door opened and out the two ladies stepped into the hallway. Now, I have seen many nice-looking young women in my time. After all, when you were our age, you never missed a chance to glance at any young woman! However, these two women looked like nothing we have ever seen before. They were both dressed in stunning dresses, their hair was perfect, the shoes, the jewelry, the smiles, they looked better than Hollywood stars! We both stood there like two dopes that had lost the ability to speak.

Even the silken-tongued Harry could not speak.

He was stunned.

"I have never seen two more lovely ladies than you two! You gals are gorgeous!" I finally dove in there for us because Harry remained stunned and speechless.

"Thank you, Paul. Harry, what do you think?" Rose asked as she spun around in front of him, displaying her attire and appearance for him.

Harry took his big, black hat off and said, "I agree with Paul, Miss Rose, and Miss Binky you are both simply gorgeous, and I cannot even describe how I feel right now. Yeeehaaww!" Harry grabbed and hugged Rose, then tilted her over and kissed her with one of his famous grandstanding kisses.

I grabbed Binky's hand, looked her straight in the eyes, and said to her, "You look stunning. You are the most gorgeous woman that I have ever seen."

Binky did look stunning. In fact, she was breathtaking; between her hair, dress, and a simple gold necklace that enhanced her long neck. She was perfect. Forget Harry's Theory; I needed to speak what I was feeling, straight from my nice guy, reliable, and boring heart.

Binky smiled and looked at me, "And you, sir, are oozing with sex appeal and are the most handsome man that I have ever seen. This suit is fabulous. I have never seen you dressed. . .."

I interrupted her, "In more than a No Way tee shirt, dungarees, and sneakers."

Binky laughed, "Or you are buried under mountains of goaltender gear and uniforms that are like a suit of armor and I cannot even tell that it is really you!"

We hugged and then shared a kiss; however, I had not yet progressed to the grandstanding level of Harry's expertise. I preferred to keep it more conservative at this point.

Rose stopped short as we were walking in the hallway and we had begun to walk in the direction of the elevator. She put her brakes on, and then she held her arms out to signal all of us to stop.

"I have to say that you two men look simply fantastic. I cannot believe how you two clean up, and how lucky Binky and I are to be with the two most handsome men in this entire club. Guys, I have to say that I may be feeling some drinks right now, and getting a little emotional, but I need to get this out here and off my chest. I treasure the relationship the four of us have together. No matter what will happen to all of us in the future, and no matter where we all go or end up, I want to say, thank you for tonight, and say that I will always remember it and love all of you forever."

Rose was without question the most emotional of us all and she looked like she was ready to cry tears of joy, so the four of us gathered around her. We all hugged her, as well as each other, and shared a special moment together.

Perhaps it was the liquid courage that Rose had indulged in, but she finally had the spirit to say what I think the rest of us had all realized now for quite a while. There was a special bond among all of us. It was there, and undeniable. We lifted each other's hearts and spirits up together and individually.

It was very special and unique; there was no doubt about that.

The four of us strode off to the elevator where we pushed the button for the lobby and rode onto our next adventure together.

Howard spotted us and hustled right over. He checked us from head to toe, dusted off our suits and shoes and said, "Right on time, perfect, perfect, no hair tie, let me touch this up, very nice, very nice, you two, look fantastic."

After Harry and I had passed inspection, Howard turned towards the women.

"Ladies, please, let me say . . . exquisite, you both look simply stunning. Cigar, Mr. Redmond?"

"No, thank you. Howie, what do you say we get this,

here measuring stuff out of the way? Then we can get to some eatin'. Being one of these, here big shots has rustled me up quite an appetite!"

Off we went for Howard to measure and have us fitted for our tuxedos for the big grand ballroom event, and we were back in no time. Howard then brought us to a huge restaurant, where we sat at a table under a fantastic crystal chandelier. It was a spectacular setting, the four of us seated at a large table in a corner with very few other tables near ours—it was perfect!

I heard Howard whisper to a waiter, "Gold" and he handed us all menus that were mostly in French, Italian, and Spanish.

"I reckon I am going to need y'all to tell me where the hamburgers are on this, here, mumbo, jumbo menu there, Howie!"

Harry was staring at the menu, and he was turning it around and around in his hands, working hard to figure out some words.

A bottle of champagne was uncorked, and we made a toast to the evening. Howard and his wait staff catered to our every need, and Howard missed nothing. He had my Big Boulder beer chilled to the perfect temperature and ready to drink, Harry's Wall Crawler iced to perfection, as well as the ladies' drinks waiting. Howard would not allow even the smallest of details to be missing and Howard was a whirlwind of attention, while he made sure that every other dinner or drink item was ready and waiting for us. He followed Harry to the restroom and carefully checked him for any "malfunctions" before he returned to the table. Harry and his reputation for trouble with zippers had preceded him.

Howard, of course, already knew that fact.

As we studied the menu, I became aware of some young gals walking around serving drinks. They were the famous Black Bear Ladies who walked around for not only serving drinks and food, but for a lack of a better description, and to be quite frank . . . the ladies were there for the gentlemen's viewing pleasures. They dressed in very small outfits that were, of course, black, low cut around the neckline and they wore black, furry, bikini type bottoms with black stockings on their legs.

All the ladies were gorgeous.

The moment of potentially explosive lust had finally arrived for Harry. I breathed deeply and exhaled as we all remembered his pledge. It became a little more serious as one of the girls wiggled up to our table. Howard stood off to the side, watching the situation carefully unfold, and I held my breath as the young Black Bear Lady approached. Binky reached over and grabbed my hand as we all knew that the pressure gauge inside of Harry must have been ready to blow. Rose frowned, then folded her arms across her chest with an air of antagonism and prepared herself in anticipation of Harry's usual reactions.

"Another round for this table. My, oh, my, hmmm, what a good-looking group we have here," the young gal said, as she walked and swung her hips up to the table.

"Why thank ya ma'am. I appreciate the fine service that y'all provide here," Harry said as he kept his eyes locked straight forward as the young lady bent over right smack in front of his face and placed his drink down.

That was all he said!

Now, to be quite accurate in my description, she let it all hang out right then and there next to Harry's face. There were various female body parts bursting and bulging right there in front of Harry!

"Here you go, you big, awesome, handsome, Texas cowboy."

Harry remained locked on straight forward, not moving a muscle or even twitching. Harry then looked at Rose and smiled. No lewd comments, no whoops or hollers, no crazy explosions. It must have taken all of his inner strength and restraint, but he had been true to his word! We were all amazed at the remarkable performance by Harry under such extreme duress.

The Black Bear Lady then wiggled over to Rose, placed her drink, then over to Binky with her Martini (shaken, not stirred) and then she moved over to me.

"Now, I have heard everything about you there, handsome and sexy. I cannot believe my luck to serve you over all the other ladies. I get to swoop in here and see you close for myself!"

The woman said as she came closer to me and was turning up her wiggle and bounce knob over to maximum, "All the Black Bear Ladies spotted you when you came in and let me say with that hair, beard, and body, you just ooze sexy. That hair is incredible. I just want time alone with you to run my hands through it and hold on for dear life. If you get my meaning?"

I was stunned and did not say a word. I knew it was part of the culture and the act here, but this was a little more than I had ever expected.

Binky's eyes were as wide as saucers.

When the Black Bear Lady set my beer down, Binky grabbed her by the arm, "Let me tell you something there, you scantily clad, little flirt, if you, or one of your so-called bear gal friends, so much as come near my man, I will have no qualms about ripping you, from limb from limb. Back off!"

Howard swooped in, ushered the stunned young woman off, and led her to the next table. Howard returned, very flustered and in a bit of a tizzy.

"Please, Ms. Hobnobber. I apologize, but the Black Bear Ladies are part of our culture here. I assure you that she meant no offense. After all, Mr. Henson is indeed attracting quite a few of the young ladies' eyes this evening."

"Yes, Howard, I am aware of that, but the only eyes involving Mr. Henson that count around here are mine."

I looked at Harry and Rose, who were wisely not risking jumping in on this situation at all.

I spoke up here, "Howard, maybe you can just have our drinks brought over by a regular waiter, and in the best interest of all of us, maybe the Black Bear Ladies . . . can kind of go around us?"

I was once more problem solving.

"I reckon that, there is the way to go there, Howie, make it happen. I told you not to rustle up ole Bink-a-roo-ski; she is a lot tougher than she looks. After all, she carried that luggage of hers by herself that took y'all ten men and a fork truck to handle!"

"Certainly. I will be glad to make the requested adjustments, Mr. Redmond." Howard scurried off as he headed in the direction of the lounge and bar area.

I spotted out of the corner of my eye, Binky smile, and then she smoothed her dress out, shifted back to her patented prim and proper mode, and fluffed her hair.

"Now that we have those horrid bear ladies out of the way. Please, let us enjoy our dinner."

Binky reached down in her purse and pulled something out.

"Dear Paul, could you please lean over just a little?"

I was puzzled, but I scooted over close to her and leaned in. Binky grabbed my hair, pulled it all back, and took a little tie that she had in her hand. She then tied my hair off in a tail, as she happily said, "Thank you. I will be sure to let Howard know that I would like you to keep this tie in for right now."

I knew when to say something to Binky and when to keep my mouth shut. This was a time to let her handle it and keep my mouth shut. I sat there and could not help but smile at Harry, not only at the way he had handled himself, but also over the fact that Binky had stepped in and showed some of her true feelings for me. Harry tipped his hat at me and winked. He and I were on the same page.

The dinner was wonderful. It was by far the finest meal that I had ever had. It sure was a long way from burgers and the Big Bob's Griddle Franks at the Redmond's backyard cookouts, or a pizza at the Greek joint in Paterson. Howard had interpreted the menu for us, the newly assigned wait staff, which did not include any Black Bear Ladies, served us appetizers, then soups and salads, and then we ordered main courses that included steaks, fish dishes, lamb, veal, and other fabulous dishes. Howard made sure that all the food preparation was perfect. He precisely checked every single item for temperature, presentation, and whatever else Howard's eagle eye may have spotted, in which he deemed to be out of place.

The conversation and atmosphere were lively and the entire experience was something very special. We were indeed having the time of our lives.

There was no entertainment during this dinner, only some very soft background music. The Black Bear Club knew how to do it right. We all drank a lot more than we would usually do, and perhaps, we all might have all been feeling pretty good, but none of us was over the top by any means. We completed all the courses of dinner except for desserts and after-dinner drinks when a waiter came and placed a small plate of brown biscuits in front of Harry.

Howard announced to Harry, "Your special biscuits, as requested, Mr. Redmond. I made sure they were served right before dessert just as you like them."

"Why, thanks a lot there, Howie old boy," Harry said as he picked one up and popped it in his mouth. As soon as he started crunching and chewing it, all of us at the table knew what the special biscuits were, but no one said a word. The three of us just stared at him.

"What? I reckon y'all do not know what you are missing. These things are great, you need to try them," he said as he offered the plate up to us.

None of us took him up on the offer.

We had selected desserts and were waiting for them when a man came up to me, touched me on my back, and greeted me. Howard flew in on his jet plane to intercept him.

When I turned around and saw whom it was, I smiled and said, "Jim, what on earth are you doing here?"

I put my hand up to Howard to indicate that it was fine, and Howard went back to his post.

"Hey there, Paulie. I am very sorry to bother you, but I saw you sitting here, and I just had to come over and say hello." Jim was very soft spoken and quiet, and it was hard to hear him even over the soft music that was playing. He was dressed very nicely, and he was well groomed and neat.

"Hey, Harry. How are you? It has been a very long time since I have seen you. How is the nose these days? Can you still move it like that?" Jim made a little motion over his own nose to simulate as Harry does when he is cracking his own beak.

Harry put down his special biscuit and waved.

"Hey there, Jim. How y'all doing? Been great, Jim. Just great. I reckon that I am a lucky guy. Here I am, having dinner in a joint like this here, surrounded by these fabulous young gals."

Harry reached over and shook his hand.

"Yeah Jim, I can do the nose cracking, y'all want to see?"

All of us screamed, "NO" at the same time!

"I did not realize before now that you were from Texas, Harry," Jim said while shaking Harry's hand. "This sure is some extraordinary place here isn't it, for us old hockey players?"

"It sure is, Jim. I would also like you to meet my date for this evening. Ms. Binky Hobnobber, and the lovely woman with Harry, is Ms. Rose Rose. And I cannot forget our friend and associate Mr. Howard Pailet standing over here." Jim turned and greeted Howard with a handshake, and then he greeted the ladies with a handshake and a humble bow.

"Well, it is very nice to meet everyone, and like I said, I am very sorry to disturb you. I will move along and let you enjoy the rest of your dinner. The owner of the Colonials gave my wife and me a free bronze key pass for the weekend, after my performance in the game last week, so we are celebrating a little. He thought my game last week was awesome, so here we are, courtesy of the team owner! You're playing great this year Paulie, your footwork around the net is awesome, I cannot get a marble by you this year."

"Oh, thanks Jim, I ran a lot in the off season, and I think it helped me with some more quickness around my feet."

"Well, whatever you did, you are playing fantastically. I took enough of your time. I will see you next week. I think we will play you next Saturday. Paul, you should not tie your hair up like that. I hear your gal here does not like it when you do that."

I just nodded.

"Enjoy yourself, Paul, ladies, Howard. It has been my distinct pleasure. Harry, it is always nice to see you. Please forgive the interruption, have a pleasant evening everyone, thank you." Upon his goodbye, I stood up and shook his hand. He gave a little wave, and he was off.

"See ya around there, Jim!" Harry said, and he popped another special biscuit in his mouth and started to crunch it.

The desserts came right after Jim left, and as we started to sample them, Rose commented, "I must say your friend, Jim, was a very nice man. I take it he is a hockey player that you both know and apparently, Paul plays against. What a kind, gentle, polite gentleman, unlike a lot of the roughnecks I have met and seen going to Paul's games."

Binky then added, "I agree, it was very unusual, usually the hockey players I have witnessed while attending Paul's games are nothing but horrid brutes with foul mouths and terrible attitudes. This man acted like a refined gentleman."

Harry finished chomping his biscuit. "I reckon he seems nice now, but O'Malley is sure a different guy off the ice, then he is on."

At the mention of the name O'Malley, Rose choked and coughed up her dessert and Howard ran over to assist her.

Binky dropped her fork and shouted, "O'Malley!"

We were now attracting attention, and Howard was doing his best to triage the situation.

I saw the shock on the girl's faces so I explained, "Yes that is Jim O'Malley. You did not recognize him without his uniform. Actually, to be honest, you probably did not recognize him because you usually see him beating the stuffing out of someone, sticking the butt end of his stick in an opposing player's mouth, calling other player's relatives terrible names, or chasing another player around the ice with blood pouring out of his head, while he beats the hell outta the guy with his stick. I heard that in the game last week that he was referring to, the local police had to come out on the ice and take him out in handcuffs, because he got a little extra carried away."

"Excuse me, Mr. Henson, I hate to interrupt. It is really none of my business, but did you really say that chap who came by was Jim O'Malley?"

"Yes Howard, he is a real-life Jekyll and Hyde type guy." Howard just shook his head and went back to his post.

Binky shook her head and said, "That is remarkable. These people, who have the ability to change their personality from being refined, proper persons, to wild and excited personalities one minute to the next, are certainly amazing."

Once more, I knew when to comment or say something to Binky, and when not to say a word

I did not say a word.

Rose recovered, and we finally finished our desserts, after-dinner-drinks, and meals.

Howard ushered us off after dinner. He then checked Harry and me, as well as our suits for the slightest errant crumbs from dinner, dusted us off, and explained, "We will now meet in the front of the main hotel lobby and we will close this evening with a scenic and I might add, very romantic horse drawn carriage ride through the resort grounds and roads. I do apologize as in a few weeks we will have some more snow cover and this will be a sleigh ride, but we only have snow on the upper trails of the ski resort now, and on the toboggan runs, so we will utilize the carriage this evening."

I spotted Binky's head spin, then her ears perked up. Her eyes darted back and forth at the mention of toboggan runs. Ah yes, the deeply hidden alter ego of speed and thrill-seeking Binky was never very far away.

"Ladies, and Mr. Redmond, I advise you to wear your winter coats, as the temperature is now around twenty degrees Fahrenheit. I will arrange for delivery of the overcoats in the front of the hotel immediately. Mr. Henson, I know that you do prefer the cold weather and that you will not require an overcoat until it is around fifteen degrees or just slightly below that figure."

Three men appeared like magic, carrying the overcoats. I was amazed because it seemed as though a bunch of mind readers and magicians must staff this place. Howard took Harry's coat, placed it on him, dusted it off, and checked it for fit. Harry then took Rose's coat and covered her. Howard handed Binky's coat to me and assisted Binky in wearing it. Her coat was a long, black coat trimmed with white fur. She looked fantastic in it, with her blonde hair hanging down over the collar and in the front. Howard led us to the front of the hotel where under the canopy there was parked a black carriage with lantern lights on the sides, a driver in a top hat and tails, and a majestic black horse. Binky and I climbed up into the back and Harry and Rose sat in the middle.

"Have a wonderful tour. I will meet you back here to see if you require anything else before we all retire for the evening," Howard explained.

"Well, hold on there, just a doggone, rootin', tootin', minute, Howie, old boy!" Harry took his hat off and waved at Howard to return.

Howard hustled back and stood next to the carriage. "Yes, Mr. Redmond."

"Where y'all think, you're going? Y'all going back in the lobby?"

"Why yes, Mr. Redmond. I will return to the lobby and wait there for your return."

Harry was shaking his head back and forth.

"I don't think so there, Howie. Y'all climb on up there in the front seat of this here fancy, carriage thingy and come on along with us."

Howard folded his hands in front of his body, tilted his head slightly away from us, and stood at attention, while he explained, "Oh, I am very sorry, but it is strictly forbidden for me to participate in a guest's event. It is not allowed."

"Not allowed? Who says? You are part of the team here Howie, y'all climb on up in here! What if the girls or I get a spot of ice on our coats, my nose is a'snifflin,' or the ladies need something? You will not do us any good standing in the lobby, now will you?"

"You do have a valid point, Mr. Redmond, but it is a major breach of policy and procedure."

Harry laughed and smiled broadly. "Now y'all have known the world famous, ole twenty-seven and me for just a few hours, but I will ask you, Howie. Do we look like the kind of guys that have never broken a policy or procedure before, or even care about them?"

Howard seemed to break his professional stoic behavior

for just one second, and he almost smiled.

"I am one of these, here big shot, gold key guys, and I say that you come on along. Now, go get your coat and jump on in here and let's have a ride to remember."

Binky, Rose, and I joined in the cheer to urge Howard to join us.

Rose yelled out, "Come on, Howard! Go get your coat! There is no way we will leave without you!"

Howard's posture changed and you could see he had softened. "Well, indeed, you are exclusive gold key guests here at the Black Bear Club, and if you insist, then I will join in the ride to attend to your needs. Driver, please hold the ride, I will be right back while I procure my overcoat."

We all let out a cheer and waved Howard on.

He appeared back in a snap, climbed up in the carriage, and sat in the front seat next to the driver.

"Atta boy, Howie old bean. How about a light for this, here, ceegar?"

"Of course, Mr. Redmond. Thank you for allowing me to share in your special evening. No one in all my years here has asked me to do such a thing. I usually just provide services."

"Yeah, yeah, yeah, well, we aren't exactly your normal, stuffy, gold key types there, Howie. I reckon we are just getting started. It is one adventure after another with Harry and Paul, so come along for the ride and see where it all takes us."

"Why of course, Mr. Redmond. That is what I am here for." The flame from the lighter lit up the cold night sky for a moment, and I saw a puff or two from the cigar rise above Harry and his big hat. Rose leaned in close to Harry and he pulled her close to him as the driver snapped the reins and we felt the carriage lurch forward.

Binky slid in close to me, grabbed my arm and hand, and held on tight. She then rested her head on my shoulder as she asked, "Do you ever get cold there, number twenty-seven?"

"Only when you are not close by," I said. I smiled at her as she reached up in the back of my head and pulled out the hair tie and threw it over the side of the carriage.

Harry let out a loud, "YAHHOOO" and off we were, for the ending to another perfect Harry and Paul day.

9

How it will Never be the Same

The ride in the carriage was spectacular.

A cold, clear, starry night, great conversation, some warm O'Blabby's special, Irish Cream liquor, and beautiful ladies. I assure you that in our world, it could not get any better than that. Even Howard seemed to break the mold and I could not be sure, but I think I actually heard him laugh once. Harry was singing Christmas songs in the middle seat and telling stories of our adventures together, so I had to assume that even Howard could not hold back a chuckle or two. I think the story of the time bomb in the cupboard might have put Howard over the top.

We all retired after some long goodbyes. It had been a very long day, and we were all very tired. Howard had instructed us to meet in the lobby at nine o'clock and to be dressed for outdoor activities on the ski slopes.

We met in the lobby at the appointed time, and I must admit we all looked a little worse for the wear, as I think we could all have slept a bit more. While we all were excited to see each other, we walked around and greeted each other as if we were all half-asleep.

"Good morning and greetings to all! Here are aspirins, tomato juice and vodka, seltzer pills, and glasses of water for everyone who may have indulged a bit too much last evening."

Howard had a waiter standing by with the hangover remedies. The Black Bear Club even delivered aspirins, as if it was fine wine. Howard came in loud in voice, eager and ready to organize, research, and explain. He was dressed in another perfect black suit with a matching overcoat and he held his winter's hat in his hands. It looked as if he was planning to be outside today with us to make sure our day went smooth.

The man never stopped.

Harry was the only one who took an aspirin; the rest of us seemed fine, just a little sleepy. Binky just hung on my arm and smiled. She seemed like she needed to hold on to me so she did not fall down.

"I reckon you're a little loud there, Howie. Could you tone it down just a hair on the volume control? Thank you for the aspirin," Harry said as he swallowed the aspirin.

"You are welcome, Mr. Redmond. Now, we will enjoy a full course breakfast and then we have a full day of activities planned. After breakfast, we will head for the toboggan run, where I know Ms. Hobnobber and Ms. Rose will have a thrilling time careening down the slopes at high speeds, while the men hold on for dear life. I have procured extra strong, denture cement for Mr. Redmond so we do not lose his plate on the slopes, and earplugs for Mr. Henson and Mr. Redmond, as I know Ms. Rose will be terrified and will scream at the top of her lungs. We do need not to worry about any neck or arm welts due to the nature of the toboggan seats and your heavy overcoats."

Howard turned to me and spoke in an apologetic manner.

"I am very sorry, Mr. Henson, but you will need your overcoat today, or at least what you call an overcoat, as the temperature at the top of the run is only ten degrees Fahrenheit this morning."

Howard Pailet was a human reference book. He knew everything!

"Ms. Hobnobber, I feel you must know the height of the toboggan run already, so I will defer to you for further explanations of your imminent, death-defying adventure."

Binky perked up, fluffed her hair, and cleared her throat. She was on the stage now, and it was her turn to match Howard on the research and reference level. Binky did seem to relish the bantering back and forth with Howard on referenced and researched facts. She was surely in her safe zone with Howard.

"Yes, Howard, thank you. You are correct, I checked that last week, and it is a two-hundred-foot vertical drop. Therefore, according to my calculation and research, and with the cold overnight temperatures freezing the toboggan run surface into solid ice, we should easily hit speeds of sixty miles per hour or even more."

Oh no!

I was having flashes of the Flipper in my mind's eye. I wondered if The Grim Reaper and his toothless assistant worked here in the winter.

The ladies were thrilled.

Binky was going to get her speed fix, and Rose will be able to release all her inner tensions back all the way to her first horrifying day at kindergarten when her crayons broke and she could scream at the top of her lungs for an hour or two.

Howard nodded in acknowledgment of the accuracy of Binky's research, and he continued to explain the events planned for the day.

"After the fun and excitement of the toboggan runs and hopefully, no severe mishaps or accidents, it is off to lunch in the ski lodge. There, Mr. Redmond can jam with some other musicians who will gather around the lodge's famous open pit fireplace to sing, play some music, and provide casual entertainment for the lunch and lodge crowd. We all hope to hear a little of the favorite old car song that is still under development. Then, members of my salon and health staff will usher the ladies off to an afternoon in the beauty spa for a full expert treatment and pampering. Expert hairdressers and beauticians will assist in your every need and provide the best in hair preparation. The men will be groomed, shaved, and trimmed in our gentlemen's hair salon."

Binky cleared her throat and raised her hand. Howard held his hand up to her. "No worries please, Ms. Hobnobber. I will be there in order to provide personal supervision and make sure they just barely even out Mr. Henson's hair and trim his facial hair. I assure you that there will be no mistakes or errors today."

"Thank you, Howard."

"Then we will pick up the tuxedos for the gentlemen, and the ladies and men will prepare for this evening's grand ballroom dinner and dance. Are there any changes or questions?" Howard finally took a deep breath and stopped rattling off the day's schedule.

"I think ya covered it all there, Howie. I agree that we should get some grub and make off for the slopes."

Howard led us to the restaurant for breakfast, and we followed.

"I sure hope my choppers stay in there, Howie. What do you have? Some of that, there, high tech, epoxy stuff?"

Off we went. We followed Harry, who had put his one arm around Howard and his other around Rose, while we walked to the breakfast table. Binky put her arm through mine as I could tell she was already dreaming of speed and thrills. Her transformation from prim and proper Binky into speed enthused, wild Binky had already begun.

The breakfast was wonderful, as was all the food that the Black Bear Club prepared. Honestly, I never enjoyed such a glorious selection of food. The Black Bear Club could even make serving and eating waffles and eggs elegant.

It was a clear, cold, perfect day with a blue sky and bright sun. It was an ideal day to attempt to survive a toboggan run, hopefully, without an emergency room visit. I tried to be optimistic and look on the bright side. If we all crashed, and were brought to the hospital for treatment, then at least it was a nice sunny day to crash on.

Off we went to the slopes for some fun and joy of hurtling down an icy, treacherous slope of groomed ice and snow at supersonic speeds in a wooden sled. A sled, which you steered by holding onto rope handles and then leaned together in one direction or another.

How did Harry and I get into these situations?

One consolation was that at least Harry came along this time and did not go off to leave us alone for sure annihilation. It was pretty much exactly like Howard had predicted, with Binky entrenched in a major speed thrill, Rose screaming at the top of her lungs and Harry and I just holding on in order to survive the ride. Binky was in her glory. She was sitting right up in the front of the snow missile, with me second in line, followed by Rose and Harry.

The ear plugs that Howard had slipped to us worked great. Rose did complain occasionally of Harry holding on to her body in certain unmentionable locations. Harry then claimed that it was an honest mistake, and it was because of the tremendous speeds and the force in which we hurtled down the icy hill. As usual, Rose went with it and forgave Harry after a few minutes of lecturing and complaining.

After a few hours of the toboggan runs, Howard gathered us in to head for the ski lodge and lunch. At least both Binky and Rose had grown cold on the slopes and they went along willingly; otherwise, we may have continued for a few more hundred runs. Harry, Howard, and I were just happy we all survived with no wipe out or injuries and that Harry kept his teeth in his mouth.

Off we went to the ski lodge, which was a large, rustic cabin structure decorated with what seemed like hundreds of black bear statues, figurines, and paintings. There were also some moose, deer, and other wildlife decorations. The décor included festive Christmas trees, wreaths, and other holiday displays as well as huge stone fireplaces lit with roaring, blazing fires for everyone to warm up to.

We had another fantastic meal for lunch, and then we gathered around the open fire pit in the center of the lodge, while a large group of musicians tuned up their various instruments and discussed what to play. The open fire pit was made of stone and was about eight feet in diameter. It had a copper chimney suspended about five feet above the fire to carry the smoke and soot up all the way to the top of a tepee roof that had to go up at least thirty feet in the air. It was quite an impressive structure. The ladies had now warmed up after the morning out in the severe cold, and they were in great spirits.

As usual, Binky looked marvelous.

She was dressed in a wool brown turtleneck sweater with her long blonde hair tumbling down over her shoulders. She had on tight fitting dungarees that showed off her figure, along with pull-on boots with some fur along the top. Rose was dressed in similar casual clothes, she also wore her trademark, large hoop earrings that displayed her short hair, and dark features. Harry and I were very lucky to be in the company of such gorgeous women.

Howard, of course, was working hard to organize this event, scurrying about, fiddling with this and that, and providing instructions and directions. He had arranged for Harry's banjo to be hand-tuned and then brought to him. Harry had his big hat on now, and after some warm-ups, he looked like he was ready to go. Rose, Binky, and I sat Indian style together on a woolen rug around the pit along with many other spectators to watch the jam session. Rose marveled at how I could fold my legs up like an accordion, until she realized that in order to play the goaltender position, you had to be a little flexible!

Harry was the only banjo player, and along with him, there were several acoustic guitars, some electric guitars, and one electric bass. There were some string bass players, a violin or two (or as Harry called them in his phony accent, "them, there fiddlers") and a few flutes and recorder players. The lodge had a piano on the floor, and we had one young woman in the group who played it quite well. It was quite a collection of assorted players and soon after some fumbling, and stops and starts, they were playing everything from rock-and-roll to folk and then on to some Christmas songs.

Amazingly, they all started to blend, and they actually sounded very good. Harry had been playing the banjo for about four years now, and he had taken some lessons, but mostly he had just learned on his own. He could finger roll and pick very well, and his ability to pick up music very easily was just like his sister, Linda. Linda could really sing well, she had a sweet, captivating, voice. She had studied music in school and she could read as well as write music.

I loved all kinds of music. It was a big part of my life, but other than a little guitar strumming, I was not very good at playing any instruments. I had known for quite a while that the entire Redmond family had a flair and natural ability for music. It was always a joy, and very memorable listening to them whenever they decided to play or sing at the Redmond household.

It was a very enjoyable afternoon, and the three of us finally pleaded with, and then convinced Howard to join us on the floor as we sang, held hands, and rolled with the music along with the rest of the people watching and enjoying the music. Howard tried hard to hide it, but he loved sitting there, singing and holding two pretty ladies' hands all afternoon.

When I was able to, I leaned in and whispered to him, "Don't worry, I will never tell Mrs. Pailet that you spent the afternoon holding hands with two gorgeous, young ladies."

"I do appreciate that very much indeed, Mr. Henson,"

he whispered back.

At a break in the music, Harry asked if anyone could read sheet music, and a number of the musicians raised their hands. Harry summoned Howard to make some photocopies of the sheet music, which contained the song that Harry and Linda had been working on for the past six months or so.

"Take these, here sheets Howie, those other books in my case are for something different," Harry explained as he handed four sheets to Howard for copying. Howard, of course, returned in no time flat, as it always seemed that he had a jetpack on or could transport himself magically through time. Harry handed out the music to those musicians that wanted to give it a shot and could read the sheets.

Harry then explained, "This here is a song that my sister and I wrote together. She sings, but we can just play the music, we keep changing the lyrics, anyway."

Linda had apparently written the tune and created the original sheet music, but the lyrics seemed to be a project that Harry was working on. Harry was a pretty good singer, but I noticed the sheet music had no lyrics on them. They only contained the musical notes for the song, so this was going to be an instrumental version.

After a few starts and stops and some rehearsing, the makeshift band broke into the song. Now, I had heard pieces of this song forever, but I never actually heard the entire tune played through. Harry led with his banjo, accompanied by some guitars, the pianist, a string bass, and one gal on the flute, and before you knew it, the song blended and they did a great job of playing it. I was very impressed; it was really a nice piece. The melody was great, and the tune stuck in your head right away. When it ended, we all stood and gave them a big round of applause.

The song was actually very good.

Of course, Harry ate it all up, especially the part where

all his fellow musicians came up and patted him on the back. To be honest, I think he really enjoyed the part when Rose jumped up to hug him and give him a "congratulation" kiss right in front of everyone. Harry, in the spotlight . . . right where he liked to be the most.

It was getting later in the afternoon now, and Howard reminded us that it was time to head off to our appointments in the barbers' salon and the ladies had to head for the spa, so we all packed up and walked back to the hotel. So far, this has been another day to remember. After all, what was not to enjoy? Hmm, let's see now, a day on the slopes, sitting around a fire listening to music, eating a fine lunch, and enjoying the company of beautiful young ladies. Yes, this was indeed something to remember. It really did not get much better than this! Our attention was now turning to the big dinner and dance planned for this evening in the grand ballroom.

We returned to the main hotel and resort, and we all sat in some big chairs in front of the lobby fireplace, next to a newly decorated twenty-foot-high Christmas tree. It sure was a cold day for late November, as even down at the base of the mountain it was still quite cold. I thought about how tonight may prove to be an even colder night than last night. This was just the setting I loved, mountains, snow, cold weather, and warm fires. It was perfect!

"Now please, remember that this is one of only four other grand balls we hold during the year here at the Black Bear Club," Howard explained. "This is the winter kick off ball, and only gold and silver members, and their friends and families may attend this very exclusive event. This event is extremely formal, and that is why evening gowns as well as tuxedos are required. There will be a cocktail hour in the grand hall, then we open the grand ballroom and the staff will serve a full, formal meal, drinks, followed by elegant and delectable desserts served to finish a miraculous and memorable meal. The entertainment for the ball will be provided by the world famous, Black Bear Orchestra, led by Maestro Davis."

An animated and excited Howard explained the ballroom festivities to us. I could tell that this was one of his favorite events.

"The guests are announced individually and formally, with the ladies entering the hall by the right side, and the gentlemen on the left side. I will also be in a tuxedo, and I, of course, will guide you this evening. I suspect that you will be able to meet many of the other gold key personal assistants this evening, as you will see them serving their assigned members tonight in this setting."

Harry tilted his head back. "I bet you got them all beat there, Howie! Have y'all ever won like the most valuable personal assistant of the year award or something like that? Because y'all are the best in the business!"

Howard cleared his throat.

"Thank you for asking, as well as for the compliment, Mr. Redmond. Yes indeed, as a matter of fact, I won the personal assistant of the year last year and I was awarded a very nice cup for my mantle at home."

Harry shook his head back and forth violently, and dramatically as only Harry could and he yelled back, "I reckon they gave you a lousy cup? C'mon there, Howie! Squeeze them up for some dough so you and Mrs. Howie can go howl at the moon together! I can see I have to teach you Harry's Theory too."

Howard, as usual, did not react to Harry and his outlandish advice, but the three of us could not help but steal a smile at Harry's predictable reaction to the awarding of a "lousy cup."

"I sure hope this ball thingy is not too stuffy there, Howie. You know old twenty-seven and I like to loosen it up a little if it is Boresville."

"Oh, I can assure you, Mr. Redmond, that this is a very formal event, and you will all enjoy yourself tonight. It will be an evening to remember."

Harry seemed to be a little suspect of this evening's plan, as he did not have his usual enthusiasm for this particular event. Howard then added a final tidbit that this was like meeting your bride at your wedding, as the next time we will see the ladies will be when they announce them at the ballroom. He explained that there was an individual and formal announcement of each of the couples who are present during the grand entrance ceremony for the ballroom festivities.

Howard stood straight up very proudly and announced the information, "It is a Black Bear Club tradition, and it adds to the anticipation and formality."

Harry let out with a big sigh, "I reckon that, there, tradition seems a little over the top there and pretty high on the stupid meter, Howie."

Binky and Rose immediately disagreed with Harry while they proclaimed their support for the traditional idea.

"I think it is hopelessly romantic, what a wonderful tradition," Binky said as she loudly voiced her support for the tradition. Rose was nodding her head and smiling, as it was clear that she also felt it was a great idea.

Binky turned towards me and she grabbed my hand tightly. I could tell that she was about to put me on the spot.

"Twenty-seven, do you not agree how wonderful and romantic that sounds?"

Oh boy, another major test of my role within the hopeless paradigm known as Harry's Theory!

"Well, I, well. . .."

"Oh, y'all can't ask Paul, he is a hopeless softie and a cupcake romantic at heart!" Harry jumped in and rescued me. "Oh well, since it is one of them, there, traditional things, then I guess that we can go along with it, even if it seems like it is pretty stuffy to me."

The girls smiled. We received a few goodbye hugs and kisses, and off the ladies went.

Harry, Howard, and I stood there and watched Binky and Rose walk off merrily to the spa. Harry scratched his head and looked at us.

"I dunno, men. I reckon I am a'thinkin' that this here ball thing is going to be a little on the yawning side of life. Did y'all see the stars in our gal's eyes?"

Howard first looked at me and then at Harry and he provided his wise, old sage, Howard type, advice, "I must advise you, Mr. Redmond, that the ladies generally find the grand ballroom dance and the event to be one of the most wonderful of all of the events here at the club. I am sure that once Mr. Henson and you share the experience, you will also find it to be most enjoyable."

Harry shook his head and put his arm around Howard. "All right there, Howie. I reckon I am not convinced, but we will take your word for it. To me, it sounds like sitting around and watching a checkers match between two old battle axes." Harry screwed his mouth up like a corkscrew. Then he suddenly smiled and his entire face lit up. I saw his eyes looking across the lobby. Howard and I both noticed the change in his face, and we turned to see what Harry was looking at. A Black Bear Lady was strolling across the lobby in her full swing, shake, and bounce mode, serving cocktails to some older men sitting in front of the fire.

Harry looked back at us with the smile still on his face. "Well, I guess one advantage of that, there, silly, tradition is that I reckon by not having Rose or Binky around, I can steal a quick drool and ogle over them, there, fine looking, bear gals without gittin' in a heap of trouble."

He pulled off his hat and watched as she moved away and he whistled.

"Y'all check out that train and that fine little caboose in the back of it!"

I could not help but laugh aloud at the comment, and Howard broke into a chuckle, which he was working very hard to suppress.

"What?" Harry put his arm back around Howard's shoulders, "Now Howie, I cannot imagine that all these years of training to be stuffy and unemotional, have dulled y'all's senses that much now, has it? I bet when you go home after watching these, here bear gals wiggle around all day, y'all chase Mrs. Howie all over the house and try to catch her!"

Howard could no longer hold the laughter back as he burst out laughing, as did I. Howard was very embarrassed at his failed efforts to resist the outrageous Harry comments.

"Oh, Mr. Redmond, you are indeed a wonderful and unique person. I apologize for my nonprofessional reaction!" Howard was now turning multiple shades of red. We all stood there enjoying the moment together. Same old Harry. Polished up a little, a different shine on him, but the same old Harry.

Howard led us over to the barber and hair salon, and as I walked in and sat down, a man who introduced himself to me as Frank met me. I greeted him and he led me over to a large leather barber chair. Howard was in tow, right behind me to make sure not to face the wrath of Binky.

"Step up here, twenty-seven! Boy, oh boy, that was some great playoff game last year when you shut down that escapee from the insane asylum, O'Malley! Hey, I heard that your gal hates when you tie all this long hair back. Is that true or not? How do you see while playing goalie with all this hair if you cannot tie it all back?

It surely was nice to be famous for something.

The barber's session went well, and Frank did a great job under the watchful eye of Howard, although having Howard hold a small tape measure up to the ends of my hair might have been overkill. When I protested to

Howard, he simply mentioned and reminded me of the now famous Black Bear Lady incident.

I heard Harry yell over from his chair, "Y'all have a point there, Howie!"

We picked up our tuxedos, showered, and changed. It took Harry and me a little time to figure out what all the parts and pieces of the tuxedo were. A quick call or two to Howard provided us with the required information, and soon Howard had managed to have two-novice tuxedo wearers all assembled properly. For both of us, it was the first time we had ever worn a tuxedo. The two of us really looked great in our suits the other evening, but to see us in tuxedos was a remarkable sight.

Harry looked at me and I looked at him. "I reckon that I feel like a giant stuffed penguin, there, twenty-seven. This, here, suit is not exactly my style."

I had to agree with the big guy, he and I looked like fishes out of the water.

We met Howard in the lobby, and he was dressed in his tuxedo. He, of course, looked very distinguished; however, we still looked like oversized stuffed penguins. Howard checked every inch of us and adjusted our ties, our jackets, our cummerbunds, and all other details. Howard pronounced us ready to go, convinced Harry that he could not wear his ten-gallon hat, off the three of us went, and we headed for the ballroom.

I had a question for Howard. "So, Howard, if the personal assistants funnel the men into the ballroom, then who guides the women in?"

"The ladies are brought in by the world famous, Black Bear Ladies, of course."

Harry and I both stopped in our tracks when we heard the words, "Black Bear Ladies." I had horrible thoughts and a vision of Binky dressed in her fantastic evening ball gown, her hair perfectly prepared, her golden jewelry around her neck, ripping the flirtatious Black Bear Lady limb from limb, behind the scenes in a hallway leading to the ballroom. She might even summon O'Malley to jump into the behind the scene melee!

Howard read our minds, "I have taken all precautions to ensure that the young lady who approached Mr. Henson last night is not working this assignment tonight."

Harry nodded his head in approval and said, "Good job, Howie. Otherwise, I reckon you might need to call an ambulance or a morgue wagon."

We walked into a hallway that led to the ballroom. Howard and other personal assistants were carefully listening to instructions from a gentleman who appeared to be in charge of the event. He had us all lined up in a specific order behind many other haughty, unfriendly, looking men dressed in tuxedos. Most of the other men were older, and the few men who looked our age, or close to it, appeared as if they were very well to do. They scanned us up and down as if we had some unknown disease.

They were all aloof and very arrogant when we attempted to greet any of them. I am sure my long hair, beard, and general hippie looks were painfully apparent even dressed up in this penguin suit.

This could be a case where we were fulfilling one of the more famous sayings of Ronzo when he would announce, "Y'all can put lipstick on a pig, but he is still a pig!"

Harry and I were very uncomfortable, but we played it cool. Once or twice, due to some obnoxious stares, whispers, and general attitudes towards us, I was afraid that Harry might go off on one of the pompous guys, but I could see he was doing his best to blend in and not cause a scene. For Harry, this was a major show of restraint; after all, this type of event was not really in the Harry and Paul's playbook.

Howard stood on the side, along with many other personal assistants, and he watched us carefully. A monotone, bored voice was droning on-and-on from inside the ballroom. When the announcer called your name, you strode out a door and into the open floor of the ballroom where you met your woman about halfway, and then you walked arm in arm as you strolled together through the ballroom to a grand hall where the cocktail service was. It did seem awful formal and pretentious, but we were stuck, there was no going back now. We could hear the introductions of the names of the attendees whining off in the distance. The announcer sounded rather unenthusiastic in conducting his introductions.

One-by-one, the disinterested voice called out the names, and the man who was next in line, would walk out and disappear into the ballroom beyond our vision.

"Dr. and Mrs. Everett Johnson, the Honorable Benjamin A. Strauss, and Mrs. Strauss, Mr. Walter Spence E.S.Q and Mrs. Spence."

On and on, we could hear the announcer calling the names of doctors, judges, lawyers, bankers, and other high rollers, as we grew closer to the doorway. Here we were. Two bums from Paterson, a welder who makes believe he is a cowboy from Texas, and an electrician by day that earns eighteen dollars a game as a long-haired hippie, ice hockey goaltender by night.

Oh boy, this is going to be good.

The big moment was near as I could now see the ballroom floor from the doorway.

Harry was next in line. He turned and gave Howard and me a quick thumb up.

I heard the bored voice call out, "Ms. Rose Rose and Mr. Harry M. Redmond Jr."

Out the door, fraudulent, Texas Harry went . . . cast into the world of pretentious honor!

Howard and I watched from afar and we saw him almost stumble at the sight of Rose. To say that she looked stunning and beautiful would not do her justice, she was out of this world! Rose strode across the floor earning gasps and whispers throughout the crowd at her beauty. Poor Harry was weak in the knees and fading as he met her in the middle of the floor, and even the stuffy attendees had to struggle for breath at the sight of the two of them together. Those aloof and snooty men we had tried to rub elbows with, in the hallway, now gasped in horror, at the sight of Harry with this gorgeous gal.

I was next, my long hair, beard and my six-foot four-inch frame stuffed into a penguin suit. To top it all off, I had to meet Binky in the middle of this floor and then into the ballroom with all of these eyes upon the two of us! My knees were shaking worse than facing O'Malley on a one-on-one breakaway.

"Ms. Binky Hobnobber and Mr. Paul John Henson."

Out the door, I went, and when I saw Binky out on the floor, I felt as if a one hundred mile an hour slap shot had hit me in the head!

She was radiant. Stunning. Absolutely, stunning was the only description required.

Everyone could hear the flattering comments coming from the crowd loud and clear. Her stunning appearance, sexy walk, ear-to-ear smile, and presence as she walked across the floor were like something out of a Hollywood movie.

Here is this gorgeous, classy woman, and she is meeting this long-haired, hippie goaltender out in the middle of the ballroom floor. Something is very wrong with this picture! I was more than lucky; Binky was like a gift from Heaven. I could not help feeling deep down that I was inadequate, and that I did not deserve to be in the company of such a lovely woman.

Every man in the entire joint had become immediately jealous of Harry and me. If generations of men in our era had never recovered from the sight of Crystal Zirconium in, Cruising, coming down those stairs in her black leather after her makeover, then I can guarantee there was a whole load of men who saw Binky and Rose that night who had the same experience. I know that Harry and I never recovered because they were the two most gorgeous women we had ever seen.

I met Binky in the middle of the floor; she took my arm, smiled at me, and winked. I heard Howard clapping behind me; I think Howard may have never recovered from the sight of Binky and Rose either.

Howard met us out on the floor after the introductions had finished, and all he managed to say was, "Ms. Rose and Ms. Hobnobber, please forgive me, but you are both stunning. It is remarkable how the four of you look, I am so proud!"

"Thank you, Howard, you look very handsome tonight also," Rose said. Howard thanked Rose and smiled at the compliment. We each received our favorite cocktails and at Howard's suggestion, both Rose and I shifted to mixed drinks rather than beer for this event. Rose was enjoying a gin and tonic and I opted for bourbon with a little splash of water.

It was quite remarkable how the same men that had snubbed Harry and me when we were in the hallway, now circled and wanted to meet us. The two most gorgeous women in the place on our arms had a little to do with our newfound popularity, I am sure.

"You are stunning Binky, simply stunning," I managed to say. Binky smiled and complimented me on how nice I looked in my tuxedo. She was clearly on cloud nine for this event. We mingled a bit and met many folks; all of a sudden, we had achieved a new lofty respect from some of the same people who had just a few minutes ago, wanted nothing to do with us. Looking back, I am sure that many of these people were very unsure of whom we exactly were. There were some strolling violinists in and around the crowd during the cocktail hour and they circled playing classical music for a backdrop. Not exactly, "Close to the Crevice" that was for sure.

Binky, Rose, Harry, and I hung together, chatted, and sipped our drinks. We were on our best behavior, as Harry and I both made our best attempts at fitting in and being gracious to each and every, snobbish buffoon, who came by to introduce themselves to us. We knew they just wanted to catch a close-up glimpse of our ladies. We also realized that they were only pretending to be interested in learning who these two bums were.

After all, you could never fit in with them once they asked the fateful question of, "What line of work, are you two, fine gentlemen engaged in?"

Harry of course, expertly spun it with his best phony drawl combined with vague, widely exaggerated, and broad answers such as, "I am in the construction business, and my buddy here is a professional athlete."

The stares I received when Harry proclaimed my so-called, professional athlete status was an emphatic, and shocked, "Him?"

I do not think anyone was buying it.

Howard leaned into Harry and me for some protocol type advice, "We are about to move into our assigned table for the dinner. Please be sure to carry the ladies' drinks into the ballroom setting. I assure you, gentlemen that it is the proper way to enter."

We nodded our heads, and we both followed Howard's drink etiquette instructions. Harry took Rose's cocktail, and I carried Binky's Martini, (shaken, not stirred) as Howard escorted us to our table on the outskirts of the grand ballroom. The girls were having a wonderful time, and Harry and I felt just a little out of sorts. It seemed like the girls and this entire event was so much above us at this point! As usual, and consistent with the décor of the rest of the club, the grand ballroom was spectacular, with hanging chandeliers and all the flamboyant furnishings of the other locations inside the club.

Assembled in the front of the grand ballroom was a full orchestra and the conductor began to lead them in some classical, string-dominated music. There were violins, cellos, harps, the full strings along with pianos, percussion, cymbals; it was unreal to hear such lush music live. I had never even seen a real orchestra in person, nonetheless heard one! Even for a progressive rocker like me, it was an impressive sound to experience live. After all, my beloved band, No Way, had adopted a huge number of classical overtones into their music, so I did have some appreciation of classical influences.

I needed to give this music a chance; I thought in my mind. Not exactly my cup of tea, but give it a chance there, Henson, just give it a chance.

Binky held my hand as we sat at the table as we took it all in, and Rose and Harry sat close to each other on the other side. Howard took his usual post on the side, watched us, and offered his advice.

Harry seemed to be a little in awe. "I reckon this is unreal, guys, I never dreamed it would be like this. I am stunned at how fancy it all is. I think we will need to get up and dance some type of waltz or something. Paul, can you and Binky do that? I will need to follow you, twenty-seven. This is something I will be lost on for sure."

"Oh, Paul, I hope you know how to do it. I have never danced a waltz before either," said Rose, who now was studying my face for guidance.

I suddenly felt my confidence build, as I knew this is where I can show them that I may be some hippie, hockey goalie from Paterson with a gorgeous girlfriend, but as hard as it will be for folks to imagine, I can nail it on a waltz. Binky also seemed to become a little concerned. And she turned, gave me the famous Hobnobber stare, and got right up in my face.

She then asked, "Can you lead me? I am not sure I can

do a ballroom waltz properly. I guess I should have researched the subject last week."

She locked her eyes into mine as she studied my face for an answer, and she closed in deeper for the famous Hobnobber stare.

Here was my big chance to play it cool. I smiled, as my sister and I had actually won the waltz entry in a dance competition we entered a few years back, so I was very confident and very relaxed that I could handle this. It may have been another major mistake on my part, or a miscalculation, but rather than answer Binky as she stared at me, I decided to shift gears into playing the part within Harry's Theory of being cool, calm, and collected. I never said a word. I just sat back, nodded my head, and smiled. Binky looked at me and she must have sensed my confidence as she also sat back in her chair and smiled.

She was going to be fine.

"Just follow, twenty-seven there, Bink-a-roo-ski. We have done this all before."

Harry also caught my confidence, and he knew and agreed with the angle I had decided to work at this time. I had easily passed the Harry Theory test this time around. Be cool, mysterious, and never let them know exactly who you are. I caught Howard out of the corner of my eye, and he winked at me. Howard knew the drill.

Dinner was pure culinary perfection, as all the food was superb as usual. The dance floor opened up as dinner was completed. A few folks went out on the floor, and when I heard the waltz music start, I grabbed Binky's hand and out we went. Harry and Rose waited, but then they followed us out on the dance floor. Binky and I faced off, and she followed my lead perfectly as we flowed into the waltzing dancers across the floor.

We nailed it! Harry and Rose flowed behind us. Binky was enthralled, and it was pure magic. There was no other way to describe it.

She just stared at me and smiled as we moved across the floor and finally, she managed to say, "I am so happy to be with you. This is the greatest night of my life. You are even more handsome than you were the other night, and it is amazing to me that you can dance like this."

Women enjoy this kind of thing. It may not have been my bag but holding a gorgeous woman that was smiling at me, and saying passionate things, sure was starting to grow on me. I had to admit that it sure was a lot better than sweating, or bleeding on the ice in my goaltending gear, while O'Malley did his best to put a dent in my head with a hockey puck.

When the waltz had ended and we returned to our table, Howard met us and congratulated us.

"I must say that all eyes were on the four of you, the other dancers could not hold a candle to your performance."

Howard was acting as if he was a proud parent.

The night went on and on, slow dances, waltzes, music, drinks, food, and elegant desserts. Harry had a bit of a rough time with some flaming cherry, something or other, but after failing to blow it out, he smothered it with his napkin and a splash of water. We danced when we could; we enjoyed a few cocktails here and there, and then, we ate in between. The orchestra was extraordinary, but I felt myself growing weary of the endless strings and same old music going on and on endlessly. There were no melodies to the music, just endless notes that all sounded the same. To a progressive rocker like me, it all had started to sound like drudgery.

Where was The Soda and Beer Caps Band or No Way when I needed them?

Rose and Binky had moved over to sit next to one another at the table to talk and now, they were staring out starry eyed with quixotic looks at the orchestra, while watching a handful of dancers going around the floor like hands on a clock.

Harry and I sat next to one another.

"I don't know, Harry, this is sure getting a little boring, and the girls are overjoyed by all of this. Look at them, they look like they are lost in the romance of the whole thing, if they get used to this we are doomed."

Harry looked over at the girls and then he whispered to me, "I reckon you're right, Paul. At this rate, Rose will never allow me ever to wear ma' big ole' hat anymore, and you can forget about listening to No Way. Ole Bink-a-roo-ski will make you throw all your No Way records out and join her in researching waltz music."

I nodded my head in agreement.

Harry tapped me on the forearm and said, "Let me test the situation and see where we stand, Paul. Say . . . Rose, honey . . . you having a good time?"

Rose turned around, and smiled a big, broad, wide smile and answered, "Oh, Harry yes, thank you! It is so dreamy that I am getting lost in the music."

Harry smiled a fake and forced smile and said, "Great darlin,' I am glad you are enjoying it!" He leaned back into me and spoke in a low whisper, "We are in big trouble here twenty-seven, and the gals are lost in some fantasy dream world. I reckon it ain't old Paterson town either."

I then elbowed Harry and pointed out a man sitting a few tables away. He was an older guy dressed in his tuxedo and sitting perfectly upright in his chair with his head tilted all the way back. His mouth was wide open, and he was snoring his brains out. Harry signaled me with one of our famous hand and head signals for a restroom meeting, so we both excused ourselves from Howard and the ladies and headed for the restroom. As we passed by the sleeping man, Harry rolled up a little piece of a napkin and bounced it off his forehead. The guy did not even move, he was so out of it.

We made a beeline to the men's restroom.

"I reckon this, here, waltzing stuff is getting like watching paint dry there, Paul, I think it is time for one of our famous action plans."

Some stuck-up old guy was listening to us as we stood near the sinks in the restroom, and he frowned a little at us as he heard what we were discussing. The restroom attendant came over, and he was dusting off our shoes and tuxedos while we tried to discuss our game plan.

Harry quickly grew impatient with him. "Hold on there, Elroy, my pal and I are coming up with a game plan here, go check out that guy over there. I see a crumb on his collar."

The attendant believed Harry, and he actually headed off in the innocent man's direction to check his collar.

"I have an idea, if you are up to it. I think it is time we get this, here, joint more like a party, rather than a funeral home!"

"I am with you, Harry. What do you have in mind?"

"Well, I will need you and Binky to follow my lead, so just watch. You can jump in when the time is right. If I play it perfectly, you will know when that is. First off, I need to get old Howie to buy into the gig, and I think I may have just the remedy for this bore fest."

I never really enjoyed it when Harry gave me vague details, as these events usually ended with me in some tough or difficult situation, but as usual, I was ready to support the plan.

When we returned to the table, Harry grabbed Howard, put his arm around him, and pulled him aside.

"Yes, Mr. Redmond. How may I be of assistance?"

"Howie, twenty-seven, and I am in big trouble. Look at the ladies over there. They are submerged in orchestra and waltz heaven. Paul is going to look pretty weird going to hockey games in a tuxedo. I am a'thinkin' that we might have created an uncontrollable monster here."

Howard glanced over at the ladies and then back at me.

"Well sir, it is a magical night for them, but I can see where this type of entertainment does not exactly fit in with your, as well as, Mr. Henson's primary interests."

"Howie, please let me have a piece of paper and your pen." Howard instantly produced the items, and Harry wrote down some information on the paper and handed it back to Howard.

"I need you to go to my banjo case and find this book and make copies of the sheet music inside. I then need you to convince old Maestro Puss over there that he may be good at that, there, waltz-a-roo-ski music, but he is putting everyone to sleep, and this sheet music is the perfect remedy. After all, an orchestra is an orchestra. He should not have that much heartburn about this. Please make enough copies of that entire book for the orchestra, Howie."

Howard shook his head.

"This is highly irregular, Mr. Redmond, this is a formal ball, and I do not know how this is going to go over."

"Oh, c'mon, Howie, this place looks like half the people are dead and you have to admit that you are also bored stiff standing here on the sideline like a penguin. Howie, the carriage ride was irregular, the holding hands and singing with the ladies, was not in the manual either."

Harry put his arm around Howard and pulled him close to him. "Howie, life is short, and twenty-seven and I play on the edge all the time. Loosen up your collar and just go with it."

Howard covered his mouth and pondered for a moment.

"I have heard it said of you that you could sell ice to an Eskimo, and based upon your actions, I feel that is indeed very true. Mr. Redmond, you are a magnetic personality and you have presented quite a convincing argument. I suppose it would not hurt . . . at least . . . to give it a try. Maestro Davis does owe me a favor or two, so I may be able to pull a few strings here and there."

"Atta boy, Howie! Call your cards in on him and work the deal. This is New Jersey where backdoor deals are a way of life! I reckon you need to trust me, Howie! This here show is turning into a real yawn-fest. Half of these folks have never even lived in their lives, and the other half does not even realize they are even alive."

Harry closed in and put his arm around Howard once more.

"The first time some of these old boys even knew they had a heart, and some other male body parts, was when they spotted Rose and Binky on the floor tonight in the grand entrance. I can promise that if we pull this off, then we are going to give these stuffy, old mummies a night to remember."

Remarkably, Howard was in, and he smiled and shook Harry's hand.

"I will need a minute or two at the microphone to kick this all off, so you need to work the deal with Maestro Puss for me to have some air time. Please bring my hat back too!"

You could see that Howard now had a mission, and that Harry had convinced him.

"I will do my best, sir," he answered, and Howard was off.

Back at the table, we continued to enjoy drinks, some dessert, and the music droned on in the background like fingernails on a blackboard. The romantic atmosphere had captured our two lovely ladies, and the gals did not seem to mind, as they were in another world. Harry and I felt like our tuxedos were strangling us and like we could not get enough air. I did not even dare even to ask Harry what his plan was. Years of going along with his wild ideas and schemes had taught me just to go with it. Advance notice of his schemes caused undue anxiety.

I would learn soon enough.

Howard returned carrying the hat and a box. He waved

to us and gave a quick nod of his head. Howard headed for the side of the orchestra stand. At a break, he pulled Maestro Davis aside for a discussion.

Howard handed him the sheet music and you could see Maestro Davis shaking his head as he glanced at the music. The two men went back and forth until you could see the maestro scan the audience. Howard was pointing to the crowd and speaking with him in what appeared to be a rather intense conversation. As you looked around, you could see all the dead expressions and quiet atmosphere of the half-asleep attendees across the ballroom floor. Howard was working him hard for the deal. Maestro Davis then turned to Howard, nodded, and took the music out of his hands. The maestro moved some of his orchestra members around, and I saw him bring in some extra musicians with horns and trumpets. He was studying the sheets of paper that Howard had given him, and then he assigned a few assistants to distribute the sheets throughout the orchestra.

Maestro Davis strolled to the microphone, turned it on, and tapped it.

"Good evening, ladies and gentleman. I would like to thank you for a remarkable evening. Tonight, we have some special guests that I would like to present as a prelude to a slight change in our musical program. I would like to introduce a gold key guest and hand the microphone over to him for a special announcement. Please welcome Mr. Harry M. Redmond Junior."

Harry jumped up from the table as Binky, Rose, and I sat in stunned silence. Howard threw Harry his big ten-gallon hat, which Harry effortlessly plucked out of the air.

Harry leaned over to me and whispered, "Be ready to come out here."

He put his hat on his head, ran out onto the floor, and grabbed the microphone. The crowd went silent as the stuffy people were in shock.

"Howdy everyone! I want to take just one minute here

to say that I am one of the luckiest people in attendance here tonight. I have a gorgeous lady at my side. I know some of you stuffy old boys out there have spotted her and checked her amazing backside out already! I have the greatest personal assistant, Howie, watching for any crumbs that get behind my cummerbund, and making sure that I pull my fly back up after a restroom trip. I am having a great time. The plain truth is, though . . . just a little tough to accept. I have to admit that I am just a poor, old, schlep from Paterson."

The crowd sat there, stunned.

"I am lucky, because I have the best buddy in the whole wide world sitting with me at our table. He has put up with me through all my crazy antics, selfish moves, and motives, stupid ideas over a lot of years and he is the nicest, smartest, and greatest guy in the world. We have been best pals since we were ten years old and I love him like a brother."

Binky looked at me and grabbed my hand.

Rose leaned in and asked, "What on earth is he doing? Is he drunk?" The crowd grew a little restless as you heard some murmurs go through the crowd as to what this speech was all about and where it was leading.

"He is here tonight with his gorgeous woman, and I have to tell you he has an awful lot of talents. One of which, he is the goalie for the Long Island Roosters that finally stopped O'Malley in the playoffs last year!"

As soon as Harry said that, an old man stood up, waved his cane, pointed at me, and yelled out, "I knew that I recognized him, that's number twenty-seven, the guy with all the hair there at your table! He played the greatest game I have ever seen a goalie play in the net. I can't stand that lunatic O'Malley and he shut him out in the playoffs! He is the best goalie that I have ever seen!"

Then another stuffy, pompous man lost his cool also, as he stood up from his seat, and shouted out, "O'Malley is a wild-ass-hockey goon and a jerk! Up your ass, O'Malley! Go, Roosters!" All the time, his wife was tugging at his tuxedo tails, and she tried to pull him back down to his seat.

The Long Island Roosters fan club had a team chant that they would do at the games. It was not my favorite thing because it seemed pretty stupid to me. One section of the club would stand up and yell out, "Roosters! Roosters! Roosters!" and then the other section would answer with three rooster crows in a row. It was pretty dumb, but it was what they did to fire up the crowd.

It was obvious that there were some folks from the island here tonight, as well as some hockey fans. A tall woman dressed to the maximum with a huge chest, a big string of white pearls around her neck, and her glasses on a string hanging around her neck, then stood up and yelled out, "ROOSTERS! ROOSTERS! ROOSTERS!"

As the two old men stood up and answered, "COCKLE DOODLE DOO, COCKLE DOODLE DOO, COCKLE DOODLE DOO!"

I was glad O'Malley only had a bronze key and was not in attendance, or this might have turned into a hockey brawl.

"I love this! I reckon that's what I am talking about!" Harry yelled while putting his hands up over his head. "Like I told you, he has many talents. If you think that he is hot in the net, then just watch when he gets out here with his super, sexy, dancing machine woman!" Harry whirled around and pointed to Maestro Davis. "Ole Maestro Puss! Hit it!"

Maestro Davis tapped his baton on the stand, and the horn section and violin section of the orchestra stood up. As soon as the horns started the first few notes, and then the violins came in, I looked at Binky, as I knew what Harry had done.

Binky smiled and said, "You have got to be kidding."

"Let's go!"

I grabbed her hand, and we ran out to the middle of the dance floor and faced each other off just as the horns hit the intro for the Spanish section of "Living Love."

If we thought we had nailed it that night at the Surf Club at Seashore Heights, then we really nailed it tonight. We had a full orchestra led by Maestro Davis with full strings, full horns, and the whole ensemble going full tilt for us, as they had dumped the stifling waltz music in favor of the Electronic Transistor Orchestra playlist!

Binky and I danced as we had never danced before, with all the eyes of the doctors, lawyers, judges, big shots, little pistols, high rollers, gold keys, silver keys, personal assistants, and everyone else in gowns and tuxedos watching us. It was just the two of us out there, as Binky wiggled, I swung her here and swung her there, I spun her, I leaned her over, and I wiggled a little as well. I flipped her. We danced close, we danced apart, and just as the song ended, we nailed the ending perfectly, as though we had practiced it for years.

The song ended, the last notes hit, and the entire place stood up and gave us a standing ovation. Binky and I held each other and then bowed for the crowd as the grand ballroom had exploded into applause. The maestro and some musicians came out, congratulated us, and shook our hands. The whole ballroom had come alive, from an oppressive, boring waltz snooze fest into a full tilt nightclub bash!

When Maestro Davis hit the baton and started the notes for, "Mr. Clear, Clear Skies," all the people ran out to the dance floor. Before you knew it, everyone, and I do mean everyone, from the waiters, to the snobbish people, to the personal assistants, to the Black Bear Ladies, to the cooks, to the chefs, to the security guards, to a maintenance man who was changing a light bulb in the hallway, and anyone else that may have come by, was out there dancing.

Harry grabbed Rose and hit the floor and Binky ran and grabbed Howard. I would never have imagined it, but Howard Pailet himself, dressed in his fancy, smancy, tuxedo, was out there on the floor with everyone else, and he danced as if he had not a care in the world.

Now, we had a party!

It went on, as the world-famous Black Bear Orchestra played all the hits that were in Harry's Electronic Transistor Orchestra songbook like, "Sad, Sad Women," "Does the Wind Spin You Around," and many others. A crazy, fraudulent cowboy, a long-haired hippie goalie, their super-efficient personal assistant, and two gorgeous, young women turned the grand ballroom of the Black Bear Club upside down on this glorious night.

It became a night for all of us to remember.

Harry and I stood on the side of the ballroom, watching as the entire ballroom floor jumped around and danced. Old men, young men, old women in gowns and some in-between men in tuxedos, cooks, and chefs and waiters, and servers, all out there, jumping around, having the time of their lives.

We watched on the sideline as our two gorgeous, young ladies danced with Howard to, "When You Are Feeling Loose." Harry put his big arm around me, squeezed me until I felt my chest crush, and he smiled.

"Well, the night always comes there, twenty-seven, and this one looks like the end to another perfect, Harry and Paul day."

10

Double Disaster

After turning the entire Black Bear Club upside down, we all retired for the night. Howard advised us that we could sleep late since the checkout time was not until eleven in the morning. He told us he would meet us in the lobby for one last special event, and that casual dress was fine. Harry and I were up early, and I had to admit there remained a little pang of sorrow inside me at thinking that it was time for us to leave. We met the ladies, and the four of us strolled into the lobby to find Howard.

As we walked towards the lobby, a young male employee of the club stopped us and he said, "Excuse me, but I heard about last night." He turned towards me and handed me a piece of paper and a pen. "I know you are a famous ice hockey player. Would it be out of place for me to ask for your autograph? Could you also ask your movie star female friends and Big Tex to sign the paper for me?

I took the paper and pen from his hand and smiled at him. "Why sure, thank you," I said as I signed it, and put number twenty-seven below my signature.

I then handed it to Harry.

"Why sure, there partner," Harry said as he scrawled "Big Tex" on the paper and handed it around for the rest of us to sign. Binky and Rose giggled at the thought of them having become "overnight celebrities."

The young man received his paper back. "Thank you, we have never seen anything like youse guys around here. It usually is pretty boring. It sure has been fun," he said and off he went.

"I reckon we are like celebrities around this here joint!" Harry proclaimed while he beamed at the thought. This weekend had more than fulfilled his voracious appetite for the spotlight.

"Good morning," Howard greeted us as he was standing by dressed in his normal suit attire and he was back to his normal self. I imagined it would take a bit of time for poor Howard to recover from his breach of proper procedures, but perhaps I was incorrect. His usual faithful waiter, displaying the hangover remedies, accompanied him, but today we were all fine.

"Our last event is for the Black Bear Club resident photographer to take pictures of the four of you and create a lasting record and memory of your visit here. Please meet, Mr. Gene W. Oliver. He will guide you for the posing and photographs. I will stand here on the sidelines and leave you in his more than capable hands."

Mr. Oliver greeted us all and then ushered us off to various places in the club, utilizing different backdrops, as he snapped pictures of the four of us together, Binky and I together, Rose and Harry together, and then each of us individually. The ladies looked lovely. I am not sure Harry, and I looked really swift, but it had been a long weekend.

He was almost finished when I jumped in and pulled Howard over. "C'mon Howard . . . get in here."

There was only a short protest this time, and Howard joined with all five of us in a group picture. Then Mr. Oliver snapped some pictures with Harry and me, shaking Howard's hand, and then my favorite, as Howard joined the girls, and they took the picture as the ladies each kissed Howard on his opposite cheeks!

"Oh, boy Howie, I reckon that one is going to need some serious 'splaining to do for Mrs. Pailet!"

Howard was clearly embarrassed, but we knew deep down that he loved it. He had become used to our tradition of bending and breaking the rules. Once the pictures were finished, we circulated the lobby and said goodbye to some of the Black Bear Club staff. Some club members also snapped our pictures when they saw us and recognized us.

It was quite the scene.

It now came time for us to leave as Howard led us to the front lobby where we saw Binky's luggage go by with ten men and a Substantial Industries hand truck wheeling it out to the Trans Whizzer. I saw a young staff member carrying my Long Island Roosters' number twenty-seven bag and as he passed me, he pointed at it, and gave me a thumb up signal. The car was shining from a recent polish and wax, warmed up, and parked right at the front door.

Howard led us to the front door, he stood at attention along with some other staff members who were assisting him, and stoically delivered a pronouncement, "On behalf of the entire staff here at the Black Bear Club, I would like to thank you for visiting with us. I hope you enjoyed your visit as exclusive gold key guests. My expectation is that we provided satisfactory service for all your needs, and that we created a lasting memory for you and your party."

"Howard, please . . . a canned speech," I said as I pulled him close and shook his hand. The four of us then gathered in, gave him a warm hug goodbye, and the ladies kissed him again and thanked him.

"Howie, y'all are the best! We will never forget you!" Harry said as he put his arm around him and almost knocked poor Howard over when he squeezed him.

Howard Pailet stepped back and pulled his handkerchief from his suit pocket. He wiped away some tears that were coming down his cheeks.

"I do apologize . . . Mr. Redmond . . . for the breach of emotions, but I have to say that in my sixteen years of service here at the Black Bear Club, I have never had a more enjoyable group than you and your friends. I shall treasure this weekend as a fond memory all my life, as I never had more fun, or was treated with more respect, and dignity than I was by this group. It was indeed, a magical time. You are very special people, and I know that no matter where life takes all of you, you will always be together in your hearts, because you have a special bond. I shall miss you all greatly."

Howard sniffed, took out his handkerchief, and wiped his eyes.

"I have learned a valuable lesson from this weekend. I learned that life is an adventure, and sometimes you need to go along for the ride and see where it all takes you."

The girls were now also crying, and they gave Howard one last hug, and Harry and I shook his hand. Howard leaned into me and with a voice choked with some considerable emotion, he whispered, "Mr. Henson, one last thing."

"I know. I will keep the tie out of my hair, Howard."

"Oh, no sir," he shook his head gently, "good luck next Saturday beating that miserable, O'Malley."

I smiled and patted his shoulder. "Thanks Howard, I will do my best."

We walked to the Trans Whizzer as the staff opened the doors, dusted us all off and closed the doors for us. Harry gunned the big engine, put it in gear, and peeled a long strip of rubber out of the canopy and onto the road. Binky and I turned to wave goodbye to Howard as we saw him wave back while wiping his eyes with his handkerchief.

I had a vision in my mind and a hope in my heart that Howard Pailet was forever changed. We would never know for sure, but it would be nice to think that the next day he marched into his management office and demanded money instead of that lousy cup.

I wondered if the Black Bear Club would ever be the same.

We filled the ride home with conversations, laughs, and a few sobs from the four of us while we looked back on the weekend; it really was, as Howard would say, "Magical." Harry dropped Rose off first, and Binky and I said goodbye to Rose. Harry carried her luggage in and he was gone for quite a while. He must have had a long goodbye, and after this weekend that was understandable. Off we were to Binky's house, and after Harry and I struggled to get Binky's luggage up the front walk and into the front hallway, Harry left us alone so I could say goodbye to her.

I was a bit surprised, as she seemed sad and very quiet, but when I questioned her about it, she said she was just sad that the weekend was over and she was tired.

We had a long embrace and shared a goodbye kiss, and then she looked at me and said, "Thank you, Paul, I will never forget this weekend, it was the time of my life." After a quick glance down at the ground, then back up to my eyes, she spoke in almost a whisper, "And you are the man of my dreams."

She opened the door and stepped into the house, and she was gone.

"Oh well, emotional women," I said aloud to no one. I hustled out of there in case Mr. Hobnobber was hanging around in his hand cast and wanted to shoot hockey pucks around. I climbed in the front seat of the car and Harry reached out and shook my hand, then grabbed me around the neck and squeezed me until I could not breathe.

"You know that I meant that mushy stuff I said last night about you at the microphone. Especially, the part about you being the best!"

"Thank you, Harry, but I sure do enjoy breathing as well." Harry was a strong guy! "You know . . . Binky was very quiet, and she seemed sad."

"Oh yeah, I reckon Rose was too. I think they just are coming down from such an emotional high. It sure was a weekend to remember. I do not think any of us will ever forget it to be honest with you, twenty-seven."

I had to nod my head in agreement. It was quite an

adventure and experience.

We returned to Harry's house. We sat around the old kitchen table and filled Ronzo and Linda in on all the details of the fantastic weekend over a few Dingleberry and Big Boulder beers. Ronzo loved it and he wanted all the details, so we went on for hours, telling him all about it. We owed him, for sure, we owed him, and we had not wasted a minute of it, just as Ronzo had advised us.

"It sounds like you boys did me proud. Nothing, like a few old Paterson boys to tear the joint up."

We thanked him once more for what he had done for us, and I excused myself to head home. It had been a long couple of days, and I had to go to work tomorrow, and then get back to hockey practices and my training. I knew that I needed some time to unwind.

I went home, unpacked my bag, and put on, "Close to the Crevice" on my record player. I put on my headphones and settled in my bed to listen. I did not make it past the first five minutes, and I was sound asleep.

I did not speak to Harry, Rose, or Binky on Monday, as it was tough to make it through work, since I was still pretty tired from the weekend. I am sure that all four of us felt the same way as we all recovered, so I felt it best to leave everyone alone for a day or so. I knew I had practice on Thursday night and the big game with O'Malley and the Colonials on Saturday, so I needed to rest and get back into the swing.

It was Tuesday at dinnertime and I was going to go for a run before dinner when the phone rang. I answered it and it was Harry. "Hey come on over, whatcha doing?"

"I was just going for a run."

"Well, run over here to 20 John Street and that will be good enough. You are in great shape, y'all wear yourself out and then you get slow on your stick side low near the ice."

"Click." The line went dead.

I hung up and jogged over to Harry's house, and I was surprised to see Rose there with Harry.

"Hey guys . . . what is going on?" Rose waved weakly at me and forced a very slight smile, but she did not say anything.

Harry came over and put his arm around me. "C'mon in, buddy. We need to talk and show you something."

I was wondering what was going on, as Rose seemed sad and aloof, and Harry was speaking New Jersey, which meant he was serious.

"Hey, why is everyone so sad and serious?"

Rose and Harry did not answer me, but we walked into the house and then went to the kitchen and sat down at the table. No one was home, and it was a Tuesday at dinnertime at the Redmond house, so I really thought this was unusual. I began to get an ominous feeling over all of this. . ..

Rose looked at me and slid an envelope across the table to me.

I could see her eyes fill with tears and they started to fall down her cheeks.

"Binky asked me to deliver this to you in person, Paul. I promised her that I would. I feel so bad right now that I cannot even stand it!"

She abruptly stood up from the table, and Harry grabbed her and held her.

"I have to wait outside," Rose said, while she ran out of the room.

I looked at Harry and then at the envelope.

"What is this all about, Harry?"

Harry shook his head. "You better open it, and I will leave you alone. I need to check on Rose."

Harry left. I heard the front door open, and then close behind him. I stared at the envelope, then tore it open and pulled out a handwritten letter. I recognized the handwriting on the paper as Binky's writing; she wrote with a picture, perfect handwriting. I started to read it:

Dearest Paul,

This is by far the hardest thing that I have ever done in my life, but this past weekend made me really realize where I was in my life, and how you fit into it. I have made the very difficult decision to enroll in a university on the west coast in California and leave New Jersey. I plan to enroll in law school to study law and follow my father's example as an attorney. This past weekend made my mind up. I cannot emphasize enough how wonderful it was, and how I will never forget it, or any of the times we spent together. The truth of the matter is that I have fallen so deeply in love with you that I cannot stand it. You are everything a woman could ever want in a man. You are reliable, smart, trustworthy and strong. You are incredibly handsome, sexy, and a lover beyond compare. That is the trouble as we met excessively early in our lives. My research indicates that you are, in fact, the kind of man that a woman wants to marry, but not to date. How I cried each night, wishing that I could have met you five years later and then it all would be perfect. Right now, either right or wrong, I still have a lot more of life to experience. Although, I am sure this is the worst decision I will ever make in my life; I ask that we never see each other again, and that I leave in silence. I know that a very smart, lucky woman will recognize the prize that you are, and grab you, and you will be very happy for the rest of your lives. My compilation of recent statistics, show that usually happens within one or two weeks after a break up of a relationship. I may end up an old maid, never married, and regretting the day I signed this letter. Time will tell, but right now, I have to do this and break my heart at the same time. I shall always treasure our time together and I will have those memories forever.

Love Always,

Binky

I dropped the letter on the table and thought, 'Harry and his stupid theory'! All this time, he was right; I am nothing but a reliable, honest loser. I should have listened to him! It felt like I had just faced two hundred O'Malley's and that all of them had beaten me over the head with their sticks. I did not cry or even feel any emotion; I was too numb even to react. I stood up, folded the letter, and put it in my pocket. I walked slowly out to the front of the house where Harry and Rose stood next to the front gate. They both looked up when they saw me. Rose came over. She was sobbing almost out of control, as Harry stood next to me, and did not say anything, but he did place his hand on my shoulder.

Rose hugged me and then said, "I tried to talk to her. We talked for hours, but she is convinced that this is the right way to go. And she did not even have the courage to come here and tell you in person. She made us give you that stupid note. It is pitiful. I cannot believe it after the weekend we had together, what we all have is so special, and now it is all over!"

Her own emotions had overwhelmed poor Rose.

"It is all right, Rose. Sometimes, people make decisions, and they have to go where they think that life leads them. I am going to be fine . . . it will all be all right."

Rose looked up at me and said with the tears running down her cheeks, "It will never be the same Paul, never, ever. You two are perfect for each other, her quirky personality and your steady, calm, and honest approach. It was amazing the chemistry that you two had. All of your life, you look to find a love like that . . . something so special with someone . . . you just do not toss it away. She loves you with all of her heart. It makes no sense what so ever, it is just her stupid research. Sometimes, I swear, I want to stick a sock in her mouth when she starts with that stuff!"

It seemed as if Mr. Hobnobber had some company in the sock stuffing department; folks were now lining up to stuff them in Binky's mouth.

Rose then turned, walked away, and she got into the Trans Whizzer, and sat in the passenger seat. I could hear her crying even with the door closed.

"Hey, are you all right, buddy?" Harry said as he placed his arm around me. "I tried to tell you, but you would not believe me that my theory was right. I am sorry, twenty-seven that I was dead on and pegged you as a doormat."

That comment sure made me feel a lot better.

"I am good, Harry, and no, you were right. I was dumb not to listen to you. It may take me a little while, but I learned my lesson. No more, Mr. Nice Guy for me. You had better take Rose home, she is pretty torn up."

I sighed and looked up at the sky for no real reason, and then back at Harry. Maybe I just needed to collect my thoughts.

"Hey, do I really get soft on shots low on the stick side when I am tired?"

Harry nodded his head to indicate yes. He looked at me as if he did not believe that I was going to be all right, but he gave me a little punch in the arm and walked away. He went in the Trans Whizzer, pulled something out, and then came back.

"Here, you will need these more than I will, so you can borrow them for as long as you want." I looked up and saw that he was handing me the Crystal Zirconium cassette tapes.

I took them and said, "Thanks, Harry."

"Sure thing. I will call you, or you can call me if you need me. I am here for you, Paul."

Harry and Rose took off in the Trans Whizzer and I watched as it went down the road and then turned the corner onto Geyer Street.

I was alone now on the front doorstep of 20 John Street, right next to where Harry used to tie poor Mr. Bug up on the front railing. I actually wished he were still there, so that I could punch his face in and watch all of his air go out. I sat down on the step and sighed. I had so many happy times here at this house over the years, but this one is going to have to go into the bad memory book.

It is amazing how a moment can change everything. One stinking little moment in time comes along, and everything changes, just like that.

Actually, it is very profound.

I stood up and started to jog home, and I thought to myself, well at least, I have some more time now to work on that low stick side location.

This time, it was not another ending to a perfect Harry and Paul day.

I played the game on Saturday against the Colonials like a man possessed. I refused to lose this one. There was no way, no how, that I was going to lose. I did it for all the folks at the Black Bear Club. I did it for Howard, Harry, Rose, Binky, the old man, the guys from the shop, and Mr. Hobnobber.

Most of all, I did it for myself.

I had found that hockey eased the pain deep down in my stomach that had appeared when I had read the note from Binky. Now, this dull ache just would not go away. There was no way that O'Malley and the Colonials stood a chance, thirty-five shots on goal and I allowed zero goals. I was so in the flow that even my teammates were afraid of me. O'Malley was wild out there, ransacking the ice like an out of control, wild barbarian, crashing around, serving two fighting penalties before finally earning another classic, obscenity-laden ejection from the game with a double major set of penalties. It was an ugly display, even for a seasoned goon like O'Malley.

No one could get a marble by me, nonetheless, a hockey puck. I looked up in the stands to see Harry, Rose, the old man and some guys from the shop cheering me on, and for a second, I thought about how Binky would usually be there too, but I shook it off. After the game, I showered, dressed, and met Harry and Rose out in front of the arena.

"Wow, no more Mr. Nice Guy. I reckon you were fired up tonight Paul. Great game, man alive—you even taunted O'Malley from the goal. I never saw that before," Harry praised my performance.

Rose just smiled, held my hand, and weakly spoke, "You played great, Paul."

She still seemed so sad. It seemed the last few days as if her spirit was lost. I thanked them and they invited me out for some drinks and music, but I told them I was tired and had to get home. I just did not feel like it right now.

I went home and spoke to the old man about the game for a while. He was thrilled that I had taken out the Colonials and O'Malley. I think he sensed some of my pain about Binky. I had not given my parents any deep or in-depth details, just a vague story about how she was moving away to attend school. The old man did not press me; he kept the conversation strictly about the game.

We said goodnight. I climbed into bed, and fell asleep very quickly, when I heard the telephone ring in my sleepy mind. I was half-awake when the old man burst into my bedroom and shook me.

"Hey wake up, it is Rose. She's on the phone and sounds really upset, something about an accident."

I jumped up and quickly got to the phone.

"What is wrong, Rose?"

By now, my old man and my mother were standing right next to me.

"Oh Paul, please come quickly over to the Willow Brook

Tavern. We went for some drinks after the game, and someone rammed into the Trans Whizzer in the parking lot. It is so bad."

"Are you hurt? Is Harry hurt?"

"Oh, we are fine. We were not even in the car. It was sitting in a parking space in the lot, and some hippie chick in one of those weird, hippie, wildly painted, Wagon Bus things, rammed it in half. The car is bad and Harry is a wreck."

"I will be right there."

I hung up the phone, filled my parents in, and assured them that no one was hurt. We all were relieved about that, but the fact that the condition of the Trans Whizzer sounded as if it was a total wreck—well that might be a little more pain than Harry could handle.

I jumped in the jeep and took off towards the tavern. The old Paul would be a good law-abiding citizen, but the new Paul was going to break some speed limits here and there, or at least as many of them that my old jeep could actually exceed. I thought if a police officer pulled me over, I would tell him the truth, that I was on a rescue mission for my best friend and his gal.

No more, Mr. Nice Guy!

I made it there in no time to find a wrecking truck with flashing lights turned on, and a police car in the parking lot. I pulled my jeep over to the side and I saw Rose running up to me.

"Oh, thank goodness you are here, Paul," she said as she hugged me when I stepped out of the jeep.

"Sure, Rose, are you ok?"

"Yes, yes, I am fine, but Harry needs you. He is over here." Rose led me by my hand over to the side of the police car where Harry sat in the back seat with his hands covering his face.

"Hey Harry, it is all right, you guys were not hurt that is the main thing." I knelt down in front of him and put my hands on his arms.

"Paul, thanks for coming. What a disaster," Harry said as he took his hands away and then shook my hand.

"Look at what is left of my glorious machine, come over here and look at what some spaced out hippie chick did to the world's greatest car."

We walked over and looked at the Trans Whizzer as the hook and winch pulled the car onto the back of a flatbed wrecking truck. It was bad. The impact of the collision, folded the Trans Whizzer in half like an accordion as it looked like the hippie chick had hit it full force right in the center and "t-boned" the car. Due to the roof being a T-top roof, it folded the car in half at the weak points.

"Hey Harry, cars can be fixed, people cannot always be fixed. The main thing is that you and Rose are safe, and that no one was hurt."

A big heavy-set guy, smoking a smelly cigar, working the wrecking truck hydraulics handle, heard me say that you could fix the car, and he piped in, "A lot of cars can be fixed pal, but this is not one of them. I can tell it is a total wreck job, once these Trans Whizzers bend like that you cannot straighten them out, even with a frame machine."

I frowned at him and waved my hand at him to shut his big trap. "Thanks a lot pal that makes my buddy feel a lot better."

He shrugged his shoulders and went back to operating the handle, "Just sayin' the truth, man."

When Harry heard that, he wandered back in a daze to the police car. Rose and I tried our best to console him. The policeman came over and looked at me.

"Hey pal, are you the friend that he said would come?"

"Yes officer, I am."

"Good, I need some info and they are pretty torn up so maybe you can help."

I answered many general questions. He told me where Harry could pick up the police report and where the Trans

Whizzer was going to be towed to.

"Such a shame, I did not want to say it in front of your friends, but what a fabulous automobile."

I looked at the policeman who was around forty years old or so, with close-cropped hair under his police uniform cap and a full round face. He looked like he was a very kind man. I could tell that he had some feelings for the sad fate of the beloved Trans Whizzer.

"I am afraid they cannot fix that one."

"Yes, there sure were a lot of memories in that car, sir."

The officer looked at me and put his pen down. He seemed to sympathize. Perhaps he recalled a classic car that he had at one time.

"I bet so. You must have owned the world with a car like that at your age."

"We sure did, sir. What happened to the chick that rammed the car? Was she stoned or bombed out of her mind?"

"No, she was not. She was straight as an arrow. I tested her for everything but diabetes since I felt so bad for your pal. She was just dreaming, misjudged the turn, hit the Trans Whizzer in the center, and folded that car right up. It sure was strange that a hippie bus could do that. The bus hardly had any damage. I was amazed that she was able to drive it away with just a crushed in front bumper. The thing is built like a tank." The policeman looked at his paperwork and then back up at me.

"I wrote her a ticket for being a dreamer and having the accident and told her that she had better take off now, because your buddy was pretty upset. She wanted to apologize to him in person and give him some hippie, lucky charm or something, but I chased her off. She had bright yellow hair man, bright yellow hair." The officer looked at me and my hair and I knew he was enjoying utilizing the word "hippie" in this conversation.

He smiled a little out of the side of his mouth as he said,

"She was weird, but cute. She was very pretty, and I could tell she felt really bad. She seemed nice and let me tell you again, she was really pretty."

I now understood that the police officer felt the hippie chick was pretty. He had mentioned it to me multiple times already.

"I searched that bus for everything. I was sure I could bust her for dope and earn a big promotion. She was clean as a whistle, I could not find a single thing, just a bunch of hippie books, music, cardboard cards that she called tallower cards or something like that, and some candles she said she used in her yoga class."

"No kidding, well that just fits with things that happen to us, we always seem to have a cloud of weirdness that follows us around. This has been a bad week, to say the least."

The officer finished writing down some info and handed me a paper with the towing company's contact information.

"Sometimes it is like that, young man. It cannot always be perfect, you know. Hey, get this. The hippie chick's name is Sky Blue."

"Sky blue?" I had never heard a name like that before.

"Yeah, yeah, yeah, first name spelled s-k-y and last name b-l-u."

I wondered why some folks named their kids such strange names and then I thought of Mr. and Mrs. Hobnobber. I thanked the officer and told him I would take Rose and Harry home in my jeep.

I started to turn away when he tapped me on the arm and said, "Say, not to change the subject, but I think I know you. Don't you play goal for the hockey club out on the island that plays the Rockets once in a while over in Great Falls at Ice Land? I go to a lot of those games. They are wild."

I was amazed that he had recognized me.

"Yes, officer, that is me. You have a good memory. Most people do not recognize me."

"Nah, it is easy. It is all that hair. Say, aren't you supposed to not tie that all up because the chick you are dating, hates it like that?"

"Not anymore, sir, I tie it up all the time. In fact, I am thinking of cutting it all off next week."

The officer looked at me a little strange but he continued, "I have a police buddy who works in Rockland County in New York, who has to drag that crazy O'Malley out of fights on the rink all the time. That guy is a nutcase, but my buddy tells me you are the best goalie in the league."

"Thank you, sir, I appreciate that."

I shook his hand again, and I met Harry and Rose. We all climbed into the seats of the jeep and we took off. Harry sat in the back and Rose sat in the front. It was a depressing, long ride home, as Rose was very upset and Harry did not say too much.

Rose spoke softly, while we rolled through the night, "I just cannot even believe how badly things have gone since we were all so happy one week ago, tonight. It is almost like some horrible twist of fate or something that all this bad stuff has happened. Now some strange, hippie chick with yellow hair, destroys the Trans Whizzer. I hope Binky is happy at all this bad luck that she started." Rose looked over at me and was very stern. "I told you, Paul, things would never be the same."

I reached out and took Rose by the hand to comfort her, as I had to admit she was right. Sometimes, you have to realize that things will never be the same ever again, and accept the changes as hard as they are to deal with. We pulled into the driveway of the apartment where Rose lived. She leaned in the back seat, kissed Harry goodnight, and held his hand.

"Stay here, I will call you tomorrow to check on you."

"All right there darlin.' Paul, please walk Rose up to the door for me and make sure she gets in safely will you," was all the stunned Harry could manage to say.

I walked Rose up to the front door and she held my hand when we got to the door.

"Paul, I cannot tell you how badly I feel about all of this. You are the best, and I swear if Harry and I were not in a relationship, that I would chase you myself, now that Binky went off and lost her mind. I do not care if she is my best friend. I swear that girl is crazier than O'Malley."

"Rose, I know I can say this without you or Harry taking it wrong, but I love you as I love Harry. You two are my best friends. You are very special to me. We have shared an awful lot of adventures together over the last year or so. You and I are so much alike in our roles, you working hard to keep Harry under wraps, and me in my role of keeping Binky on track."

I looked down, and even in the darkness, I could see the tears building in her eyes.

"Remember what Howard said about the four of us having a special bond. You said yourself, no matter what happens, they cannot take our memories away from us. You are also very special for putting up with Harry, being the steady guiding light in his wild and rocky world, you are great."

She had tears on her cheeks now, and she reached up and gave me a hug. I could feel her body shivering in the cold air. Rose was a very emotional young lady who always carried her emotions on her sleeve. I may have been wrong, but I saw in her eyes that perhaps the whirlwind lifestyle and constant action and drama of Harry and his world had finally taken a toll on poor Rose. I had seen that same look in Joyce's eyes once before, and I always knew that it would take a special woman to calm Harry down once and for all.

She wiped the tears away from her eyes and laughed.

"You are so tall, and I am way down here. I understand Paul, I love you too . . . I really do. I can't even tell you how much I adore you. As of late, in fact all of this week, I just do not know where Harry and I are going. Sometimes, the things that he does that I used to love just, annoy me now."

Perhaps I should not have, but I couldn't help but laugh aloud at the statement. Rose smiled, and she giggled a little.

"I am sure I am not telling you something you do not know because you know him better than anyone!" I did understand, more than what she actually could know.

"I do, goodnight Rose."

I let her hand go, she said goodnight, opened the door, and went in. I climbed back in the jeep and let Harry stay in the back seat. I reached around, picked up the Crystal tape, and put it in the tape deck.

"Thanks there, buddy. Is Rose, all right?" Harry was speaking normal New Jersey now.

"She is upset. It has been a tough couple of days."

"Sure, has been there, twenty-seven. Hey, is Trio Liquors still open? Can this old wreck make it before they close up?"

"Sure, I can make it. She is not pretty, but she still rolls."

I detected just the slightest smile on his face.

"Let's get a bottle of decent bourbon, put this old jeep in four-wheel drive and head up High Mountain in North Haledon. The two of us and Crystal, can share it up on the very top there. I bet the view tonight's pretty awesome. You love all this cold weather."

"We can do that Harry. We can do that."

11

The Night Sky Turns Blue

It had been a week or so since that tragic week as well as the demise of the Trans Whizzer. I had spoken to Harry on the phone, but between hockey and work, I had been busy and we could not get together. He had picked up a rental car from the car insurance company while they all sorted out the fate of the Trans Whizzer, so I knew he was mobile. He sounded depressed on the phone when I had spoken with him, but I guess that was to be expected.

I had some good days and some bad days, but to be honest, if I was not very busy with hockey or work, the days were mostly bad. Between the loss of the Trans Whizzer and Binky taking off, the churning in my mind and deep in my stomach just would not stop. Christmas was right around the corner now, and the Redmond family usually went crazy and all out for the holidays. We were just a few weeks away from the annual Redmond family excursion to head out to the mountains to cut down Christmas trees. I was not really looking forward to that, and it usually was a highlight of the year for all of us. This year, I just had a sense that something was different, and it was going to be very low key for Harry and me.

My parents did not push me. They had met Binky a few times, and they really liked her, but I think they had a strong sense that it was a little rough for me, so they stayed away from even mentioning her. I came home from work on a Friday and I actually mentally felt good. I thought that perhaps if Harry was not going out with Rose, then maybe we could do something together. I had off for the weekend, as I had played a Wednesday game in which I had taken a few hard shots, and I was a little sore. I had taken one hard shot under my chest protector up around the collarbone, and it was a little difficult to move my arm. I think my coach felt sorry for me, so he gave me a practice off to rest and heal up a little.

When I walked in the back door after work, my mom greeted me, hugged me gently, and asked about my chest.

"I am good, Mum. I have a large bruise there, but right now, it is just a little sore."

Mum frowned at me and waved her hand in the air. My mother did not understand hockey, nor was it her favorite thing to see her son wounded and stitched up from my latest injuries.

"That horrid game, it is so blooming dangerous. I worry about you playing all the time. Oh, you received a package today from the Black Bear Club. I put it up in your room."

"Thanks Mum."

I felt the old man's eyes watching me from behind as he studied my body language for any signs. They both knew the package more than likely was going to bring up some bad memories. I knew what it was before I even looked at it. I knew the contents of the envelope would be the copies of the photographs that they had taken of all of us.

When I picked up the envelope and saw the "DO NOT BEND" stamps all over it, I knew I was right. While I sat on the corner of my bed, I went to open it, but I just could not bring myself to do it, so I took the envelope and tossed it in my desk drawer. I put it right next to the letter that Binky had written to me.

It would suit me fine if I never opened those two packages ever again.

I sat back down on the edge of my bed in my old bedroom and lowered my head, while looking around the tiny bedroom that I had grown up in, within this old house on Belmont Avenue. I had many memories here, from being a little stupid kid to now, when I was on the edge of responsible manhood. Right then and there, I had the stark, cold revelation of just how much I had cared for Binky. It was a moment of dread that I never wanted to face or admit . . . but it was true. My own words had come back to haunt me.

She had consumed my entire soul.

I loved her with all of my heart, and now she was gone. I had to admit that it had torn me apart, and it had shredded me into pieces like no other event in my entire life.

I called over to Harry's house, and Ronzo answered. We spoke, and he told me that Linda and Harry were working on the song and that I should come right over.

"I have not seen you in a while. I reckon you guys have had a rough patch, come on over, and we can share a few Big Boulder and Dingleberry beers and relax."

"You got it, Ronzo."

The perfect remedy! A night of laughs with the Redmonds! I hung up the phone and headed towards 20 John Street. Walking in the front door, Harry was standing in the dining room, while finger rolling away on the banjo, Linda was sitting down in a chair next to him, and she was singing sweetly:

"All those things, I used to love about you now just drive me crazy. I reckon it is time for us to move on and say goodbye because our love has grown lazy. I will always care about you and miss your lovin' heart, but darlin' the sad time has come for us to part."

Linda was singing her heart out and she really had a great voice. I was puzzled because it was the same catchy, wonderful tune as the favorite car song, but it now had different words.

The song finished, and Mr. Redmond, Ronzo, and I

stood and clapped.

"That was amazing! But what is with the new words?"

Linda stood up, came over, and gave me a big hug. I could tell that she wanted to say something to me.

"Are you all right, Paul? We all loved Binky, but you are going to make some woman happy someday. I swear I cannot believe what that girl is thinking. She is crazier than that psychopath O'Malley is. If I was fifteen years younger, and I did not have old Ronzo, I would chase you myself, and so would many other women. You are going to do fine."

"Yeah, yeah, yeah, but, look on the bright side, Paul. I reckon you can tie all that hair back now anytime you want," Ronzo said as he came over and slapped me on the back. They were all doing their best to cheer me up.

"Thanks guys, I appreciate the kind words. I am doing fine. Life is full of hard lessons, but it is always good to be with great friends like all of you. I will be fine. Hey, what is with the song and the new lyrics?"

"We will let Harry tell you that, y'all want a Big Boulder beer Paul? Pop, you want a Dingleberry?"

Mr. Redmond shook his head and answered, "Get me a Big Boulder. Those Dingleberry beers are way too sweet." Ronzo nodded and then pointed at me for my answer.

"A Big Boulder, Ronzo, thanks."

I sat next to Harry.

"Well, I changed the song because Rose and I decided to call it quits. Actually, to be honest, she dumped me, Paul."

I felt my heart sink in my chest. I was right about the look I saw in her eyes that night. It was now a total tragedy, the four of us . . . our special group of people no longer existed. All the four of us had left now was a pile of spent memories and torn emotions.

"I am so sorry, Harry. I love Rose."

"Yeah, I love her too, twenty-seven. I told you that I felt it would never be long term. I guess she just could not deal with you and the Binky situation, the Trans Whizzer getting smashed, and the . . . as she said, fake worlds that I live in. She wanted me just to be myself. I refuse to do that right now at this point in my life. I have to act the way I do, at least with her I do. But on a bright note, she gave me this great line for our song when she dumped me."

Harry picked up the banjo, rolled a little over the strings, playing the main melody, and the key hook for the song.

He stopped playing and put the instrument down.

"Yup, it is perfect. All those things, I used to love about you, now just drive me crazy. So, I shot home here after we broke up, wrote all the lyrics, changed the name to the same line and we are good to go. We finished the song! Linda is having it published next week, and she and I will head for a recording studio to lay down the track."

Harry stood up and waved his arms in the air over his head.

"Big hit, buddy, a big hit!"

Ronzo returned with our beers and we popped them open.

"Thanks, Ronzo. No kidding Harry, youse guys are really going to do it?"

"Sure, Linny and I are ready. I tell you that it is going to be awesome. Hey, I know Rose will call you. She really wanted to chat with you. I know you guys love each other and are really close, so I understand."

"I will speak with her, sure Harry."

He nodded and asked, "Hey, did you get the pictures from Howard?"

"Oh boy, I would not have brought that one up, Harry," Ronzo said as he took a long sip of his Dingleberry beer.

"I did, and I did not open them, did you?"

"Nope and I reckon, at this point, that I never will!"

We slapped each other on the back. Harry went to grab me when he remembered that my chest was still sore. . .. I held my hands up in defense, so he backed off.

"Oh well, the end of the Stinky and Toes era, and on to something else. You never know what is around the corner for Harry and Paul."

Just as Harry said that, the front doorbell rang. This time of the year, the Christmas crazy Redmonds changed their main doorbell to a "Jingle Bells" doorbell, so off it went dashing through the snow for about five minutes. Ronzo got up and opened the door, and Harry and I sat on our chairs watching to see whom it was. The door opened and there stood a tall, slender young lady, wearing no hat and a light overcoat. The one thing that we noticed right away was the color of her hair. She had a short haircut and her hair was a bright, electric blue color.

Ronzo smiled as Cocoa came running in with Piggy in his mouth to see who was at the door. Ronzo asked, "Can I help you, little lady?"

"I am sorry to disturb you, but I am looking to speak with Mr. Harry M. Redmond Junior. Is he at home, please?"

"Well, c'mon in, little lady, you can catch a cold out there with no hat on, just wearing that little thin coat. Harry is in here, right over here."

The two of them walked into the house from the porch and the young lady stood in front of us, smiling. She was carrying a paper bag in one hand and she waved to us with the other. She was wearing torn up bell bottom hip hugger jeans, sewn in random locations with peace signs and a patch that said, "Peace and love." She had on a tie-dyed tee shirt with a big yellow peace sign in the center and old, dirty looking sneakers.

I vaguely remembered the police officer telling me about the hippie chick who wiped out the Trans Whizzer, but he told me she had yellow hair. Maybe this is her sister because this chick had blue hair. Harry spotted her and stood up. He was a little puzzled, but after all, she was a female, and far be it for Harry not to say hello to a female. I had to admit even though she looked a little unusual and did have short electric blue hair that she was very pretty, with sparkling clear eyes and a great smile.

Harry stood up while checking out the attractive young lady. I saw his eyes scan her up and down very quickly.

"I reckon, I am Harry Junior and this here is my best buddy Paul John Henson, the best doggone, ice hockey goalie in the world, that dog there with the Piggy in his mouth is Cocoa, the world's smartest dog, and the big guy over there is Ronzo. How can I help ya there, little lady?"

"I do not know how to approach this but I wanted to come by and apologize for what I did to your beloved car." She reached her hand out towards Harry and said, "I am Sky Blu, Mr. Redmond. I spell my name, b-l-u. There is no e at the end."

Oh no, I thought, it is the hippie chick!

I heard Ronzo let a big puff of air out when he heard her name and he held on tight for the imminent explosions. Cocoa grabbed Piggy and ran off to hide behind the couch. Harry stopped short and he put his hand down.

The smile faded from his face in horror.

"You! I reckon you have an awful lot of nerve coming here after you destroyed the world's greatest car and a part of my very soul!"

Harry waved his hands and arms towards the front door.

"I think it is time for you to leave there, Blue Cloud. What are you, some Indian chick or something? Who would name a girl, Blue Cloud? That is almost as bad as naming a girl Binky!" Harry was becoming loud and angry. This scene was turning badly very quickly.

I spotted the eye of the tiger come upon Harry in both of his eyes, and that meant some serious intenseness was upon him.

"Hey, easy there, buddy." I stood up, patted Harry on the back, and went into my problem-solving mode.

I could see the young lady was very upset, and she had tears welling up in those pretty clear eyes.

"My name is Sky Blu, not Blue Cloud, and like I said . . . I am very sorry. It was a terrible accident. I knew from my horoscope that I should not have gone out, but I just wanted to go home from my candlelight yoga class, and I cut through the parking lot and hit your car."

She was crying now, and Ronzo and I looked at each other.

"Hit my car! Hit my car! You knocked it to the next county, you crazed, horoscope reading, hippie, whacko!"

She was really bawling now. I managed to have Harry sit down, and I turned to Sky Blu.

"Look, it has been a really bad couple of weeks for the two of us and the accident is a very soft spot right now. It might be best if you go."

"I—I—I—just wanted to give you this, because I sensed that it has been a difficult time for Mr. Redmond. I pulled his tarot cards and saw that he had some turmoil in his life and I wanted to do the right thing."

Ronzo jumped in and said, "Look, please do not cry. Sit down here. Would you like a glass of water? Please do not be so upset." She nodded. Ronzo had her sit, and I handed her a tissue as she slowly started to stop crying.

"Give me what?" Harry asked her abruptly. "You said you wanted to give me something?"

Ronzo returned with the water and she took a sip, started to regain her composure, and she stopped crying just a little.

She started to speak and almost answered his question, when she suddenly stood up, took her right arm, and crossed her chest. She then placed the palm of her right hand on her left shoulder and closed her eyes. Sky Blu stood there for a minute or two while we all sat and wondered what she was doing. It looked like she was hugging herself with one arm. I just stared at her, as did

Ronzo and Harry.

Oh boy, do we ever, ever, ever have a normal stretch in our lives? On the other hand, is there always some kind of strange influence from another world that circled us like a black cloud of weirdness?

As she stood there in front of him, I saw Harry checking out her slim, trim, very attractive female figure. His eyes were going up and down her body, studying her. Sky Blu had all of her parts and pieces in all the correct places.

I have known Harry a very long time and he may have been very angry at this hippie chick, but he was not going to pass up an opportunity to check out an attractive female form, even if he wanted to strangle her. I spotted his posture change just a little. Like I said, I knew my best buddy like a book.

Sky Blu lowered her arm, opened her eyes, and then spoke, "I am sorry but I needed to heal with a quick Reiki application. I wanted to give you this sage smudge stick to help with all the negative energy around here due to my horrible intrusion in your lives."

Sky handed Harry the paper bag, and he stared down inside it. He then reached inside of it and pulled out what looked like a block of dried herbs.

"You come along, smash my car into bits, then give me a big block of some funny looking, smelly stuff? Are you for real there, honey?" Harry just stared up at her.

"Oh, it is healing herbs, you light it up."

Ronzo smiled and said, "Now you're talking there, Sky. I know we had something like that over in Nam. Can we try it now, Harry?"

"Oh no, Mr. Ronzo you do not smoke this, you light it up and wave it in the air in the corners of the house, on the porches, in the basement, and all the rooms in the house and allow it to smolder. The smoke attaches to all the negative energy around, pulls it out, and purges it to go away. That allows the positive energy to infiltrate where the negative used to be. In addition to my unfortunate accident, has there been other negative energy and happenings in your lives? In studying and looking at your friend Mr. Henson here, I see that he is a very attractive man, but he has deep sadness in his eyes. It is very powerful, like something has hurt him greatly very recently."

The four of us looked at each other, and I started to think. Who is this pretty hippie chick? How can she sense what has happened to me as well as to us? It was a little strange even for our world.

I had to admit there was something convincing about her, as well as captivating. She was not only pretty but also very well spoken, and for a hippie chick, she was no airhead. I could tell that Sky Blu was smart.

"This is the least I can do to make up for the trouble I have caused and to do my best to say I am sorry." Linda came down now from the second floor to see who was here, and Ronzo introduced her to Sky.

"I would be honored if you would let me do this, Mr. Redmond. I feel so bad about what I have done."

Harry looked at her very intensely. His eyes had changed, as well as his body posture.

I saw his expression change and his demeanor soften. "Harry, please call me Harry, please don't call me, Mr. Redmond."

Oh yes, Harry was warming up to her!

"Well, go ahead there, Sky. I guess we do not have anything to lose. It really cannot get much worse than it has been for the last two weeks, maybe this old smudge-a-dub-dubber will work."

Harry handed her back the smudge stick.

Sky smiled and explained, "They can be difficult to light up, so it may take me a few tries to get it going."

Sky reached in her pocket, took out a headband, and placed it around her head. She then placed a peace necklace around her neck. Taking the stick in her hand, Sky worked on it with a lighter and after a few false starts; she managed successfully to light the stick up. It flickered and some light smoke drifted up into the air.

Sky then walked around the house, speaking in a low, inaudible whisper, waving the stick in the air in all the rooms, lingering in the corners, and then she went on the porches and into the basement. She then let it smolder, and she placed it on a plate on the dining room table. It actually did not smell badly, but I still felt about the same as I did before, I had noticed no change. Then again, I was not quite sure what my expectations were or what was really happening tonight.

Mr. Redmond, who had come barreling down the stairs when he smelled the smudge stick, wondering what was on fire, now joined Ronzo, Harry, Linda, and me in the living room. He laughed when he found what the strange smell was, and Harry introduced his father to Sky.

I was not at all surprised at Mr. Redmond's reaction. Nothing really came as a surprise to the Redmonds.

Not smudge sticks, alien landings in the neighborhood, wild lions roaming the yards and alleys of the neighborhood, earthquakes, exploding swimming pools, they just took it all in stride. It was just another day at 20 John Street.

Ronzo was going around sniffing the smoke in his nose just in case he had a slight chance to relive his glory days. And Sky started to reach for her jacket.

"Once more, I am very sorry for the trouble I caused. I sincerely hope that the smudge stick pulls out the negative energy and that things improve for you."

I reached for her jacket to give it to her when she saw me wince and pull back and grab my arm and chest.

"Oh my, are you hurt, Mr. Henson?"

Harry explained, "He is always hurt somewhere on his body during the hockey season there, Sky. Like I said before, Paul is a semi-pro ice hockey goalie and he is a little dinged up from a game this week."

"I am so sorry. I have something in my van for you."

She was gone out the door in a flash and returned just as quickly with a little bottle of something.

"This is some essential oil, my favorite in fact. It is Lemon Herb Balm."

Ronzo circled back in to see what this was all about; I still think he was hoping for some different kind of herbs that Sky might be bringing in for us.

"You can rub it right here on your shoulder and then apply strong pressure on this spot right here to heal your chest injury. Sky reached over and placed her finger right on a spot about halfway down my shoulder.

"Thank you, Sky. I will give it a try tonight." I thought how this gal carried an awful lot in her hippie Wagon Bus; she was like a rolling hippie, homeopathic distributor.

"Well, I need to be off . . . it was nice to meet everyone. I hope that it all improves and becomes a lot better for everyone."

Harry cleared his throat. "You know, Sky, we were going to order some pizza and have some beers, and some wine. Would you like to stay and see if that smudger thing worked? We have had a lot of bumpy roads as of late, we might need a second application."

Harry was extending an invitation, and it looked like his attitude towards Sky had come around about three hundred and sixty degrees. The other thing that I noticed was that when he spoke to her, he spoke in regular New Jersey speak, suddenly, he had lost the phony twang and cowboy influences.

"Why, that is very nice of you, Harry. Does this mean I am forgiven?"

"Well, sure, I can see that you sincerely feel terrible about crushing my prized automobile and I know it was really just an accident. So, yes, let's go with forgiven."

Harry smiled, extended his hand out and the two of them shook hands. There was a sparkle in Harry's eye when he looked at Sky that I do not think I had ever seen before; it was indeed different. It was not ogling; it was not gawking. I do not know how to describe it other than it was special, very special.

Perhaps there were one or two very small ice patches forming here and there in Hades.

We ordered the pizza and opened some more beers, poured some wine, and we all laughed, talked, and had a good time. There was nothing on earth like a simple Redmond gathering over the kitchen table at good old 20 John Street. It was truly a special place. A place filled with very special people.

As the night continued, I studied Sky and watched Harry and her talking in the corner, while she sipped wine and Harry told stories. She laughed at his jokes and she was mesmerized as he went off, telling her only a small sampling of some of our adventures together. Harry was in his glory, and I noticed something very different about him as he spoke with her. He was acting like, well, for lack of a better description, he was acting like Harry M. Redmond Junior. He was not Mr. Big Shot, Big Tex, old nose cracker and teeth spitter, or any other assorted alter egos.

Harry was just being himself.

I realized how much I missed that because the real Harry M. Redmond Jr. was a special kind of guy. If he just was being his plain old self, he actually was a pretty amazing and lovable person.

Rose was right; he just needed to be himself.

Harry's storytelling contained no embellishments or gross exaggerations. He easily waltzed through story after story because, as hard as many of the stories were to believe—they were indeed all true.

We sat around and talked for many hours. Patty and the Big Spike joined Harry, Sky, Ronzo, Mr. Redmond, Linda,

Cocoa, and me as they stopped by for a visit. They were also able to meet Sky, and Sky laughed until she had tears in her eyes, when Harry introduced her in a tongue-in-cheek manner, "As the super-cool hippie chick that destroyed my beloved Trans Whizzer."

Harry just had a way that he could not stay mad at people for long, and vice versa, it was just the way that he was. Harry and Linda played the new song for Sky and the rest of the gang, and we all cheered and clapped. It turned out to be quite a night, and I was having a great time. I may have consumed a few more of the Big Boulder suds than I usually did, but it was all good. The beers made me a little numb, and that was not such a bad thing tonight.

I stepped out on the front steps of the porch for a little breather in the cold night air. I thrived on the cold; I took a deep breath and looked up at the clear sky. So many memories right here on these front steps. I thought about how much this old porch had seen; from Mr. Bug, to unloading pool parts with a rope over the big tree in front of me, to Ronzo carrying his precious jar of Christmas cheer to that old bomb of a work truck under the watchful eyes of Mr. Redmond and Mr. Porter.

So many good times, but now, I just did not know, it all seemed so bad.

I wondered where Binky was tonight and what she was doing right at this very moment. The night was fantastic and John Street twinkled with Christmas lights that lit up all the houses in a festive glow. Even in this worn out, gritty neighborhood there was beauty all around. I could not even imagine how things had changed in just a short period of a few weeks; it was like one big, long blur. I was just looking out at the sky, thinking, when the front door opened behind me. I tried to shift gears and hide my mood when I saw that it was Sky.

"Oh, I am sorry. I was just catching a little air here," I said as I moved over to let her down the steps.

"Excuse me, Paul. I just needed to get something out of my bus for Harry."

I moved over to the side so Sky could pass by me. She stopped and looked at me. She was indeed very pretty, her eyes lit up in the cold dark evening air.

"They are all wonderful people, aren't they?"

I smiled, "The best. You cannot even describe them to anyone. It has to be experienced. I would do anything for them. They are like a second family to me. I have known them all since I was ten years old."

Sky leaned on the rail and looked up at the Christmas lights twinkling on the house. She seemed to be searching for a moment or two for some words.

"Harry is amazing. He makes me laugh so hard. He is so handsome, gregarious, and unique."

I thought that was a very good description of Harry. This hippie chick was dead on. She seemed star struck by Harry. I almost wondered if it had been a classic case of love at first sight.

"He speaks of you with such admiration, such an honor. It is as if you both are one, even closer than brothers are. You are a dedicated friend to Harry and I have only heard a few of your adventures together."

Her face took on a deeper, more serious expression.

"I can tell you are a great man, Paul. I can tell by your aura, by your inner strength. You are a great athlete. I can tell by your muscle tone and build."

I was a bit puzzled at her comments, and I tilted my head and raised my eyebrows a little to her. Sky Blu's forthright and open analysis of me surprised me quite a bit.

"Do you always analyze people that you just recently have met?"

Sky came off the rail a bit, and she laughed. "I am so sorry. I should have explained, but that is what I do for a living at the Center for Learning. That is where I work, you see, I help people to be in touch with whom they are, and where they may end. May I continue or am I offending you?"

I nodded to show that I was fine with this. In fact, now I was intrigued.

She then continued, "You are very spiritual, you believe in God and what is right and kind. There is an inner light and fire inside of you Paul, you can feel it, and others can sense it. You would make a great religious leader."

I turned and looked at her. I felt a cold shiver go down my spine. I did not say a word or change my expression.

"Harry taps your inner strength that is why sometimes you feel drained. He only pretends to be strong, but he looks to you for the strength, reliability, and the steadiness that he sometimes lacks."

Sky looked at me and smiled.

"When were you born? Do you know your zodiac sign?"

I did not know why, but I answered her right away. I had no qualms about telling her.

"November. I am a Scorpio."

Sky nodded her head as if that is what she had already known.

"That makes sense, from some stories I have heard. You are indeed a born leader, a great lover, an insightful person who is in control and who solves problems."

This was becoming a very interesting situation. Who is this chick with this electric blue hair that she can detect some of our innermost traits after only a few hours of knowing us? Even for our world, this was very strange.

"Some young lady somewhere has made a terrible, terrible, error."

Sky put her hand on my shoulder and gently turned me a little towards her.

"You know, it is good to cry, Paul. You will cry again someday."

I had not fooled her . . . she knew my mood.

"When I pulled the tarot cards for Harry, I also pulled

cards for his friends that I may have affected due to my driving error. Your cards showed strength, but sadness over love, and Harry's cards had told me he was in turmoil and searching for all kinds of direction. After meeting you and Harry, I could easily make the match when I saw the sadness in your eyes. You are like a lot of people, where their eyes are direct windows into their souls, and they tell their entire story."

Sky now was looking directly into my eyes and I did not blink or attempt to hide them.

"You miss her terribly, don't you?" Sky had hit the nerve dead on.

I now looked away and made a rather obvious attempt to hide my eyes.

"Yes, more than I can ever describe."

"People never really go away forever. Even when they die, they return to us, somehow. We remain together forever with the people that we love. She will return to you someday, I can tell." Sky reached and took my hand in hers and said, "Believe it and it will happen."

I smiled at her kindness, and she smiled at mine. I liked this gal. She had a heart of gold, and she calmed your soul. That may be just the combination that we all needed right at the moment.

Sky picked up what she needed out of her Wagon Bus and we went back into the house. The rest of the night was fun and relaxing.

I had a chance to speak with Harry alone in the kitchen, and he was smiling from ear-to-ear while he poured a glass of wine for Sky.

"She is really nice Harry, and very pretty too."

He looked at me and smiled, "Yes, she sure is! I sure know how to pick the right chick to smash up my car!" He was very excited. I could feel his enthusiasm over meeting Sky.

"I guess that is one way to look at it." I patted him on

the back and told him I had to take off.

I excused myself to everyone, and then went over to Sky and said goodnight to her. "It was my pleasure, Sky. I hope we can chat some more in the future. Goodnight, now."

"We will, Paul. I have invited Harry to come by our Center for Learning, to learn more about some of the things we do, so I am sure we will be seeing each other soon."

"I would like that, thank you."

"Be sure to use the oil and apply that pressure." I assured her that I would and I walked out in the cold, crisp air.

It was an easy walk, the two city blocks or so to my house from 20 John Street. I had walked it so many times in my life that I could do it blindfolded. Before I went to sleep, I applied the essential oil and pushed as hard as I could on the spot that Sky had shown me.

It may have been a coincidence or my imagination, but when I woke up the next day, my sore spot was gone.

I called over to Harry's house to see if he wanted to go out on Saturday night, but Linda told me he had gone over to meet Sky at the Center for Learning that Sky had mentioned.

"I really like her, Paul. She is a lot of fun."

It seemed like Sky had made quite an impression with everyone in a very short amount of time. Good for Harry, I thought. I resigned myself to hanging around at home and having a few Big Boulder beers with the old man, and watching the hockey game on television, when Rose called. We made plans to meet in an hour or so and have a few beers together.

I was glad we did, as it cleared the air for both of us. She cried a little, we laughed a lot, and told stories. She told me that she had also received the pictures from Howard at the Black Bear Club but did not open them, either. We talked for hours until the bar was ready to close. When the night ended, we promised to stay in touch and that was very special to me. Oftentimes, best friends who go in different directions due to life's crazy twists and turns promise to stay in touch, and they never do. I knew it would be different with Rose; we would always stay in touch.

When I returned home from work on Monday night, there was a message from my old man to call Eddie Austeri, who was the general manager for the Long Island Roosters hockey club. He had been the man who actually signed me up after watching me in a goalie clinic when I was seventeen years old.

I called him back the first thing the next morning.

"Paulie, I've got great news for you, but bad news for the Roosters. The owner of our club also has some ownership in a club out in Kansas City. The Roosters are actually part of the farm system for this team out there."

Mr. Austeri was very excited and you could hear it in his voice over the phone.

"They need a goalie badly . . . the first-string goalkeeper went down with a severe knee injury and he will be out for a while. The team in Kansas City has been struggling big time and attendance is down. The big boss is convinced that you can help them turn it all around. He wants you out there immediately. Big step up, Paulie! This is two rungs up from where you are now, big arena, big exposure, a step or two away from AHL, or OHL young man."

"Wow, I am shocked, Mr. Austeri. That is great news."

"Can you get away from your full-time job, Paul? I can get you a few thousand dollars in your pocket as a bonus, daily expenses, and a hotel room for this gig. The pay is a lot better too, Paul. You will make a fairly decent buck out there."

"Hey, I have no ties here right now. My boss loves hockey and we are slow right now with the holidays coming, so I am sure I can work it out."

Mr. Austeri was thrilled, "Perfect! Look, this league has specific rules about injury call ups during the season, so you can only fill in for about a month or so, but if you do well, I bet you can get a contract in the spring."

"I am ready. Tell me what to do, and I will go."

"All right, I will make the arrangements, pack your stuff, and get to the airport on Tuesday morning. I will have a plane ticket ready, and we will contact you with the arrangements. I will clean out your locker and ship your gear, just pack your skates and civilian clothes. Hey, good luck kid, I know you are on your way. The scouts drool over you. All of us knew that you were the real deal years ago when we first saw you. Size, speed, smarts, and you are the most fearless goalie, I have ever seen, and kid, let me tell you that, I have seen a lot of them."

I thanked him and hung up the telephone. He was always a very nice man to me, and I owed him a lot for giving me a chance two years ago. A moment really does change everything. Maybe I really was on my way, and this hollow pit in my stomach would finally go away.

I told my parents, and the old man's excitement overwhelmed him. He was calling all his buddies from the shop and telling them that his son was practically in the big league and on a roster. My mother was a little sad about me leaving and missing Christmas and Boxing Day at home, but she was excited about the chance the team had offered to me for a huge career opportunity. She knew it was my dream since I first strapped on the goalie pads and donned the mask. I wanted to be a professional goaltender and my dear Mum understood that fact, maybe more than anyone else did.

I actually felt happy about missing Christmas here at home and being busy, because I was dreading the holiday, anyway. I called to tell Harry the news, but he was out at the recording studio with Linda, recording the new song. They were really doing it! Everyone was suddenly living his or her dreams.

I spoke with Ronzo and told him all about my call out to

the team in Kansas City.

"I reckon that smudge stick thingy that Sky brought over really worked, Paul. It sure seems like things have turned around since she came over to our house and waved it all over the place. I really like her and she sure is nice to look at too!"

Ronzo's excitement and joy over the song coming to life was apparent, and I sensed his excitement at my sudden opportunity for hockey fame and fortune. He was as excited as everyone else was, and he promised to tell everyone when they all returned home.

"Good luck there, Paul. I know it has been a little rough for you the last few weeks, but it looks like things are getting better. Just know that all of us here at 20 John Street are always rooting for number twenty-seven."

I thanked him and promised that I would call from Kansas City to provide my contact information and to catch up to Harry.

I felt bad that I missed Harry, but as I hung up, I had to agree with Ronzo that things had really turned around since Sky came and smoked the house up with that smelly bag of herbs. Either it sure was a strange coincidence or perhaps it really was a little more than that.

I called my boss, and he supported my opportunity and granted me a leave for a few months from my position. I was a good worker, so I knew he would take me back when I returned to town. He used those dreaded words about me all the time. He always said, "I was honest and reliable."

I had no hesitation about packing my bags up and heading out of town as quickly as I could. I hoped deep inside that this sudden change in scenery was just what I needed.

In the morning, the old man and Mum drove me to the airport. They hugged me and they both had some tears in their eyes as we said goodbye. Before I knew it, I was off on a plane to Kansas City to play goal for a team called the Kansas City Hawks. I had dressed nicely for a change. This time, I lost the rock-and-roll band tee shirts, and I ditched my usual canvas sneakers. I felt it was time for an image change, so I put on my suit and tie.

Despite my threats, I had not cut my hair, but I did tie it back all the time. I had no reason not to anymore.

As I sat in the seat, flying out high above New Jersey, I fingered the little number twenty-seven tie tack and wondered if I would ever wear my Long Island Roosters jersey ever again. Maybe that manager of the surf club had made the right move after all when he asked for my autograph back in the summer.

Wow! That sure seems like years ago. It really does.

I arrived at the airport in Kansas City, and a Hawk's coach met me at the airport gate. It was a small airport compared to New Jersey, and it seemed like a small metro area to me when I compared the area to Paterson, New Jersey, as well as the metro New York City area. The coach drove me first to the hotel where I was going to stay, and then to the arena to meet the head coach and my new teammates. They all seemed like great guys and very supportive.

As we dressed in the locker room for practice, a tall, lanky, defenseman with really big, strong arms came over and stood next to me as I dressed for my first practice.

"Hey, welcome to KC. I am Jazkot, Henry Jazkot."

I stood up and shook his hand. "Paul John Henson. It is nice to meet you, Henry."

"Wow, strong handshake, and you are tall and big, too. We heard a lot about you. Man alive, I tell you, we need a good goalie, we have not played well this year, and the pressure is on now. Big time, New Jersey accent, eh? I cannot ever remember a goalie or hockey player that was from New Jersey before."

I smiled as I pulled on my chest protector. "Yeah, not

exactly a hockey hot bed, but it is home. How about you, Henry? You sound Canadian."

"Yes, I grew up near Regina, in Saskatchewan. I am a prairie boy."

If Henry could only see where Harry, Jeff and I started playing street hockey on Geyer Street in the old neighborhood, he would be shocked. So, there we were together, dressing for ice hockey in an arena in Kansas City, a prairie boy from the flat lands of Canada, and a long-haired city kid from the streets of Paterson, New Jersey.

Life sure has a way of putting different people together in a big, giant jigsaw puzzle.

A short young man with a pile of hockey jerseys in his arms came in and yelled at me, "Hey, new long-haired goalie guy, twenty-seven, they told me." He threw me a jersey and I pulled it on.

It felt good, really good.

Henry sat down next to me and asked, "Hey did you really play against that mass murderer, guy O'Malley, and shut him and his team out to win it all in your league last year? We heard about him all the way out here. Is he really that crazy and did he go to jail for manslaughter?"

I laughed and said, "Yes Henry, he really is a piece of work, that is for sure, but no, I do not think he is in jail. At least not yet that is."

I tugged at my skate laces and checked the blade edges on them. I looked at Henry over my shoulder and asked him, "Hey Henry, let me ask you since you have heard of O'Malley and about me all the way out here, have you ever heard that my girlfriend doesn't like when I tie my hair all back like this?"

Henry looked at me a little strangely, but he finally said, "No . . . I do not recall that I ever heard that one, Paul. I heard a lot about you, but not that one."

"Thanks, Henry."

I was beginning to like Kansas City already.

Practice went well, and I did fairly well in the net, or at least my teammates and coaches seemed to think so. The speed of the game and the skating abilities of the players were a lot better than the Metropolitan League. The shots were a lot quicker, and the skill levels were certainly a step up from where I had been playing, but I handled it. It was a light workout because there was a game that night. As we changed back into our civilian clothes, many of my new teammates came over and thanked me for coming out so quickly and joining the team.

Henry sat back down next to me and started to change out of his uniform as he told me, "You're as good, Paul, if not better than they told us. Number twenty-seven . . . the real deal! Great feet and you attack the puck like no goalie I have ever seen. You have an edge."

"Thanks, Henry."

I liked that when he said that I had an edge. That is how I felt these days, like I have an edge and that people and pucks should stay out of my way. I think it was a way for the pain inside of me to come out. No more Mr. Nice Guy on or off the ice.

I checked into the hotel, called my home, and spoke with my parents, and then I called over to Harry. He answered the phone and he was overjoyed.

"Twenty-seven! I am so sorry I missed you, but we were in the studio all night. It was fantastic. The song came out great!" Harry was babbling now in his excitement. "My old man knows some guy at the shop who knows a big shot at W.N.H., and he is going to give him a copy of the record. You are on the way, Paul. I cannot believe it! Soon, you will be in the big leagues."

He went on and on, ranting and raving as if he was out here playing alongside me. He asked me a thousand questions about the team, the rink, the dressing room, and I tried to calm him down, until I finally had to stop him short.

"Hey Harry, this phone call is costing me a lot of dough, I need to go, but I wanted to ask you, how is it going with Sky? Did you get to see her after you went out to the Center for Learning on the weekend?"

"Oh, yeah, Paul, we have seen each other every single day since we met. She is fantastic, and where she works is really cool. You cannot believe the stuff I have learned. Look, since she came over and waved that stinky bomb thingy in the air, we cut our song, and you made it to the big time." (Harry and his typical exaggeration, soon I will be in the hall of fame before I even played a game.)

"All of our lives seemed to have turned around in just a moment. Things are going great, and this stuff that Sky is teaching me is tremendous. She is like no other woman that I have ever met. I am weak in my knees around her."

Now, Harry has said that to me for years, in fact I would certify on a hundred Bibles that he has said that about every woman that he has ever met. This time his voice sounded so different, so calm, so relaxed.

"That's great, I am so happy that you are enjoying each other's company."

We said our goodbyes. I promised to call him when I could, and he did the same. As I hung up the phone, I realized that he never once said, "I reckon" or "y'all" or any other of the phony drawl slang. He spoke with a heavier New Jersey accent than I did. I just spoke with the real Harry M. Redmond Jr. and that was a great feeling.

My debut game went well. The arena was packed, and while standing in the net waiting for the national anthem and then the opening faceoff, I was not nervous at all. I had some type of inner fire that was very hard to explain. I could not help but think, as I scanned the crowd and the whole atmosphere, how far away I was from knocking around with Harry and Jeff on Geyer Street with the ends of Christmas tree trunks that we cut off as our homemade hockey pucks. I smoothed the ice in front of my net with my stick, crouched down in my stance, and I was ready.

I scanned the crowd at the first stoppage of play. This was a hockey town, and the fans were rabid. It was as if I had made it to the big time. I looked up at the faces of the people in the crowd and I sure missed seeing Binky, Rose, the old man, the guys from the shop, and Harry up there, clapping their hands.

I let a goal in my net, about five minutes into the game on a power play, but there was very little I could have done to stop it. I was down low on the ice, with a screen in front of me, and a slap shot from the point was tipped and changed direction on me. I lunged and just tipped it with my catching glove, but the puck still trickled into the net. The crowd moaned, and I heard a strong round of boos from the homers. I knew they had been suffering from poor goaltending play as of late, and they were hoping that this new number twenty-seven guy could do a little better.

I understood how they felt. I really did, but there was very little I could do with a shot like that one. I managed to crack a smile under my mask as Henry skated by and tapped my pads. I shook off goals scored on me and moved on rather quickly in my focus. I was used to facing tons of abuse and heckling from tougher crowds than these folks could have ever imagined in their wildest dreams. At least the crowd was not pelting me while I stood in the net, with half-eaten hot dogs and half-full beer cups!

That was it.

I shut them down after that, save after save, some routine, some spectacular, and before you knew it, we fought back and scored two goals to take the lead, and then an empty net goal in the final minute to ice it. One game, one win, and my new teammates surrounded me after the game.

Henry grabbed me by my ponytail after I pulled my mask off and he shouted, "Hey, the Hawks finally have a goalie and he is the real deal!"

The home team crowd was going wild. It seemed like I was somehow a new hero to this little city so far away from my home. We all skated off, and then we made our way up the runway to the locker room. Fans were reaching down to me, yelling and looking for fives as they hung over the railings. I pulled the hair tie out of my head, smiled and yelled back at some crowd and high-fived the spectators back. A few folks dropped papers and pens over for me to sign them and a bunch of young women, including one gorgeous, dark-haired gal, dropped papers with their phone numbers written down on them to me. It was a little wild, and in fact, I had to admit it felt really good.

Therefore, it began—my little stint with the Kansas City Hawks.

A far-off place and a new beginning. I sure was a long way from 20 John Street. I felt like it was a great adventure for me to begin and an escape for me to try to rejuvenate my spirit.

I called Rose on the weekend. She was thrilled for me, and she filled me in on what was happening in her life.

"Will you ever ask me, Paul?" Rose asked.

"Ask you what? If you have spoken to Binky? No, Rose, I will not. I really do not see the point. Binky made her choice and we all need to live with that."

"I understand," was all Rose could say. I had been honest to an extent, as I really did not want to know. The pain was a little too tough to handle right at the moment.

I spent Christmas Day with Henry, as both of us were far from home and had no plans. There were not too many places open on Christmas Day, but we went to a steak joint in downtown Kansas City. It was an excellent meal and a good time. Kansas City steaks are pretty darn good, and the downtown area was small, but it was a nice place to hang out. Henry was a cool guy, and we got along well. I shared some of my Harry and Paul adventures, and he told me about life on the Canadian prairies.

Henry was amazed at my stories because it was hard for him to imagine such a life in such a different place than he grew up in. I told him the story of how Harry, Jeff, and I started playing hockey with sawed off ends of Christmas tree trunks for pucks, on the dead-end street around the corner from our homes. We called it "Geyer Street Gardens," and it was our first hockey rink. He marveled at how far I had come from such humble beginnings.

I told Henry, "But is that not a true fact of so many things? Often, great adventures come from such quaint ideas or experiences. A moment changes everything Henry, it really does."

He agreed. "You know, Paul, you are really smart for a goalie. I would think with all of your smarts, you would have picked a safer position!"

We shared a good laugh together; looking back, Henry had a good point! We both would not admit how lonely we both were, but at least we could pass the time together.

Time went by fast.

This hockey life was a lot more demanding than my time with the Long Island Roosters. It was now a full-time job of course. The practices were long, and we traveled farther for away games. I saw some places that I never dreamed of ever seeing. Most of all, it kept my mind very busy, and that was a very good thing. I had been playing very well in the goal. At one point, we won eight games in a row, until we all had a horrible night and we suffered a bad loss. The coach rode us hard over the next few practices, and we rebounded with another winning streak.

I had developed a little fan club and the local press covered me in a quick story. I fit the media hype bill, strange, long-haired, hippie, guy from New Jersey, funny way of speaking, playing well; it was right up their alley. I was a frequent guest on the little radio station that covered the games and did the live play-by-play, and the broadcast team interviewed me often. I told the story of Geyer Street Gardens so much that I was sick of hearing it myself.

I spoke with Harry when I could, but he always seemed to be out with Sky. When we did speak, he was bouncing off the walls with enthusiasm at his relationship with Sky, as well as my success. I also spoke with my parents, Ronzo, Linda, and Rose once a week. It was fine when I was busy or on game nights, but the time alone in the hotel was brutal. My mind continually filled with memories and that deep, dull pain in my stomach dulled a bit, but it never went away. I didn't even bring any of my beloved No Way recordings to help me pass the downtime, so I had to suffer through listening to music on the radio.

Soon, it was mid-February; the Hawks had climbed into second place and secured a playoff spot. Most of my coaches and teammates told me I was the reason, but I think it was more that we just all came together at the right time.

One morning before practice, the Hawk's general manager called me into his office for a meeting. He was a middle-aged man named; Andy Lord, who was a little nervous and jumpy, but he had always been a nice man to me. My head coach was also sitting in the office.

"Sit down, Paul." Mr. Lord motioned to a chair in front of his desk.

"Well, the time has come for us to send you back to the Roosters. By the time, you get back there—the season will be over for them. They did not hold up so well once you left. I do not think the Roosters are making the playoffs this year. It kills me to do this. It just kills me! Nevertheless, we all knew the rules ahead of time. We just did not know how good you were."

Mr. Lord shook his head back and forth while he spoke, and I could tell that he was a little upset.

"This is a crazy league, and they have rules for roster moves, so that we all do not bring in ringers and stack the teams for the playoffs. The only reason we could bring you up, was that the Roosters are in our system, and because of the injury to our starting goalie. I have had to prove that a number of times since you came since you have done such a fantastic job for us in the net."

Mr. Lord looked straight at me and then at my coach.

"I think Coach Bossard will agree with me when I say, you are one helluva goalie, son. It is going to be tough to let you go." The coach chimed in and agreed.

"Thank you, I have really enjoyed it here, and I hope I was able to contribute."

Mr. Lord grew louder and a little more animated.

"Contribute! Man, you did more than that! You are like Mr. Hockey here. I bet you could go grab any young woman you want from those stands every night. However, you stay away from that stuff and keep your nose on the game, and that shows you have your head on straight. We went eighteen wins and three losses since you arrived here and became our net minder. You are fearless in that net, Henson. I do not ever recall a goalie that plays as fearless as you do. It is a little remarkable how you stand there. I know you have as good a chance as anyone that has passed through here to make it to the big league."

"Thank you, sir, that is very kind of you to say."

"Look," Mr. Lord leaned over his desk a little towards me, "I will offer you a nice deal in the spring, but I know that you will have a better deal on the table in April than I could ever offer. The scouts are drooling over you now. They call my telephone all day long asking what your contract language is. Henson, you have all the tools, strong, big, fast, and reliable."

There was that horrible, reliable word again!

"To top it all off, you are a really nice, polite guy too."

Oh well, despite my best efforts, I am still Mr. Nice Guy.

"The club owner really appreciates your efforts, and he made out another bonus check for you."

Mr. Lord handed me an envelope, and extended his hand. "You will go back home with a nice, little, amount of money there twenty-seven. You deserve it. Our attendance is through the roof because of you. The fans are going to be screaming for you, it will be difficult to explain."

"Thank you, Mr. Lord, it has been a wonderful experience here and everyone has been great, I certainly will miss this place and the team."

I shook hands with the coach and Mr. Lord, and they explained that in the envelope was a plane ticket back to New Jersey for a flight in the morning. He also explained that they would ship all of my hockey gear, equipment, and my skates to New Jersey for me. I told him I would take my goaltender skates home with me. I did not trust anyone with my skates; they were my livelihood! I went down to the locker room and said goodbye to all my Hawks teammates. I made plans to meet Henry for a few beers that night. Henry was a good man, and we had some good times together. We wished each other good luck and exchanged contact information for the future.

I called my parents and the old man said he would pick me up at the airport. I called Harry, but as usual, he was out with Sky, so I spoke with Linda.

"It will be so nice to see you, Paul. So much has happened in the months since you've been gone. It is going to be great to see you!" I also called Rose. She was happy to hear how well it went, and I promised that I would see her when I returned. I packed my gear and said goodbye to the hotel staff, who all gave me a nice send off.

There was an older woman who worked at the front desk who was a big Hawk's fan, and she was very upset that I had to leave. She even ran out to her car and came back wearing a brand new, Hawks Jersey with twenty-seven and my name on the back that she had just bought.

That was really cool.

I hailed down a cab in front of the hotel and threw my

gear in the trunk.

"Heading to the airport there, long hair?" The driver was looking in his mirror back at me.

"Yes sir, the airport, thanks."

It was a cold frosty day here in Kansas City and it looked like it could snow at any minute. I sure hoped that my flight would get out on time. The driver of the taxi was listening to the radio, tuned into a country station, and I could hear the music playing as he drove and whistled.

All of a sudden, the driver said loudly to me, "Oh, I love this song, this is a good one," he said as he turned up the volume on the radio. I was just staring blankly out the window when I heard a tune come on the radio that made my head lean in, and I nearly jumped out of my seat:

"All those things, I used to love about you now just drive me crazy. I reckon it is time for us to move on and say goodbye because our love has grown lazy. I will always care about you and miss your lovin' heart, but darlin' the sad time has come for us to part."

I could hardly believe my ears at what was coming out of the radio at me, but it was Harry and Linda's song! It was really Harry on the banjo, backed up by an assortment of different instruments and Linda singing! I sat back and was stunned, but then I started to laugh until my eyes had tears in them. The driver must have thought I was out of my mind, but I did not really care.

The disc jockey came on as the song ended and he announced, "That is the number one song that everyone is calling for, 'All Those Things I Used to Love about You Now Just Drive Me Crazy', by Big Tex and Linny."

Big Tex and Linny!

Unreal. It is really unreal, I thought.

Who knows? Who can say? You would think that after all of these years of dealing with madness, nothing about Harry and the rest of the Redmonds would be a surprise to me.

Maybe that smudge-a-dub-dubber, as Harry called it, really did work.

12

Hades Freezes Over

I arrived back in New Jersey and I had to admit that it was nice to be back in Jersey. The New Jersey Turnpike, pollution, mobsters, the shoreline, the woods, New Jersey has it all, and I missed every inch of it!

My old man and Mum met me at the airport gate. It was great to see them and they made me feel like a hero coming home from war. The old man made out as if I was a big superstar. He would inflate my status to strangers and any passers-by whom he could engage, and may have wondered who I was and what I had just returned home from doing.

We walked together to the baggage claim to find my luggage, and we talked the entire way. After a million questions from them about hockey, Kansas City, as well as my health, my old man piped in, "Did you hear about the song that Harry and his sister recorded?"

"I can't believe it, Dad. I heard it on the radio, on the way to the airport in a cab, and the disc jockey said it was number one!"

"It is incredible. Just when you think the Redmonds run out of steam, they come up with another crazy angle. It is a huge hit, I heard it, and it actually is very catchy, I have been singing it all day."

The old man looked at me over the top of his glasses. "I do not want you to be more surprised than you are already by the crazy world of Harry and the rest of the Redmonds, but please be prepared for some changes. He came over to say hello to us last week, and he introduced us to his new girlfriend, Sky."

My mother turned around, "Oh, she is so pretty, and nice Paul, even if her hair was orange, she is still so cute."

"Orange! It used to be blue."

"Well, you missed a color or two in the rotation since you left, because I met her before your mum did. I went over and had a few Big Boulders with Mr. Redmond and Ronzo, and I met her over there. She had purple hair that night."

Yes, I am sure I missed quite a bit; after all, even ten minutes can bring big changes in the world of the Redmonds. My parents then told me to be ready to go over to the Redmonds after I went home, washed up, and had settled in. We all had invitations to a big, "Welcome Home Paul" party at 20 John Street. No one threw a better party than the Redmonds, so this should be a good one! I really missed Harry and the rest of the gang. It will be good to see them after almost three months away.

It was good to be home and back in my own house. Skippy greeted me, and it was nice to see my old dog. He was slowing down now, but he was happy I was home. I stowed my gear, took a shower, and dressed for the party. I did not really care what I looked like. I was just happy to be here, so I put on a No Way tee shirt, my old canvas sneakers, and I tied my hair up. My parents wanted to leave earlier than I did; they had already driven over in the old man's faithful 1964 Putter Classic model 200 car.

I could not believe that he still drove the same old vehicle after all these years.

I preferred to walk, it allowed me to retrace my steps and remember all the times I walked over to the Redmond's house since I was just a little kid. When I turned the corner, I noticed cars lining both sides of the curb up and down John Street, from Belmont Ave to Geyer Street. I thought how these cars cannot be all for the party. I went up the steps and I could hear music playing and a lot of talking inside. I tapped on the door, opened it up, and stepped inside the familiar front porch.

When I walked into the living room, the room exploded with shouts and cheers.

"Here he is! Welcome home, number twenty-seven!"

It seemed like a hundred people were screaming at me. Cocoa was running around, jumping, leaping on me, and barking. Ronnie, Linda, Patty, Mr. Redmond, the Big Spike, and the kids instantly surrounded me, and they were all hugging and grabbing me. I heard the camera's shutters snapping and saw flash bulbs popping.

Then out of the kitchen, ran Harry, and he came barreling up to me like a freight train. He picked me up in a big bear hug and almost broke me in half.

"Welcome home there, twenty-seven! Man, we all missed you!"

After we embraced for a while, Sky came over to me with her orange hair; she smiled and gave me a big hug and a kiss on the cheek.

"Welcome back Paul, you were really missed but we all are so happy for you!" She looked at me closely and quietly asked, "Your eyes are still sad. Are you really doing all right, Paul?"

"I am fine, Sky, it is nice to be home and see you again."

It was neighbor after neighbor, Father Mark had come, my parents, friends old and some new, all of them coming up and greeting me like I was some famous movie star. They all came by shaking my hand and patting me on the back. Then the biggest surprise came, as emerging from the crowd was Rose! She screamed, she ran over, and hugged me and as usual, she was crying her eyes out.

It was something else! Let me tell you! I felt like I really was a hero. They had big banners up, signs and streamers everywhere. The food was flowing nonstop from the kitchen, the Big Boulder and Dingleberry beer were cold, and the party was on.

When I finally recovered from the welcome home onslaught, and Ronzo put a beer in my hand, I noticed that things had really changed here at 20 John Street. As I had a chance to breathe and look around, I realized something was different. Ronzo was dressed in torn blue jeans with a bunch of peace sign patches sewn on them. He had a blue, faded tee shirt on with bleached yellow stripes and on the back, it said, "Give peace a chance." He wore old, dirty sneakers and a large pewter peace symbol around his neck on a long chain. Linda had a similar outfit on, but her shirt was a black tee shirt with the famous logo from No Way's latest record on the back. She had a hair band embroidered with the words "rock on" in her hair.

Harry came over to me and now that things had calmed down a bit, I had a chance to study him. He was dressed in blue jeans with canvas sneakers on like mine. He wore a blue, purple, and red dyed shirt with a large peace sign on the front. On the back, it said, "Make Love Not War." Around his neck was a chain with a pendant of his zodiac sign hanging on the end. I then realized that he dyed his hair a light blonde color, and it was longer than I had ever seen it.

Harry smiled at me and grabbed me once more. "It is so good to see you. It seems as if you have been gone forever. You were really missed."

I was shocked and did not know what to say right at the moment. I just stood there and smiled.

Gone were the cowboy boots, gone were the ten-gallon hats, the big belt buckles, the bolo ties, country and western records, the western belts, the silver studded western shirts, and the banjos. No more, I reckon, no more fixin', no more y'all. All of them had their New Jersey accents restored.

I had missed the passing of a phase while I was gone!

This was a significant event, and I had missed it. This

was what the old man was warning me about when I first came home. It was all gone, tossed out, and moved down in the basement alongside Mr. Bug, bowling bags, and the old billiard table.

Mr. Redmond walked by and I noticed he had on old, torn blue jeans, with a bright blue tee shirt stenciled in the back with "The Center for Learning." He was wearing open-toed sandals, and he had grown his hair longer too. The record player was blasting out some type of chanting music with sitars and some weird, wind instruments playing an obscure tune. The Redmonds had moved into the hippie phase, and I could only surmise that Sky was the driving influence behind this.

It took me a little time to digest all of this and as people were talking to me, I must have looked like a dope, as I was in such a daze. I was working hard not to be in shock at the ushering in of a new phase and era in the perpetual, Redmond phase, rotation, evolution. You just never know with the Redmonds, but after all, the country and western phase had lasted a very long time.

My old man came over and whispered to me, "I told you, things had changed. No more cowboys, they all are a bunch of want-to-be hippies now. All these years of hanging around you, I would have thought they would have picked up this hippie thing sooner."

"I see that. It is amazing, Dad. Simply amazing."

I recovered, found Harry, and asked him the famous question. Even though I had been through the passing of phases, many times before and I already knew the answer, I still had to ask.

"What happened to all the country and western stuff?"

"Oh, we are still into that, we just all go over to the center with Sky now and we are not into the country stuff as much as we were."

Yup, same answer!

At least Mr. Bug had more clutter to keep him company,

and he did not stand out so much down in the basement now.

It was hard to mingle and talk to everyone. They all asked a million questions over and over, and it was difficult to speak with everyone and still be polite.

I found Rose in the kitchen and signaled for her to step out to the back patio. We bolted out the back door and headed for the patio to talk. I was looking to catch up with her and recover some more.

"It is great to see you here Rose, thanks so much for coming."

"I would not miss it for anything in the world. When Harry called and invited me then I knew I had to come. You look great Paul, just great, handsome as ever."

"Thanks Rose. You look as pretty as ever. Harry looks wonderful, I know he has this hippie thing going on, but he seems so relaxed, so calm, like he is being himself for a change."

Rose smiled. "I agree. He is very happy, and she is perfect for him, calming, pretty, smart. She is wonderful . . . I wish . . . them the best."

For one second, it seemed like Rose was not truly sincere, but it could have been my imagination.

I changed the subject and took a long sip of my beer. "The whole song thing is wild too. I could not believe it when I heard it out in KC." Rose took a sip of beer and nodded. I smiled at her and then asked, "So, how are you?"

"I am good Paul, I miss the old days, but I am good. I have a new job and I met a real, nice, guy there who I go out with here and there."

"I hope it is a little more normal than Harry and Paul adventures!"

Rose laughed, "It is, but in a lot of ways that is why we all were so special together, because it was always exciting and never was very normal."

I leaned back on the wall of the patio and sighed.

"Do you still miss her, Paul? I thought about you all the time, out there by yourself, in a strange area, it must have had some brutally lonely times."

"Oh, Rose. I do not know, anymore. Some days, I just want to stand and scream up into the air so loud that the entire world hears me, and other times, I just want to be alone and cry."

I stood up and turned towards Rose.

"Do you know that I never cry, Rose? I cannot, even though sometimes, I want to. I never really feel anything, but a dull ache deep in my stomach that never really goes away. It seems as if playing goal has numbed my emotions, Rose, I am always focused and numb."

Rose came over. She hugged me, and I held her. It felt good just to be with a friend who understood that it was not all glory and fame. It was, at times, brutally lonely.

"I understand Paul, in many ways I wish just the exact opposite."

I was not following her, so I asked, "The opposite?"

Rose looked up at me and said, "I wish I could stop crying." We stood there for quite a while, each holding on to each other. Not only were we holding on to one another, we also were both holding onto memories that swirled around us like a thousand ghosts in the cold night air.

I finally whispered to her, "Let's go back inside. Thank you Rose for being here for me."

"Thank you, twenty-seven, for always being there for all of us too."

We went back into the house, I grabbed the both of us another beer, and we mingled. Sky came over, and we all sat at the kitchen table and talked for what seemed like hours. The crowd thinned down now, and my parents left. Father Mark came over and had some kind words for me before he left. I told everyone about Kansas City and some places that I had played in and visited. Harry and I shared with Sky some more stories and amazing adventures of our past together. Sky listened with great interest and laughed at all the right times. Rose was right because Sky was wonderful. Harry, Ronzo, Linda, Patty, the Big Spike, and Mr. Redmond joined us around the table and we talked and shared stories, just as we had for so many years. We talked about the song, the center, and they asked me about the Kansas City Hawks.

Patty and the Big Spike also wore hippie-type of clothes and attire; they had joined in the latest phase too! Everything was well in the world once more!

Most of the crowd had left now, and it was getting late. Rose said goodbye, as she had an appointment early the next day. It was almost eleven o'clock when the entire gang moved to the living room, took off their shoes, and sat in a circle on the living room floor. Sky showed me where I needed to sit next to Linny. We all sat on the floor and joined hands together. Ronzo put a record on the player that had some type of low chanting going on, and then he joined the circle on the floor. Harry took a candle, put it in the middle of the circle, he lit it, and then turned the lights off in the room. He reached down and put a wide headband on around his head. I could see even in the darkness that it had peace signs all over it.

While closing her eyes and rocking a little as she sat on the floor, Sky said, "Now let's all breathe and relax and thank the universe for returning Paul to us safely."

Everyone closed their eyes except me, and they began to breathe deeply in and out, as they all started to sway back and forth slowly in unison. Sky coached us with the breathing and some kind of chanting, but I really did not get it, so I just faked it and went along with the whole thing.

Oh boy, where was Mr. Bug when I needed him?

It was nice to sleep in my own room, in my own bed, and there was no doubt that I had been exhausted, because I slept for about fourteen hours straight. I did not wake up until late afternoon when I wandered down to the kitchen and saw my mom at the table.

"Would you like a cup of tea, Paul?"

"Sure, Mum."

I missed English teatime with my mother.

"Are you hungry Paul? would you like a scone? I baked them for you special."

"Maybe later, Mum. Thanks. I appreciate that."

"I will make some roast dinner for you tonight and maybe some lemon tarts tomorrow? Would you like that?"

"Sure Mum, I missed your English cooking."

We sat for a while and I did not say too much.

"You were tired. It was good for you to sleep."

"Yes, there is a bit of a time change too, Mum."

My mother nodded as if she did not realize that.

"That was quite a party last night. They are such nice people. They do seem a bit over the top with this new hippie thing, eh? Dad says you came home with a good bit of money, eh? What are you going to do with it?"

"Nothing, Mum, I just am going to bank it all. Please bank it all for me if you go. Would you please? You still are named on my account."

"Sure, that is nice to save it, Paul. I will watch it all for you. What are your plans now that you are back?"

"I am going to go back to the electric shop next week. I already talked to my boss, and he has some projects for me. I need to stay busy, Mum . . . you know that I cannot just sit. It sounds like the Roosters year is over—maybe they need me for some mop up duty for a few weeks. They did not make the playoffs. Then I need to find an agent. It looks like I will have some offers on the table for a new team or contract for next season. I know at the very least, the Hawks will have a deal out there for me, but I do not know if I want to go all the way back out to Kansas City."

My mother fiddled with her teacup, then she looked at me. "You really were in love with Binky, weren't you? I see the pain is still in your eyes."

"I rather not talk about it, Mum. I need a bit more time to think it all out."

"Are you feeling all right? You did not get hurt badly out there, did you? I worry about you playing that dangerous position. How you stand in front of that bloody, awful puck thing is frightening to me."

"No, I am fine Mum, actually, I am in great condition. All the bumps and dings have healed. Only about twenty stitches so far, this season. I really am in the best shape of my life."

I smiled at my mother, who just sat and stared at me over her tea. She did not say anything, but I could feel her desire to speak.

"Thanks for the tea. It tasted good. I missed you, Mum. I love you. It is nice to be home."

She weakly smiled at me.

"I think I will go for a run." I stood up and kissed her on the top of her head, and she grabbed my arm gently and held it.

"Why don't you ask Rose for her telephone number, and call her? What could it hurt?"

I shook my head to indicate no, smiled at her and patted her arm, but I did not answer her.

I changed into my old Long Island Roosters warm up suit and was ready for a run when Harry called. He asked my mother if I was around and if I could come over.

"Tell him I am out for a run and I will head that way!"

Out the door, I went, and I was over to his house in no time flat. I walked in the front door and there in the living room was a strange sight even for 20 John Street. Ronzo, Linda, Patty, and the Big Spike were all sitting in chairs with their pants rolled up and their feet in some type of footbaths. The baths were making some small bubbles around their feet, but there was no noise that I could hear. They all had their eyes closed, as if they were meditating.

Mr. Redmond was lying on the sofa with some headphones on and some type of device next to him, with wires that went up and under the sofa cushion and his pillow. I did not say a word, but slipped quietly around them and headed for the kitchen.

I found Harry at the kitchen table dressed in his hippie outfit but without his headband on. He was reading some type of book and I tried to catch a glimpse of the title, but Harry closed it when I walked in.

"Hey Harry, what's going on with the foot bath things in the living room?"

Harry looked up at me and smiled.

"Oh man, you have to try that Paul, it is the greatest thing. Those are ionic footbaths and they remove all kinds of toxins and impurities from your body by ionization. You fill it with a special salt that the Center for Learning imports from Tibet, and then you drop this ionizer thingy in there. Wait 'till you see it. You stick your feet in there and the water changes all kinds of colors as the salt cleanses all the bad stuff out of you. My water was black yesterday and Ronzo's was an orange color. Sky taught us all to do it at the center, so we all ran out and bought our own baths. They make you feel like a million bucks."

Somehow, I knew that they had all run out, and each bought brand-new baths of their own. I just knew it.

"It has to be special salt from Tibet? You cannot just use salt from the grocery store, Harry?"

"Oh no, we ordered boxes and boxes of the special salt. We stored it all in the basement."

I tried very hard to hide my lack of surprise at the storage location.

"What is your old man doing there on the sofa?"

"Oh, that is something very different. He is doing neuro-acoustic bio tuning. He recorded his own body frequencies and now he is listening to them so he gets in tune with his life and his own body. This is incredible stuff Paul. You really have to try it."

I then feigned some very polite interest in this latest phase, "Wow, I never heard of such things, it sure sounds like great stuff." I noticed the cover of the book that Harry was reading as it sat on the table, The Beginner's Guide to Twisting Yoga by Candlelight. It had a picture of some chap, all twisted up like a pretzel on the cover.

"So how rough was it out there in KC? I bet you ran into some wicked, hard slappers?"

"It was not that bad, Harry. Some big boy shots and one guy who played in the big time and was on a rehabilitation stint, working his way back to the big league. Now, he could shoot!"

Harry smiled, and I could tell that he was recalling our playing days together.

"I held my own, Harry. It was not as bad as you think."

"I am sure proud of you, twenty-seven. It is a long way from Geyer Street and us guys knocking some sawed off ends of Christmas tree trunks around when we were just stupid kids."

Harry got up from the table.

"Would you like a beer, Paul?"

"Sure thanks, Harry."

"You want a Big Boulder, right?"

"Yes please, those Dingleberries are way too sweet."

He grabbed a Big Boulder beer from the refrigerator for me and a soda for him. I now knew Harry had something on his mind. I knew that body language and the way he moved his eyes when he had something to tell me.

"So, I see that things are going great with you and Sky. She is a wonderful lady."

"That's why I asked you to come over. I need to tell you something, Paul."

Harry sat back down next to me, slid the beer over to me, and looked at me very intently.

"I asked Sky to marry me last night, and she said yes. Both Sky and I wanted you to be the first to know out of the entire world. We have not told anyone other than you right now."

I sat back in the chair and I had to admit I was stunned. I really wanted to scream out at the top of my lungs! Harry was going to marry the hippie chick who wrecked his beloved Trans Whizzer. What an incredible twist of irony that out of such a catastrophic event, Harry meets his future wife. Oh well, why on earth would I be astounded at anything that involves Harry or the Redmonds? I bet that policeman I met the night of the accident sure would not believe this one. A whirlwind romance, and the guy who swore he would never get married, has finally met the girl of his dreams.

I broke into a smile and wanted to yell out again, but I did not want to disturb the foot bathers, so I just reached over and grabbed Harry, shook his hand, and enthusiastically patted his shoulder and then we stood up and embraced each other.

"Oh, Harry! Fantastic! I am so happy for you. She is perfect for you, and you are for her. I have never seen two happier people in my life. Even speaking with you on the phone all the way from KC, I could tell you had really fallen for her."

Harry was smiling broadly and listening to my excitement at the news.

"Harry, this is just great. She is pretty and smart, but I also love her sense of humor. I have to tell you that Sky has the most wonderful calming effect on people, she is very special."

Harry was beaming ear-to-ear as he told me, "It is true that ever since she came here, all of our lives have changed. She waved the smudge stick thing around and you go to the big time in hockey. The song goes to number one, and we fall deeply in love. Take my word for it . . . you are, as usual, right on the money. Sky is special. Beyond words."

I was never one to believe in that kind of stuff, but I had to admit he was right. There seemed to be something to it for sure.

"Paul, she is the one. I can be myself around her, no phony accents, no fake New York Bug uniforms, no big hats, no fancy cars, and we drive her old Wagon Bus around. I just can be me, fun, relaxed, and calm. I can just be Harry. You are the only other person in this world I can be myself around, only you and now, Sky."

Harry sat back and took a long sip of soda, then he set the can back down on the table. I thought back to the years and years of conversations and memories, both good and bad, that we had shared as friends over this table in this old house. It was like a sacred place and in reality; it was just an old kitchen table.

Harry looked down at the table and then back at me while he explained, "I have to tell you that it was just like you told me it would be. She consumed my soul, Paul. Sky and I became one. All we think about is each other. It is an amazing feeling to be this much in touch and in love with someone."

I smiled at his heartfelt honesty, and said to him, "It is simple. You love her, she became part of you, and you became part of her. She now consumes your heart as well as your soul."

Harry nodded, took another very long swig of his soda and I chugged the beer a little.

It tasted cold and good.

"You know what, Paul? I owe you a major apology for what I have told you in the past."

"For what, Harry?"

"I was wrong to call you a doormat and a loser Paul, you are anything but that. In fact, it really is the opposite. You are the biggest winner I know, and you have always been there for me. When we were just little kids and my mom died, you were there to tell me she was watching us from Heaven. When Joyce and Rose dumped me, you were the guy who was there to support and encourage me. You came the night when we wrecked the Trans Whizzer and stood by me. When I was in that hospital bed, while the docs tried to put me back together after the hockey puck accident, you were there for me then too."

Harry looked away from me. I think he was tearing up just a little.

He continued, "You were, and always are, there for me. No matter what half-crazed idea I came up with, or how selfish I was being. You put up with me when I was working on some dumb idea or stupid scheme to whip up, like putting ETO's music in some fancy pants ball room orchestra's music and making you dance first, or when I skated in that crazy, forty-hour marathon roller skating fund-raiser to raise dough and to win back Joyce."

He laughed aloud now. "In fact, I cannot even count how many things I put you through, yet you are still my friend. You never complained, and you always went along with it all. You are always there to either guide me or support me, just as you are now. I feel terrible for calling you that, Paul. The Harry Theory is stupid, and it is wrong."

I appreciated his kind words and friendship, and I tried to convey that to him. "I only ever wanted to be your best buddy Harry, that's all. We will be friends forever, no matter what."

He shifted uncomfortably in his chair and pushed the soda aside. "You told me once that someone would come along and I would fall for her. I told you that Hades would freeze over when that happens. I think old Satan had better find a blowtorch now. You were right, and I can tell you that you are the smartest and best buddy anyone could ever ask for. I tell you Binky is sitting somewhere reading about how those young ladies were taking off their bras for you to sign after a game, and she is thinking how badly she blew it by writing that stupid letter and taking off."

I laughed a little. "Who told you that ladies were taking off their bras for me to sign?"

Harry smiled, "Well, didn't they?"

I nodded my head a little and admitted, "Once or twice yes, I admit they did a few times."

"I knew it." Harry gently punched me in the arm.

"Someday, she will know what the rest of the world knows, that you are a great guy."

I leaned back into another sip of the Big Boulder beer. "There is no need to apologize, Harry, and I still think your theory is right. I am not the same guy, I learned, and I have moved on, Binky made her choice, and now I have my own life to live."

Harry was shaking his head. "Don't change, Paul. Just because some crazy gal lost her mind, please don't ever change. I swear that Binky is crazier than O'Malley."

The jury was in now, and it was a unanimous ruling all in favor of Binky surpassing O'Malley on the nutcase level.

"I will try, but it is hard. Really hard."

Harry looked at me for a long time but he did not answer me. He was studying my face for evidence that my feelings for Binky were still as strong as they always were. I knew I was not fooling Harry at all. He decided not to pursue the conversation and changed the subject.

"We are getting married right away, no bridal showers, and no long engagements. We just want to be together. We hope to have the wedding right here in the living room next weekend. Money is not an issue right now. The dough is rolling in for Linny and me on the song so that will not be a problem for us right now."

"Harry, the song is a remarkable story. One minute you are hacking around on the banjo, and then, the next minute, you're on the radio."

Harry laughed. "But I did work on it for a few years now. I just needed Rose to dump me for the final inspiration!"

"Sky, and I . . . well we are both Catholic, so I am sure Father Mark will be good to go right away. Of course, I want you to be my best man at the wedding."

I was happier for Harry than I could ever say.

"I will be proud to be your best man and I can think of no better place than right here to be married. After all this wonderful, old house has seen, it would be only appropriate."

It was a crazy week as the Redmond house turned into a wedding chapel and the party was prepared. If it had been warmer outside, then it would not be a problem as we all could gather out in the backyard as well as the house. That was not going to work because it was the first week of March and it was still cold outside. I went over every day after work to help everyone with moving furniture out in the garage, cleaning, and to assist with the preparation for the wedding.

I was thankful, as Sky selected for Harry and me to wear a plain white dress shirt, no ties, black dress pants, and black shoes for the ceremony. I was hoping that she did not want us to wear old tattered jeans and dyed tee shirts or something like that, but we were off the hook. Harry kept his hair dyed the lighter blonde color and Sky did her hair exactly to match Harry's hair color.

Sky only had her mom and dad, and one younger sister. Her sister was going to be her maid of honor, so it was a small wedding party. It was going to be a small reception, family, and some close friends, nothing fancy. This type of ceremony was all that the two of them wanted. It seemed as if Harry and Sky just wanted to be husband and wife as quickly as possible. We had the chapel set for the wedding so that the front where we would conduct the ceremony was in the living room, and the guests could line up all the way into the dining room. It actually worked out really well.

Father Mark agreed to conduct the service and the only, "Sky like" addition to the service, was that we all had to wear peace sign necklaces in addition to small-carved wooden crucifixes around our necks. Even Father Mark agreed to wear the peace sign along with his priest garb. All the guests would also receive peace sign necklaces to wear. Harry had picked out a very high-class engagement ring that Sky received on the night they decided to get married, and the wedding rings were simple gold bands. Before we all knew it—we were all set to go as far as the ceremony planning went.

We had a quick rehearsal on Friday night, then we all hung around and enjoyed some beer, wine, and some catered food for dinner.

I had the chance to speak with Father Mark for quite a while and I enjoyed that. I had known him through the family for a long time, and we had a good laugh over what he proudly had labeled the now famous, "Harry road rage incident."

It was a great night, and we were all very excited about the big day that awaited us.

Taking a break, I poured a hot cup of tea and went out in the backyard with Cocoa. I grabbed a chair and sat on the back patio in the cold. Cocoa and I went back a long time with each other, in fact, since the day that he was brought home as a little pup. He and I had shared many quiet times as well as many fun times together over the years. Cocoa sat next to me with his Piggy in his mouth.

I petted him and rubbed him under his neck, and together the two of us looked over the yard where Harry and I grew up together, playing everything from hide and seek as little stupid kids, to bringing our first dates over for summer picnics as awkward teenagers, to hanging Christmas trees upside down in the big oak tree in front of me. Those ghosts that always hang around me in my life, and are never very far, decided to return once more. A thousand ghosts of the past floated around us, they circled all around in the cold, night air. I could see and hear them clearly as I am sure Cocoa did too. I could hear our laughter, our shouts of joy, the kicking of cans in the driveway, the sound of hockey pucks, basketballs, baseballs, and the splash of the old swimming pool. I saw Jeff Porter shooting a slap shot in the driveway. He was wearing his ball cap backwards on his head . . . just as he always did.

Clear as a bell, I heard Jeff's father, Mr. Porter's voice saying, "Bite the bullet, kids."

I heard Harold Clipclock calling out for another beer, and Ronzo shouting to be careful of his car parked in the driveway, that we did not scratch it, or break a windshield with our puck. I saw my old man rushing across the yard to rescue the Big Spike from the collapsed and broken pool! There was Sal Zucchini, the old mobster with a heart of gold, and all of his henchmen! They were right there in the driveway, speaking with Mr. Redmond! There was the steel barrel with a warm fire in it, smoking and burning, the sparks floating high up into the Christmas-laden air, until they disappeared from sight. Ronzo and the rest of the men stood in the snow in front of the barrel, laughing, smiling, and recalling the legendary time bomb in the cupboard.

They were all there in front of us, talking, laughing, and they seemed so real that we could both see and touch them all.

Then they all disappeared, and they faded away once more. It was a joyous, yet sad reunion of memories.

Now tomorrow, it was all ending, as Harry would begin the next phase of his life, and it would change the famous duo of Harry and Paul forever more.

I heard the back door open, and I saw Sky come out. She spotted us and slowly walked over to join us.

"Hey, what are you two doing out here?" She wrapped a sweater around her as it was a cold March night.

"Oh, Cocoa and I were sharing some time together. He and I do this every once in a while, now for the last ten years or more."

Sky laughed, she came over and sat next to us, "You are thinking about all the three of you have shared here, now aren't you Paul and Cocoa?"

People always knew to speak to Cocoa as if he was a human, because he was indeed, the world's smartest dog.

"You two are not losing, Harry, you are gaining the both of us you know."

"Oh, I am fine, Sky. It is just when you have shared what the two of us, oops, sorry Cocoa, the three of us, have shared for all these years, it will be a big change. I am fine."

Cocoa looked up at me as if he agreed with my statement.

"You know, Sky . . . I knew the first night when you came over that Harry fell for you. He stopped talking as if he was from Texas with that phony act and he just changed back to being Harry. You captured his heart and soul and I could not be happier than I am for the two of you."

Sky leaned over close to me and spoke in a low voice that was almost a whisper.

"Paul, please know that I love Harry with all my heart. He is all I ever dreamed of when I thought of meeting a man and getting married. He is my life now."

"I know. That is why I am so happy for the both of you. I can tell it is real."

She reached down and petted Cocoa as he looked up at the two of us.

"Are you happy for you though, Paul? I am sure that all that success in hockey comes with a price of some pain and some loneliness. I cannot even imagine how hard it was to leave your home, friends, and family at such a hard time in your life, travel halfway across the country to a strange place, and then perform as well as you did."

I shifted a little uneasy because I knew that Sky could see things that most people could not. I tried hard once more to hide my eyes.

"I stay busy, Sky and that is the key, but some nights like tonight, I cannot help but think how great it would be if things had been different, and Binky could have shared in the joy of tomorrow with all of us. I feel like she stole happiness away from me. Does that make any sense to you?"

"Perfect sense, but I tell you someday it will change. Paul, time is the only real enemy we all have, but you will recover all that happiness. You are too wonderful not to."

I smiled at her and stood up.

"Thanks, Sky. We should go in now. You have to be fresh for tomorrow, but not frozen."

Sky took my hand and smiled, and the three of us went back inside. I stopped on the stairs and gently pulled her hand back. Sky stopped, and she looked back at me.

"Tomorrow, you know that a new life begins. Life with Harry is one adventure after another, so my best advice is to go along for the ride and see where it takes you."

"I know, Paul. I know."

I was up early the next morning because I wanted to get going right away. My parents were, of course, also attending the wedding, so it was a busy day at our house. We all had breakfast together and then I showered, trimmed up, and got dressed. The wedding was at one in the afternoon, but I wanted to be over to the house earlier to help in any way that I could. I did not tie all my hair up, instead, I left it long and loose. I think I looked good, at least that is what my mother told me, but she always said that, anyway.

I was over early, and Harry was pacing the floor in his room. He was all dressed, and he looked great, even in his new color of hair. I checked his clothing for any of his famous, "malfunctions."

After all, I was the best man!

"Hey relax. It is all right, Harry."

"That is easy for you to say, you are used to standing in the net with thousands of people screaming at you, while guys try to knock your head off your shoulders with a frozen hockey puck."

I had to admit that he did have a good point. Regardless, Harry was very nervous, and there was not much for me really to say that would calm him down. I just listened as he was working into some type of therapeutic frenzy, telling stories of us together, "Remember when we did this and when we did that." He was a wreck, so I just let him go on and on spilling his memories.

The women chased us out of the second floor because Sky was arriving and the women did not allow Harry to see her. They placed us into exile in the kitchen where Ronzo, the Big Spike, the old man, Father Mark, and Mr. Redmond came and joined us. Harry was still pacing the floor and talking a mile a minute.

Ronzo got up from his chair, opened up a kitchen cupboard, and pulled down a bottle of whiskey. He poured us all a shot and Harry a double.

"Here, drink this. It will help you relax and maybe give our ears a rest."

We all toasted Harry and down our throats, it went.

Father Mark provided clerical guidance, "Give him another one, Ronzo. He still looks like he wants to talk."

Soon it was time. All the guests lined up, I had the rings, Father Mark was in place, and the music had started on the record player. I shook Harry's hand, and we walked out together to take our places in front. We walked side-by-side, to this next phase in Harry's life, just as we had done together so many times before.

Cocoa sat down at attention to watch, with his faithful Piggy at his feet. Cocoa had picked a spot right next to us on the side of the living room.

Sky appeared and slowly walked down the stairs, followed by her sister. She was gorgeous; she was dressed in a white dress with a headband of flowers. She was more than a knockout; she was a triple knockout with a hippie twist. What a woman! Harry was weak in the knees when he saw her and I could not help but think about Harry's favorite singer, Crystal's appearance in the movie, as well as the famous grand entrance at the Black Bear Club. This time was different though; Sky was going to be his wife.

As I stood there next to Harry, a million adventures ran through my head as I reflected on all that we had done together for us to have finally arrived at this point in time.

Father Mark ran the show. You could hear the weeping, the crying, and sniffles in the background and in no time at all it was, "The rings please Paul," and then it was over. Mr. and Mrs. Harry M. Redmond Jr., now officially married. It was a done deal.

I think somewhere down in the deep depths of the basement of 20 John Street, in and amongst the clutter of past phases and smelly, old bowling shoes; even Mr. Bug shed a tear.

The reception was a blast. As I have emphasized, no one on the entire face of the earth could party as the Redmonds could party. The music blasted, the beer flowed, glass after glass of wine poured out of bottomless carafes, and the booze downed. The food was catered in, and it was very good, everything from main food courses to cakes and ice cream. The wedding cake had a huge peace sign on top above layers and layers of cream and sugary goodness. We cleared the serving table out of the rooms and everyone danced after the "official" first dance for Mr. and Mrs. Harry M. Redmond Jr. was completed.

Sky came over to me and she asked with some extreme prodding from Harry and Patty, "I have only heard of the legendary dancing ability of twenty-seven, but I have never had the pleasure of actually seeing you dance. Would you dance with the bride?"

"It would be my pleasure, Sky."

Ronzo played a loud, fast, rock-and-roll record on the record player, and Sky and I cut the rug together in the living room of 20 John Street. She was a very good dancer, she moved really well, and I really enjoyed the dance.

Sky warmly hugged me after our dance, gently kissed my cheek, and thanked me.

"Wow, you can really dance. I could not even keep up with you, and I know you were going easy on me. I swear that woman is crazier than O'Malley to have walked away from you."

Ding-ding! Another vote for old Bink-a-roo-ski and I know that Sky did not even know who poor O'Malley was.

The dance floodgates opened; the very foundations of the old house shook with joy, as I now had to dance with Patty, Linda, my mother, and even Ronzo. Patty insisted on a slow, sexy dance, as she grabbed my hair and held me so close in jest that I felt I was going to break.

Patty was a riot, as she screamed out to her husband, "Are you jealous yet, Big Spike? Are you jealous yet?"

We took a ton of photos; many tears were shed, people laughed, people hugged, and people cried. The night rolled on and on. It was the greatest party ever seen at 20 John Street, and believe me, I had attended a lot of them.

Like all weddings and receptions, it went by all too quickly. Soon the day had passed into night, and the night was early morning. It was time to wrap it all up and after tearful goodbyes and best wishes to all, Mr. and Mrs. Harry M. Redmond Jr. now prepared to depart for their honeymoon. They were riding up to Vermont to a cabin up on Millington Mountain, a wonderful place to be in the late winter and early spring. I had given them a card with some money, a large box of assorted wines, and two necklaces with golden peace signs on the end of them for a gift collection. We piled all the wedding gifts in the Wagon Bus, I helped Harry with the luggage, and it finally came time for us to wish them all off.

Out in front of the house, Sky and Harry thanked each person, hugged them, and kissed everyone goodbye. When it came time for Harry and Sky to walk over to me, Harry grabbed me and hugged me so hard I thought he would snap me in half. I could feel his tears rolling off his face and dripping down upon my shoulder.

"The end to another perfect Harry and Paul day," was all I said. Harry could not even answer me. Sky hugged me, kissed me, and they were off.

I held Linda and Patty's hands as we watched the taillights of the Wagon Bus disappear around the corner and leave John Street. Hades had officially frozen over solid, and still, I could not cry.

13

All the Seasons That Pass You By

Life settled in for Harry and Sky, as well as the rest of us. They rented a small house from one of Harry's distant relatives up in a nice little borough out of the city, off to the north, about five miles from where we grew up. After a vacation for the honeymoon, Harry went back to work at the welding shop, and Sky was back working at the Center for Learning, tending to yoga by candlelight, reading tarot cards, and assisting people with their ionic foot baths. I went over to the Redmonds here and there to have a beer and chat with Ronzo and the rest of the gang. They were still deep in the hippie phase, so not much had changed over there.

Sky, Harry, and I went out to dinner now and then on weekends, but I always felt like the third wheel. It was awkward as I felt they were just being nice to go out with Paul when they would rather be alone. After all, they were young newlyweds, enjoying themselves.

I had hired a managing agent, and he was sorting out the offers and contracts that I had coming in from various teams. I was not happy about going to Canada, for not only dealing with some of the border crossing laws, and for taxes that you had to pay, but also it was so far from home. He was working on a decent deal with a team that would be in a league one-step up from the Hawk's system. It was within the Boston Bear's farm system and the team's home base was in Albany, New York. They had to travel to away games in New England and one stop in Ontario province in

Canada. That was very appealing to me; I could be home from Albany by car in about four hours, so that was ideal.

I worked out hard, ran all the time, and did a lot of lightweights and flex training. The old man helped keep me sharp, as he worked with me on some shooting drills that we had come up with together in our driveway to keep my reflexes sharp, and my eyes tuned.

My father did not really know how to train for hockey, but he had been an excellent baseball player, so he understood coordination and training mechanics. I was feeling good and on top of my game; I was ready.

The fire was burning hard, and I was in the flow.

Still, that empty pit and ache down deep in my stomach never went away. No matter how I tried to forget, the pain never really went away.

To be honest, the best times I had were when I spoke with, or got to go out with Rose. She was still dating that same guy she had mentioned, but every once in a while, we would meet up for a beer. We would talk until the bars closed down and they kicked us out. Next to Harry and Sky, Rose was my comfort zone, and with the two newlyweds always busy, it was nice to hang out with Rose and laugh.

I signed the deal in late April for the team in Albany, and I picked up a nice signing bonus, as well as a solid one-year deal. Even after paying off my agent, I banked a nice chunk of money for a poor kid from Paterson. I was now a member of the Albany Flying Dutchman. Oh well, weird name. But after all, I had been a Rooster for two years, so this was not that bad. I found a nice little apartment in a small town outside of Albany called Latham, New York.

I was off in early September 1980 to my next stop in my hockey career. It sure was a great location as I could easily drive straight up and down the New York State Thruway back and forth to Paterson.

I quickly worked through all the goodbyes, and once I

had them out of the way, I packed up my old, faithful, MJ-17 jeep and the two of us rolled north. I enjoyed it in upstate New York. It was cool, the late summer was nice, not very humid, and it was very cold at night.

I liked it when it was cold.

The culture was the same as New Jersey and I noticed very little difference, unlike when I was in Kansas City. Not many folks pointed out my heavy accent and asked, "Where are you from long hair?" They rooted for the Canaries, Bugs, Lasers, Rovers, and all the New Jersey, New York and Connecticut teams that I grew up watching and following.

No one here previously had heard that much about my past or my career, so I was very happy. It was a fresh start. I did very well in early practices and I liked the coach, team, arena, and my teammates. I had settled in; it had been the correct choice for me.

What I really enjoyed the most was having my own apartment. I had my own space, and I enjoyed being alone. I played my No Way records, read many books, and worked out a lot. I was in the best shape of my life, my body was toned, and I was ready to take on the best hockey shooters from anywhere in the world. I had no one to answer to, and no one bothered me.

I spoke with Harry and Sky on the phone here and there, but honestly, we talked less and less all the time. I spoke with Rose when I could, but for the most part, I had grown accustomed to the loneliness.

After all the years of family and close friends surrounding me, it was a very different life, but I slowly accepted the change. In fact, I grew to enjoy it. I was alone with my memories and I could stay focused on my job and mission.

Hockey was now my life. It was where I felt safe and secure, I could hide behind my goalie mask, and the world did not know who I was. In some ways, it felt good to be number twenty-seven, and Paul John Henson was gone. He was nowhere where anyone could find him, and I really liked it that way.

Two or three apartments away from mine lived a young, dynamic, red-haired gal. She was very nice; she would flirt with me and come over to talk to me whenever she would see me. She pretended that she was into hockey when she heard that I was a professional player, and she tried very hard to connect with me. I was polite to her and tried not to be rude as she was very pleasant and very attractive, but I could not really be bothered. She hinted a lot about going out for dinner and tried to coax an invitation out of me. One day, when she did not receive any of the desired results from me, she just outright asked me out for dinner. I declined as nicely and politely as I could. I did not want to hurt her feelings, but I was just not interested in any relationships at this time.

I was a long-haired hippie hockey goaltender, and I stayed focused on my mission.

The Albany Flying Dutchman hockey club listed me as the starting goaltender for the opening game, which was against a team from Portland, Maine. It was opening night in our home arena and the place filled with hometown fans and visitors right to capacity. The Maine team had a tall and strong center iceman whom my teammates had warned me about before the game. He had a big-league caliber slap shot, a mean streak, and a big mouth.

From the opening faceoff, he taunted me, looking hard to see if he could find a weakness in the new, hotshot goalie that the Albany hockey team just brought in here. He commented whenever he could as he skated by, on my hair, my New Jersey roots, and other general trash talk. The first chance he took to take a headshot at me, he did, and rather than aim at the net to score, he aimed to see if he could get me to flinch, kill me, or just to put fear into my heart. He ripped a rocket of a shot that he carefully aimed at tearing my head off, which I easily gloved, and then dropped and passed the puck off to one of my teammates to create a scoring opportunity.

The strategy had backfired as the Dutchman's best scorer scooted down the ice with my pass and he scored down at the other end. The poor decision at trying intimidation enraged the big center as he jawed at me, working hard to get a reaction. I just laughed at him, I had no fear at all of this idiot, and he was in the minor leagues compared to Jim O'Malley.

O'Malley would have eaten this guy for breakfast, sliced him up, and then had him for dessert after dinner. I had trained under the best hockey lunatic available in all the land. I played with such a fire, such a lack of fear, and such high confidence; it was as if I had been waiting my entire life for this moment.

Making saves in the net was my release, and it was now easy to hide behind the goalie mask, stare down life, as well as the shooters, with an edge that I never had before, and it made me satisfied. It was where I felt the most comfortable, and I could hide that persistent pain that I had learned to ignore, but never went away.

I cemented my status as the starting goalie for the Albany team and I was on my way.

It was a week or so before Christmas, in December 1980, when we were in Burlington, Vermont, playing an away game. Our team was in first place, but this Vermont team was hot on our heels in second place, so this was a big game for us. Late in the second period, we were protecting a three to one lead, when the action caught me a little out of position at the top of the crease. A hard slap shot came out of a screen in front, and it caught me directly on the tip of my left skate. I could not get my stick down in time, but I made the save. The pain was immediate even through the thick, white, plastic shell that surrounded my goaltender skates.

I knew something bad had happened.

I held the puck for a faceoff and managed to coax the referee into a whistle for a play stoppage. I tried to skate the pain off, but it did not feel very good.

When the period ended, I headed straight for the locker room, grabbed the team trainer, and asked him to call the team doctor. Sure enough, by the time I got my skate off, I knew my big toe and the toe next to it were broken. In fact, the toe next to my big toe was pretty well smashed.

The doctor checked me in the locker room and he gave me the straight scoop. "You are done for tonight, Paul. This is all swelling badly now, and I have to straighten the smaller toe out and splint it. We cannot risk losing you for any longer than we have to. Paul, you are the leading goalie in the league right now. I know you are a tough guy, and you want to play, but let's get you to the hospital, get this fixed, and get you healed up and ready to go for the next games after the holidays. We can send you back to Albany early and you can start your Christmas break."

The head coach was there, and he agreed, "Look, we are ahead here, Paul. I think you kept us in the game long enough. We can stick Raymond in the net and finish this game and then we are off for fifteen days for Christmas break." The coach turned to the doctor and asked, "Will he be good to go by then, doc?"

"Sure, he will be able to be back in the net in ten days, so you should be fine." I was not happy, but they were in charge. It was out of my control.

"Let's do it, put Paul on the disabled list, and let's cruise into the break."

The disabled list! I had never ever missed a game! However, if it had to come, then it came at a good time when we had no games scheduled, anyway. I went to the hospital, they x-rayed me, and splinted my toes, and I was good to go back to Albany a few hours early. The doctor told me that I was to stay off it as much as possible, but it would heal fast and really was not a big deal. In fact, it did not even really hurt that badly anymore. We had won the game, so we ended in first place going into the break, and I was heading home for the holiday, anyway.

Sooner than I had thought, I was back in the apartment in Latham, packing my bags to drive back for Christmas. I was thinking how lucky it was for driving that the toes were broken on my left foot when the telephone rang.

I picked it up and heard Sky's voice, but I could barely hear her, as she was speaking in a low, weak whisper, "Hello Paul, it is Sky."

I could tell by her voice that something was seriously wrong. "What's wrong, Sky?"

"Oh, Paul. Can you come home right now? I am afraid that Harry is going to need you badly in the next day or so. He will need your strength and courage. You will be his resource so that he can go on. Can you come home, Paul?"

"I will come right away. Sky, what is going on?"

"Paul, I have been very sick as of late. I have been in and out of the hospital for the last month or two. The doctors admitted me yesterday, and I feel that I will never leave here alive. We did not want to tell you, and get you upset while you were away and playing so well, but we need you now, Paul. It is something beyond what I can do at the center to heal. The doctors have found a large growth in my female organs, and they are going to operate tonight. Paul, they want me to go in right now for the operation. I feel like this is so very serious. I am so sick and weak. I can feel it Paul, and I am not afraid for me, but I am so worried about Harry."

"I am on my way, right now. I will leave right now, Sky. It will be all right, Sky . . . you are going to be all right."

"I do not think so Paul, I feel something very bad within my body. However, I know you will take care of everything that I cannot. Come Paul, I am in Wayne General Hospital on the Hamburger Turnpike. Drive safely, but please come quickly. I love you, Paul. Always remember that we all love you."

"I love you too Sky, I am leaving now."

The line went dead. My heart was beating a mile a minute. I grabbed my bag, threw it in the jeep, and tore off for the New York State Thruway southbound. I rode off into the night with a thousand thoughts going off in my head, of which the last was the pain in my left foot.

A moment changes everything once more, one stinking, awful, horrible moment.

It was the longest four hours of my life as I drove down to New Jersey and finally arrived at the hospital.

I found the correct area from the woman at the hospital information desk, and I hustled off to the wing and waiting room that she had given me. While walking down the hallway, I spotted Linda and Ronnie, who saw me and ran up to greet me. Linda hugged me as Ronnie held her.

They were both crying.

"Oh, Paul! Thank God, you are here. Thank God that you are here, Paul."

That was all I could get out of Linda. I looked over her shoulder at Ronnie, who was wiping away tears as he shook his head back and forth to me.

We walked over to where Patty, George, and Mr. Redmond were sitting, and they all hugged and greeted me. They all were crying, too.

"Please, Paul, come over here." Mr. Redmond put his arm around me and led me away from the rest of the family.

"It is not good, Paul. Sky has been so sick for the last few months. They decided to operate to try to cut out the cancer. When they opened Sky up, they closed her right away. She is full of cancer, and she must have had it for a very long time and did not know it. The surgeon said there was nothing he could do. She was so weak that her heart stopped on the operating table, and then started back up, but she slipped into a coma. And it is not looking good. Father Mark was here and performed last rites. It is not looking like more than a day, or so, her organs are shutting down since the air hit them, and the cancer spread even more."

I felt my knees going weak and my throat closing around me.

How could this all be happening? How could no one have known? How could this really be all true? Still, I could not cry, but I felt an anger rising up in me, anger at the injustice of it all, an anger that I could not even describe.

"Where is Harry, Mr. Redmond?"

"He is in the room, sitting right next to her bed. He needs Paul, as he has never needed you before. We all need you, Paul."

I breathed deep and hugged the kind, gentle soul who was like a second father to me, and I had known since I was just a little squirt.

"I am here, let me go in and see Harry and Sky."

I walked towards the room when a nurse came over and stopped me.

"Please, only, immediate family, sir. Are you a member of the immediate family?"

In all my years, I have never even heard Mr. Redmond raise his voice. Nonetheless, get angry, but he heard what the nurse said, and he shot right over to us.

"He is in the immediate family. He is Harry's brother, and he is my son. Now, let him in!"

The nurse backed off, and I walked into the room. It was horrible. Attached to Sky were all kinds of tubes, monitors, and all sorts of other medical instruments. Harry was sitting in a chair next to her bed, holding her hand with his head down on the bed.

I walked over, put my hand on his shoulder, and said, "I am here, Harry, I am here."

Harry did not move, but I heard him sobbing his eyes out. "Please, Paul," his voice cracked, "you are the smartest man I have ever met, and you make saves in the net all the time. You always solve problems . . . do something Paul . . . save Sky. Please Paul, save Sky."

He was rocking back and forth with his hands folded together as he trembled.

"I wish I could Harry, but it is out of my hands, oh, how I wish I could, but it is out of my hands."

Harry sat there next to her, and I stood there with him. I kept my hand on his shoulder, supporting him and comforting him, standing by my friend, just as I had always stood with him through the good and the bad.

I stood there and stared at Sky; how peaceful and beautiful she was. I stood there for six hours straight, right next to Harry, holding him up as he held her hand. We watched her breathing become shallower until she slipped away from us forever.

I did not cry. I was hollow and empty inside, emptier inside than I had ever been before, but I did not cry.

I held Harry as his body heaved in sorrow and God, how I wished I could have made this one save, just one save God. Why could I not have made one more save?

The funeral was the most heart wrenching experience of my life. It took all of my inner strength and courage to guide Harry through it. It was pure anguish; there was no other way to describe it other than pure anguish. I would have rather endured any punishment on Earth than go through what we all were going through on this horrible day. The families were a wreck. No one could even function or speak. My parents were both in shambles; they had known Harry for so, so long, through such joy, and now, through such sorrow. Rose was there as well as lots of other countless friends and family, but it was surreal, and beyond intense.

It was a blur in time.

The intensity of the sorrow was something that you could not imagine, or even feel, or I could ever describe. It was like agony that you could not endure anymore. You wanted to fall on your knees and plead for mercy. We had all seen such joy in Harry's heart since Sky came into his life, and now it was so cold, dark, and awful.

It was a cold, horrible, overcast December day as we walked out of the limousine and climbed up a long hill in the cemetery to the gravesite. I carried Harry and physically held him up as we followed the casket up the hill behind Father Mark. I held him as his entire body heaved in sorrow while Father Mark conducted the graveside service. I held him as we turned and walked away, and I dragged him from the grave, a sobbing, twisting mess of humanity.

I still never shed a tear. The numb feeling and twisting pit I used to call a stomach lingered within me. I loaded Harry into the limousine and Father Mark walked over to me. His face wore the anguish of the day.

"You need to have a doctor come by Paul and give Harry a sedative. I will make the arrangements. Are you going to bring him to his house, or yours?"

"I will bring him to his house. Father Mark, I will be staying with him for a while, and I do not have to go back to New York for a week or so . . . I will not leave him. Please come by, Father Mark . . . I am not sure I can take any more of this, I need help."

Father Mark looked at me as the cold, bitter wind blew as hard as it could at the both of us on that horrible hillside. He put his hand upon my shoulder.

"Paul, you can take it. You are strong, and God gives you special strength. He always has ever since you were just a little boy, and he always will. I have watched you two grow up together, and you are steady, strong, and the rock of them all. When Harry would act out on some fantasy, and the Redmonds were off on their next phase in life, you always held them all steady. Your parents named you well, Paul. You take after another Paul that I have read a little about. God bless you, Paul John Henson, I will be there soon and meet you at the house."

We drove to Harry's house, and I managed to get him a drink of water, which he sipped between sobs. He did not speak; he only cried and moaned my name as well as Sky's name repeatedly. I managed to get him undressed, and in bed, when Father Mark and the doctor arrived. The doctor gave Harry an injection and soon he mercifully drifted off to sleep. The doctor gave me some pills and instructions on how to keep him sedated and calm for the next few days. I thanked him and told him that I would call if I needed any more assistance or advice. Father Mark and I let the doctor out and we sat in the living room. Cocoa came in and sat next to me. The poor dog was also devastated, and he really needed our companionship.

The afternoon was creeping on now, and the overcast skies had cleared a little before the sun had a chance to go down. I could see some rays of sun peeking through the breaking clouds as it sank low in the sky.

"Paul, I know you are a Lutheran, and we will both break some rules here. But would you like to partake in communion?"

"I will, if we can commune together Father Mark, I can say the Lutheran liturgy from my memory for you, if that will work."

"It will work, Paul."

He went out to his car and brought back his communion kit. We served each other communion and then we prayed together. Father Mark, Cocoa, and I then sat in silence in the living room as we watched the sun go down through the windows.

"Tell me how something such as this can happen in this world, Father Mark. Tell me how a loving God takes someone like Sky from someone like Harry. Tell me that

Father, so I can understand."

I have never seen a priest or a pastor cry, ever, not in even the worst of times. The tears rolled down Father Mark's cheeks like a waterfall. He motioned for me to stand up, and then he grabbed me by the shoulders and led me outside on the porch as we faced the sunset.

"I will show you why, Paul . . . that is why."

He pointed at the rays of sun just setting and the faint pieces of blue sky illuminated for a last curtain call before the night came.

"That is why, Paul, because God decided that Heaven needed more pieces of blue sky, so that her beauty could light up every day in both Heaven and on Earth."

I then remembered as I stared at the blue sky, what Sky had told me on the first night that I had met her, "People never really go away forever. Even when they die, they return to us, somehow. We remain together forever with the people that we love."

I smiled at Father Mark, he smiled at me, and we put our arms together and interlocked our hands. The two of us stood there for a long time, until the sun had faded and the night finally came.

I stayed with Harry, both day and night, and he slept most of the time. Family came by and checked on us; all of them, from Ronzo and Linda, Patty and the Big Spike, my parents, Mr. Redmond, Father Mark; everyone. I called Rose and filled her in, and we talked for a little while. Cocoa and I just hung around, watching Harry together.

Harry got up occasionally, and I managed to get him to eat some toast and soup and to take a shower. When he began to get upset, I had him take some more pills and go back to sleep.

Sleep seemed to be the only peace he had.

It was only a few days until Christmas now, and Harry and Sky had a little Christmas tree they had put up in the corner of their living room, which I plugged in and let it twinkle in the night. Little peace signs and other little wooden signs that simply said "Love" decorated the Christmas tree.

I almost lost track of the days; they all were the same.

I was sleeping on the couch in the living room and really sacked out as I woke up to the sunlight peeking down on me and to the noises of pots and pans banging in the kitchen. I moved and looked ahead to the kitchen, and saw Harry moving around in there, and Cocoa sitting next to the kitchen table.

I stood up and wandered over.

Harry was standing in front of the stove working a frying pan with some eggs in them.

"Hey, twenty-seven, man, I thought you would never wake up. Are you hungry? You want some eggs?"

"Sure, Harry, let me wash up. Did you let Cocoa out?"

"Yeah, yeah, yeah, we went for a long walk early this morning, he is good."

I went to the bathroom, washed up, dressed, and came back to the kitchen.

"How do you feel?"

"I feel a little better. I am just kind of hungry now, you know."

"I guess so. You only would eat some soup and some toast here and there. It has been a bit rough."

Harry dished out some eggs for the both of us and some toast. We sat at the table together.

"When do you have to get back to the team?"

"I have until the twenty ninth of December. I broke two toes and I have to rest anyway, so I cannot skate until then."

"Ouch, big slapper, eh?"

"Yeah, yeah, yeah, big shot, and I just caught it right, I could not protect myself."

Harry took a deep breath and I could see his body shudder and quake; the pain was still trying to leave him.

"Oh, what is it like two days until Christmas, Paul?"

I looked up at the calendar on the wall to double check.

"No, Christmas was yesterday Harry, you slept through it."

Harry looked at me and dropped his fork as he said with shock, "You have been here with me the whole time? You did not visit your folks on Christmas Day. Today is your Boxing Day holiday that you always spend with Mum."

"No, I am good. I have had a lot of Christmases and Boxing Days. Harry, it just was not that important this year. They are just days, like any other day."

Harry looked at me through deep, sad eyes that seemed like they had no more tears left in them.

"You guys are in first?"

"Yeah, only by three points though . . . tough league."

"I looked up your stats in the beginning of the year, then I lost track when Sky got. . .." His voice trailed off before he could say the word sick. We finished our breakfast in silence and cleaned up the dishes together. It was good, though, to see him up, moving around, and eating.

"Twenty-seven, you need to go home and visit Mum on Boxing Day." Harry was walking slowly to the living room, barely moving his feet with his head down.

"I am good, Harry. Mum understands she really does."

Harry stopped and looked at me.

"Father Mark is coming over. I spoke to him early this morning when you were sleeping and he and I will spend some time together. I will be fine. You have done so much. Please go, and see your parents before you have to head back up north. I will see you in the morning. Please, it is what I want, and it is what Sky would expect."

When Harry muttered Sky's name, his eyes welled up. He collapsed in his easy chair, and he stared at me.

"Are you sure?"

"Yes, yes, please, I am sure."

"All right, Harry, if Father Mark is on his way, then I

will call my folks and then head over to see them. Just call me right away if you need something. I can be back here in fifteen minutes."

Harry extended his hand out to me, and I grabbed it and shook it.

"You are the best Paul, and someday when I can think straight, I will find the right words to tell you how much I owe you, and how much you mean to all of us."

"Harry, you owe me nothing. Like I told you before, you only have to be my friend, that is all you ever will owe me."

I gave Cocoa a quick pat on the head, I grabbed my gear, and out the door, I went. When I was pulling my jeep out of the driveway, I spotted Father Mark parking his car out in front of the house. I waited until he got out of the car and he was walking towards the house.

He stopped when he saw me and asked, "How is he, Paul?"

"Finally, he is up and he ate, he is still shaky, but he is at least speaking."

Father Mark waved and nodded, "I will call you, thank you."

I pulled out and headed to my parent's house. They were happy to see me, as was old Skippy. It was a very solemn and quiet day. We usually had a nice roast beef dinner with Yorkshire pudding for Boxing Day, some beer, and some good times. It was so brutal that we all did not even eat that much. We just sat around and mostly stared at each other as the day slowly ticked away. The conversation we had was entirely about how we were dumbfounded at the horrible events of the last two weeks or so. I gave my parents a rundown on how Harry was doing, but for the most part, I hardly spoke.

We passed the time by sitting together in silence. My mother cried a lot. In fact, at times, she sobbed her eyes out, while my father and I did the best we could to comfort her.

It was a strange way to spend time with my parents; it was really under the worst of situations.

Father Mark called me. He told me that Harry was doing all right, but he had gone back to bed early and seemed to be sleeping soundly now.

He said they had settled some things and that Harry would fill me in when I came in the morning. I did not really understand that statement, but I thanked him and assured him that I would be there early in the morning.

I had not been home in six months or so, so it was surely different sleeping back in my old room and in my old bed. Sleep did not come very easy. I had forgotten about my broken toes, and they throbbed a little tonight, but it was mostly the pain in my heart, and in my stomach, that kept me awake. All of our lives had changed so much in such a short amount of time, it really made my head spin.

I was over at Harry's house bright and early. I was very surprised when I met him in the driveway of his house carrying some items to the Wagon Bus. I noticed the little Christmas tree sitting in the driveway.

The tree still had all the decorations upon it, and the little tree was sitting next to a few boxes and some suitcases.

"Hey Harry . . . what is going on?"

Harry stopped, and he put down a box that he was carrying. "Hello Paul, I was just loading up the last of these boxes here."

"Boxes? What are you doing?"

Harry shifted on his feet as if he was uneasy.

"Paul, I cleaned the house out yesterday. Father Mark and the Catholic Charities helped me. I donated everything to them except for a few odds and ends, my own necessities, and my clothes. It is all gone. Furniture, pictures, pots, pans, forks, knives, Sky's clothes, all of it, gone. I called my Aunt Gracie, who we rented the house from, and told her that the house would be vacant. I told her I would wire her the entire balance of the lease money tomorrow. I am gone, Paul. Cocoa and I will be leaving."

"Leaving? Why? What are you doing? Where are you going?" I was puzzled.

Harry walked over to me and stood in front of me.

"I am taking off. The house has been swept clean of everything left of our lives together. I have to go, Paul."

"Go where, Harry?"

I was now confused and concerned.

Harry came over and put his hand on my shoulder as he explained, "I have a distant uncle out in Michigan. He lives out near the border with Canada. I have decided to head out there and stay with him for a while. I just have to get out of here, Paul."

Harry looked away from me for a second, and then he looked right back at me and stared into my eyes.

"There is nothing here for me except ghosts and bad memories. I cannot take it. I need to go, be out on my own for a while, and just think. I have plenty of money from the song. I do not even have to work right now. I have to get out of New Jersey. I know that you, of all people . . . I know that you understand, Paul."

I was not saying a word, but deep down, I did know what he was feeling. I knew how much some things hurt and how good it felt to get away. I also knew very well of the ghosts and how they followed us both around.

"Why don't you come along with me to upstate New York? You would love it there. We could hang together, go to the games, and tear up some joints. I have an extra room in my apartment. It would be a new start. Harry and Paul, and Cocoa, together like we always have been."

He smiled. It was the first time that I had seen him smile in a long time. He shook his head as he started to bend down to pick up the little Christmas tree.

"I can't, Paul. I have to make a new start. We can't ever go back to the way we used to be. It has all changed now.

All those things we did, all those great times we had, I will never forget them, but it all is so different now. Nothing . . . will ever be the same, we could never go back."

I knew he was right.

He reached down the rest of the way, picked up the little Christmas tree, and he carefully put it in the back of the Wagon Bus. He turned and looked at me and said, "I will never take this down, or put it away, Paul. It was the last real thing we did together. We decorated this tree. She was so sick, but we did this together. Then we sat in the living room, and turned all the lights out in the house, and we held each other and cried as we looked at how perfect it was glowing in the night. I will keep it forever more. I swear I will move it from town to town, house to house, from state to state, from country to country. It will never leave me no matter where on the Earth that I go. It will be a memorial to her wherever I go. I will die and ask you to bury it with me."

Harry stood there in front of me with the tears running down his face.

"This little tree is all I have left of her, Paul. All I have left of my dear wife . . . is this perfect, little Christmas tree."

I nodded my head as if I could really ever feel even the smallest amount of pain that Harry was feeling right now.

"When will I hear from you or see you again?"

"I don't know, Paul. Maybe soon or maybe never again."

I stood there not saying anything because I had run out of words and thoughts to say.

Harry lifted the last of his bags into the Wagon Bus and he came over to me.

"Always remember twenty-seven, no matter where you are, or I am . . . we will always be together forever. For Harry and Paul, the night always comes, and that is when we are out there, running around, doing the things that we always did, and taking on the world together."

I held him, and I could hear him sobbing as we

embraced. He let go of me, turned, and whistled for Cocoa. Cocoa came, stopped running, and placed Piggy on the ground. He jumped on me and I held him as he licked my face for one last time. Then he picked up Piggy, and jumped in the Wagon Bus.

Harry climbed in and closed the door. He started the vehicle, put it in gear, and he drove down the street slowly. I watched the taillights for a long time until they disappeared and I could no longer see them.

I stood there alone in the street, and I finally felt some tears running down my face. I stood there crying, as I had not cried in years. It was as if the seal finally broke on my internal tear valve, and I could not shut it off.

I cried, as I never have in my entire life.

14

Believe It and It Will Happen

It was early November in 1984. I had returned to Paterson in the late summer after being away for the last four or so years. For some unknown reason, I always kept coming back here. I am not sure why, but I just always did. I really wanted to go back to upstate New York, back in the capital area around Albany. I liked that location better than any other place I had ever lived.

I guess there was some type of comfort factor, or fate of some sort, that always brought me back to Paterson.

I had no solid explanation for it.

An awful lot had happened to me since Sky had passed away and Harry had left New Jersey. Neither his family nor I had heard a spoken word from Harry since we parted that day out in front of his house right after Christmas in 1980. All of us, including, Mr. Redmond, his sisters, my parents, Father Mark, Rose, and me, received a postcard from him about two years ago, that just said, "Thinking of you" with his signature on the back. It had no return address on it. That was all we had heard since he left. No one had any additional contacts with him since we received those cards.

The loss of Harry in my life created a void that I just could not describe or maybe even understand or accept. Loneliness is a pain that I cannot clearly convey. It tears away at your very heart and soul. We had both shared so much together since we were about ten years old, and now he was gone.

It was as if a part of me went with him.

I was just not the same person. I felt empty, and at times cold and uncaring.

The memories of all of our adventures together were something I carried with me wherever I went; they were just there all the time in the back of my mind. Just like this whole story has been for so very long.

Sometimes, these memories were a curse that I knew I would never shake.

Now, when you add to the fact that I missed Binky every single hour of every day, then it was even more of a burden. I never really could figure it all out. The sadness ebbed and flowed, but it was something that I could not entirely control.

Perhaps I never would.

I had returned to Albany and had a very successful year there. Our team won our league championship, and I won a league MVP trophy and received some great publicity. The management of the Bear's organization in Boston offered me a contract to play in the Atlantic Coastal League for a team in Norfolk, Virginia in the farm system of the Boston Bears. Before I even realized it, I was within one-step of the big time. I hated to leave upstate New York, as it was the best place I had ever lived, and I really enjoyed it there.

Virginia was not my favorite place. It was terribly hot and humid, and I despise the heat. I did play well there for two years straight. I was within a week or two of a call up to the big time when I was involved in a terrible collision in front of the net. I was sandwiched between two players, and I felt my knee tear in half.

It was not good. I had to have extensive surgery to repair both my ACL and MCL ligaments on my right knee. The rehabilitation took forever. By the time I got back into the game, time and the team had passed me by.

To be honest, my heart for the game had finally given

out. I did not have the flexibility I had at one time, and my skills were not the same.

I never made it to the big time, but I had come close. I had played goalie for a very long time. The aches, scars, and pains from years of playing goaltender remained a constant reminder to me of the time I spent between the pipes.

I could never forget even if I tried.

I received a contract buyout due to the injury, and a settlement from some insurance I had taken on myself in case of injury.

I retired from professional hockey in April 1984. I had banked an awful lot of money over the years of playing. I never spent a dime of my contract signings; it was all there in the bank, never touched. I had no real regrets. A kid from the streets of Paterson, who started playing hockey on the streets using the sawed-off ends of Christmas trees for hockey pucks. In addition, I came within a step or two of the big time.

Some folks said I had a bad break. They would shake their heads and tell me how I had suffered such bad luck because I would have been one of the best of all time. I say no, I lived my dream, I did the best that I could, and I have all those memories to take with me forever. I traveled all over North America, lived in different places, had been interviewed on television and radio, met different people; it had been a good run.

I would not have traded the experience for anything.

Well, come to think of it, that was not true. Looking back, maybe I would have traded it for a few things. The hurt never left me, even after all these years; my stomach always had that same dull ache deep inside of me. It never left me, ever. Not a day went by that I did not think about Harry, Sky, Rose, the Redmonds, 20 John Street, or Binky.

Not a single day.

I came back to no fanfare like the shindig I had when I

came back after my stint with the Hawks in Kansas City. Mr. Redmond had retired and moved to a retirement community in Florida. We had spoken on the telephone many times, and he never got over the loss of Harry in his life and the grief we all felt. I guess he had the same ghosts chasing him around that I had seen and experienced.

Linda and Ronzo took all the money from the song and moved out to the woods in the Pocono Mountains in Pennsylvania. The Big Spike and Patty moved all the way to the west coast when George took a job out there.

The house at 20 John Street was sold a year or so earlier and a young family moved in there. I wondered how they moved all that clutter and stuff out of there and where Mr. Bug ended up. I somehow had hoped that he did not end up tossed into the trash somewhere in an unceremonious manner. My hope was that some other New York Bug fan grabbed him, and he once more was hanging out on a porch somewhere proclaiming his love of the Bugs to the world.

I rode by the house at 20 John Street a number of times after I returned to the city. I stood out in front of it . . . and just remembered. I wanted to ring the doorbell, and tell the young family that lived there now about all that had happened in that wonderful old home. I would tell them all of it, from exploding swimming pools, to picnics, the old kitchen table, to parties, to weddings, to time bombs in cupboards, to Christmas trees that hung upside down in the big oak tree in the yard.

I came close to ringing the doorbell once or twice, but I never had the courage to do it.

The old man retired, and my parents moved out to Sussex County in rural New Jersey. They bought a nice, small, comfortable home that was low maintenance and perfect for them. The old man was now living his dream as he had finally received a promotion at work the last five years or so that he worked at the shop. He had received a promotion to a general foreman, and he finally made a good amount of money. That, combined with Mum's fantastic money handling skills, gave him a nice chunk of change to retire on.

He finally sold the old 1964 Putter Classic model 200, and he bought a brand new, Substantial Industries Rhino 400. It was the car of his dreams, and the old man was in his glory tooling down Route 23, just daring folks to try to cut him off or run into him. After all of those years, of other cars running the old man off the road into ditches in the powerless Putter, the old man was finally on top of his game.

I was very proud of him.

I swear that he washed, and he polished up the Rhino every single day.

There was a strong sense of sadness the day he sold that old Putter, and he put away his Super Deluxe, Whiz-Bang, tool set from Substantial Industries for the last time. Many wars the old man had fought on that old car, from water pumps to steering boxes, to exhaust systems, and there was somehow a strong love-hate relationship between the old man and that old car. He stood in the driveway for a long time watching it for the last time as it rode down the road with the new owner at the wheel.

I swear that I saw a little tear appear in the old man's eye.

To this day, I think he secretly wishes that the old Putter were forever more rolling up and down the roads somewhere in automobile heaven, rather than having come back to life as a recycled trash can, or something worse than that.

Father Mark had retired, and he was no longer in the area. I missed him; we shared some wonderful discussions over the years in both very good times, and some very bad times. He was a special guy. He sent me many notes, cards, and letters over the years, and I always wrote him back.

I even exchanged letters with Henry Jazkot way out on the prairies in Canada. He had torn his Achilles tendon a few months after I left the Hawks and he had to retire. He had followed my career and congratulated me on how far I had made it. He was a good guy.

I had always kept in touch with Rose and even came back to New Jersey to attend her wedding a few years back. She married that chap that she had dated for years, and they seemed somewhat happy. The three of us went to dinner one night, and we shared many of the old times. His name was Daniel, he was an all-right chap, but he seemed a little on the stuffy side. He corrected me rather adamantly when I slipped up at dinner and called him Dan rather than Daniel. Oh well, I did have to give him some credit for sitting there as Rose and I talked about all the old adventures that I am sure made no sense at all to him.

Maybe I was wrong about him, but he just did not seem like a fun person. But he went along with us, anyway. Rose seemed happy enough, but I always detected such an inner sadness to her. Maybe Rose and I had the same trouble.

We could not forget.

I still spoke to Rose about once a month. She was one of my dearest and best friends, and that would never change. I never asked her about Binky and she never mentioned her to me. It was an understanding that we had together.

I had a little apartment not all that far from where Harry and I grew up, and it was very nice. It was all I needed and wanted. I lived alone, kept to myself, and that is how I liked it. Once or twice, I debated taking some of my money and buying a little house, but I never did it. There was no real reason to.

My knee healed up fine. In fact, I could run, work out, and do my old drills. I was still slim, trim, and strong. I could have gone back into the net, and I am sure that I could have played very well for some local teams, but I had no real desire. It was an agreement that I seemed to have reached with myself. It was as if I had achieved what I needed to in my heart, and I was satisfied.

Occasionally, I ran into some folks who knew me and of my hockey career, and they treated me like a celebrity, but it was not very often. I dated a few gals here and there, but never more than once or twice, and then it was over.

Once they became too clingy or attached to me, I took off.

I had gone back into the electrical service business, worked my way up to an operations manager and estimator, and made a decent wage. The work and my job were very enjoyable, but I had another crazy idea that I was pursuing. I told no one about it. Even my parents, my sister, or Rose did not know. I kept it to myself because it seemed so off the wall.

I had steadily gone back to church after I retired from hockey since I now had the time to go on Sundays. It had strongly affected me spiritually. I enrolled in a local college part time, and I was taking some night and weekend courses as a prelude to thinking about going on to a seminary and becoming a Lutheran minister.

I had Sky, Father Mark, and believe it or not, Jim O'Malley to thank as my inspiration for this crazy idea. I attended a reunion of our old hockey league and ran into him at the dinner. He had retired from hockey and he had become an evangelical pastor for a nondenominational church. After I had stopped laughing, I figured if O'Malley could do it, then so could I.

Life sure is strange.

I would not only have been a long-haired hippie goalie, but now I would have to convince folks that I was a long-haired, hippie, pastor. It was a little crazy, but still, I stayed in school and studied.

After work on Fridays, I would frequent a little bar and grille right around the corner from my apartment. If it were hockey season, I would watch the New York Rover games on a big television screen they had in the corner.

A waitress named Mary would always take good care of me and I would take care of her.

Mary was on the payroll, as Harry would say.

She would keep my table aside over in a dark corner by myself, so that I would not be bothered, and bring me my beer and my usual food. Besides, Mary kept the lounge lizard women away from me, and any other floozies, who would happen to come by. She was middle-aged, big and tough, but she was very kind. Mary knew that I rather be left alone to watch my game and dwell on my hockey and other memories. She would make sure that was always the way.

This particular Friday was no different from any others; well, I should not say that. It started out the same. After work and a shower, I dressed in my usual No Way tee shirt and old worn dungarees. I still had all that long hair all tied up behind my head, and my beard and mustache. Some things never changed, I guess.

For some reason, though, I could not find the last piece of my usual outfit. I could not find my old canvas sneakers and I went on a search. I found them in a closet, and when I picked them up, I spotted a long-forgotten paper bag.

Hmm, what is in this?

I opened it up and found a bunch of old candles, a few peace sign necklaces, and to my surprise, a smudge stick of dried sage herbs. I smiled, as it must have been something Harry or Sky had given me a long time ago. I stared at the smudge stick and thought of that night so long ago.

Oh, why not, I thought. I sure could use a dose of positive energy.

I put one of the peace necklaces on, said a short prayer aloud, fought to light it and when I finally did, I walked all over the apartment. I walked into all the rooms, speaking aloud, good thoughts and short prayers. I went into all the corners and then set it on the table in the kitchen as it finally expired.

I felt a tingle of sadness at remembering the original event, but I also felt good. I was relaxed. I headed out to the gin joint; the game tonight should be a good one.

I walked in right before the opening faceoff; Mary waved to me and brought my Big Boulder beer over. After some small talk, she dropped the beer and left me alone. I became engrossed in the game. The New York Rovers versus the Philly Comets, cold Big Boulder beer, a big screen; fantastic stuff.

Even after all these years I still loved it, I could feel even through the television screen, the ebb and flow of the game.

It was magic to me.

It was where I escaped. If I closed my eyes, in my head, I could hear the noise that the ice made when players cut edges hard, I could hear the special sound that the puck would make when it hit a stick, and I could pretend that I was still following the action from behind that fiberglass mask that I would hide behind.

It was the second period; the game was close, and I kept my focus on the action. Both goaltenders were hot, and they were standing on their heads making saves. I knew that feeling so well when you were in the flow and nothing could get by you . . . in fact; even a marble could not roll by you.

I heard a soft woman's voice behind me ask, "Is this seat taken?"

Initially, I did not take my eyes off the screen, as I knew that Mary would be swooping in to chase her away. Then, for some unknown reason, I pulled my eyes down from the game and over to where the woman was standing. I then followed her up from her shoes to her face. When I saw who was actually standing there next to me, to say that my heart came up in my throat, or that my stomach turned over would be an incredibly vast, as well as a gross understatement. A much better description would be that once again, Jim O'Malley had returned to me, renounced his new life, and he had just given me a giant whack over my head with his stick for old time's sake.

You see . . . it was Ms. Binky Hobnobber that was standing there in front of me.

Mary came in from the side. "Please miss, that seat is taken, please we have a seat over here in the bar."

I held my hand up to Mary, and she stopped short.

"It is all right, Mary. The seat is open. It is all right. Thank you."

Mary looked puzzled, but she stopped short. "Are you sure, twenty-seven?"

I smiled at her and softly said, "I am sure. Mary, please bring the lady a Martini . . . shaken not stirred."

Mary nodded, and she was off. I turned to Binky and did not say anything, but I pointed at the open seat. Binky, very weakly, smiled, she pulled the seat out, and sat down. She let out a deep sigh and folded her hands in front of her. She looked even more beautiful than she did the last time I saw her.

The sight of her stirred my very soul.

As gorgeous as she looked to me, her eyes were void of feeling and her expression was flat, almost lifeless.

Mary brought the Martini over and I thanked her.

"Sure, twenty-seven. Are you good?" Mary asked, as she pointed at my beer.

"Good, thank you."

Binky picked up her drink and took a sip.

"Hello Paul, it is so nice to see you. You look wonderful."

"Hello Binky, you are looking well, too. It sure is a surprise to see you. How did you find me?"

She leaned back in her seat, rolled her eyes away from me, sighed, and stuttered on her exhale. I saw her eyes fill with tears as she said, "Oh, I never stopped trying to find you, Paul, be it in Albany, or Kansas City or Norfolk, or Paterson. I never stopped, so it was easy. You see, you were never, ever very far from me, no matter where I was. You were locked in my heart and in my mind."

I stirred uneasily in my chair.

"How's, Harry? Have you heard from him?"

Rose must have kept Binky in the dark to some extent.

I shook my head to indicate no, and then asked, "How was school? Are you going on to law school now?"

"I decided against attending, I have gone into research sciences."

Despite the intenseness of this discussion, I almost smiled. Yes, she was still Binky!

I did not know what to say. It was like a dream that she was sitting across from me here in some gin joint in Paterson, New Jersey. After all those days, nights, the pain, the agony in my stomach that never left, all the things that have happened since she left, and there she was. I did not know whether to run out the front door screaming or to grab her in my arms.

It was unreal to me.

After all this time, there she was, right in front of me. My memories had not failed me as I studied her; she was just as perfect and gorgeous as I had remembered her, in fact, maybe even more so.

I then remembered the smudge stick. I recalled what I had done to spread some energy this evening, right before I left the apartment. I felt my spine shiver, and that feeling you get when something stirs your very soul.

"I had to come and see you when I returned home. Rose helped me with some of the details, but I researched the other information that I needed to find where you would be. I am so sorry about your hockey career, you were right there, so close to the big league. How is your knee?"

"It is fine. I could still play if I wanted to play. I still run, I still stay in shape and have no regrets. I enjoyed it all

Binky, it was my escape, and hockey was my life."

I knew it was time; it was time to spill my guts. I finally had to say what I felt so deep inside of me. I knew that she had come here looking for finality. Maybe in my heart that is what I also needed. The words just came out; I was not going to continue with meaningless small talk, not after all of this time.

"It was all I had after you left and the four of us fell apart." Binky looked down at the table and then her eyes looked up towards me. Our eyes locked, and I noticed her body shudder a slight bit. It seemed like the mention of the breakup had struck a despondent nerve.

I continued to bare my soul. I just had to do it. "Then after all the other horrible events that transpired, I could hide my pain behind that mask. On the ice, I was numb and focused. And all the other millions of ghosts of you, and would have, could have, should have and why, they were just not there. The genuine pain came when the game was over. When the lonely times began, that was where the pain came. If a song came on the radio from ETO, then I would have to dive for the off switch. It was a slow torture for years. I cannot describe it, but it is crazy stuff inside of my head. Hockey was my only escape from it all, my relief from all the pain and memories."

I moved in over the table and stared deeply into those perfect, clear blue eyes of hers.

"You know, I have had this dull ache in my stomach now for almost five years. It came the day that I read your letter, and it has never left me."

I felt some anger inside of me, so I stopped speaking and took a long sip of the beer. It was bitter confession time now; I had just taken in some more liquid courage.

"It became very wearisome standing alone in front of that net as well as being so alone in life. I told Sky once that I felt like you stole happiness away from us both. Everyone counted on Paul. My teammates, the fans, the coaches,

Harry, Sky, my parents. It was always, Paul will know what to do. He will come along and make the big save. Yet, when it came time for me to make the big saves in life, like when you left as you did, when Sky died, when Harry was in such pain and he left, when my knee exploded, I was useless, I was a bum, and I was powerless."

I moved my eyes away from her and then back again. Binky was not saying a word; I could only see the tears welling up in her eyes. Our eyes locked again.

"Do you not see, Binky? I was at my best playing in the net. It was where I could hide from you, from the memories, and from life."

Binky put her eyes down again, and she took another sip of the drink. I had not held back, but I had spoken deeply from my heart. After all, she had come to see me, and I was compelled to tell her what I had felt for all of these years.

I saw more tears forming in her eyes. Her mouth twitched and her hands shook.

"I had to come here, Paul, to tell you how sorry that I am. How I feel so bad that I cannot stand it anymore. I can no longer stay away because I can no longer cope with the pain and knowledge that I left you to deal with all that you had to handle by yourself. I did not come here to ask you if we could pick up where we left off, but I just wanted to tell you how very sorry I am for what I did to you, Harry, and Rose. Not a day goes by that I do not regret ever signing that stupid letter, leaving without another word, after such a wonderful time for all of us. I received the package from Howard that had our pictures in it from the Black Bear Club and I never even opened it, I could not stand to even look at them."

Binky breathed deeply, and then she sighed. She also was speaking from her inner soul.

"I acted like a scared coward to the man who is the most fearless person I have ever known both on the ice and off of it."

Binky's eyes filled with tears now. They ran down both of her cheeks, and she wiped them away with her hands when she felt them.

"I am so sorry for not being able to stand with you, love you, and share and support you when you would have needed someone so badly in your life during the good times and the bad."

Binky was now searching for the strength to continue speaking. Her hands were trembling badly, and she started, and then stopped a number of times, before she was able to find the strength to continue. I felt her suffering and pain, and it was very difficult for me to see her in such emotional anguish.

"I feel like I wasted the time that we should have been together. It was ludicrous, telling you how much I cared, and then leaving you with such a silly research explanation. It was such a terrible error. The fact is that I could never, ever look at another man, I never even dated anyone else, and all I can ever think about is you."

Hmm, so she did not run off with the dangerous criminal guy from around the corner after all. She started to sob heavily, and the tears rolled out of her eyes and down her cheeks even harder than before.

"One thing in that letter was true, even to this day. I still love you with all my heart. However, I have no false expectations after all this time. I do not ask for anything, except forgiveness for the pain I caused. If you can just tell me that you forgive me Paul, I will walk out of here and be satisfied."

I took a long look at her, and I could see the pain in her face, and the longing in her heart. I felt a calm peace come over me. It was something that I had been waiting for to happen to me for such a very long time. In fact, it was a feeling that I had longed for since the day I read that letter that Binky had written while I was sitting at that sacred kitchen table so long ago.

My voice grew soft and quiet, and it reflected the calmness that had now overtaken me. I knew that despite the pain and the years of loneliness, I never harbored anything but love for this woman. It was true, and the calm feeling inside of me now was remarkable.

I knew that God had finally sent peace and rested my soul.

"You see, that is what you do not understand, Binky."

I took her hands in mine and held them tightly.

"That is where this ache in my insides comes from. It comes from the fact that I forgave you the very second, I finished reading your letter. If I could only have been angry with you for writing it, and leaving, then I would have been fine, but I cannot, because I love you. I love you with all of my heart, and I have never stopped, despite all the pain and loneliness."

I handed Binky a napkin from next to me.

"Really, Paul, you do? Even after all you have been through, all the wrong that I have done, and all this time?"

I nodded my head, took her hands, and squeezed them even harder.

"Please don't cry. I hate to tell you, Binky, but your research was wrong. In the letter, you indicated that a new relationship would be right around the corner for me. Well, it never happened."

She dried her eyes with the napkin and seemed to become composed. I could see that she was working hard to shift back to her traditional prim and proper mode. I had to be realistic. This was the one, and only Binky Hobnobber, and she was not going to be down for very long. That is why I loved her with all of my heart.

"I am so glad that my studies were flawed on that one, Paul." She took the last sip of her drink, and I finished my beer.

I waved to Mary, who waved back to me. She had been watching this scene unfold from afar, and Mary had anticipated that I was going to need some reinforcements. Mary quickly brought over some more drinks.

Binky looked at me and she smiled while her eyes darted from her drink back to my face.

"So, where is it that we are now Paul, where do we go from here?"

That was the exact question that I was hoping she would ask me.

"Binky, Sky taught me a lot about fate and the mysterious things in life that are all around us. I never put much credence to all of that stuff, but some of it I could never explain, that is for sure. I surely cannot explain some of what happened tonight. Sky was a wonderful person."

I stopped and thought about that for a second or two.

"Correction, she is a wonderful person. I know now that people never really go away forever. Even when they die, they return to us, somehow. We remain together forever with the people that we love. She told me that you would return someday or somehow, and even though I never knew it until now, inside of me, I did truly believe that."

I could see Binky studying my face very carefully; in fact, she was hanging on my every word now.

"What I am certain of is that God's hand is on all that we do, and be it fate, or whatever you believe in, people are brought together in this world, and things happen all according to a plan. Did you ever really think about the odds of that canned looped tape that night at the Surf Club playing, 'Living Love,' rather than some meaningless disco dance song? You and I had committed to dancing to the next song no matter what, and fate dialed up, 'Living Love.' I may never figure out the meanings to the lyrics of, 'Close to the Crevice' but I sure know what 'Living Love' is all about."

Binky sat up and the normal happiness of her blue eyes came back to life right in front of me.

"I understand the lyrics, Paul. I have researched that

extensively."

Now this was getting good. Binky was back in her comfort zone. I decided to challenge her research skills. There is nothing Binky enjoyed more than a debate on her research.

"So, what is it about?"

Binky leaned in, and that old familiar wide-eyed stare started to appear, "It is about how love is a living, real thing, and that it should not be thrown away, or tossed aside for any reason."

"Very good, so looking back at all that has happened, do you really think it was not a stronger force than we will ever understand that had that song play for us that night? To answer your question, I say we listen to the song and finally take the advice. We need to forget about lost time between us. We need to forget about lonely days, pain, and sadness and go on from here. All of that no longer matters anymore, it is over."

I had grown more animated, and I waved both of my hands over the table, as though I was symbolically wiping and swatting away all the old tears, memories, and loneliness.

"What matters is now, and that we are sitting together, right here and now, and we are meant to be here. Life is short, time is the only real enemy that we have, we now just need to go with it."

Binky smiled and her eyes returned to life. My words had struck a chord, and her mood changed. It was so good to see her smile. I knew that somewhere, Sky, Rose, and Harry were all smiling with us, too.

"Harry is right, Paul. You are the smartest person we all have ever met."

I got out of my seat and went around the table.

"I am warning you, but I have been drinking beer." She smiled and reached up for my hand and I slid in next to her. I embraced her, and we shared a long, overdue kiss.

Binky pulled away a little, and she became a little coy and excited.

"Can I show you something that you will laugh at and be very surprised to, see? It is especially surprising, given my general approach at being refined and proper in all that I do."

"Sure, let's see."

I was a little mystified as she undid the button at the end of her shirtsleeve and rolled up her sleeve, exposing her right arm. All the way at the top, near her shoulder, was a little tattoo of a red heart. Inside were the numbers: twenty-seven.

I grabbed her and laughed. Binky was now laughing hysterically.

"I did it one night when I was so depressed and Rose had told me you had made it to the ACL team in Norfolk."

Same old Binky, a woman with a wild side, who hides behind a prim and proper disguise. She was turning all kinds of different shades of red, and she looked really cute and coy in her outright embarrassment.

"Wow, now, if this all didn't work out, then it would have been an easy solution to just find a long-haired, hippie goaltender who wears the number twenty-seven, that would not have been too difficult to do now would it?"

"Impossible, there is only one on Earth."

I grabbed her hand and pulled her up out of the seat, and told Binky, "Let's get out of here, Binky. You and I need to go somewhere, anywhere, let's ride, howl at the moon or whatever. For us, the night always comes, and that is when we are out there, running around, doing the things that we always did, and taking on the world together. You know, I just had a terrible thought, but when we get married, will your father always come over and want to take shots on me?"

Binky stopped getting up out of her seat and she seemed

to be thinking.

"Well, he was very excited to hear that I was coming to see if I could find you tonight. He told me he had researched the statistics on restoring broken relationships, and that there was a very good success rate in the recent patterns. Therefore, I suspect there is a very real possibility that he might be practicing his slap shot right now. Once he gets it out of his system, we should be all right though."

"Good, I will just let him score a few shots right away, and he should be good then."

Binky nodded her head very quickly as she did when she had agreed with what you said. We got up, and started to head for the front door.

I handed Mary seventy-five dollars as we passed, and she whistled at me.

"More generous than usual there, twenty-seven. What is the occasion?"

"We left some tears on that table, Mary. There is some extra cleanup so that will cover it. Mary, please meet Binky, you will be seeing quite a bit of her in the near future."

"Hey, wait a minute, I have had my sights on this long-haired, hockey goalie for a while there, Binky. What makes you think that you can just waltz in here and steal him from me?"

Binky smiled and rolled up her sleeve and showed Mary the tattoo.

"Sorry, but I have had my sights on him for longer, Mary."

Mary laughed, and she hugged me. "It is nice to see you smile, twenty-seven. You have a good night. I have to go clean that table of spent memories and tears. Do you want me to save them in a bottle?"

"No, Mary, we no longer need them, you can wash them away."

We walked out into the night and headed for my old jeep. I then realized that for the first time in years and years, that dull ache in my stomach was gone. In fact, it had left the second I saw Binky standing next to me.

One little, stinking flash of a moment had changed everything once more.

"Paul, I see your license plate is still, goal 27. You have had this old jeep forever. I bet it has seen a lot of things with you over the years and carries a lot of memories."

Binky was right. I guess I was now just like the old man. He had the 1964 Putter Classic model 200 forever, but now, I had my old 1975 MJ-17 jeep for almost as long. It must have been a Henson family tradition never to sell old wrecks of vehicles.

"She is not fast or pretty anymore, and she sure is not a 1979 Trans Whizzer, but she still rolls. What do you say, we go up to Shadow Lakes and roll down the hilly Ewing Ave exit ramp on Route 208 southbound, and stop at the traffic sign at the end of the ramp? I have heard there is the strangest thing that happens if you stop there, put your vehicle in neutral, and watch as the vehicle goes backwards up the hill."

Binky smiled, "I have heard that. We should go. I see you still know how to dress when you want to impress a young lady on a date."

I stopped and looked down at what I was wearing. "Sure, I do, it worked, didn't it?"

"Paul, when the summer comes, can we go down to Seashore Heights and ride the Flipper again, that was such fun."

I sighed and breathed deep, "I do not know. Binky, you might be pushing your luck on that one."

We got in the jeep; I started the engine and pushed the clutch down to the floorboards.

"Hey, wait a minute!"

Binky put her hand on mine as I reached for the gearshift. "Did you just propose to me there, when you asked me if my father would come over after we were married?"

She leaned in with that famous wide-eyed stare and zoomed in close to me, waiting for her answer.

How I had missed that stare from those fantastic blue eyes!

"Well, I reckon I just might have there, Bink-a-roo-ski. Y'all might have to do a little research and figure it all out now, won't you?"

I slid the Crystal Zirconium tape into the player. Binky looked at me, pushed the stop button on the player, and searched around on the floor for the tape box. She picked one out, and she popped out Crystal and replaced her with The Big World Record by the Electronic Transistor Orchestra.

"Please be ready to pull over on the side of the road there, twenty-seven. My research indicated that, 'Living Love' is the sixth track on this recording, so you need to find a safe spot on the side of the road. You can lead, of course."

She reached behind my head, pulled out the little hair tie, and tossed it out the window of the jeep.

I put the jeep in gear, popped the clutch to get a little squeal of rubber, and we disappeared off into the night.

The End

Epilogue

It was winter in 1985, and I was working in the basement doing my best to pull a frozen bolt out of our furnace blower motor. It was not going really well when I heard my wife calling for me from high up in the house somewhere.

"Down here Binky, I am in the basement here." I heard her come down the stairs and walk into the workshop.

"What are you doing, Paul?"

"Well, I can't seem to get this bolt out to replace this motor. Until I do, you will have no heat in the house."

"Oh, I see, well you like it cold, anyway. Do you want me to look up how to extract frozen and stubborn bolts?"

"No, I have it. I will let you know. Say what is up? Why were you calling?" I had tied all my hair up behind my head to keep it out of my eyes while I worked on this stubborn contraption. Binky reached behind my head, pulled out the hair tie, and put it in her pocket.

"Oh, I almost forgot. How could I forget? The prospect of researching something diverted me, look what came in the mail today."

Binky dropped a postcard on the bench in front of me, put her arm around me, and hugged me. I looked down and saw that the front was printed with, "Thinking of you." I turned it over and the only thing written on the back was a signature that read, "Harry M. Redmond Jr." and a phone number with an area code that I did not recognize. The address on the envelope was "To: Mr. and Mrs. Paul J. Henson."

This time, the card had a return address on it as well as a phone number. I put it down on the bench, folded my hands together, and smiled.

ABOUT THE AUTHOR

If you ask Paul John Hausleben, he will tell you that he is not an author, he is just a storyteller. His mission is to continue to write and tell stories to warm your heart, make you laugh, and sometimes make you cry, just a little. Most of all, he deals in memories, and helps you to remember the good times of your own life, and the special people who touched you along the way. Paul was born and raised in Paterson, and then nearby Haledon, New Jersey, and began writing at an early age. He revisited a writing career later in his life, and he now is the author of a number of novels, compilations, short stories and audio and video works. Most of his work, touches upon nostalgic remembrances of simpler times, and tells the stories of heartfelt, humorous, and special human relationships. Other than writing, among many careers both paid and unpaid, he is a former semi-professional hockey goaltender, a music fan and music reviewer, an avid sports fan, photographer and amateur radio operator. He now resides in Somewhere, U.S.A., but his heart always remains along Belmont Avenue in good old Paterson, and Haledon, New Jersey.

Titles by Mr. Hausleben that you also will enjoy:

The Time Bomb in The Cupboard and Other Adventures of Harry and Paul.

Reunion, A sequel to the Night Always Comes and Another story from the Adventures of Harry and Paul

The Autumn Collection

The Christmas Tree and Other Christmas Stories. Tales for a Christmas Evening

Ye Olde Book Shoppe
A Story for the Christmas Season

The Miracle Tree, Another story from the Adventures of Harry and Paul

The Summer Collection

And many others

Coming Soon?

You may contact us via email at ctte27@gmail.com

www.ingramcontent.com/pod-product-compliance
Lightning Source LLC
LaVergne TN
LVHW020659110826
845149LV00012B/2050